Praise for THE HALCYON DISLOCATION

"In a truly original sci-fi fantasy that literally transcends space and time, Kazmaier hurls readers into a world with shady morals, dubious friendships and exotic surroundings. It's one turn after another as this colonization epic unfolds."

—Robert McCallum, Dirctor/Writer of *Unearthly*

"In his first novel, Kazmaier combines the knowledge of the scientist with the imagination of the story teller. *The Halcyon Dislocation* is an incredible tale that seems frighteningly credible, thanks to its compelling insights into human nature. It's an adventure; one that progresses on the weighty consequences of moral choices made without regard to morality. This novel will leave you thinking about freedom; what it really is, and how to preserve it."

—Patricia Paddey, Freelance Writer

"In the great tradition of cautionary tales, *The Halcyon Dislocation* explores the intersection of faith and science when the world of its protagonist is turned upside down. Chilling and relevant, this story is a wild ride that shakes the foundation of its characters' faith and world view."

—Scott Weisbrod, *Experience Planner*

"A gripping story with great ideas and insightful characterization."

—Mark Jokinen, *Mark Jokinen Books*

"This novel deals with important issues for older teens and undergrads. The Christian message is clear and unambiguous, and the author avoids anything graphic or explicit. Though a bit rough around the edges, with too much "show" and not enough "tell", it is well enough written to be recommended to those who enjoy science fiction."

—*The Curious Presbyterian*

"I was drawn in by the author's vivid descriptions and imagination in this new world that is Middle Earth-like."

—Lisa Hall-Wilson, *Maranatha News*

"For his first novel, Kazmaier does well at quickly getting the plot in motion and describing the new world. The science makes for good reading, too; perhaps no surprise, since Kazmaier is a working and teaching scientist. He makes dimension and time travel seem plausible and comprehensible."

—Lloyd Rang, *Faith Today*

"Throughout the novel there is a keen and vital sense of adventure and discovery with elemental forces at work, both in a material and metaphysical/religious sense. The interest level is sustained throughout."

—*Writer's Digest*

"An original, exciting novel."

—Kevin Miller, *The Word Guild Canadian Christian Writing Awards*

"The universe that the author creates is one that I can only best compare to Tolkien's epic ... It's often a tall task for any author to portray a simple world around [its] main character, but in Tolkien fashion, Peter Kazmaier creates a vivid universe filled with multiple cultures, philosophies, character-types, and story-lines, all handled with care representative of someone who truly understands and loves the characters and universe that they have created. I give this novel 4 out of 5 stars, and highly recommend it."

—*Confessions of a Dangerous Mind*

Book 1 of The Halcyon Cycle

The HALCYON Dislocation

PETER KAZMAIER

THE HALCYON DISLOCATION
Copyright © 2012, Peter Kazmaier

For more information or to order additional copies, please contact:
Wolfsburg Imprints
2421 Council Ring Road
Mississauga, Ontario, Canada
L5L 1E5
http://www.peterkazmaier.com

ISBN: 978-1-77069-705-8

Word Alive Press
131 Cordite Road, Winnipeg, MB R3W 1S1
www.wordalivepress.ca

WORD ALIVE PRESS
Just Write!

Library and Archives Canada Cataloguing in Publication
Kazmaier, Peter, 1951-
        The Halcyon dislocation / Peter Kazmaier.
(Halcyon cycle ; bk. 1)
ISBN 978-1-77069-705-8
        I. Title. II. Series: Kazmaier, Peter, 1951- . Halcyon
cycle ; bk. 1.

PS8621.A96H35 2012   C813'.6   C2012-904701-5

Dedication

To Kathy and my other book club friends (Doug, Patricia, Dwight, and Hope), for your encouragement to follow my dream...

Contents

If quantum mechanics hasn't profoundly shocked you, you haven't understood it yet.

—Niels Bohr

The Island University of Halcyon

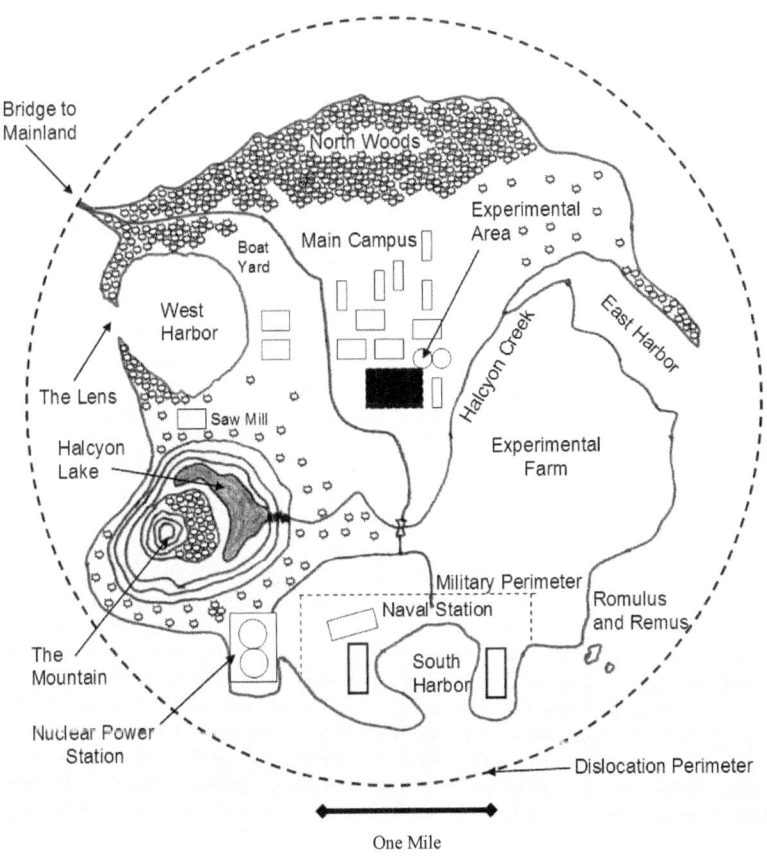

The Bridge to
The Mainland

North Woods

Experimental
Area

Boat
Yard

Main Campus

West
Harbor

East Harbor

The Lens

Halcyon Creek

Saw Mill

Halcyon
Lake

Experimental
Farm

Military Perimeter

Naval Station

Romulus
and Remus

The
Mountain

South
Harbor

Nuclear Power
Station

Dislocation Perimeter

One Mile

The Halcyon River Region

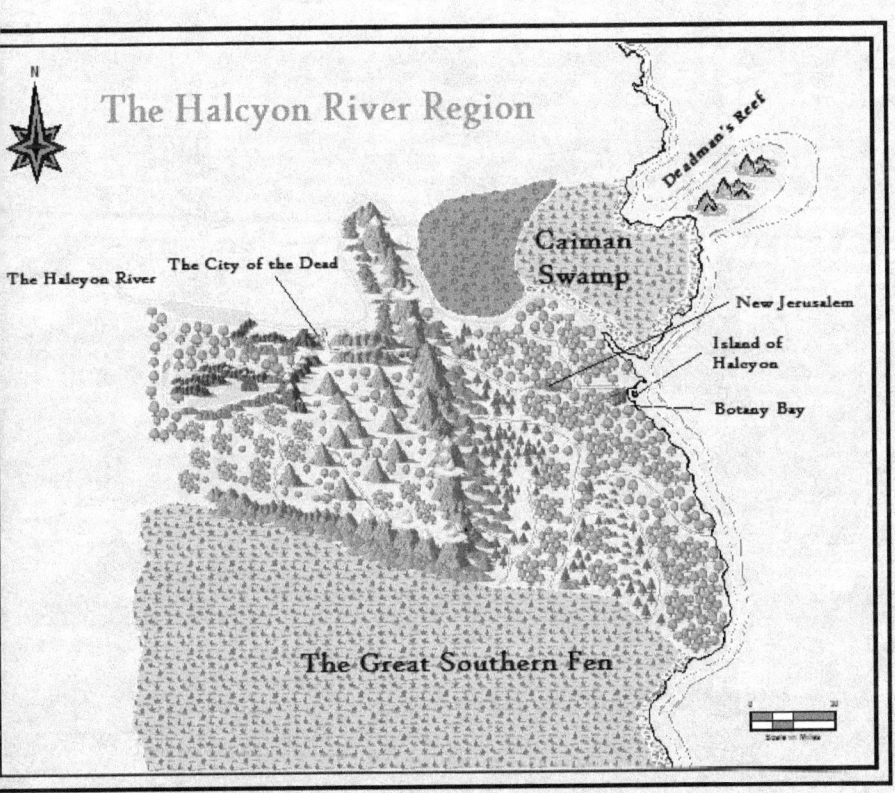

The City of the Dead

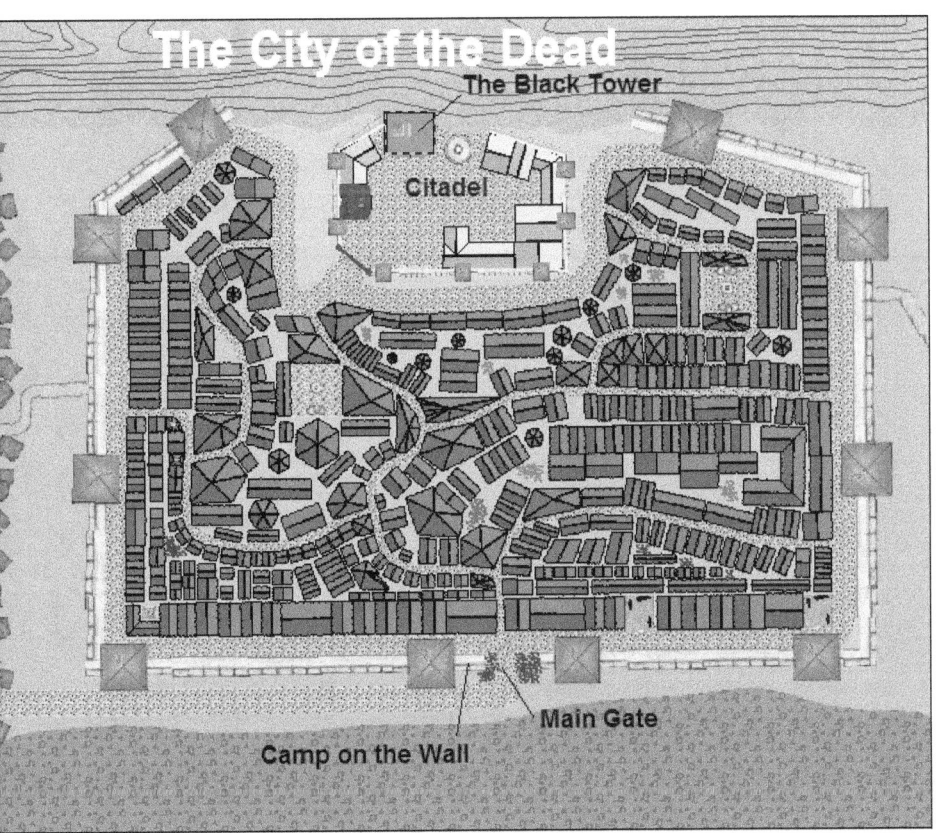

The City of the Dead

The Black Tower

Citadel

Main Gate

Camp on the Wall

Chapter 1

The Dislocation

Dave Schuster sat in the chancellor's office drinking coffee. The conversation had lapsed. Pushing back a strand of unruly black hair, Dave looked at his uncle across the desk and waited, respectfully, for the older man to say something.

Chancellor Charles O'Reilly lounged back in his chair. Fifty-three and clean-shaven with gray hair, O'Reilly had maintained his trim military build. While admiral of America's Sixth Fleet, he'd had few opportunities to visit Dave's home. Nevertheless he still enjoyed a close relationship with his sister, Dave's mother. With O'Reilly's recent retirement from the navy, his appointment to the University of Halcyon as chancellor, and Dave's arrival as an engineering student, they had determined to get to know each other better. However, the demands of the chancellorship and the frenetic pace of first year engineering had conspired to make this visit—on Wednesday, March 2—their first since Dave had arrived to live on the island campus in September.

"Are you still interested in astronomy?" O'Reilly asked warmly, gazing at his nineteen year old nephew.

Dave was jarred from his train of thought. "Yeah, I am. I didn't bring my telescope, but I still can't get enough of it."

"If you love it so much, why did you go into engineering?"

"I didn't think I could get a job in astronomy," Dave laughed. At six feet two inches tall, with the broad shouldered physique of a linebacker, Dave was as large as he was practical.

O'Reilly rubbed an old scar on his chin. Suddenly, he bolted upright in his chair. Dave followed his uncle's eyes and stared through the large balcony doors across from the desk. Angry gray storm clouds had replaced the bright sunlight of only a few minutes ago. Immediately, a flash of lightning followed by a crash of thunder rent the air. The lightning lit up the room in a dazzling display, as one bolt followed another in rapid, artillery-barrage succession.

"What in the world—" began O'Reilly.

A bright flash of red light blazed through the glass doors, giving way a moment later to a tremendous shock wave. The room shuddered. Several books fell to the floor from the shelf behind O'Reilly's oak desk. Dave's stomach lurched as if he were falling through the floor.

Startled, both men jumped to their feet and moved to the glass doors. Half a mile distant, a fireball rose from the experimental field in the center of the island campus. Smoke from the explosion had already begun to obscure their view.

The phone rang. O'Reilly darted back to his desk.

"O'Reilly!" he barked. He listened, grimfaced, to the caller, only occasionally grunting assent into the mouthpiece.

Placing the receiver on the cradle, his eyes hard, he squared his shoulders.

"Dave," he said, "I'm going down to the emergency response center in the basement. I don't want you out on the street until I know more about what's going on. Come with me, but try to stay out of the way."

"Yeah, sure." Dave bit back the temptation to ask questions when he saw the set of his uncle's jaw.

Uncle Charlie's military face! Something big is going on, and I get to be on the inside of this emergency.

Glancing at his phone for messages and updates, Dave thought it odd that there were none, and returned the device to his pocket. He followed the older man as O'Reilly left the office, turned first toward the elevator, and then changed his mind, headed toward the nearest stairwell, and raced down the stairs, two at a time. Reaching the subbasement, O'Reilly entered a key code into a keypad. The door clicked as the lock disengaged. Dave kept pace as they hurried down the long corridor, and then passed through an open door into a large room.

Dave quietly slipped in behind his uncle and took a seat just inside the door at the back of the room. As he sat down, he glanced at his phone again. Still nothing. Two more people came in, and sat down at a bank of consoles facing a wall-sized display at the front of the room.

The buzz of conversation stopped as O'Reilly strode to the center of the room and approached a tall man in a white shirt. After a lengthy whispered conversation, O'Reilly turned to address the emergency response team, his expression grim.

"For those who have just arrived," he began, "there has been an explosion at the experimental area. Do we have any word on casualties?"

"No word on casualties," said a man wearing earphones.

"Is our nuclear power station still on line?"

"Yes," said the man, peering briefly at his monitor. "There was a power surge from the experimental area, but it didn't overload the safety systems, and power generation at the nuclear plant is nominal. That power surge ended abruptly at about the time of the explosion."

"Has the campus fire department been dispatched to the experimental field?"

"The first truck has just arrived. I'm in contact with Chief Gamble, but he needs a few minutes to assess the situation."

O'Reilly rubbed the scar on his chin. "Have we requested support from the mainland?"

"We've tried, but our communication links have been disrupted. We can't get through," said the communications technician.

"How can that be? Was every microwave tower knocked out?" exclaimed O'Reilly.

"I don't get it, either," answered the communications technician. "One of the towers is clear on the other side of the island and couldn't possibly have been affected by the explosion. I can reach the naval station on the south side of our island, but even they can't communicate with anyone on the mainland."

At least that explains my phone, thought Dave.

The wall display showed the firemen scurrying to deal with the blaze in the experimental area.

"Could you search the camera archives for the footage prior to the explosion?" asked O'Reilly.

"Yes, of course!" said the technician.

The video on the screen flashed backwards in time. The technician expertly froze the video frame at the point when the explosion had started, consuming part of the experimental field building.

"Go back two minutes and let's run forward," said O'Reilly.

The intact experimental field building appeared on the screen, surrounded by a spherical bubble shimmering faintly, like air over a ribbon of blacktop in hot desert sun. In the distance, the sky was blue, dotted with small cumulus clouds, but directly over the experimental building a black storm cloud was roiling violently.

The cloud grew more turbulent, and lightning flashes lit up the dark mass. Soon lightning began to hit the experimental building, and the shimmering bubble expanded rapidly outward, passing beyond the camera as the lightning strikes increased in intensity.

A short time later the explosion occurred, and the whole sky turned coal black. A moment later, like a television changing channels, a bright blue cloudless sky appeared, marred only by the black smudge of the explosion.

"Where did the clouds go?" someone asked.

The phone rang. "It's Professor Hoffstetter," said the communications technician, handing the phone to O'Reilly.

"Bertrand, are you all right?" O'Reilly asked. "What about the rest of your people?" O'Reilly's face gradually relaxed as he heard the answer.

"Calm down, Bertrand. What do you mean by 'have you seen the bridge?' What bridge are you talking about?"

O'Reilly listened for a few moments more, then cupped his hand over the mouthpiece and said to the technician controlling the view screen, "Ed, would you display the bridge to the mainland on the screen? Hoffstetter seems to think that something is the matter with the bridge."

The main screen shifted from a picture of fire trucks working at the explosion site to a view of the bridge to the mainland. Everyone gasped. The bridge was only half there. The camera showed the familiar blacktop running in a smooth curve to the bridge at Causeway Point, only to end abruptly after a few hundred yards, as if sliced off by a knife. Five people had emerged from their vehicles and were pointing at the truncated end of the bridge. But it was not only the bridge. The mainland of North Carolina, only half a mile away twenty minutes before, had disappeared and been replaced by an unfamiliar shoreline that could be seen as a hazy shadow across miles of sea.

Dave was stunned. His heart raced, the room felt hot, and sweat beaded on his forehead. He had been following the accident with the detached excitement of a television viewer watching a disaster movie, but when the truncated bridge appeared on the screen, his mind reeled.

What's happened to the bridge?

O'Reilly, still holding the phone while staring over his shoulder at the main screen, was first to recover.

"I'll get back to you, Bertrand," he said softly into the mouthpiece and hung up.

"Where are the students now?" he asked in a deliberately calm tone. None of the staff answered. O'Reilly scowled at each person in turn. Every eye was transfixed on the amputated bridge.

"Where are the students now?" he asked in a louder tone. Still no one answered.

"Most would still be in class," answered Dave from the back of the room.

"Ken, get what's-his-name, the head of the campus patrol," ordered O'Reilly.

"That would be Ben Wychek," said the communications technician, tearing his eyes away from the bridge.

In a quiet voice O'Reilly continued, "Use the public address system. Tell the students we've had an explosion. It's under control, but for their safety, all classes are cancelled. They should clear the streets for the movement of emergency equipment, and return to their dormitories. Then call Ben Wychek and ask him to round up all the stragglers and get them back to their dorm rooms. For once I'm glad all of the students live on campus."

"Will do!" returned the communications technician. In a few moments his voice was blaring over the campus public address system at a volume so high they could hear the echo from a distant loudspeaker. The main screen shifted from campus camera to camera as the group clustered in the emergency response center watched the campus patrol begin to implement O'Reilly's most recent instructions.

"Go back to the camera observing the bridge," said O'Reilly.

"Yes," said the communications technician.

"Retrieve the footage from the archives, and roll the video from the point where the bridge is still intact."

In a few seconds they saw the bridge as it had been, spanning the strait. Nothing changed for some minutes. Occasionally a car crossed the bridge and headed toward the mainland.

"The explosion happened at 14:31, according to the other camera," said the technician.

The time counter at the bottom of the screen passed 14:30. Suddenly a curved, shimmering curtain appeared, passing the camera as it expanded across the bridge. As it did so, the whole screen turned coal black. In another moment, the blackness vanished and bright, clear blue sky appeared. The bridge was truncated, and the shoreline had receded.

The room was silent, deathly silent. The video clip ended, and the screen again showed the live video feed from the explosion site.

Dave saw another man, whom he recognized as Darwin Blackmore, the vice-chancellor, silently enter the room and approach O'Reilly. Blackmore was a tall, thin, impeccably dressed man with a sallow face ending in a goatee. He carried himself with the easy confidence of a man aware of his gifts and the power he wields.

"What seems to be the trouble, Charles?" he asked.

"Eh, what did you say?" said O'Reilly as he turned around and pulled his attention away from the video screen.

"What seems to be the trouble? Why were the students sent back to the dormitories?" repeated Blackmore, an icy edge to his voice.

His tone caused O'Reilly to give Blackmore a searching look. "I'll tell you what I know, Darwin. Hoffstetter was running a full-scale test of his force field generator as a run-up to the Department of Defense demonstration next month. Somehow, during the test, there was an explosion," he gestured to the screen, which was still centered on the experimental area. "But we have an even bigger problem. Show him the bridge!"

The bridge reappeared on the screen, truncated as before, except that a few more cars and people had gathered to stare at this concrete evidence for the unbelievable.

Blackmore was puzzled. "What am I looking at?"

"The bridge, man, the bridge to the mainland!" said O'Reilly, his voice rising.

"Oh my god!" said Blackmore, turning white as a sheet. "Where's the rest of the bridge? Where's the mainland..."

"Exactly!" said O'Reilly. "Darwin, you take over for me here."

"Where are you going?" asked Blackmore sharply.

"First I'm going to drive out and inspect the bridge myself, and then I'm going to the hospital to talk to Hoffstetter. I'll have to be able to give our people answers!"

With that he strode out of the room, beckoning Dave to follow. Using the same stairwell as before, they went up one floor to the first basement, and then to the underground garage.

Not given to ostentation, O'Reilly drove a small, well-used Toyota. The car emerged from the underground parking lot into bright sunlight, where smoke from the explosion, driven by the wind, formed a long, slanted column to the west. They drove slowly past the patrol cars of the campus police, who were already beginning to clear the streets, and headed for Causeway Point. There, more cars choked the approach to the bridge, and curious onlookers were gathered into groups, as if talking would shield them from the terrifying evidence of their senses.

Parking at the side of the road, O'Reilly and Dave got out of the car and walked past the groups of students to the bridge. The concrete structure, resting on large pillars buried in the ocean floor, seemed undamaged, extending ahead of them into the strait like the bowsprit of a ship. Fear gripped Dave's stomach as he walked out onto the bridge and saw the ocean, hundreds of feet below him. He tried not to think of the height but concentrated on putting one foot in front of the other. After a couple of minutes, they approached the end of the pavement. O'Reilly, about ten feet ahead, continued to the very end of the bridge, where he crouched down on his hands and knees to examine the severed edge.

"Cut as cleanly as if with a sharp knife!" he muttered. "Not so much as an impact fragment."

Dave kept his eyes on his feet, determined not to betray his fear to his uncle. Suddenly the end of the bridge yawned before him, and he looked down into the foam flecked sea, churning against the last remaining bridge pillar at his feet. Dizziness and nausea washed over him. He would have toppled forward, but for the firm hand that pulled him back.

"Dave, don't stand so close. I don't want to have to explain to your mother…" O'Reilly didn't finish the sentence, but pulled Dave away from the edge. "Maybe you should sit down." Dave obeyed. O'Reilly looked at his nephew him for a moment with concern, and then returned to examining the bridge.

Uncle Charlie, we're both wondering when we're going to speak to my mother again. Where are we? How do we get back?

O'Reilly stood up. "Let's go back," he said in a subdued tone as he extended his hand and pulled Dave to his feet. They walked back to the car in silence, ignored by the clusters of people whose frightened, animated discussions buzzed in the background. Grateful his uncle didn't ask for an explanation of his behavior on the bridge, Dave left O'Reilly to his thoughts.

Chapter 2

A New Beginning

From the bridge O'Reilly drove straight to the university hospital, now alive with frenzied activity in the aftermath of the explosion. Dave followed his uncle as he strode into the main foyer. The woman at the reception area was speaking frantically into the telephone. Her eyes widened when she recognized O'Reilly.

"I've really got to go!" she said to her caller, and hung up.

"Chancellor O'Reilly." The receptionist straightened her blouse and returned a recalcitrant wisp of hair to its rightful place.

"I need to see Professor Bertrand Hoffstetter right away. I understand he has been admitted."

The receptionist quickly tapped the name on her keyboard, hesitated a few seconds, then, "He's in room E-241. Down that hall to the end. Turn left to the elevator."

Thanking her, the two men hurried to follow her directions. The nurse at the station on the second floor of the E-wing showed them to Hoffstetter's room.

The door was slightly ajar. They could hear a muffled, repetitious sound coming from inside. They paused to listen. The indistinct sounds rose and fell in pitch like a chant.

O'Reilly glanced at Dave, and then rapped smartly on the door. The chanting stopped.

"Just a moment!" a gruff voice called out, then, "Who is it?"

By way of an answer, O'Reilly pushed the door wide and strode into the room. Dave followed. A portly man was just leaning over the far side of the bed. Dave saw him drop an angular, foot-long black object into a bag on the floor.

Hoffstetter's black hair was beginning to recede. In stark contrast to his hair, his beard and moustache were ash gray. His eyes were hard, trumping any joviality his corpulence might have conveyed.

O'Reilly offered a hand to Hoffstetter, who had recovered his sitting position in bed. "How are you, Bertrand?"

"Charles—I didn't expect to see you here. I'm fine, of course. I should be back at the experimental area, but these medical cretins insist on keeping me here under observation."

"What happened, Bertrand?"

"Who's he?" asked Hoffstetter sharply. Dave had again tried to make himself inconspicuous by quietly taking a chair at the foot of the bed.

"My nephew. He was in my office when the explosion hit." O'Reilly paused. "I want to keep him with me until I've had time to assess our situation. So what *has* happened, Bertrand?"

O'Reilly pulled a chair close to the bed, sat down, and leaned forward intently.

"Charles, I must tell you that I have made the most momentous discovery of my career," said Hoffstetter in a conspiratorial tone.

"What do you mean?" asked O'Reilly.

Hoffstetter looked at O'Reilly's face, as if trying to read his thoughts, and then continued. "I can say matter-of-factly, without prejudice or exaggeration, that I am the most brilliant physicist of my generation—arguably of all generations. But even I could not have predicted what happened today—"

"What *did* happen today?" interrupted O'Reilly.

Hoffstetter was annoyed at the interruption. "To put it simply, when I was powering up the Hoffstetter field generators"—he seemed to relish the sound of his own name—"the apparatus behaved errati-cally and eventually detonated."

"But you had tested this before! What was different this time?" asked O'Reilly.

"As far as I can tell," continued Hoffstetter, "in constructing the larger unit, we seem to have crossed a scale threshold of some sort. In all of the smaller experiments, the force field bubble appeared and could be controlled. This time, to put it as simply as I can, the field generators seemed to interact with the atmosphere and triggered an electrical storm, which overloaded the system. When the field collapsed..." Here he launched into unintelligible jargon.

O'Reilly put his hand up to stop the verbal deluge. "Bertrand, you're far beyond me. I need to understand this catastrophe in plain language so that I can communicate to the students and faculty. What do I tell them?"

"Don't you see, man? It wasn't a catastrophe; it was a breakthrough! I've made physics history! I deserve a second Nobel Prize..."

"Bertrand! What is 'it'? What has happened? Forget all this other crap."

"Do you know how the Hoffstetter force field generator works?" asked Hoffstetter petulantly.

"No!"

"The Hoffstetter force field causes a time lag or time shift inside the bubble. Oh, it's very small; it's in the range of about ten to the minus thirty-second of a second behind normal time, but that's enough to stop projectiles. Firing into the Hoffstetter force field is like trying to fire into yesterday—you just can't do it. At our time offset, air molecules and light can still tunnel through the time barrier. If I could draw 1,000 times more energy from the power plant, and if I had the equipment to increase the time offset, we could even stop the penetration of air molecules. An even larger time lag would stop radiation, such as light or even gamma rays."

"So how does that relate to what's happened?" asked O'Reilly.

"Charles, with due respect, you simply don't have the understanding to comprehend what happened. How can you expect me to explain it to you?"

"You need to try," said O'Reilly. "You can't drive us on a lee shore like this and then tell me it's too hard to explain."

"All right, all right," said Hoffstetter. "Give me a minute to decide how to explain it to you." Hoffstetter's eyes closed as he paused.

Dave's eyes wandered around the room. Next to Hoffstetter's bed on the floor was an open duffle bag. A jet-black obelisk jutted out of the bag. The obelisk, square in cross section and tapering to a pyramid at one end, had curious red letters on it in a script Dave did not recognize. He was just wondering about the nature of the object, and why Hoffstetter had appeared in such a hurry to put it away earlier, when Hoffstetter resumed his discourse.

"Think of it like this, Charles: electromagnetic radiation, such as light, has both frequency and intensity, which can be controlled separately. Frequency determines the color of the light. Intensity determines the brightness. Each can be modified independently. We have the same sort of control over the force field. The intensity determines the diameter of the force field bubble, and the frequency is analogous to the time offset. When the storm hit, it overloaded our intensity control and expanded the force field far beyond the experimental field. At some point in the expansion, the frequency control was also overloaded. First the time offset increased; then the force field collapsed precipitously as the generators exploded."

"That's why we saw the bubble expanding past our cameras, and when it turned black, that was the increase in the time offset?" asked O'Reilly, understanding beginning to dawn.

"Exactly!" declared Hoffstetter. "I can see my explanation's been clear."

"So what happened when the force field collapsed?" asked O'Reilly.

"Normally when the force field collapses, we return to our normal time. This time, however, the collapse of the very large time offset—we still don't know how large it was—did something to the matter inside the Hoffstetter field. Somehow it dislocated us; that is to say, it transported us to another place or perhaps another time. I don't know where."

"But that's preposterous!" exclaimed O'Reilly.

"Use your eyes! Use your head, man!" Hoffstetter shot back, sneering. "Where's the rest of the bridge? What happened to the mainland?"

"So where are we then?" asked O'Reilly, his eyes hardening at the contempt in Hoffstetter's voice.

"Well," said Hoffstetter, "let me work it out for you. The amputated bridge is incontrovertible evidence that Halcyon has moved. The alternatives are: we moved in space, we moved in time, or we moved right out of our space-time. Let me analyze these alternatives in turn. If we moved any great distance in space, Halcyon would be a small, airless, hemispherical asteroid drifting through space, the dead companion of our sun or some other distant sun. If we had been dislocated a shorter distance so that we remained on the surface of our planet, the sun would have been displaced in the sky at the time of our dislocation. I've run the video files. The clouds changed, but the sun remained exactly where it was in the sky. That may mean we've moved only a few miles, and that's why everything looks the same. The other part of the bridge is probably only a few miles away."

"If we had moved only a few miles," said O'Reilly, "the airwaves would be buzzing with communication, and a Coast Guard helicopter would have already arrived from the mainland. I don't think we've moved just a few miles! Remember the change in the cloud patterns? The weather doesn't change that much when one only moves a few miles. So what about your other alternatives?"

"I suppose," said Hoffstetter, "preposterous as it sounds, Halcyon could have moved forward or backward in time. That might explain the radio silence. If we moved to an earth in a parallel universe—"

"Backwards or forwards in time, parallel universe—are you serious?"

"Of course I'm serious!" snapped Hoffstetter. "Use your brain! Radio silence when there would be all kinds of squawking on all major frequencies—everything from short wave to radio to maritime communications. The sky changed, the shoreline has receded—how much more evidence do you need?"

Dave's head spun. He had the sensation of trying to escape from a trap. *This can't be true! This must be some kind of a joke. There must be a reasonable, logical explanation for this. Hoffstetter is a crackpot—no, he must have been injured by the explosion. They'll laugh about this tomorrow.* But in the back of Dave's mind there was the picture of the bridge, a phantom that wouldn't go away, a phantom that demolished every rationalization.

O'Reilly sat in stunned silence, and the silence became uncomfortably long. "How do we find out what's happened? How do we test these hypotheses?" asked O'Reilly at last in a weary voice.

"Well, if we're on the earth at a different time, we'll know when we examine the stars in the night sky. If we're on a sister earth in a parallel space-time, who knows what that may mean."

O'Reilly sat back in his chair by the bed and scowled. "Time travel seems pretty farfetched, but since we don't know, let's hope for the best and plan for the worst. If we are displaced in time or in a parallel world, can we get back?" he asked grimly.

"I suppose, in principle," said Hoffstetter. "At least I could replicate the experiment and take us somewhere else if I had the equipment. But frankly I don't have a clue how to control this dislocation. There is no assurance that initiating another dislocation will take Halcyon home. Anyway, I have to assess the damage, and the sooner I can get out of here, the sooner I can begin."

"I see," said O'Reilly. He rubbed the scar on his chin and watched a nurse enter the room, deposit a tray of food on Hoffstetter's table, and leave. "I suppose our first order of business would be to figure out where we are. I'm going to talk to the staff in astronomy. What resources do you need to get us back?"

Dave saw the hint of a sly smile creep across Hoffstetter's face. "I'll need someone high up in the administration to help me get whatever resources I need. How about Blackmore? Can he be spared?"

"If that's what it will take," said O'Reilly evenly, "then you will have him to help you. Just get us home!"

Hoffstetter started to eat with appetite.

Why isn't Hoffstetter more upset? wondered Dave.

O'Reilly looked as if he was about to get up and leave, but changed his mind.

"How are the others?" said O'Reilly.

"Oh, my team is fine," said Hoffstetter absently, with a mouth full of food. "The control center is well protected, and the explosion didn't damage it. They have all of us here at the hospital only as a precaution."

"From what you said, you must have had some inkling that this experiment entailed some risk. How could you go ahead with it?" said O'Reilly, his exasperation growing.

"Of course there was some risk. We didn't know exactly what would happen if the field collapsed suddenly—that was one of the things we were going to test—but we knew there was a very small probability that if the field were to collapse precipitously, some unusual things might happen."

O'Reilly choked at the euphemism *unusual things.* "And shouldn't this have made you more cautious?" he sputtered.

Hoffstetter bristled. "Chancellor O'Reilly, it's easy to second-guess my decision after the fact. Without courage and a willingness to take risks, science cannot advance. Don't you know your history? You're a military man. Do you remember the Manhattan Project? Physicists had calculated that there was a low probability that the first atomic bomb explosion might set up a chain reaction in the atmosphere and destroy all life on our planet. But they conducted the test anyway because the need was great. I was faced with the same dilemma, and I didn't flinch from my duty to advance the cause of our knowledge and science." Hoffstetter bellowed for a nurse to adjust his pillow. No one came.

"How did you know about the bridge?" O'Reilly asked suddenly.

There was the slightest hesitation before Hoffstetter responded. "We have the same video camera links in the control room that you have in the emergency response center. The bridge happened to be up on one of the monitors, since we were keeping an eye on the weather from that quarter, so we saw the truncated bridge right away, after the field collapsed."

"Yes, yes, of course." O'Reilly sighed wearily. "I'd better be on my way." He motioned for Dave to follow. Once outside the room he shook his head in disbelief. "Somehow our intelligence and cleverness always outstrip our moral judgment and our good sense!" O'Reilly said, more to himself than to Dave. "Doing his duty to knowledge and science! I wonder what he's not telling me…"

As O'Reilly drove Dave back to his dormitory, Dave noticed his uncle's face looked drawn and gaunt in the afternoon light. He had aged several years in the space of a few hours. Dave thought about raising the question of the black obelisk in Hoffstetter's bag but decided now was not the time.

They arrived at a large multistory building with the name "Socrates" in bold relief above the doorway.

"Dave, I'm sorry to leave you like this. I know all this uncertainty about what's happened makes it very hard. But I need some time to make plans for Halcyon. Since I need to speak to the people here on our university television network tonight, I have to figure out how to come to grips with our situation. I need to think about a possible course for Halcyon that will bring us back home…or one that will at least let us survive."

"If anyone can get us out of this mess," said Dave, "it'll be you!" O'Reilly smiled for the first time since the explosion and squeezed Dave's shoulder affectionately. Dave started out of the car.

"One more thing, Dave. Please don't say anything to anyone until I've had a chance to make an announcement. I'll tell everyone tonight anyway. This accident and its implications will stretch the psychological fabric of our people to the limit. It's almost like telling them that their closest relatives have died. If this leaks out prematurely, we may have a riot on our hands before we can be ready for it."

Dave's mind was reeling as he walked up the stairs to his dorm room, checking his phone again, just in case. Of course, there was nothing. Fear hovered at the edge of his mind like a vampire bat. If he allowed it to settle, it would attach itself and suck the life out of him. *I've got to keep busy and not think about it.*

When he entered his dorm room, Glenn Thompson, his roommate, was sitting on his bed studying the topography of Miss Arizona.

"Hi, Dave!" Glenn said. "Hey – is your phone working?"

"Hi." Dave said without enthusiasm. "No, it isn't."

"That's weird. Neither's mine. Internet's down too. Must have something to do with the explosion. What's eating you?"

Dave evaded the question by asking another question. "What do you think about the explosion?"

"Well, it got me out of sociology today. Professor Aberhardt was continuing to rail against the twin social evils of religious fundamentalism and the nuclear family. I was glad to get a break. That class is a bore."

In an effort to stop thinking about the dislocation, Dave turned his attention to one of his favorite pastimes, baiting Glenn.

"Glenn, why are you spending so much time studying that skin magazine? Can't you get a real date?"

Glenn, who was used to this banter, feigned irritation. "As a matter of fact, I can get a date anytime I want. Sociology students are in great demand by the fairer sex. Women are social creatures, and that gives us a great advantage over social Neanderthals such as you engineers." He spat out the word *engineer* as if it were a disease rather than a discipline. "No," he continued, "Miss Arizona is a work of art, and she's low maintenance. Why shouldn't I enjoy her? Life is short, and I ought to get all I can in the time I have. So go for it! That's my motto."

Dave decided to escalate. "Glenn, when you sociologists think that women appreciate your social prowess, you're overlooking one important fact."

"What's that?"

"It's true sociologists are on the whole more sensitive and tender-hearted than engineers are."

"Yeah?" said Glenn suspiciously.

"Women relate well to you because they're beginning to mistake you for other women. Engineers, on the other hand, could never be mistaken for women, except for those who really *are* women, and if women are looking for real men with none of that warm wishy-washy milquetoast feeling about them, they turn to us."

Glenn's riposte was laced with expletives. The exchange ended with Dave hitting Glenn in the head with a small pillow he kept handy for just such an attack. After the errant return shot upended several books from the bookshelf next to his bed, Dave thought it was time to turn to something else. "Anything on TV?" he asked, turning on the set in their room. Only the university channel was broadcasting, and there was no programming except for a message saying that an important announcement was coming at 9:00 p.m. and everyone should tune in.

"I think I'll go downstairs to the store and buy a sandwich," said Dave, turning off the TV.

"Do you know when they'll let us out on campus again so we can go to the cafeteria to eat?" asked Glenn.

"No," said Dave, "that's why I'm going to get something now rather than wait for them to open the cafeteria."

"Always thinking about your stomach," groaned Glenn.

"Why don't you come down with me?" asked Dave.

"I told some of the guys I'd join them for supper," said Glenn, returning to his magazine.

As Dave left the dorm room he felt much better. He went down to the main floor that housed the dormitory store and sandwich outlet. But his mind kept going back to the accident, so he bypassed the store entrance, went outside and looked for the moon. It was a sliver, late in its last quarter and getting ready to set in the west, just as it should. Nothing seemed to have changed! He went back inside. There was only one other person in line ahead of him, a pretty brunette wearing a doctor's uniform. He caught sight of her nametag; it read "Pamela Lowental."

"Hi, Pam," said Dave as if he knew her.

"Oh, hi," said Lowental in a tone of familiarity. She looked at him closely. "Do I know you?"

"I don't think so," said Dave, "since I would have remembered you. Do you live in Socrates?"

"Yes, on the second floor."

"You're a doctor?"

"Nope, I'm a premed student."

At that moment a woman appeared from the back to give Lowental her order.

"See yah!" Pam said as she left with her food.

Dave nodded and smiled. It was his turn to order. He had just purchased two sandwiches, one for himself and one for Glenn, since he had doubts the cafeteria would open that day, when a campus patrol officer came in and asked the employees to close the store so he could talk to them.

Dave sat in the common area, looking out the large glass windows to the grass commons outside. The campus was deserted except for the occasional patrol car that passed in the street. He noticed that the officer who had closed the dorm store did not leave but stationed himself outside of the dormitory to enforce the curfew. Dave decided to go to the dorm weight room.

Chapter 3

Mobilization

At 8:50 p.m. the campus public address system began urging everyone to turn on their televisions. Ten minutes later, Dave and Glenn watched the university station's broadcast as Chancellor O'Reilly and several other university dignitaries filed into the briefing room to face the cameras. Of particular interest to Dave was the presence of a naval officer, whom he did not recognize. O'Reilly came to the podium and looked squarely into the camera.

"This afternoon," he began, "a commissioning test of a new force field generator, carried out on behalf of the Department of Defense in our experimental area, had some serious and unintended consequences. The experiment triggered an electrical storm, which ultimately led to a detonation that damaged the force field equipment. Furthermore, unbelievable as it may seem, this explosion at 14:31 hours has dislocated—that is to say, moved—the whole island of Halcyon from its original location. We have not yet determined our new coordinates, but I can say that Halcyon's very best minds are working out our location and how to get back home.

"Let me tell you what we know. The air, the ocean, and even our preliminary astronomical data indicate that we have been dislocated to a part of the earth very close to our original position near North Carolina. It is puzzling that we have so far not been able to communicate with the mainland, but it is likely that the failure of our communication equipment is a consequence of the dislocation process."

"If this is a joke, it's a very bad joke!" sputtered Glenn as he jumped up from his chair.

"It's no joke," said Dave softly.

O'Reilly continued as a picture of the truncated bridge filled the screen. "The bridge to the mainland has been neatly sliced in two. Fortunately the whole island was dislocated, so all of our resources are intact. The nuclear power plant is still operational, and our self-contained island infrastructure is functioning well. We do not have to worry about running out of electricity, since there is enough nuclear fuel on site for about fifteen years.

"However, the geography around our island has changed. It is my belief, based on discussions with my advisors, that the island has moved only a few miles from its previous location. The coast is now six miles away. If we cannot reestablish communication with the mainland over the airwaves in the next few hours, then we will send a boat to the mainland.

"As I have said, our best evidence indicates that we have moved only a few miles. However, until we have confirmed this conjecture by communicating with the mainland, we must take steps to ensure the orderly functioning of our small community.

"As chancellor, I—together with the senate and Commander Sanderson from the naval station at the south end of the island—have taken it upon ourselves to form an interim government to ensure we continue to conduct our affairs in an orderly manner under the rule of law during this interregnum. It seems prudent under the circumstances to act as if we might be without communication or support for a protracted period of time. We will work to assure our basic necessities. Once we have taken steps to ensure our survival, if we have neither been rescued nor found a way to return home, then we will hold elections and operate as a freely democratic country.

"For now we will declare martial law. All food will be used to carry our population through the next critical few weeks. There will be no hoarding. I repeat, all food will be shared equally. If we have to go hungry, we will all go hungry together. In addition to the 15,000 students housed in dormitories on campus, we have about 5,000 faculty and support personnel. Many of these support personnel lived on the mainland. They will be housed mostly with the faculty in the faculty district, but some will also have to be placed in your dormitory rooms. If you have a large room and must accept a third person, please do so with goodwill.

"Finally, you will ask, 'What are our next steps?' To that I would respond that our most immediate need is food. We must look first to the sea to support us. Securing our food supply will buy us the time we need to reverse the dislocation or await rescue. To buy us this time, I am suspending all classes, and we will assign everyone to necessary tasks. It is essential that we work together and put our community ahead of our own personal wants and needs. It is only by this kind of unselfishness that we will pull through this crisis. May God have mercy on us!" O'Reilly took a sip of water from a glass and cleared his throat.

"We are all asking what has happened to us. Dr. Blackmore, the vice-chancellor, and his team of physicists and engineers will take personal responsibility for investigating the accident. I have asked him to keep us informed of his progress on an ongoing basis.

"I will take personal responsibility for our survival. I have asked Trevor Huxley, who will take responsibility for food procurement, to provide some of the details on logistics. Trevor?"

Huxley, a short, heavily jowled, overweight man with a red face, took off his glasses to clean them. His voice was unexpectedly thin and reedy, despite his flabby appearance, as he read from a prepared speech. "I am sure that everyone is as shocked as I am at what has happened. I'm sure you will understand me if I say that we must all pull together. What I say may seem high-handed to some, but it is essential to our survival."

Dave saw O'Reilly shift uncomfortably at the longwinded preamble. Huxley noticed the motion, cleared his throat, and applied himself to the written text. "It is essential that we keep all the critical departments functioning: engineering, the physical sciences, and medicine. We will also give priority to the support functions that keep our buildings lit and infrastructure operative. This will mean that additional personnel with the right expertise will have to contribute. If you are asked to lend a hand or take a shift, I would ask that you do so.

"We hope, of course, that we will be rescued soon, but it would be wise and prudent to act as if we might be cut off from home for some time. As the chancellor has pointed out, our critical need is food. We estimate that we have about two weeks worth of food in storage. If we ration it carefully and collect all of the food in the various campus stores, we may have enough for three weeks.

"Those of you who are not directly seconded to the critical support activities that I have already mentioned will be asked to perform one of three functions, and we will assign these by dorm. First, every available boat will be used to bring fish back to campus. We will convert one of the warehouses at East Harbor into a fish process-ing plant. The dorms Aristotle, Aquinas, Bacon, Bentham, Descarte, Fuerbach, Hegel, Hobbes, Kant, Locke, Machiavelli, and Mill are on fish procurement duty.

"Second, dorms Nietsche, Peirce, Plato, Sartre, Spinoza, and Vol-taire will lend support to our experimental farms and harvest the food that we have in the ground, planting new crops if necessary.

"Finally, the dorms Schopenhauer and Socrates have been desig-nated to travel to the mainland.

"If you are contacted by one of the departments to contribute your particular skill, please do so. Otherwise, please contribute to the assignment given to your dormitory. The senate respectfully asks that you provide your full support."

So my dorm is assigned to exploration. I wonder if Uncle Charlie had me in mind when he made that choice.

O'Reilly approached the microphone and nodded curtly to Hux-ley. "One more thing," said O'Reilly. "The naval station at the south end of the island will be considered a critical university department and will be responsible for the defense of the island. Commander Sanderson is now officially in charge of the campus patrol, and he is now also a member of our senate. I believe he would like to say a few words. Commander Sanderson."

Sanderson, a broad shouldered man in his mid-forties with short hair graying around his temples, strode briskly to the podium. "In view of the seriousness of our situation," Sanderson said, "as part of the martial law Chancellor O'Reilly has already announced, a curfew at 21:00 hours—that is 9:00 p.m.—is now in force. Please return to your dormitory rooms by that hour. That's all that I have to say at this time."

The broadcast went off the air, replaced by a message saying that regular programming would resume the next evening at 7:00 p.m.

Glenn was so angry he stormed out of the room. Dave rose from his chair and began pacing. Ever since the sight of the bridge and the interview with Hoffstetter, he had been trying to explain away the evi-dence for the dislocation. The official announcement robbed him of the solace of denial, and he was angry.

Why am I angry? If we have been dislocated, why blame them for telling me?

One thing had surprised Dave. He had never heard Uncle Char-lie refer to God before. At Halcyon, reference to God was regarded as unscholarly, unprofessional, and anachronistic. Certainly, there was more than one side to Uncle Charlie.

I wonder what other surprises this crisis situation might yet reveal?

Dave's thoughts were interrupted when Glenn stormed back into the room. "No way am I going to be ordered around," snarled Glenn. "I know my rights. I don't have to do anything." He picked up the phone, changed his mind, and slammed the receiver back onto the cradle.

"Look, Glenn," said Dave, "we don't really know where we are or how much trouble we're in. Wouldn't it make sense to cooperate?"

"I know how these military guys think," continued Glenn. "The first hint of an emergency comes along, and they go on a power trip, declare martial law, and begin ordering everyone around. I want no part of it."

When he saw the anger in Glenn's face Dave knew that Uncle Charlie had been right. If there were more like Glenn, then the university stood on the brink of a riot. *Oh boy, I don't think I've heard the end of this. I hope this doesn't lead to trouble!*

The rest of the evening was spent in small groups in the dorm common area. The group seemed evenly split: there were those who, like Glenn, were angry, those who denied the whole thing, explaining it away as a practical joke or a colossal misunderstanding and those whose fear was palpable.

About midnight, despite the curfew, Dave went out into the dorm courtyard. He realized that even though he had argued for co-operation, the imposition of a curfew rankled him. He looked up and saw the Big Dipper and Polaris. Nothing seemed to have changed. If they had been displaced in time by 50,000 years, he remembered from astronomy class that the Big Dipper handle would be distorted. If it weren't for the bridge and the mainland, he would think his parents were still only a phone call away. He sat outside looking at the stars until 1:00 a.m. They made him feel as if he were home.

Chapter 4

Fish Tales

Al Gleeson had had a sinking feeling something was seriously wrong ever since he'd heard the call to return to his dorm room. Now the television broadcast he was watching confirmed it.

Lord, what do I do now? What do we all do now?

Al ran his hand through his hair and turned to his roommate, Brendon Monk. Brendon had the pasty white complexion of a man in shock.

"Are you all right, Brendon?"

"I don't believe it! I don't believe it! This can't be happening," said Brendon, clenching and unclenching his fists. They could hear the buzz of animated conversation as students on the fifth floor of Socrates left their rooms, chattering in the hallway about the news. Al and Brendon were just going to join them when Al's phone rang.

"Hello," said Al as he watched Brendon head out into the hallway.

"Did you watch the news?" asked a familiar voice.

It was Tom Chartrand, a close friend. "Can you believe it?" said Al, by way of affirmation.

"I don't know what to believe," continued Tom. "Listen, this isn't a good time, but I have to ask a favor."

"What is it?" asked Al.

"I just got a phone call from Sturgeon, my biology prof, and he's asked me and a bunch of the other students from my class to help him with today's catch. He's been out in a trawler with his grad students since the classes were cancelled, bringing in whatever fish he could find, and he needs help sorting and classifying the catch. Since you are the fount of all wisdom and a fisherman by hobby, I thought I'd ask you to come along and lend your prodigious talent to this exercise."

Tom's optimism was good medicine. Al jumped at the chance to get away. "Your unabashed flattery has won the day. I'd like nothing better right now than to get out of the dorm and do something useful."

"Okay, I'll meet you downstairs. Wear your old clothes; you're going to be a mess when you get back."

Al changed and headed downstairs. Tom was waiting for him; together they left the building and began the walk to East Harbor, about three quarters of a mile away. A short way from the dormitory they were stopped by a campus patrolman.

"What are you guys doin' out after curfew?" he growled.

"My name is Tom Chartrand, and this is Al Gleeson. We've been seconded to biology, and I just received a call to go to East Harbor to help unload a catch of fish."

"Who are you working for?" asked the officer in a suspicious voice.

"We're to report to Professor Sturgeon in biology. He took out a trawler this afternoon and has just arrived back."

"Wait here!" The officer walked out of earshot and spoke at length on his communicator. Al saw him keep his eyes fixed on them as if he expected them to make a run for it.

The patrolman ambled back. "Okay, you're good to go! Your story checks out. Here, take these passes and show them to any other patrolmen you meet so you don't waste their time reporting in. You're supposed to have these before you head out." He scrawled a signature on a couple of pieces of green paper and shoved the passes into their hands. "Fill in the blanks later."

After about twenty minutes they arrived at East Harbor. The quay was deserted except for one lone trawler. A huge tube from the hold of the trawler was spewing fish onto a tarp on the wharf.

"Professor Sturgeon!"

A figure cloaked in rainwear turned toward him. "Oh, hello, Chartrand! Glad you could make it. Can you believe it! I've been trawling off these waters for more than ten years, and this is the first time I've run into a school of fish like this. I filled up the whole hold in four hours!"

Al studied the professor. In addition to his rain gear, Sturgeon had fine chainmail gauntlets on his hands, like a butcher's cutting gloves. He was bearded, and his head was framed by bushy long hair that made him look like a bear in his hood. A hook-like nose protruded from the hairy shrubbery of his face, which was broken only by a smile that revealed crooked teeth. His eyes were a contrast to his austere face and showed an uncommon friendliness. Al's interest was piqued by the conversation.

"Normally, it would take me a week of trawling to catch what I caught today in an afternoon," said Sturgeon. "You know what else is funny?"

"No, what?"

Sturgeon picked a couple of fish from the mound. "Not only did we catch a lot quickly, but look at these. We have a lot of species mixed in together." At this point he noticed Al examining the fish. "Who's your friend?" he asked, pointing at Al.

"Let me introduce Al Gleeson. He's a fisherman by hobby and has come along to help."

"Glad to meet you!" said Sturgeon, affably taking off his gauntlet to shake Al's hand. "Please help me sort the species into piles so we can make a tally. If you need any help identifying a particular fish, ask one of the grad students. I'm afraid I'm going to have to go back to supervise the discharge. Use gloves. Some of the fish have spines. There's a pile of spares on that box." He waved in the general direction of a forklift, then turned and bellowed instructions to a student standing on the deck of the trawler.

Al followed Tom as he picked up two pairs of gloves. They got to work on opposite sides of the enormous mound of fish. Al pulled two large Atlantic mackerel out of the pile. Indeed it looked like his area was mostly mackerel. He found a large tarp that already had several hundred mackerel on it, and added his to the growing pile. He found the occasional black sea bass in among the mackerel. It gave him an odd sense of security since he had often caught black bass off Halcyon near the causeway bridge, when he could get away for an early morning fishing trip.

On his third trip back, he saw the tail of what looked like a small black-tipped shark sticking out of the pile. He carefully gave it a pull. It didn't budge. He pulled harder, and the pile began to shift as the fish came out.

It can't be! I don't believe it. His mind reeled as he looked at the forty-pound monstrosity he was holding by the tail. The fish was about three feet long with the dorsal and tailfins of a small shark. But instead of the jaws and head of a shark, he saw a mass of ten tentacles crowning the creature's head like the snake hair of a Medusa.

Al let the bizarre creature slide to his feet, and then stood there dumbfounded, looking down at the jumble of tentacles. One of the graduate students brought Professor Sturgeon over.

"May I have a look?" he asked gravely. He bent down and grabbed the heavy fish by the tentacles using both hands and spread them to reveal a blunt shark's mouth with razor sharp teeth.

"I've never seen anything like this before," he muttered. He flexed the fish torso. "It's clearly a chordate. How can this be? Where are we? What's happened to us?" He looked around at the gathering crowd. "Just an unusual specimen," he said in a loud voice. "Please get back to work. We don't want to be here all night."

Exhausted and covered in scales and fish oil, Al and Tom walked back to the dorm. Although most of the fish had been familiar Atlantic species, there must have been two dozen examples of species that Al had never seen before.

"So what happened back there?" asked Tom at last, breaking the silence.

Al drew a deep breath and ran his hands through his hair. "From what I can tell," said Al slowly, "Halcyon is not just a few miles from our former location, as O'Reilly was hoping. We found a good many fish tonight that, as far as I can tell, have never been reported off North Carolina, or anywhere else on Earth. Sturgeon said as much."

"What are you saying?" asked Tom, a current of fear in his voice.

"I do not think the senators were quite accurate in their assessment," said Al. "When we travel to the mainland, I do not know what we're going to find, but I do not think it will be North Carolina."

Chapter 5

Calm to Chaos

Dave woke from his sleep in a cold sweat, his nightmare still vivid. He and his older brother Joe had been on a rock wall of the quarry near home, climbing, as they often had, without ropes. In the dream, Dave was looking up as his brother shifted his handhold and a piece of rock gave way. Joe slid down a steep incline and snagged a rocky projection only six feet away. He looked at Dave, his eyes pleading for help, as he clung desperately.

"Dave, help me! Please help me!"

Dave was too terrified to move over and grab his wrist. He saw the disappointment and despair in Joe's eyes as his grip weakened. Then in an instant, without another cry, he plunged to the bottom of the quarry. Dave woke with the thud of the body ringing in his ears.

I couldn't have helped him! I couldn't have helped him!

Steady old fellow; get a hold of yourself. It's been a year since I last had that nightmare. I guess being at the edge of the bridge with Uncle Charlie brought it back.

It was still dark outside. Glenn was gently snoring. Dave went over the funeral in his mind. Mom and Dad never said anything to him and never questioned him about what exactly had happened. Although he and Joe had strict orders not to climb there, they never blamed him. Dave made up for it by blaming himself.

When the first light of dawn crept through the window, Dave was startled by a knock on the door. "Dorm meeting in twenty minutes," said a voice.

Dave got up. Glenn groaned, sitting up in his bed, holding his temples. "I could sure use some coffee," he said.

The events from the day before came flooding back, and Dave realized there would be no coffee, and probably no breakfast. He got up and looked in his small fridge. There was half a carton of orange juice and two pieces of cold pizza. He offered a slice to Glenn, but when he declined Dave was more than happy to eat both slices himself.

They both threw on some clothes and rushed downstairs to the large auditorium on the main floor where dorm rock concerts were usually held. The auditorium was nearly full, with more and more people arriving every minute. The dorm president, Clive Henderson, stood on the stage, preparing to speak to the audience through the public address system.

Henderson cleared his throat loudly to get everyone's attention. "I have a few things to say. As you heard on the TV last night, Socrates was selected to begin exploration of the mainland." There was a murmur of opposition, and Henderson held up his hand for quiet. "Here's how we're going to organize ourselves. Each of our five floors will represent a separate company or unit of operation. Tomorrow, weather permitting, the Fifth Socrates will head to the mainland. We will be joined by a small company of naval personnel, who will be armed. If we make contact with North Carolina, our mission will be over—"

"What do you mean 'if'?" said a voice from the back.

Henderson stared at the questioner and said slowly, "We're not 100 percent sure that we will make contact."

The murmuring grew louder. Henderson pounded on the podium with a gavel. "Silence!" he roared. The sounds stopped as if a loudspeaker had been switched off.

Henderson continued more quietly. "Because of the food situation, we don't have a lot of time. If we don't find—that is to say, if something unexpected happens—we plan to make camp on the mainland and make that a base for exploration. We don't know what we're going to find there, and we're all rookies, so let's keep our heads and learn fast.

"Every week, as our transportation permits, we will send one dorm floor over to the mainland and rotate one floor back to Halcyon. Your floor dons will fill you in on the details and tell you exactly when you're scheduled to leave. Any questions?"

"I paid tuition to come to university," said Glenn. "What if I don't want to go exploring?"

Henderson looked Glenn squarely in the eye. "That is your choice, of course. However, if you don't work, you don't eat." More murmuring. He waved some papers in the air. "These food vouchers entitle you to eat. If you sign up, then you'll get two meal vouchers today. As long as you keep working, you keep eating."

"When *do* we eat?" shouted out Dave.

"Ah, I can see we have at least one veteran among us," said Henderson with mock gravity. "After your floor meeting, your don will pass out the signup forms and the meal vouchers. Any other questions?"

"Where do we get the equipment for this camp we're supposed to set up?" called a voice from the back of the auditorium.

"We hope that each of you has some equipment of your own, since backpacking and rock climbing are popular activities. We can get some tents, bows, and arrows from the physical education center. We are currently collecting all of the fire axes from the fire safety stations, and we will send some of those along with the first group. In addition, the metallurgy department is even now converting scrap metal to useful implements."

"How are we supposed to cross the six mile channel?" queried another voice.

"We only have a few Boston Whalers and precious little fuel. But we have about 200 dinghies. We will cross with about 60 and try to establish a beachhead."

There were a few more questions, but Dave and Glenn went back to their room. About twenty minutes later, another knock on the door told them that Floyd Linder, their fifth floor don, had called the much awaited floor meeting.

After about 200 people had assembled in the large common room, Linder climbed onto a small platform at the end of the room, and whistled to get everyone's attention.

"First things first," he began. "If you sign up, you'll receive your meal vouchers from Al Gleeson. You'll have to come to him every day to get your food vouchers. There are only two meals per day until we get our food situation sorted out, so don't miss your chance!

"We'll be the first group to go to the mainland. Our job is to learn to sail well enough to get across the channel. While we're learning, the navy guys will be exploring the coast with the few powerboats we have available. If they make contact, our training will have been a waste of time. On the other hand, if we have to go ahead, a contingent from the naval station will join us, and their responsibility will be to protect us while we do the grunt work of establishing a camp. How many have sailed before?" A few hands went up. "All of you please come and see me after the meeting. We'll all meet at West Harbor after lunch to watch training videos, and then we'll take up sailing in earnest tomorrow morning. Clive was overly optimistic about our crossing to the mainland tomorrow. It's my call, and we won't try the crossing until we're reasonably proficient and the weather's good."

Dave and Glenn signed up for duty and received their food vouchers. They made their way through a sleepy crowd of students to the cafeteria for a meal of day old hamburgers and reheated fries. Nevertheless, they were so hungry, any meal would have tasted delicious. They were still quite hungry when they finished their portions, and they couldn't help ruing the complaints they'd made in the past about cafeteria food. After brunch they walked to West Harbor and spent the rest of the day in class watching sailing videos that described more than they'd ever wanted to know about sailing.

Late that afternoon, word raced across campus that the first boats had returned from the mainland; no trace of North Carolina or any human habitation had been found.

Tired and hungry, Dave and Glenn returned to their room and turned on the TV to see if broadcasting had resumed. To their surprise Jennifer McCowan, the blonde talk show host of *Halcyon Music*, was on the air.

"Even without social media," said McCowan in her gentle, lilting voice, "I know that everyone is asking 'where are we?' and 'what's happened to us?' To answer those questions I've asked a friend of mine to the studio. Please welcome Vlad Sowetsky."

Canned applause welcomed Vlad.

"So, Vlad," said McCowan, "please tell our viewers what you do."

Vlad, a tall, big boned youth in his mid-twenties, had a long, narrow face and close-set eyes, so that the overall impression vaguely reminded one of a horse. He had shoulder length hair and stubble on his face.

"To cut to the chase, I'm a graduate student with Professor Hoffstetter, and I was in the control room when the dislocation occurred."

"So what actually happened during the accident yesterday?"

"Well," said Vlad, "we were running the largest test on the force field to date. The plan was to—"

"Whoa," said McCowan, "I think you are going much too fast. Tell the audience how the Hoffstetter force field works, but no jargon, please!"

Vlad screwed up his face as if he were being asked the impossible. "The force field appears as a bubble about the size of a soccer ball when we first generate it. The time inside the bubble is slightly behind our time. When we first make the bubble, the time delay—or offset—is very, very small so that the field is thin. That is to say, anything can cross it. We expand the bubble to the desired size and then thicken it. By 'thicken' I mean that we increase the time offset so the field begins to have an effect. First it stops large objects. If we increase the time offset even more, we could theoretically stop air molecules or light from crossing the force field boundary."

"Field boundary," said McCowan. "Now you're lapsing into jargon again and losing me."

"By field boundary I mean the edge of the force field bubble. Shooting a missile through this barrier is, as Hoffstetter would say, 'like trying to shoot into last week.'" Vlad was beginning to get exasperated.

"Okay," said McCowan, "please go on. Even if I don't understand all of the physics, I'm sure there are many listeners who will."

"Well, we had intended to expand the force field so that it enclosed the central building in the experimental area. However, while we were expanding the bubble, the first lightning strike overloaded the equipment and the expansion continued unabated."

This was followed by a momentary pause and a baffled look on McCowan's face. "How big did the bubble get?" she finally asked.

"I think it expanded to a sphere about four miles in diameter," said Vlad.

"Then what?"

"Then a second series of lightning strikes overloaded the offset controls, and the time offset increased enormously," said Vlad. Beads of perspiration had appeared on his forehead.

McCowan uncrossed her legs and leaned forward. "Tell the audience what you think happened next," she prompted.

Vlad took a deep breath. "I only have a half-baked theory. Do you know about quantization of energy?"

"Vaguely," said McCowan, a blank look on her face.

"Let me see if I can make it as simple as possible. Macroscopically, that is, in the world of meter lengths and kilogram masses, energy seems to be continuous. It flows like a stream or a river. So if I ask how much energy it takes to lift this book," he lifted a book from the table, "you can calculate the energy in joules to as many decimal places as you like. I can lift the book to any height and calculate the lift energy for each height. But when you go down in size, ten orders of magnitude to angstroms, the world changes. When lifting electrons away from the atomic nucleus, all the rules change, and one can only 'lift' the electron to discrete 'heights,' or energy levels. It's like being able to lift this book in little jumps." He demonstrated by rapidly lifting and stopping the book at various heights.

"Yeah, I know what you're talking about. You're bringing back unpleasant memories of first year chemistry. But what has that got to do with the Hoffstetter field generators and the accident?"

"Everything!" said Vlad. "I think time is also quantized."

"You've lost me again. How can time be quantized?" asked McCowan. "And if it is, what difference does it make?"

"Well, think about it in relation to the quantization of energy that you learned about in first year chemistry. We think of time flowing past us like a stream moving at a constant rate. That may appear true in our macroscopic world, but what happens if, at very short time intervals, one reaches a minimum time (I call it a *mintival* for *min*imum *ti*me inter*val*)? What if our existence at the time interval of a mintival consists of little jumps, like a jump second hand rather than a sweep second hand? Or putting it another way, what if instead of a flowing stream, time consisted of a series of pools," and here he paused to let his words sink in, "and our existence is a discontinuous series of jumps from one pool to the next?"

"Your theory is fascinating, Vlad, but what has that got to do with the Hoffstetter field generators?"

"I just told you that the Hoffstetter field generators cause the matter inside the field to lag normal time by a very small amount, say ten to the minus thirty-second of a second—that's a decimal point with thirty-one zeros after and then a one. Now let's suppose…" Sowetsky turned and kneeled on the sofa and drew three contiguous rectangles on a white board behind his seat "…that these three rectangles represent three sequential mintivals in our world, or universe, if you like. Another world can coexist with ours, as long as the mintivals of that world are offset from those of our time." He drew three more rectangles adjacent but offset to the first three, like bricks on the side of a building. "It would be like a single reel of film containing two movies, with the odd numbered frames representing our world and the even numbered frames representing another world. If two protectors played this interlaced film with one displaying the odd numbered frames and the other the even numbered frames, one film could give rise to two motion pictures. Similarly, although two solid objects cannot occupy the same space at the same time, they can occupy that space at different times, so to speak."

"Keep going," ventured McCowan doubtfully. "I hope our viewers are following you through all this."

"Well, normally, when the Hoffstetter field generators shut down, they collapse back to the nearest quantized mintival. When the field generators overloaded, I believe we kicked over into the trailing mintival—hence the new world!"

"Well, I'll be!" said McCowan, genuinely shocked. "Can we get back?"

"I don't know," said Sowetsky, frowning. "We only know how to make the Hoffstetter field lag time, not precede time. If we tried it again, we might jump into yet another world that lags this one!"

"You can't be serious!" said McCowan.

"I'm deadly serious," said Sowetsky evenly.

"We're never going to get back, are we?" asked McCowan, her voice fading to a whisper as tears began to fill her eyes. She turned away from the camera for a moment. "I have one final question, Vlad," she said, regaining her composure with obvious effort. "Did you tell Professor Hoffstetter about this possibility?"

"Of course! I told him not once but several times!" said Sowetsky. "That's what burns me up so much."

"What did he say when you told him?"

"At first he told me 'science requires us to take risks,' and finally he told me to stop raising the matter."

Back in the dorm room there was brooding silence as the interview on the television drew to a close. Glenn suddenly got up and threw a magazine as hard as he could against the wall, cursed, and stomped out of the room. Within minutes, Dave heard the sound of an ominous rumble, like the growl of a giant beast being roused from a troubled slumber. He went out into the hall to investigate. Students were everywhere. Approaching the common room, he felt the air electric with tension. The fear and anger that had been building over the last two days was growing, and students were gathered in groups. Most had seen the television show, and they were loudly blaming Hoffstetter for their predicament.

The discussion grew increasingly heated. Some of the students began yelling and cursing Hoffstetter. Finally their anger reached a crescendo when someone shouted that they ought to storm the experimental area control building and make Hoffstetter pay for what he had done to them; the crowd surged downstairs.

Dave thought about saying something, but he knew he wouldn't be heard. He went back to his room. Whatever these angry students did would add to Uncle Charlie's heavy load of care. The loneliness of Dave's position washed over him like the tide coming in. What if they couldn't get back? He would never see his parents or siblings again. He began to think of his home and of times they had shared together. He tried to tear his thoughts away, but they kept going back to the home he might never see again. He remembered reading *Mysterious Island* by Jules Verne. How he'd loved the thrill of imagining himself one of the Americans learning how to survive with only his wits. Now he lived that dream. That cheered him up a little bit, but the dark thoughts that he might never see his parents and siblings again kept assailing him. Convincing himself that Sowetsky could be wrong provided the only relief.

What does Sowetsky know? He's only a graduate student. Uncle Charlie would tell us if this were really true, he thought. With that, he dozed off for a couple of hours.

It was almost midnight when Dave was awakened by his roommate's return. Glenn lurched against the doorway. His unruly black hair was matted, and there was an ugly purple bruise on his forehead. He was drunk. Torn and muddy as he was, Glenn flung himself into his chair by his desk.

"Ohh, my head!" he groaned as he gingerly felt the bruise. "I'm going to be sick."

Dave helped him across the hall to the bathroom where Glenn vomited, then removed his soiled clothes and staggered into the shower. Dave returned to their room. When Glenn came in, looking somewhat revived, he appeared to want to talk.

"So what happened?" Dave asked.

"Those bloody physicists," slurred Glenn. "Always trying things without thinking about anybody else. Look what they've done now. Stranded here and no way to get home."

"So what did you do?" repeated Dave.

Glenn looked at him from under the bruise, which had now grown to cover a good part of his face. "We tried to get at Hoffstetter. Everyone was saying he was over at the experimental control center, so we went over there. The campus police and the navy guys were waiting for us. We tried to break through, but we couldn't. They had stunners, and several of us got hit. They've converted the new zoology building into a temporary jail and dragged several of us back there. We regrouped and tried again. Reinforcements kept arriving. Finally, old O'Reilly, the chancellor, arrived and tried to talk to us. Somebody clipped him with a bottle and knocked him down. I'll say this for him; he has a lot of guts. He got back up and told us we had to pull together and we ought to go home. After we saw him knocked down and get back up, we quieted down and decided to listen to him and give up our assault.

"I happened to be with a bunch of guys from Locke. They all went back to a keg party over in their residence. Apparently they had planned it before the dislocation and had quite a lot of beer. I had a good time!"

"Yeah, I can see that," said Dave. "Let's get some sleep."

Chapter 6

Training for Sea

Just after sunrise the next morning, Dave sat shivering in the cold—on the heights overlooking West Harbor—along with 180 recruits from Socrates. West Harbor Bay reminded Dave of the two-dimensional diagrams he had seen of the human eye. The bay was approximately three quarters of a mile in diameter, and the shoreline was nearly circular. The mouth of the bay, located at the west side of the harbor where the pupil would have been in Dave's diagram, was bounded on the north by Causeway Point and on the south by Lighthouse Point. The stubby remains of Causeway Bridge could barely be seen from the heights behind the harbor.

When the naval personnel finally arrived, they announced that the recruits would be assigned to boats in groups of three. Names were called out, and the newly minted mariners made their way to their designated dinghy. When Dave's and Glenn's names were called, they joined a third fellow, a slender youth just under six feet tall, with light brown hair and glasses.

"Hello. My name is Al Gleeson," he said by way of introduction as he extended his hand first to Dave and then to Glenn.

"I'm Dave."

"And I'm Glenn."

"Have you fellows sailed before?" asked Al.

"No, we haven't," said Dave. "Have you?"

"Yes. I can't say that I'm experienced, but I've done some dinghy sailing with my brother." A shadow passed over Al's face, as if a painful memory had sprung up to trouble him. He appeared to shake it off. "Anyway, we're in dinghy number forty-one, so why don't we go and check it out to see if it's in good shape and ready to sail."

He led the way down the hill and along the quay to a dinghy. Al helped them check out the rigging and showed them how to raise and lower the centerboard. When it came time for them to cast off, he gave Dave the tiller and helped Glenn raise the sail. They left the quay and followed the boat ahead of them without incident. All day they practiced tacking, wearing, and learning to capture the wind efficiently. Al was a patient instructor. They didn't seem to encounter anything he hadn't seen before, and he seemed to know how to accomplish each maneuver. The sun was shining, and when the breeze picked up, the singing of the rigging and the whoosh of the bow wave made it exhilarating. Dave found it much more fun than watching endless video clips describing the various parts of the rigging and specific sailing terminology.

While the three companions felt good about their sailing accomplishments, the instructors, racing back and forth in Boston Whalers, worked overtime to cut them down to size. Many were from the naval station at the south end of the island and, exercising the prerogative of experienced sailors, they shouted rude remarks about the landlubbers' lack of sailing prowess. The novice sailors took all these insults good-naturedly, occasionally throwing them a deliberately contorted salute. Toward the afternoon, the wind veered to the east and clouds rolled in and it began to rain. The instructors had gathered the boats together and were showing them how to dump their dinghies, and how to use the centerboard to right them again before the dinghies "turtled," with mast pointing straight down. Wet from a combination of their time in the water and the cold rain settling in, Dave lost his morning cheerfulness and grew increasingly weary. When it was time to quit, the three headed home, too tired even to talk.

The next morning began very much as the day before, but after a short time of sailing in the bay, the instructors headed the lead boats out through the lens. Today, they would practice sailing in the rougher water of the channel as preparation for the six-mile trip to the mainland. When Dave's boat began to pitch more vigorously in the rollers of the strait, they put her on a course that gave them an unimpeded view of the mainland.

"I wonder what we're going to find when we get over there," said Dave.

"Have you ever read Jules Verne's *Mysterious Island?*" asked Al.

"I love that book!" said Dave.

"Maybe we'll get to live that story," said Al.

"I'm looking forward to paradise," offered Glenn. "With our technology, we won't have any trouble being 'king of the hill.'"

"Why paradise?" asked Al.

"Oh no!" groaned Dave. "Don't get him started!"

"You may have noticed," said Glenn, "that there are many good-looking, nubile females in our company."

"Go on," said Al, glancing sideways at Glenn.

"Well, on the mainland, as the terror of the unknown settles on them, they will increasingly seek out the protection of the alpha male."

"So why does an omega male like you think he has a chance?" fired back Dave.

"You'll see!" said Glenn unmoved. "I'm going to be in my glory!"

"I'm sorry I asked," muttered Al.

"What do you think we'll find over there, Al?" asked Dave.

"The naval guys have scouted the shoreline using one of the Boston Whalers, and they reported nothing unusual—just virgin forest coming right down to the shoreline. Yet even *Mysterious Island* had its mystery and its secret. To tell you the truth, I'm filled with misgivings, and the foreboding that the secret this place holds isn't going to be nearly as pleasant as finding a guardian captain Nemo."

Halcyon had begun to settle into a routine that blunted the edge of the crisis. Everyone was busy with their survival assignments, and there were no more university classes. Every night, there were keg parties that ended with a portion of the student population drunk. Some of the lecture halls had been turned into impromptu theaters that showed canned movies. Halcyon Television began broadcasting regularly from 7:00 p.m. to midnight. At Darwin Blackmore's insistence, he was given a one-hour slot on Friday nights to keep Halcyon up to date on Hoffstetter's efforts to return Halcyon home. That show was avidly watched by anyone who could get to a TV set.

Dave went to a keg party one night to help stave off the gloom and loneliness he felt when he had time to brood. But the next night he decided to go to a lecture by Frederick Aberhardt on the family of the twenty-first century. The lecture hall, which had more than a thousand seats, had at most 200 students clustered near the raised platform. Professor Aberhardt, an austere speaker, fixed his piercing eyes on the audience and spoke in a nasal tone while information was displayed on a screen behind him. In rapid succession, he reviewed selected segments of human history from the dawn of civilization to the beginning of the twenty-first century.

After forty minutes he came to his point. "Ladies and gentlemen," he droned, "I have recounted our history filled with war, injustice, slavery, prejudice, and intolerance to impress upon you the incontrovertible conclusion that religion, far from being a unifying and enlightening element in our existence, has been responsible for many, if not all, of the sordid events that make up our past. Behind the power of religion lies the nuclear family, in which the hierarchical authority structure that is the true power of religion is propagated to defenseless infants. Thankfully, we see significant evidence from sociology that this state of affairs is changing, albeit very slowly. Here in Halcyon, we have a unique opportunity to make a break with our past and develop a truly scientific society where our technology and understanding of human behavior can be harnessed to help us evolve to a new modality of social interaction, where we can realize the potential of our human spirit."

Dave would have found this boring except that the reminder of his lost family made it distressing. He was sorry that he'd come. All this talk about the family reminded him of his former life and awoke his loneliness. He missed his parents and siblings acutely. The thought that they might never really know what happened to him, and that he might never see them again, formed an impenetrable fog around him.

Aberhardt was finishing up. "As I have said, here at Halcyon, we have a glorious opportunity to make a break with our past. You students are choosing your futures. You can choose to build a new society that has forever thrown off the shackles of religion. Overturn the family. Embrace new relational structures that do not bind you to one another for life. Choose freedom!"

There was polite applause and then time for questions.

One student raised his hand. "Professor Aberhardt, how are we to bring about these transformations in Halcyon society? Shouldn't we outlaw the nuclear family and religions?"

Professor Aberhardt cleared his throat. "Although I think you would acknowledge that the terrible legacy religion has left our species would be justification enough to outlaw Christianity in particular, or even religion in general, I don't think that approach is the best one. Outlawing religion provokes public debate of these actions, and since 'any advertising is good advertising,' any attempt to ban religion overtly, even in a forward thinking place like Halcyon, may actually increase its influence. There are many fundamentalists in our midst who will seize any opportunity to proselytize, and they would use this kind of legal opposition as a call for greater activity. There is much sociological and statistical evidence to support that observation, especially in Marxist countries where religious suppression was tried for many decades with little success. To my mind, a much better approach is to make religion disappear from view. We live in a secular society, and we should avail ourselves of every opportunity to use the doctrine of separation of Church and state to make religion a private matter, and then make sure that the privacy that's left can't be used to propagate religion to others. By slowly eradicating religion from every aspect of public life, and then making all social interactions 'public life,' one can accomplish this ban quietly but effectively without ever triggering a public debate on the ramifications of a legal ban on religion.

"However, to make the elimination of religion complete, one also needs to eliminate the nuclear family. Even if we fully remove religion from public life and prevent the acquisition of new adherents from the public at large, the creeds will still propagate through the nuclear family. As a rule, birthrates are usually quite high among fundamentalists of all stripes, and so, over time, they take over a population.

"I'm sorry my answer is so long, but this is a very important point. The elimination of religion really comes down to the elimination of the nuclear family. When parents stay together for a long time in a marriage, and are able to teach their children—from an early age—their own prejudices, they are able to build a cocoon or scab around their children's minds so that it's very hard for educators and sociologists to circumvent the parents' dogmatic religious teaching. However we've found that if we can encourage couples to explore their desire for new, fresh relationships. That is to say if we encourage them to change their partners every couple of years, or even better, every few months, then the children arising from these liaisons are much more open to our guidance. Thus, encouraging promiscuity will effectively destroy the nuclear family and the ability of the family to inculcate religion in their young. We've moved a long way down this path, extolling the virtues of a free and liberated lifestyle. Continuing to do so, I believe we can be rid of the twin evils of religion and the nuclear family in our lifetime."

Another hand went up. Dave saw that it was Al. He hadn't known that he was also coming here after a hard day of sailing.

"Professor Aberhardt," said Al, "from my knowledge of history before the twentieth century, with the possible exception of France under Napoleon, there wasn't a single government that did not overtly or tacitly align itself with religion. In the twentieth century, those governments that were blatantly atheistic were, if anything, much more tyrannical and brutal than governments that had gone before. Don't all the misdeeds in our history that you are casting at the feet of religion really constitute a problem that finds its source not necessarily in religion but rather in human nature?"

Aberhardt leaned over the podium and glared at Al as he gathered his thoughts. "Sir," Aberhardt began at last, "tell me; were you raised in a traditional family?"

"My mother and father have stayed together to raise me, if that's what you mean," said Al. "In fact, they're still married."

Aberhardt smiled. "I'm afraid, young man, you bear the marks of your prejudiced upbringing. It's precisely these kinds of pathological delusions that we're seeking to rectify and eradicate. It's not really your fault. You had no choice. It's so very difficult to break out of the shackles of the ideas forced upon us while we were children and unable to defend ourselves intellectually. To escape the kind of indoctrination that you've experienced in your family is precisely why we strive to eliminate the twin evils of religion and the nuclear family. I believe there was a question at the back."

There were more questions, but Dave didn't listen to them. He admired the courage Al had shown in asking his question, even if Aberhardt had made him look like a fool. But was Aberhardt right? Were Dave's thoughts really the consequence of parental manipulation? Were the love and appreciation he felt for his parents only the products of conditioning that occurred when he was unable to defend himself?

Chapter 7

Botany Bay

On Monday morning just after dawn, a knock came on Dave's door.

"Rise and shine!" said Al cheerfully as he looked in. "Linder has decided we're crossing over to the mainland today."

The announcement gave Dave a shot of adrenaline. He was wide-awake in the twinkling of an eye.

"Have they scouted a landing site for us yet?" Dave asked.

"Yes," said Al. "Linder went over yesterday in one of the Boston Whalers with some of the naval personnel, and they've chosen a preliminary site for the colony, almost directly across from us. Why don't you fellows head down to the wharf? I'll meet you there after I rouse the others."

After a hurried breakfast, the two roommates finished packing their belongings, carried them down to the wharf and stowed their supplies in their dinghy. Dave sat on the wharf, dangling his legs over the edge, waiting for the others to arrive. The morning was bright and clear—ideal for sailing. With a gentle wind blowing out of the north they ought to make the crossing without much trouble.

Al and the others arrived and stowed their gear. A truck came with additional supplies for each dinghy.

When this cargo was offloaded, Linder gave the signal to embark. The dinghies began to leave the quay in single file.

With the Boston Whaler for support, Dave watched as the first of the 180 sailors from Socrates dormitory set off to cross the channel. He sensed everyone's spirits were high. Maybe they would go down in the history books as the ones to make momentous discoveries in this new world.

Soon it was their turn. Glenn cast off as Dave raised the sail, and Al steered them away from the quay to take their station in line. Their dinghy, *The Pitch and Toss,* was heavily laden and sluggish. Nevertheless they were able to get out of West Harbor easily, clearing Lighthouse Point without tacking. Even though the day was fair, the swell was rougher than any they had previously encountered. The name chosen for their boat took on a connotation none of them had intended. Both Glenn and Al became seasick, and they alternated between leaning over the gunwale and lying miserably on the mound of supplies. Dave, who was less prone to motion sickness, was left by himself to keep the dinghy on course.

They completed the crossing in about two hours. The Boston Whaler, worrying them like a dog herding a scattered flock of sheep, led them to a single island at the foot of a shallow bay. The island was shaped like a boomerang, with the apex pointing west toward the mouth of a creek. At low tide, the creek flowed around the island on its way to the retreating sea. The drop-off on the seaward side of Boomerang Island, as they named it, was steep enough that the fleet of boats could be moored there without grounding as the tide ebbed. The anchorage wasn't ideal, since the boats were exposed to an east wind, but it seemed the best that the coast had to offer.

The armed naval personnel scouted the small island and took up guard positions. The colonists in turn unloaded supplies as rapidly as possible, and late in the afternoon, the Boston Whaler escorted fifty dinghies back to Halcyon. Al was taking their dinghy back, and as Dave said goodbye to him, a pang of fear gripped his heart. There was no escape. A door had closed. They were committed. With about 130 colonists and only ten dinghies, only a few could retreat back to the safety of Halcyon if disaster struck.

Dave didn't have long to think about the danger, since they had to work quickly to set up their campsite. After the navy personnel chose a command center in the middle of the island, at the apex of the boomerang, Linder allotted the rest of the expedition four campsites that were arranged in a ring around the naval camp. The naval personnel worked efficiently and set up a solar powered communication center that would provide contact with Halcyon.

As Dave set up their tent, he was surprised to realize that the vegetation here was much like home. *I'm forgetting this is a new world. It's so similar to home; I was thinking I'm just on another camping trip.*

He looked at the vegetation with new eyes and recognized ash, beech, and oak trees. There were also plants Dave didn't recognize, but he wasn't sure if they were truly alien or simply less familiar plants from home. Near the shore was a low shrub, with shiny leaves like holly and beautiful red berries. He looked at it briefly. It had a pungent but not wholly unpleasant smell.

The tents erected, Linder and the naval commander, Glenn Mac-Donald, called everyone together. MacDonald addressed the group. "I want to stress that we need to be very careful in this new environment. Although many of the plants appear familiar, we're going to take no chances. We've brought two dogs and several rabbits along, and they'll try all of the local food before we do. After the food passes that test, a small number of volunteers will try the food for a week before we inflict it upon the whole company. Any questions?"

Dave thought wistfully about the departed boats.

But his fears appeared unfounded. Game was plentiful, and the dogs didn't get sick. They explored the immediate area of the mainland near the island. They followed a creek for several hundred yards into the abundant woods that surrounded Boomerang Island. A plant, which looked identical to the potato plant from home, grew in abundance in the sandy soil along the bank of the creek. The rabbits thrived on it.

The next few weeks passed quickly as they built their colony, which they named Botany Bay. Daily hunting expeditions and the abundance of white-tailed deer meant that meat was never in short supply. But the deep, narrow creek that flowed around Boomerang Island made crossing to the mainland difficult, even at low tide. So the colonists constructed a bridge over the creek and tidal flats. Dave worked long and hard driving wooden poles deep into the mud and securing the bridge to the supports.

Even though they had seen neither natives nor dangerous carnivores, Macdonald insisted they build a stockade with a fifteen-foot palisade on a promontory overlooking the creek. After Dave's team finished building both the bridge and the stockade, they moved on to build other structures: smokehouses, dormitories, and a large dining hall. Botany Bay began to look like a small village.

Every Friday all the radios would be tuned to Blackmore and Hoffstetter's joint broadcast from Halcyon. The colonists were heartened to hear that not all of the force field equipment had been destroyed, and Hoffstetter spoke confidently during the broadcasts of having them home by Christmas, or by next summer at the very latest. Everyone's spirits lifted at the prospect.

By the time the stockade was complete, Botany Bay had already grown to almost 600 inhabitants, as more and more recruits from the dorms Schopenhauer and Socrates were trained to sail and then ferried to the mainland.

Most of the trees in the vicinity of Botany Bay had been felled and used in the construction of the first buildings. A cry for wood from Halcyon had also been received. Clive Henderson, now the Governor of Botany Bay, decided that a lumber camp was needed farther up the creek. It could be used to supply logs for the construction of a large cookhouse on the mainland, and also to meet Halcyon's need for wood. Dave was chosen to join the construction crew for this new undertaking.

Chapter 8

Happy Berries

It was early in July before Dave returned to Botany Bay. Although late in the evening, a party was in full swing around the campfire at his base camp on Boomerang Island. Someone had brought a keg of the new Halcyon beer to the mainland, and the revelers were consuming the beer with great liberality.

"What's going on?" asked Dave, taking a seat beside Darryl Wyndhurst, one of the fellows from his camp.

"This is what's going on," said Darryl. He held out a handful of beautiful red berries, smaller than cherries but the same deep red color. "These are all the rage! We call them 'Happy Berries.' Try some."

Dave experienced a sense of misgiving, yet he also felt the weight of months of deprivation that made him yearn to try something daring and adventurous. He knew if he thought about it, he would talk himself out of trying the berries. In a rush he ate them before he could change his mind. He was disappointed and relieved at the same time. They were bitter. "They don't really taste very good," said Dave.

"Just wait awhile and you'll see why we like them," said Wyndham. "How about some supper?"

As they crossed the bridge to the mess hall, Dave felt his heart begin to race. He was feeling warm, but there were other changes too, feelings he wasn't used to but which weren't entirely unwelcome. Self-confidence, wellbeing, and power seemed to rise up within him. No obstacle seemed too hard to overcome; no task was beyond his reach. He had never felt so positive about their future. The venison they ate for supper tasted particularly delicious, Dave thought, and he really enjoyed the stimulating company of his comrades.

That night as he was lying on his bedroll, sleep would not come, even though he had worked very hard that day. The power and euphoria he had felt after consuming the berries had worn off by midnight, and he missed it. He got up and began to search for more of the berries along the shore. He found one of the bushes by the pungent smell, but as he searched feverishly for the fruit, he realized to his consternation, that it had been stripped bare. He swore, and began to run along the shore, heedless of the branches slapping at his face. Suddenly the smell of the Happy Berry bushes became strong. Down on his hands and knees, he wormed his way through thorn bushes until, scratched and torn, he found himself in the middle of a patch of Happy Berries. Eagerly, with shaking hands, he felt along the branches of the bushes until he found some berries. He tore them from the branch and shoved them into his mouth. He gave a contented sigh as the feeling of euphoria and power descended on him again.

Dave felt well, very well indeed. He made sure he always had a supply of Happy Berries, so that he never went through that episode of craving again. He would eat some berries just before bed and be content all night long. Not that he slept more than four hours at a stretch. He found that his strength had increased and he was able to chop wood at a prodigious rate. The days seemed to fly by.

—————

Late in July, Dave was walking through Main Street in Botany Bay after a week's work at the lumber camp when he heard his name called. Al ran up and clapped him on the shoulder.

"Dave, I heard that you were coming back today, and I've been waiting for you!"

"Al, how are you?" asked Dave without enthusiasm.

Al looked at him closely. "What's wrong with your eyes?" asked Al.

"What do you mean?" asked Dave.

"Your eyes—they have an orange tinge." Al looked grave. "You're a Happy Berry user!"

"So what if I am? What is it to you?"

Al walked beside him in silence for a few moments. "I came by to tell you it's your turn for furlough in Halcyon. We'll be managing a raft of logs, and I asked to take you along with me when we take a load of logs back home."

Dave's wave of anger gave way to excitement at the prospect of getting back to Halcyon.

Why do I have such a short fuse? Al meant no harm.

Dave couldn't bring himself to apologize. The best he could manage was an affable "When do we leave?"

"We leave with the tide. How soon can you be ready?"

"Give me fifteen minutes. I have most of my stuff on my back already."

When Dave arrived at the far side of Boomerang Island, Glenn, Al, and Floyd Linder were in deep conversation. When they saw Dave they dispersed and made ready to depart. Al helped Dave on board, and then Al and Glenn pulled the gangplank on board the raft. Linder attached a red handkerchief to a short mast and then waited until their tow would come. After about ten minutes, the fixed keel sailboat *Goin' Places* hoisted sail and passed them a line for towing. When the raft gathered way, the friends collected near the steering oar at the stern of the raft, and chatted.

Dave opened his pack and pulled out a bag of Happy Berries and popped several into his mouth. The juice began to dribble down his chin.

"So you've learned about Happy Berries, have you?" said Linder.

"Oh, you know about them?" said Dave defensively.

"Yeah," said Linder. "But don't let the chancellor catch you using them."

"What do you mean?" asked Dave, a cold hand touching his heart. "What do Happy Berries have to do with the chancellor?"

"When the chancellor heard about them, he outlawed them on Halcyon, on pain of imprisonment. We're supposed to be enforcing that edict at Botany Bay, but His Honor the Governor is turning a blind eye."

"I personally think O'Reilly is right, that we ought to be very careful with anything that addictive. If history has taught us anything, it's that these wonder drugs that seem too good to be true generally are," said Al.

"What right does O'Reilly have to tell us what do?" shouted Dave. He regretted his words right after he said them and put his head in his hands.

"Dave," said Al gently. "You know you're in trouble. You've got to stop using them!"

"But I can't!" said Dave, the misery of the last few weeks crowding in on him.

Al looked at the other two. "Dave, you're going to hate me, but we're your friends and we're going to help."

Before Dave could react, Al went to Dave's knapsack, grabbed the bag of Happy Berries, and flung them into the sea.

"Nooo!" said Dave, jumping up. The bag disappeared astern and sank.

Dave reacted instantly. In a rage he flung Al onto his back, pouncing onto his prone body. Floyd and Glenn grabbed Dave from behind. It took all their strength to get him off of Al.

When Dave had calmed down and regained his self-control, Al offered him a couple of tablets. "What's this?" asked Dave.

"It's sedovarin. It's about the only thing we've found useful at Halcyon for getting people off the Happy Berries when we lock them up. It takes away the cravings until you can handle them yourself."

Resigned, Dave took the two pills with a swig of water. "This was a setup," he said.

"Yes, I'm afraid so. Glenn told us about your condition. We figured there was nothing we could do while you were at Botany Bay, so we waited until our chance came, and your furlough seemed like the golden opportunity."

Dave didn't know whether he should be furious or thankful. In one sense they'd violated his personal rights, but if he were honest with himself, had he seen Glenn hooked, he probably would have done the same thing.

As the sedovarin took effect he fell asleep. When he awoke, he saw they were on the west shore of Halcyon and a Boston Whaler was hauling their raft close to shore. He could feel his desire for Happy Berries, which should have been overwhelming now, as a dull ache. He fought against the sensation. As he thought about the last few weeks and confronted the thought of facing Uncle Charlie, he was overcome with shame.

They anchored the raft so the logs could be hauled away at low tide. Having completed their task, the three friends waded ashore in the surf, and decided to walk back to campus rather than travel with *Goin' Places* to the harbor.

The changes that had taken place in Halcyon in the past few months took Dave by surprise. For one, the food supply had stabilized. For another, the chemical engineers had managed to make alcohol from fermented stock. This had been one of the first manufacturing processes they had brought online at the Halcyon chemical engineering pilot plant. The intent had been to process the alcohol into fuel, but it seemed that a significant fraction of the precious distillate was making its way to the campus pubs. As Botany Bay inhabitants on furlough, the three friends had received free passes to a local pub to sample some of the new Halcyon brew.

"Halcyon is in the middle of an election!" said a patron at the Phoenix, a local pub that had sprung up near the waterfront in an unused storage building. "It looks like it's going to be a close one between the old chancellor and Blackmore, the vice-chancellor." Dave heard lots of opinions on the election when the pub's patrons learned he'd just arrived from Botany Bay.

When the four companions finally left to head back to Socrates, they passed a university common where an election speech was being given. At Dave's insistence they stopped to listen. Darwin Blackmore, flanked by Hobbes, spoke at length about the excesses during O'Reilly's tenure as chancellor.

"Chancellor O'Reilly, although much appreciated for his service, is not the man to nurture our fragile democracy. He has been too ready to take action by himself without the consensus of the people; he has been too ready to fancy himself a dictator."

Dave's loyalty to Uncle Charlie flared up. "Don't they realize that O'Reilly had to do what he did to pull us through?" asked Dave.

"I agree, Dave," said Al, "but people are fickle, and it's easy to think only of what's been lost and not about what you would've done if you'd had to make the hard decisions."

Dave didn't want to hear any more. He sensed the mood of the crowd had turned against Uncle Charlie during his absence. It seemed that Uncle Charlie's efforts to pull them through the first few critical weeks after the dislocation were now being viewed with contempt and condemnation.

Who am I to talk? Only a few hours ago I was railing against my own uncle because of his stance on Happy Berries. He felt in his pocket and was reassured to find his bottle of sedovarin.

He and Glenn reached their dorm room. Al handed him another vial before he went to his room. "You'd better remember to take two of these a day until the both bottles are empty." Al looked at him for a long while. "I think you're going to be all right now. It was a near thing, but I don't think you were too far along. I do wonder what will happen to the others at Botany Bay. Many of them have been addicted since they got there, and there seems to be no way to get Henderson to stop supporting the habit."

Dave closed their door. Glenn was already in bed, snoring softly. Dave also tried to get some sleep; however the trauma of quitting Happy Berries combined with the attacks on O'Reilly agitated his thoughts to such a degree that he tossed and turned on his bed. Finally, in the early morning hours, exhaustion overwhelmed him, and he caught a few hours of much needed sleep.

Election day dawned overcast with intermittent rain. Nevertheless, the sweet fragrance of summer filled the air; someone had taken the time to plant flowers in the flowerbeds just outside of Socrates. Brilliant daylilies and snapdragons added some welcome color to the otherwise somber day.

At least we have time for a little beauty in the middle of our struggle for survival.

The lineups were short at the polling station, and showing his weatherworn student card, Dave was able to cast his ballot within a few minutes.

The dorm now had a pay center, where Dave received nominal payment for his service on the mainland. Now that food was no longer rationed, he could use the old US currency and some of the new, metal Halcyon coins to pay at the cafeteria. Socrates was only about one third filled now, since the rest of the population was at Botany Bay. Still, Dave noticed that with the advent of the Halcyon monetary system, everyone had become part shopkeeper. One couldn't go down the hallway without passing tables of items being offered for sale. Even the university commons served as marketplaces where Halcyonites could sell their belongings.

When Dave reached the cafeteria it was quite late, but he found he had a selection and chose a breakfast of eggs and fish. Eggs were an expensive delicacy since most of their chickens were kept as breeding stock and only a small fraction of the eggs were set aside for consumption. Nevertheless, like a sailor on shore leave, he felt that his long absence entitled him to spend his earnings lavishly.

During breakfast Dave watched the election coverage on the cafeteria television. Even at this early stage, the numbers were so heavily skewed in favor of Blackmore that it seemed certain Uncle Charlie would be defeated. Dave felt dismay wash over him, and with it, a renewed longing for Happy Berries. He took another sedovarin and went for a long walk, to Halcyon Lake and Halcyon Mountain on the southwestern end of the island. The rain kept most others indoors, but when he arrived at the dorm late in the afternoon, he was wet but refreshed.

He turned on the television and saw the broadcast of Uncle Charlie conceding the election and turning the reins of power over to Blackmore with a handshake. Blackmore spoke at length, praising O'Reilly and promising him a significant role in his own administration. Dave felt angry and sick. It seemed like a slap in the face for Uncle Charlie.

Glenn was still out, presumably getting caught up with his Halcyon girlfriends, so Dave headed over to the cafeteria for supper. After supper Dave remembered to take more sedovarin and went to the gym to work out. When he returned to Socrates, he was amazed to see O'Reilly on his floor waiting for him.

"How've you been, Dave?" he asked.

Dave felt himself turning red. *He must see that I have been using Happy Berries.*

"I'm so angry about the election, Uncle Charlie!" Dave sputtered. "How could they not recognize all that you've done holding this place together and getting us on our feet!"

Uncle Charlie raised his hand, stopping Dave's outflow of anger and sympathy. "Dave, I came over to see you, not to talk about Blackmore."

"Doesn't it bother you that you've been defeated?" asked Dave.

O'Reilly sighed. "It bothers me more than you could know. Blackmore is brilliant. He used his weekly television program to ingratiate himself with the Halcyonites. I'm not really a politician, and I realized too late what he was doing. Life isn't fair. We should try to be fair ourselves, but it's unreasonable to expect life to be fair to us. Even in this case, while we may inwardly oppose Blackmore and his cronies, we still have to try to do everything we can to make Halcyon not only survive but succeed as a society. I think we're in for a great many more changes, but never mind that now. I have some news.

"In view of my 'great service' to Halcyon, I've been appointed Governor of Botany Bay, replacing Henderson. They've saddled me with the unpleasant task of letting Henderson know he's been demoted to second in command, and so unless Henderson is an extraordinary fellow, he'll have great animosity towards me. They've put me in a position where I'm bound to fail. Blackmore really just wants to get rid of me so I'm not a nuisance to him. Still, I could use a break from Halcyon. The politics, which I've always found distasteful, is getting to me, and I'll be glad to be away from it.

"I have had to move out of the chancellor's residence, so I chose to come here and take an empty room on the fifth floor so I'd be close to you. I'm afraid you'll be seeing a good deal of me, perhaps more than you'll like." O'Reilly smiled warmly, and a year of care and worry seemed to leave him. He seemed younger and more relaxed than at any previous time since the dislocation.

Dave was relieved that Uncle Charlie never mentioned Happy Berries, and as he listened to the news about Uncle Charlie's assignment to Botany Bay, he realized how much he loved his uncle. It would be good to have him close.

Chapter 9

Bay Trouble

Over the next few days of furlough, Dave and O'Reilly spent time together walking in the northern woods of Halcyon, stopping at a new makeshift pub after their long walks. O'Reilly spoke of his childhood growing up with Dave's mother, and Dave talked about the happy times with his parents and siblings. The older man never mentioned Happy Berries, even though Dave was convinced the lingering orange tint of his eyes revealed his former addiction. The happy days passed swiftly, and the time came for both of them to travel to Botany Bay. Before leaving, Dave and O'Reilly visited the Halcyon armory attached to the metallurgy department. As yet, the manufacturing facility for sophisticated equipment hadn't been built, but a factory for converting scrap metal into swords, spears, and axes was already fully operational. Dave and Uncle Charlie were charged with taking a load of these weapons back to Botany Bay, along with other newly manufactured goods from Halcyon.

Although old shell casings could be refilled with Halcyon powder, bullets were in short supply. If the hunting on the mainland were to continue, bows and arrows would be needed to supplement bullets. While at the armory, they saw the first prototype of a new steel crossbow that would soon be made in quantity.

With Dave's help, O'Reilly loaded these supplies into the dinghy they were to use for the trip to the mainland. Dave was quite comfortable handling the dinghy for the crossing, and they reached Botany Bay in about an hour, a brisk northeast wind on their quarter.

The quay was on the north end of Boomerang Island. As they approached they saw a large raft about to get underway. Since the wind had backed to the northwest, Dave ran downwind to give the raft a wide berth and then ran close-hauled in along the coast to the quay. As the dinghy cut through the water, Dave had a chance to examine the southern end of the town. He could see that work had progressed even in the two weeks that he'd been away. Two new log bunkhouses had been erected at the southern edge of Botany Bay. A new pen for wild boar piglets had been built, and the first captured few now inhabited their new home.

When they approached the southern edge of Boomerang Island, Dave saw his first Happy Berry bush, and dread seized him. His supply of sedovarin was exhausted. He dragged his thoughts away from the bushes, now stripped of berries in the vicinity of the town.

"Are you expecting much trouble, Uncle Charlie?" asked Dave, resuming a conversation they'd had on the trip.

"Well, Henderson is in a difficult position," said O'Reilly. "Until today he was undisputed king of his domain. Knowing how Blackmore operates, I fully expect the sealed letter I'm carrying from the elected chancellor—explaining my new position—will come as a complete surprise to Henderson. It'll only serve to make relinquishing power more painful for him."

They reached the quay, made the dinghy fast, and scrambled onto the wooden planks. O'Reilly's suspicions seemed to be correct. There was no official party to greet the new Governor. By this time even the few colonists who had lingered to see the raft away had left, and Dave and O'Reilly were alone on the quay.

"Is there anything I can do to help?" asked Dave.

O'Reilly put down his kit, which he'd just hauled out of the boat, and turned. "There is one thing. I think it would ease my mind if Henderson didn't know that you're my nephew. When this sort of change happens, people become angry and look for a way to get even. I'm afraid that Henderson, or one of his subordinates, may take his anger out on you because it's hard to get to me." O'Reilly paused. "You mean a great deal to me, and I can't express how much the last two weeks have encouraged me—you're like the son I was never able to have—but I think it'd be better if we maintained a little distance, at least until I can see how the wind blows."

"I understand, Uncle Charlie." O'Reilly, his eyes brimming with tears, took Dave by the shoulder and gave him a surprisingly powerful hug.

Dave felt a profound sense of affection for his uncle. "Uncle Charlie, why don't you go on ahead? I can unload the supplies."

Next to the quay was a wooden shed, where wheelbarrows were kept for hauling supplies. It took four trips for Dave to get their cargo to the armory and to the general store. When he had finished his task, he walked the well-worn path back to his camp. He met Darryl Wyndhurst just as Wyndhurst was crossing the causeway from the mainland.

"Ho, Dave!" Wyndhurst said. "You're back! What's new at Halcyon?" His eyes had a bright orange tint. It gave him a malevolent, predatory look.

"Well," said Dave, "they just finished an election, and we have a new chancellor, Darwin Blackmore." He immediately regretted bringing up the election.

"I didn't even know they were holding an election," said Wyndhurst. "But I'm not sorry to hear old O'Reilly has been given the boot. By all accounts Blackmore's a good man. He's making sure we're going to get home by Christmas."

"What's new here?" asked Dave, trying to change the subject.

"Not much," said Wyndhurst. "We've managed to locate quite a supply of these along the shore farther south. They don't seem to grow inland though." He was holding out a handful of Happy Berries.

Dave's flesh crawled at the sight of the red berries. "You'd better get rid of those," he said.

"Why?"

"Since O'Reilly lost the election, Blackmore has appointed him Governor of Botany Bay."

Wyndhurst cursed. "The old reactionary! He outlawed Happy Berries on Halcyon, and he's going to outlaw them here too! Well, he's going to have a fight on his hands!"

That doesn't sound very good! Excusing himself, Dave headed to his tent to catch up on some sleep, leaving Wyndhurst to continue his rant to himself.

Dave rejoined his work crew the following day and tried to focus on his job. Even though he avoided any talk about the new Governor, he could see the agitation of the townspeople. Henderson's supporters spoke loudly and openly about putting O'Reilly in his place, even if they had to use force. Dave could almost always tell, by the orange glint in a person's eye, how strongly he or she opposed O'Reilly.

Later that week, Dave was walking home after working on a new bunkhouse when he found himself surrounded by four burly men. Malevolence poured out of their orange eyes.

"So you're O'Reilly's pup!" said the first, giving Dave a shove. Dave was big and strong, and the shove proved ineffectual. This seemed to infuriate the four, and they jumped him. As Dave was going down, he caught one assailant solidly with an elbow to the solar plexus. The fellow grunted and went down on one knee. The other three brought Dave to the ground. One had him in a headlock, while the other two began to punch him.

Suddenly there was a shout and Dave felt one of the attackers pulled off of him. Dave was strong enough to break the headlock of the other and landed a solid punch to the body of the third. The assailants had had enough and disappeared around the nearest building.

Dave looked up and saw Glenn. "Hey, Glenn, am I glad to see you!"

"What are you doin' picking fights? Aren't they workin' you hard enough? Too much excess energy?"

Dave slowly got to his feet, gingerly felt his ribs, and winced.

"I didn't. I was minding my own business," he gasped.

"I know. Let's get out of here."

Glenn helped Dave walk back to camp. "You know," said Glenn, "it's all over town that you're O'Reilly's nephew. He's not popular here, you know."

"I wonder how that got out?"

"If you ask me," said Glenn, "it wouldn't surprise me if Blackmore and Henderson had something to do with it. Blackmore still sees your uncle as dangerous competition, and Henderson is now a valuable ally of Blackmore's."

"How do you know all this?"

"Well, there's a pretty young woman at the communications center—"

"The communications center?" interrupted Dave. "I thought you were seeing that lumberjack woman?"

"I am. Don't call her a lumberjack; it sounds—well, it sounds too burly."

"Okay, okay!" said Dave. "Tell me how you found out about the Blackmore connection."

"Well, as I was saying, a young lady at the communications center has found my charms irresistible and has provided me with some useful information—as well as a good time, I might add. Being of an inquisitive nature, she managed to read some messages from Blackmore to Henderson, and she told me about them."

The next morning Dave received an invitation to have breakfast with Uncle Charlie. They made small talk for a few minutes, and then Dave steered the conversation toward Blackmore. "How are you settling in as Governor?" he asked between mouthfuls.

"It's been tough—pretty much as I expected it. But I'm worried more about Halcyon than I am about Botany Bay," said O'Reilly.

"Is it Blackmore?" asked Dave.

"Yes, it's Blackmore. I ask myself whether or not it's simply my resentment at losing the election. But I don't think so. Darwin Blackmore is a fanatic. I don't know exactly what he'll do, but whatever it is, it won't be good, either for Halcyon or for our freedoms."

"What do you think he might do?" queried Dave.

"Do? I don't really know. I think he still sees me as an enemy and as trouble. I think he's been in touch with Henderson and is working to make trouble for me here. That could just be politics—one political opponent eliminating a competitor. But my worry about Blackmore goes deeper. Blackmore isn't only ambitious, he views the world and the people in it as machines, and he's convinced that he's the one to pull the handles and push the buttons."

They resumed their breakfast. Dave enjoyed the fresh biscuits and wild raspberry jam. At last, after O'Reilly had wiped his mouth with a well-worn cloth napkin, he changed topics. "Dave," said O'Reilly, gesturing at Dave's black eye, "I heard about what happened yesterday, and I'm worried. Henderson isn't strong enough to take me on yet, but now that he knows about you, you're in danger."

"So you know about Henderson's information about me from Blackmore?"

"Yes, I do. That's the main reason I asked you to breakfast. There's no longer a need for secrecy."

"Well, don't worry about me, Uncle Charlie. I can take care of myself. You should have seen the other guys."

Uncle Charlie laughed. "Yes, I heard. But seriously, if you won't listen on account of your own safety, listen on my account. As long as you're here, Henderson will hold you as ransom, threatening to attack you if I govern according to my best judgment and eliminate Happy Berries. It would ease my mind a great deal if I knew you were out of his reach. Listen, I have an idea. Before winter, I'm sending Floyd

Linder on an exploration expedition, and I want you to go with him."
He unrolled a hand-drawn map that showed Botany Bay in the center.
"We've sent out short expeditions in the vicinity of Botany Bay looking for resources, and from the little we know, we seem to be stopped
on every side. In the north there's a great river. On the other side of
the river are marshes. If one goes south, after about sixty miles or so
one reaches a swamp. But I don't know what lies more than a day or
so inland from here. We can see the coastal mountains about sixty
miles inland, but we don't know how to get through them or what lies
beyond them.

"I'm going to send you down the coast with Linder to try to find
a path through the swamp or a pass through these mountains to the
west of us. When you're reasonably sure you've found a way out of
this box, report back and we'll be set for our next move in the spring."

"Why aren't you sending the naval guys?" asked Dave.

"Good question. I can already see I have a real problem here,"
said O'Reilly. "The addiction to Happy Berries is much deeper than
I'd figured, and Henderson is part of the conspiracy. His spies are all
around me. I really don't know who I can trust. I'm convinced the
berries are dangerous, and I'm going to stop the practice, but I don't
know how many people are hooked. In any case, I'll need all of the
naval personnel here to support me. I'm counting on the fact that I'm
an ex-navy guy to help."

Chapter 10

The Expedition Heads South

On the third of September the exploration party assembled on Boomerang Island for departure. Dave was wearing full gear, with his short sword fastened onto his hip, his pack on his shoulder, and a stout ash staff in his hand. He'd been elated to hear that Glenn and Al were coming along on the trip. He also knew Floyd Linder from Socrates and Vlad Sowetsky from that fateful television interview that had led to the riot. There were five in the expedition he did not know: Tom Chartrand, Dwight Larsen, Kyle Jensen, Brendon Monk, and Stan Bigelow. Bigelow, a powerfully built youth who was a biology major, had volunteered for the expedition in order to catalog the flora and fauna encountered on the journey.

Dave was chatting with Glenn about the new crossbows they had received from the Halcyon armory when Al and Floyd arrived at the shore carrying rifles.

"We got 'em!" said Floyd, holding up his rifle. "But we only have 200 rounds of 9 mm ammo and we were told to bring back the empty shells. Are we all here? Let's get started."

Four small dinghies had been commandeered for the journey south along the coast. Floyd dispersed the expedition members among the craft. Al and Glenn joined Dave in the third boat.

They had no sooner started their journey, than Glenn began to complain. "Why don't we have any women on this expedition?"

"I'm sure Governor O'Reilly, ever protective of the gentler sex, knew you were coming along and made plans accordingly," said Al, chuckling.

"Yeah, but in these days of equality, having ten men and no women on an expedition is simply not right," lamented Glenn. "In fact, it's downright indecent!"

"Governor O'Reilly is from the old school, and I'm sure in his view, having women along on an expedition like this would be an added complication we don't need," said Al in a more serious tone.

"I still think it's undemocratic and inegalitarian. It's also not going to be much fun," muttered Glenn.

The shore passed by slowly as they sailed south in the gentle breeze. That evening, after a long day in which they had covered only about fifteen miles, they camped on a small island just off the mainland. In two more uneventful days they completed the rest of the sixty-mile trip to the edge of the southern swamp. When they had unloaded their supplies on a sandy beach in a cove sheltered from the breakers, they bid the dinghies goodbye and organized their supplies for the trek inland.

Floyd called them together. "I want us to use the buddy system. No one is to be out of sight of their buddy for any reason."

Floyd had a compass and had been conscientiously mapping the coast on the voyage south. In his journal, he was making approximate notes of their position by dead reckoning. He made one final notation in his notebook and then indicated the direction they were to take and led the way into the forest.

Dave walked with Glenn. The ground was covered with leaves accumulated from the passage of many seasons in a forest of oak, alder, and beech. The canopy was so dense that only small bushes grew in the gloom of the forest floor. The land rose gently toward the west, and the walk was easy. In the first two hours they crossed only one stream, which flowed southeast, and they refilled their water bottles from a clear pool.

Soon thereafter the land began to rise more steeply as they approached a ridge of rock running north to south. When they reached the top of the ridge, Dave could see the same spine of rock breaking out of the green forest like a monstrous sea serpent, with loop after loop of its coils breaking out of a green sea. The spine of rock jutted into the fetid fens to the south, a narrow stone peninsula, and then disappeared as if it too had sunk into the swamp. The wasteland of pools and cypress groves stretched before them south and west until lost in a distant mist at the edge of sight.

The sunlight on the ridge top was so refreshing after the gloom of the forest that Floyd decided they should take a break. They gathered in a tight group and opened their packs for a bite to eat.

"Have you seen any new species?" Floyd asked Stan.

"No, I haven't," said Stan with his mouth full. "I saw one Happy Berry bush at the coast, and since then everything else, as far as I can tell, is the same as at home."

"Well, isn't that mighty unusual?" asked Floyd.

"Oh, I don't know," said Stan. "It just means that life here has evolved very much the same as on Earth. Besides, it's not as if things are completely identical. There are some new species here, like Happy Berries and the opera bird."

"But don't you think," asked Al, "that if you had made an evolutionary prediction before you had the facts, you would have predicted a very different set of species here than at home?"

"It seems to me you could argue it both ways," said Stan. "On the one hand, you could argue that the isolation would produce very different species, but on the other hand, since the environment is the same you could argue that the optimally adapted species would be the same."

Al looked skeptical but said nothing. Dave could tell by Stan's grimace that he didn't like Al and they'd obviously argued about this before.

"Isn't it amazing," said Stan, looking at Al, "how the fact of evolution explains everything so well? Don't you agree, Al?"

Al hesitated, as if debating whether he should answer or not. "I suppose I agree," he said slowly, "but not in the way you think. I think that anyone who wants to explain any biological fact by calling on convergent evolution to explain similarities and divergent evolution to explain differences has so many degrees of freedom available that he can use them to explain anything. The real test of a theory is the ability of that theory to make a nontrivial prediction. That's why I asked what you would have predicted."

Stan went scarlet and grew angry. "I'm not stupid! I can see where you're heading. You're challenging one of the most thoroughly established principles of science. What are you, some kind of religious fanatic who doesn't believe in the theory—"

"Hold it!" interrupted Floyd. "I asked a simple question and don't want to get into any philosophical debates—"

"It's not philosophy—" cut in Stan.

"Nevertheless, let's get going. We've got a lot of ground to cover." With that Floyd rose and headed off down the west side of the ridge. The others followed in single file.

They traveled inland for the rest of that day. The woods, now predominantly maple and ash with the occasional basswood, was open and crisscrossed with game trails. Late in the afternoon, at the far edge of a meadow, Dave saw a doe and a fawn moving along the margin of a quiet brook. The doe stopped to look at them for a moment and then bent over for a drink from the stream before she continued on. *She's never seen humans before.*

During the course of the afternoon the wind veered to the south and the heavy smell of decaying plant matter filled their nostrils. The land leveled off, and they crossed a broad plateau of copse-fringed meadows. Floyd directed them south. When they reached the edge of the plateau and looked to the south and west, they saw an unbroken vista of stagnant pools, swamp grass, and clusters of cypress trees stretching as far as the eye could see. There was no option but to continue west.

They walked along the edge of the plateau. The open country made walking easier, although the smell of the swamp was overpowering. Their path was cut by several small creeks that splashed down the steep slope to join that reeking mosaic of fetid pools and masses of decaying plant matter.

That evening they approached a tall hill, an outlier from the mountains that they could see in the distance. The north side of the hill was a steep treed slope, but the south side was a jagged cliff, as if a giant had riven the hill with a sword stroke to the rock beneath. Floyd decided they needed to climb the hill to get their bearings, to search for the best route, and hopefully to make camp above the noisome smell of the fens. They toiled up the steep eastern slope, scrambling over patches of loose soil, grabbing vines and branches to bring them over the treacherous spots. When they finally reached the top, they were exhausted and sat down to get their bearings. They searched the swamp for any sign of a route south.

"There is nothing but stinking swamp as far as the eye can see!" said Floyd as he spat to clear his throat of the choking stench wafting toward them in the gentle south wind.

"I don't see any sign of higher ground or even a water channel we could navigate for any distance," said Al.

Floyd continued to scan the swamp with his binoculars.

"No, nothin'. I can't even see the other side from the top of this hill. Just one reeking pool after another, surrounded by hummocks of trees and swamp grass. I don't even see any birds."

"So now what do we do?" asked Brendon Monk.

"Let's get some rest and keep pushing westward along the edge of this morass. I sure would be happy to see the end of it," said Floyd.

They searched for a level area to make their camp and settled on a hollow partway down the northwest slope of the hill. They were so tired that they had a quiet supper and then fell asleep, exhausted.

The next morning, while Glenn was still snoring peacefully in his sleeping bag, Dave scrambled out of their tent and worked his way back up the hill to look at the surrounding terrain in the morning light. The air was already warm, and with a gentle wind blowing from the north, the air was free from the smell of decay. The morning was beautiful. Bushes of hibiscus peeked out from among the sycamores covering the northern slope of the hill. The large trumpet-shaped flowers were a stark contrast to the green foliage. When he reached the crest, Dave looked north and saw fog, like a gray garment, covering the plateau. In the distance, first hills and then the purple ramparts of mountains reared above the mist in the morning light. In the immediate vicinity, their hill was an island rising out of a sea of fog. The stillness and beauty took his breath away.

He walked over the crest to the southern cliff. A thick ghostly mist also covered the swamp. Farther south the gentle northern breeze collided with a wind from the distant ocean, stirring the mist so that it boiled like a caldron with only the occasional cypress tree appearing and disappearing in it.

As Dave walked along the edge of the cliff he heard a voice. Rounding a rock face, he was surprised to see Al sitting on a stone with a leather-bound book in his lap. He was praying. Across from him sat Tom Chartrand and Dwight Larson in silence.

Dave felt awkward and embarrassed, as if he'd intruded on a private conversation. He quietly backed away, wondering if they would meet together every morning before breakfast.

Later, Dave told Glenn about what he'd seen, and asked him what he thought.

"Al's an okay guy, but you don't want to get mixed up in this religious thing," said Glenn.

"What makes you say that?"

"You know! If you're religious, your life is all about rules. 'Don't do this.' 'Don't do that.'"

"Maybe the rules have a purpose? Maybe they help you tell right from wrong. Don't you have a sense that one of the problems we have at Halcyon is that now that we're cut off from the rest of the world, and Blackmore has started to make up our rules, we've lost our sense of right and wrong?"

"Look, Dave," said Glenn. "You worry too much about right and wrong and the goings-on at Halcyon. What you need to do is have a little time for yourself. If you think about it, it won't be too many years before we're both crotchety old men. We need to get as much out of our twenties as we can. Look out for number one; squeeze as much fun and happiness out of this world as you can, and forget the Blackmores. They'll set themselves up so they're talking for God, and if you're listening to them you'll end up being their dupe."

"You could be right," said Dave. "I feel like I've been living under a rain cloud. I guess that's what you're seeing. I excused it because I was missing my family and I was worried about Uncle Charlie. Is that wrong?"

"I wouldn't say it's wrong exactly, but you've got to snap out of it." Glenn lowered his voice. "Look, Dave, if you don't stop taking life so seriously you could end up spending your mornings sitting on a cold rock talking to a make-believe friend, just like Al does. What you need, Dave, is a girlfriend—no, at least two girlfriends."

Dave burst out laughing. "Glenn, you're so predictable!" Then he continued in a more serious tone. "My life is complicated enough. I don't see how making it more complicated would help. Besides, there isn't a female within six days of strenuous hiking from here, so you're prescribing medicine that just isn't in the cabinet."

"Maybe so, but in a couple of weeks when we find the passage out of this box, we'll head back home and you can take my advice."

"Glenn, my parents fell in love and stayed together to raise us, and they're still in love. If I meet a girl that I could love forever, then what you say makes sense and I'd be after her like a terrier after a bone."

Glenn looked at Dave critically. "Terrier after a bone? I can see you're going to take an awful lot of work until you're presentable."

Glenn stooped down, broke off a blade of grass, and thrust it between his teeth. "Loving forever, as you put it, is precisely what you *don't* want. You want to have a bit of fun, with no entanglements. That's why I said 'two' girlfriends. It helps a young whelp like you keep things in perspective."

"I just think you're fooling yourself Glenn, if you really believe you have no entanglements. I think we often don't know the value of people until we lose them. I'm missing my family now, and maybe that's a good thing. Rather than find a girlfriend to help me get over my loneliness, perhaps I should use this time to appreciate my family the way they deserve. Maybe I should be glad I'm under a cloud."

Dave sat down on a rock and wiped the sweat from his brow with his kerchief. "I never told you about my older brother." Dave felt his eyes filling with tears. "We used to fight like cats and dogs. He seemed to always be first and in my way. I sometimes wished I could be the oldest in the family. Then one day we were climbing up a quarry wall near home. We weren't supposed to, but we just did it and didn't tell Mom and Dad. Joe was ahead of me up the wall. He lost his footing and slid down past me. He caught a rock not six feet from me. He looked at me with eyes the size of saucers, pleading for help. I was frozen. I couldn't move. Then he lost his hold and fell. I can still hear the thud that followed a few seconds later. How I miss Joe. How I wish I could have grabbed him!" Dave's voice cracked, and he wiped the tears from his eyes.

"You know I rue all those times I wished I were the oldest. I only really grew to value him after he was gone."

Glenn was quiet until it became awkward. "Hey, Dave, I'm really sorry about your brother. But don't you see how that entanglement has caused you great pain? Isn't that what I've been saying? The more distance you can keep, the less vulnerable you are."

"I know what you're saying, Glenn, but somehow the pain has to be worth it. I don't know how it's going to come out, and I can't really explain it. I'd rather feel this pain of missing him, dreadful as it is, than to feel nothing. There has to be a reason for this. I just have to discover what it is."

Chapter 11

The Southern Fens

The next three weeks were spent skirting the edge of the swamp. They managed to shoot a few wild turkeys with their crossbows, and each night they set lines with bait in the streams they came across. Invariably they would catch several trout for the next morning's breakfast.

The mountains in the west grew closer and larger with each day's journey. They passed through a country of rolling hills filled with pine forests. The fragrance of the pine and spruce masked the smell of the swamp. The best part of the day for Dave was always evening, around the campfire when the nightlines were set, potatoes had been dug, and supper was digesting with the help of Halcyon tea. As they got to know each other, the group talked about anything and everything; they talked of the families they missed, their hopes for the future, and of course, with Glenn around, they talked about girls.

On this night, Dave was just settling back when Brendon asked Floyd about a girlfriend at home. Then a debate began about "the ideal woman." "The ideal woman," began Glenn in his best imitation of Professor Aberhardt, "is one who dedicates all of her energy to fulfilling every whim and desire of her man."

"Oh yeah!" muttered Brendon. "How likely am I to find a woman like that?"

Floyd chuckled and said, "You're dreamin', Glenn. Why would any woman do that for you? What could she possibly get out of a relationship like that?"

"Why would she do that for me?" said Glenn solemnly. "She would do that for me because her biological makeup wires her up that way and because being associated with someone of my reputation, social standing, and of course general good looks, would make her the envy of womankind everywhere. Just think of how her status in the female hierarchy would be elevated."

There were guffaws all around.

"I think it would also help if she weren't too bright," Tom added innocently as an afterthought.

The others laughed uproariously. Even Floyd and Al were laughing. Dave was laughing so hard that tears came to his eyes.

Trying to divert attention from this unfortunate remark, Glenn turned to Al, who was sitting next to him, and said, "Okay, wise guy. Laugh it up. How would you describe the ideal woman?"

Al composed himself and considered Glenn's question. "I don't know, Glenn. On this subject I bow to your superior experience."

"Oh, don't encourage him!" said Tom.

"You must have had a girlfriend," said Glenn. "Tell us about it."

"Actually, I never had a girlfriend. I don't even have a sister, and my mother died soon after my father abandoned us when I was twelve years old. Even when I went to live with my father and my stepmother, I hated my stepmother so much that I never really learned anything positive about women from her."

The circle had become quiet. They had moved from raucous laughter to tomb-like solemnity in scant seconds. Pleased at the diversion of attention, Glenn pressed the matter. "But you must have had a girlfriend in high school. You must have some idea about the ideal woman."

"No, I can't say I even had a girlfriend in high school," said Al sheepishly. "But I did have a number of good friends who were girls, more like sisters than girlfriends, I guess."

There were snorts of disbelief.

"No, it's true!" said Al. "You see, my father was a professor of psychology and a Marxist. He detested all religion as the 'opiate of the people,' and he wouldn't let my mother go to church even though she wanted to. After my mother died and I became old enough to stand up to him, I went to church more out of rebellion than conviction. I met a lot of nice girls at church."

"More out of rebellion than conviction? I could find religion if there were enough good-looking women there!" hooted Vlad.

"Maybe that's where you should look for your 'compliant female,'" said Kyle, looking knowingly at Glenn. "Maybe you could find one that would satisfy your every whim and desire out of religious conviction."

"Let Al finish. We still haven't heard about the ideal woman," said Floyd.

"I don't think any of the girls I got to know as friends would have fit Glenn's description. Anyway, to me, women are an alien species. I can't understand how they think or how they react, but somehow the sum total of what they are is an inexpressible delight."

"My dear, uninformed celibate," said Glenn. "Your inexpressible delight in womankind is nothing more than your disguised sex drive."

"I couldn't disagree more!" protested Al. "If you look carefully at the woman of your darker dreams, she will be an infernal Venus. She will of course be rapturously beautiful, but she will also, of necessity, be wanton and to some extent evil. The whole point is, of course, that we could misuse and abuse this beautiful evil Venus without regret or even a pang of guilt, precisely because she is evil and deserves to be used and then discarded. On the other hand, the girls I was able to get to know as good friends were beautiful, but they were also innocent, and only a complete rogue could lie to them and steal their innocence and trust. Even if a rogue did so, I can't believe it wouldn't leave a bad taste in his mouth."

Al's exposition had been rendered so passionately an awkward silence followed. Dave, not wishing the awkward moment to linger, said, "For a guy who insists he doesn't know anything about women, you said quite a lot."

"Call it a Socratic paradox," said Al, smiling mischievously in the firelight. "Since I—perhaps only I—correctly recognize that I know zero about women, I actually know more about women than some others," here he looked at Glenn, "who mistakenly think they know a lot, but what they know is completely wrong."

"Wrong? Wrong! Your knowledge is purely theoretical, while mine is experimental," said Glenn, thumping himself on his chest.

"Anyway, Glenn, you're not doing us any favors," said Dave.

"How so?" answered Glenn.

"You've been telling us time and time again we should live for ourselves. Your philosophy is 'look out for number one.' By telling everybody around you, including the women, that they ought to live for themselves, you're actually destroying what little chance we have to find these women of our dreams who will unselfishly fulfill our every whim and desire."

After the laughter had again subsided, they headed off to get some sleep.

———————

The ten men crossed another plateau and entered the foothills of the mountains. The hills were clad in a fir wood that made walking difficult, so they faced the constant danger of losing their sense of direction and traveling in circles.

Late one afternoon, as they crossed a shallow ridge, they came upon a long narrow dell bordering a pond that was shaped like the narrow willow leaf point of a spear. At the north end of the pond, a creek from a high alpine valley cascaded over moss covered rocks. About 100 yards to the south, the water from the pool plunged over a rocky ridge to fall churning and foaming to the fens far below. On the east side of the pool, near the waterfall, there was a meadow of luscious green grass dotted with tamarack and pine.

"Let's make camp here," said Floyd, leaning his pack against a tree near the water's edge.

"Stan, you set the night lines for the fish. The rest of us will scatter and look for some food. We're running low."

Dave set his pack down at the edge of the forest as he pulled out his foldable shovel and headed back up the slope. He had seen some potatoes not far from the game trail they had been following. He found them quickly and soon had a poncho full of new red potatoes, which he carried back to his pack.

Dave set them down and was just opening his pack to look for a pan so he could wash the potatoes, when he heard Al's voice in the distance.

"What are you doing, Stan?"

Dave looked up. About twenty yards away Stan rose suddenly from the ground, holding a book. He closed the journal, tossed it onto Floyd's pack, and stretched himself to his full height.

"What's it to you, Gleeson?"

"Why are you going through Floyd's belongings?"

At five feet eleven inches, Al was as tall as Stan but much slighter of build. Stan looked him up and down.

"I hear," said Stan menacingly, "that fundamentalists are supposed to turn the other cheek if someone hammers them. Is that right?"

Stan was clenching and unclenching his fists as he slowly approached Al. Dave approached quietly from behind.

"I don't have that problem," said Dave. Stan turned abruptly, and Dave saw a momentary flash of fear cross his eyes.

"I was only kidding," said Stan with a laugh.

"What were you doing with Linder's journal?" asked Al again.

Stan looked from Al to Dave, eyes smoldering. "I've been keeping track of the plants I've seen, and I just wanted to check our location with Floyd's maps so my notations will be accurate. I knew Floyd wouldn't mind."

"But you'll tell him, right?" asked Dave.

"Yeah, I'll tell him," said Stan as he put the journal carefully back in Floyd's pack.

Chapter 12

The Worm Caves

The expedition left the willow pond and climbed a tall ridge that cut across their path. To stay near the edge of the swamp, they had to cross one deep ravine after another in seemingly endless succession. The ravines cut into high hills in the north that grew in height as they neared the mountains, which now towered over them in the west. One day they climbed out of a steep valley to see the end of a mountain chain rear up before them out of the rugged country. The last mountain broke out of the rolling hills like a giant spike that had been driven through the earth from underneath by gargantuan hammers. Perhaps the southern slopes of the last mountain would let them pass the swamp?

As Dave and his companions toiled across the tree-clad slopes, their hearts came alive with hope they had at last found a way past the dreadful never-ending swamp. However when they reached the last hill before the mountain face, they were dismayed to find mounds of broken rock—likely created by some violent tumult of ages past—heaped up against the mountainside on the fringe of the swamp.

"Now what do we do?" muttered Floyd as the party gathered at the edge of the broken rock.

"We could try it anyway," suggested Brendon. Dave was so desperate to get past the swamp, that he gave his assent even though a voice inside him whispered that it would be insane to do so. The others must have felt the same desperation to get past the mountains and the swamp, since there was general assent to the proposal.

So they began the trek across the broken rock. Floyd led the group in single file over gigantic boulders, some the size of houses. The rock field was treacherous. Glenn, wandering off the trail that Floyd had proven, stepped on a loose rock and fell heavily onto a sharp shard. The group stopped, and while Al bandaged up Glenn's leg Dave looked for a rise to get a better view of the rocks ahead. He stepped on a large flat rock, only to have it shift as the soft scree underneath gave way. It slid about fifteen feet and then stopped, pitching him headlong onto a pile of rubble. He was bruised and shaken, but hadn't broken any bones.

They continued, Floyd leading them closer to the cliff face, where the broken rock was less treacherous. After three hours they had gone less than a mile over the difficult terrain. As they walked, they heard the distant thunder of falling ice as the warm sunny day melted the ice fields far up the steep mountainside.

In the afternoon, clouds moved swiftly in and added to the gloom the travelers felt in their hearts. An impassable field of jagged boulders now forced them right up against the vertical mountainside, and they could lean on the sheer cliff wall with their right hands. A steady drizzle of rain had begun to fall, and the companions were bitterly cold. As Dave craned his neck to stare fearfully up the sheer rock wall, he could see that the rain had turned to snow farther up.

The rock before them gave way to a field of scree, much more extensive than any they had seen before. This scree, made up of small round pebbles, slid at the smallest provocation, making their footing treacherous and walking tiring. Finally, as the intensity of the rain increased, Floyd led them to an overhang, where they came upon the entrance to a cave. When Dave looked down the jumble of broken rock from the cave entrance, he saw that the area below them was one long tongue of scree, as if the gaping hole were a pipe that gave rise to a pebble waterfall. The passageway was not straight but bent in a slow curve to the right, descending gently as it penetrated deep into the mountainside.

"Let's get out of the rain and take a break," said Floyd.

They readily assented and began to explore the cave with their weapons ready. After just fifty feet, the tunnel widened into an irregular chamber with a flat, pebbly floor, then narrowed again as it rose, curving left.

"Stop!" said Floyd. "We can see far enough down the passageway to detect anything coming from that direction. Let's rest here. At least we have enough light from the entrance to see what we're doing."

Floyd assigned watches, and the rest stretched out on the floor of the chamber to sleep. Dave had the first watch, but found himself nodding off after the day's exertion. He woke with a start. He had been dreaming that he was in a New York subway station as a freight train passed the platform. The loud rumble faded. The tunnel, previously filled with the subdued light of an overcast day, was now almost completely dark, with only a pale light coming from the tunnel entrance.

Have we slept this long? Dave wondered to himself.

But the same loud rumble had also awoken the rest.

"The entrance is blocked with ice!" shouted Brendon. Together, they rushed back up the tunnel to find it blocked with ice and snow. *The sun must have come out while we slept,* thought Dave, looking at the faint light shining through the wall of ice.

"Since we can see the light, maybe we can get through this," said Floyd.

They began to chop furiously with their small axes at the ice, moving the slippery dislodged blocks back to the open space. As they worked, the ice began to melt and a stream of water began flowing down into their tunnel. As the level of melt water increased, Floyd became alarmed. When they were knee-deep in water, Floyd said, "I'm beginning to think this is a bad idea. What if we get trapped in here? Al and Dave, you go down the tunnel and see if you can get us to higher ground."

As the two slowly felt their way around the next curve, their eyes adjusted to the darkness, and they saw a greenish glow emanating from the tunnel walls.

As Dave looked at the circular shaft, it struck him for the first time how unusual this uniformity was. *What a ninny I am not to have noticed this before!*

"Al, do you think this tunnel is manmade?"

Al stopped and considered it for a moment. "I can't be sure, but I'd wager that it isn't due to pure geological events. Yet, on the other hand, if we had built this, the shaft would be square and straight. This is round, or nearly round, and winds back and forth like the trail of a sidewinder."

They began to move farther up the tunnel. The shaft climbed steadily, and finally Al called a halt. "This'll do. We'd better head back and tell the others."

They met the others as they were walking back. The flow of water had increased as the melting had accelerated, and they had been forced back into the tunnel by the rising water levels.

The group pressed on, and after another 100 yards the tunnel leveled off. Twenty minutes later, they reached a large cavern. In the dim green light, they could see that the floor of the cavern was strewn with cylindrical objects.

"What do you think these are?" asked Floyd.

"They could be some natural rock formation," ventured Brendon.

"I don't know," said Al. "Somehow the shapes seem too regular."

As the party moved onto the pebbly floor of the cavern, their examination of the objects revealed that the tubes were of various sizes, some more than twenty feet in diameter, and they were made of tightly clustered plates, like the scales on an enormous fish.

"There are a great many circular exits leaving this cavern. Maybe one of them will take us through the mountain," said Floyd.

"But which one?" asked Brendon. "I wouldn't want to get lost down here."

Floyd selected the most likely tunnel entrance and then led them across the cavern floor. The party was halfway across when they heard a rumbling from the far end of the cavern, as if giants were dragging a heavy object across rock.

"What's that?" asked Dave.

"Beats me," said Floyd, "but we're not waiting to find out."

They redoubled their pace and finally reached the circular passage that Floyd had indicated. This opening was about twenty feet in diameter. Once in the passage they proceeded more cautiously. The greenish glow gave them enough light to see. The tunnel had a damp, slightly musty smell, and water trickled from the entrance in a rivulet that collected in a small deep pool at the edge of the cavern.

"Al, you take the lead for a while. That strange sound makes me uneasy. I want to watch our rear."

"Sure thing," Al said and began walking at a brisk pace down the tunnel. The rivulet began in a small pool fed by a steady stream dripping from the ceiling. They stopped to fill their water bottles.

The passage ran on smoothly. It was uniformly circular and of a constant diameter. They moved forward quickly. Al stopped suddenly. Stan collided into his back, knocking Al forward. A black fissure yawned at Al's feet as he teetered at the edge.

Dave lunged for Al's pack and pulled him back. Dave's action twisted Al around so he stumbled over the edge, dragging Dave down heavily. Nevertheless, Dave managed to get a purchase on Al's arm and hold on.

"Help me! I don't have a very good hold," panted Dave.

Brendon and Tom reached down and secured Al and hauled him back up to the tunnel.

"Whew!" said Al. "That was too close."

"What happened?" asked Floyd, who had just run up.

"Al overbalanced at the edge of this crevice, and Dave just about knocked him over the edge as he tried to grab him," said Stan.

Dave was about to protest when Floyd said to Al, "Are you all right?"

"Yes," said Al. "Dave saved my life."

"Are you able to keep moving?"

"Yes. I banged my knee on the wall of the shaft, but nothing is broken. I'm shaken, but we can keep moving."

Floyd carefully examined the crack. It was only six feet wide but very deep; despite the greenish glow they couldn't see the bottom. However, they could hear the unmistakable sound of rushing water far below.

"I'm going to jump across this gap. It's only six feet wide, so it shouldn't be much trouble."

Floyd kept his pack on and made it easily with a bit of a run. Al insisted on going next and also made it without much trouble. Dave watched the others make the leap one at a time. His fear of heights was rearing its head, and he began to shake at the prospect of jumping that gap.

Despite his phobia, there was a part of his mind that looked at his growing fear with detachment. *Curious, when I lunged to rescue Al, I felt no fear, even though that was much more dangerous for me than this jump. Now I'm petrified.*

Dave was the last one to go. Taking a deep breath he ran at the crevice and cleared it easily.

Floyd took the lead again. The hair on the back of Dave's neck began to rise at the growing sense of danger. *I'm over the fissure. Why am I still so afraid?* The lack of side passages meant that if they encountered an enemy ahead, they would be hopelessly trapped, and that troubled him. Dave steeled himself to go forward, determined not to panic the others with his fears.

That's when they found it. Rounding one bend, they came across what seemed to be a rock wall. However, on closer inspection, it looked like the wall of one of the pipes they had seen in the cavern. A dull rumbling sound like a train in a tunnel shook the very rocks of the passage. Brendon took out his hatchet and, with the blunt end, began pounding at the scales. He had succeeded in breaking off a book sized fragment when suddenly the whole wall started to open up like a gray flower to reveal a huge mouth ringed with teeth, like that of a giant lamprey. Floyd just had time to snatch Brendon back as the huge maw of the creature began to elongate rapidly to ingest him. Four tentacles, supple in contrast to the rocklike exterior of the creature, snatched at Brendon's leg and began to pull him back to the mouth as if he were a rag doll. Dave rushed up, seized Brendon's fallen hatchet, and hacked at the rubbery appendage that had fastened onto Brendon. The second blow cut the tentacle in two. Al pulled his friend back, and Floyd pushed the two men out of the creature's reach, shouting at everyone to retreat as quickly as they could to the cavern.

"What was that?" gasped Vlad.

"Get back! Get back," yelled Floyd.

As he ran Dave felt, rather than heard, a deep regular beat fill the passage.

Is that a signal? Oh please don't let another one of those monsters enter the other end of the passage!

He hardly noticed the fissure in the floor as he cleared it at a run.

When they reached the entrance to the cavern, they noticed Al was missing.

"Where is he?" asked Floyd. No one knew. Floyd was about to lead them back when Al appeared.

"What happened to you?" asked Floyd.

"I wanted to observe the monstrosity. I figured something that large couldn't move too fast. It does move at a slow walk, though, so we'd better be moving."

"Now where?" asked Dave.

"I hope my next choice is better," said Floyd as he pointed to their left to a circular exit from the cavern. They moved quickly to this new entrance as the low frequency thumping continued. As they trotted across the floor, their feet crunching on pebbles, they realized—to their horror—that some of the circular shells were alive and moving towards them. They looked like giant, armored maggots, wriggling forward as fast as a man could comfortably walk.

Behind them, the creature with the missing tentacle had reached the exit of the passage they had just left and was beginning to move across the floor. They ran as quickly as they could with their packs, urged on by fear. The thumping of the signal and the rumble of the monsters' movement diminished in intensity as they gradually outdistanced the slow creatures. They came to another circular passage entrance and raced down it as quickly as they could. After twenty-five minutes at a brisk pace, Dave saw a patch of bright sunlight ahead of them. The next moment he and the others were squinting in the bright sun at the tunnel entrance. The huge field of scree before them lapped down to the familiar green, hilly terrain that they had struggled through for the last few weeks. Off to their right, in the distance, they could see the reeking fens. They had walked through the mountain and were now about half a mile north of the place from which they had set out.

Chapter 13

The Pass

With the late afternoon sun, the shadow of the westward mountains filled the valley before them. They stumbled and slid down the scree, looking back over their shoulders, expecting the worm to emerge from the tunnel at any moment. They did not speak, but Floyd kept them walking east, down the alpine-meadow-clad skirts of the mountain, until they came to a low, treed hill, which was crowned with a grassy knoll like the pate of a balding man's head. Here they sat down, exhausted, looking fearfully at the round hole in the mountain wall.

"What were those things?" asked Vlad.

"Beats me if I know," said Dwight, "but it certainly answers Stan's complaint about the lack of new life forms, in spades!"

No one was much in the mood for jokes.

"Now what do we do?" asked Floyd.

"We could try skirting the swamp, again," Glenn offered without enthusiasm.

"We'd be dead now," said Vlad, "if the rain hadn't driven us inside that tunnel. That whole mountainside must be under an overhanging glacier. It would be like playing Russian roulette."

"Even if we were successful in getting through alive," said Al, "that broken rock terrain is so treacherous, O'Reilly would never consider that as a route past the mountains. We would still have to find another way."

"All right," said Floyd. "If I'm hearing you correctly, we don't want to try the caves again and we don't want to attempt the broken rock. The only thing left is to head north and hope we find a pass through these mountains. We're safe enough here. Even if a worm comes, it can't get through these trees at the foot of this hill without making a lot of noise."

His words were not reassuring. They made camp and boiled the few potatoes they'd carried with them. They also had some cold, wild turkey left over from a bird they had shot and cooked two days before.

After supper, they each had a cup of tea and felt the tension of the day begin to ebb from their bodies.

"I wonder what those worms eat," asked Kyle, "that is, when they can't get 'hiker'?"

"I don't know," said Stan, "but I bet those scree beds that we see coming out of the tunnels are some of the rock that they've taken out of the tunnels."

"That can't be all of it. There must be a lot more, judging by the size and length of the tunnels," said Vlad.

"Maybe they eat the luminescent green stuff," suggested Brendon.

The night sky became dark as the clouds moved in. Floyd set guards in rotation. Dave didn't have a watch this night, so he turned in and was asleep almost as soon as his head hit his sleeping bag.

——————

The next morning the air was cold, foggy, and pregnant with rain. After a brief, cold breakfast, they descended the hill and soon were lost in the soupy fog. Dave, his sight diminished by the morning haze, found his hearing enlivened; he could plainly hear water dripping from trees and babbling in a nearby brook.

Using his compass, Floyd found a game trail that headed approximately north. As Dave began plodding along, he fell in step with Vlad Sowetsky. The others, ghostly shapes in the fog ahead, could be heard distinctly as they stepped on twig and stone.

"So what were you studying at Halcyon, Vlad?" asked Dave.

"I was a graduate physics student in Hoffstetter's group."

"Oh really!" said Dave. "Were you working on the Hoffstetter field generator or on something else?" Dave pretended he didn't know.

"I wasn't only working on the field generators, but I was Hoffstetter's right-hand man."

"So why weren't you seconded to the physics project?" asked Dave.

"Why indeed?" said Vlad bitterly. "Did you see my interview on Halcyon television right after the dislocation?"

"As a matter of fact I did," Dave admitted. "I thought you spoke quite courageously."

"Well," said Vlad, "Jennifer McCowan, who had talked me into giving the interview, was given a slap on the wrist, but Blackmore and Hoffstetter had me put in the slammer in the zoology building as if I'd started the riot! When O'Reilly found out, he had me let out. As soon as they let me out, I hightailed it to Botany Bay. Now that Blackmore is chancellor, I'm afraid to go back to Halcyon in case they throw me back in my old cage. That's why I jumped at the opportunity to go on this expedition."

"But the riot wasn't your fault." protested Dave.

"Of course not," said Vlad. "It was really Hoffstetter's stupidity that was to blame for the riot. When that came out, Hoffstetter never forgave me, even after he and Blackmore began to whitewash the deed with their weekly television program."

"Was it really Hoffstetter's fault?" asked Dave.

"There is no question that it was Hoffstetter's fault. And I'm not just saying that to exonerate myself. You see, I'd warned Hoffstetter that we shouldn't build the large demonstration field generators right away because there were too many unknowns. But he overruled me. At Botany Bay, I was afraid if I started talking, and Blackmore heard about it and found out where I was, he'd lock me up again."

Floyd called a halt by a creek, and Vlad and Dave sat down on a patch of sand by the side of a quiet pool.

Another idea began to trouble Dave. "Vlad, you used the word whitewash just now. What did you mean?" he asked with trepidation.

"Between you, me, and the doorpost, all that nonsense about being home at Christmas that Hoffstetter and Blackmore have been feeding the masses on their television show is a load of crap. I had time to inspect the wreckage after the fire department put out the blaze. That equipment was completely destroyed and can't be replicated at Halcyon. Without that equipment, we don't have a hope of getting back."

Steady, old fellow! Don't let this overwhelm you. Dave forced his mind back to the topic at hand. Taking a deep breath, he continued. "So do you still believe all that stuff you said about time quantization and Halcyon slipping into a trailing time interval? What did you call it?" asked Dave.

"Mintival," said Vlad. "Yes, I believe it more than ever. Hasn't it puzzled you why so many species here are almost identical to species back home?"

"But we've found some new ones, like the worms and that new bird," said Dave.

"Opera bird," said Vlad. "Well, that's true, and there are those Happy Berries. That's not unanticipated; one wouldn't expect the two space-times to be completely the same. But back to my question: how do you explain the amazing similarities between this space-time and ours?"

"I assumed it must have something to do with the close relationship this world has with ours," said Dave.

"What if, in the past, the time differential between this space-time and ours was much smaller? What if the wall was so thin that portals opened up, so people and other life forms could move back and forth quite easily? Wouldn't explain the similarity between the flora and fauna here and back home?"

"Hmm. Movement back and forth? Is it possible that these portals still exist?" asked Dave.

"I suppose it's possible," said Vlad. He paused momentarily, as if deciding whether or not to continue, then turned and looked at Dave gravely.

"Dave, it's very important that you remember all of what I've just told you."

"Why?" Dave asked, bewildered.

Vlad took a deep breath and continued. "I have a reason for going into this in such detail. I've had a foreboding growing in my mind that I'm not going to make it back to town, and I had to tell someone before...." His voice trailed off to a whisper.

"You're a scientist; surely you don't believe in forebodings. It's a psychological phenomenon brought on by stress."

"Maybe you're right," said Vlad, but his eyes told a different story.

The ten men spent many weeks traveling north along the eastern fringe of the mountains. The mountain rampart was unbroken except for high snowbound shoulders next to even higher mountain peaks. For the most part, they traveled in the alpine meadows on the shoulders of the mountains, where the hiking was easier.

As the weeks went by, they experienced evidence for the end of autumn everywhere. The nights were growing cooler, and many of the trees on the foothills had begun to lose their leaves.

Finally, in December, they had their first reason for optimism. They were near the great river, which they could see gleaming far to the north, when they came upon a long valley that ran westward between two mountain peaks. Out of this valley, a creek bubbled and danced over a series of waterfalls to the valley floor, then continued east to the distant sea. As they followed this creek up the steep incline, they came to a valley, which was clad in upland junipers, rising gently to a pass in the west. After so many weeks of fruitless searching, Dave noticed that the group interactions had completely changed since the pass. Everyone was laughing and joking again.

Finding a grassy meadow near a pool past the top of the first waterfall, they paused to rest. Glenn promptly dowsed Dave with water as he stooped to drink, and before long, everyone ended up in the pool except Floyd, who watched the antics with apparent amusement. The others quickly took that situation in hand, and Floyd was also unceremoniously baptized.

While their clothes dried in the sun, they sat on a rock looking east. Dave observed that the creek ran almost due east toward the coast. Beyond the creek, he could see a curious, shallow volcanic cone. But then his reverie was interrupted.

"This is the first gap in the mountains we've found since the swamp," said Floyd. "What do you think we should do?"

I'd like to go home! Dave thought, but said nothing as he waited for the others to speak.

"There's no point in traveling north," said Floyd, at last breaking the silence. "Halcyon has already sent boats along the south shore of the river mouth looking for a passage past the mountains. But the mountains come right down to the south riverbank, so there's no route west along the river's edge."

Dwight recalled their duty. "But this valley may lead to a blind canyon," he said. "Shouldn't we confirm that it actually goes through the mountains?"

"That's true," conceded Floyd. "We really don't know what lies beyond that pass ahead."

Floyd put his hand on his forehead and looked into the fire they had built. After a few seconds he said, "I'll climb up to that shoulder on the south side of this valley." He gestured to an outcropping of rock up the slope of the southern mountain. "Since the mountains bend a little toward the east, I should be able to see if there are any valleys between here and the great river. That will complete our observations of the mountains to the north. I think Dwight is right; we need to travel up this valley just far enough to establish that this is either a pass through the mountains or a blind canyon. Then we'll have done our duty and we can head home."

Al and Floyd made the long climb up to the mountain shoulder to survey the mountains to the north, while the rest set up camp beside the pond at the crest of the ridge. They spent the afternoon bathing in the frigid waters of the pond and relaxing on the grass in the bright sunshine. Floyd and Al returned late in the evening to report that mountains marched in an unbroken chain north to the river.

The thought of going home to Botany Bay brightened everyone's spirits, and Floyd's proposal to explore the pass had everyone's enthusiastic approval. This was a decision that Floyd was going to regret for the rest of his life.

The Quarry

The next morning dawned clear and cold, with a wind blowing out of the northwest. Dave went to the water's edge and broke through a skin of ice to wash the sleep out of his eyes. After a hurried breakfast, the adventurers broke camp and set out to explore the valley.

Soon dark, heavy clouds rolled in from the north. After several miles of easy trekking on a gentle rise of bare rock interspersed with juniper groves, a light snow began to fall. The valley was situated between steeply rising mountainsides about a mile apart. In the distance, the group could see a level ridge traversing the valley.

After another mile of travel they reached the crest. Dave saw that on the other side, the ground fell steeply from the ridge to a long narrow valley—enhanced by a glistening ribbon—stretching to the west.

Suddenly, "Get down!" Floyd hissed.

All ten flattened themselves against the stone on the crest. Dave wriggled forward cautiously and scanned the valley for any sign of danger.

"Do you see it," asked Floyd, "the road?"

The heavy cloud cover had significantly reduced visibility. However, below them Dave could see a road appearing from around a wall of rock to their left, bent in a long westward curve, before vanishing in a curtain of snow. There could be no mistake about it. Light snow had settled on the sparse vegetation, and the wet road appeared like a glistening gray serpent in the white valley at their feet. No one made a sound. Dave hardy dared to breathe. But the road remained deserted.

"Well," said Floyd, rising to his knees. "I've got to have a closer look at this road. Dave, Al, and Stan, come with me. The rest of you stay out of sight. If there's trouble, don't play hero. Just get out of here." With that he took off his pack and doubled back down the east side of the ridge, then ran for the cliff face at the left side of the valley. Dave loped after Floyd, and Al and Stan brought up the rear.

When Floyd reached the cliff face, he climbed back up to the ridge, and then crouching down, explained his plan. "Let's use the broken rocks as cover," he said. "Stan and I will go first until we find some cover. Then you guys leapfrog past us. That way, two of us will always be watching." He and Stan moved quickly, skirting the boulders as quietly as ghosts, in the dead air of the light snowfall.

When they had stopped, Al and Dave edged down by a different path until they were about fifty yards beyond them. Dave could see the opening to the left; it looked like a canyon with steep sides. On their next leg, Floyd and Stan made it all the way to the road. Dave and Al quickly joined them.

The road ran only a short distance into a blind canyon. The canyon walls were smooth, the unmistakable signature of a rock quarry. Stacks of squared stone stood on the valley floor, lightly covered with snow. Large slabs of mountainside had fallen, and broken rock, some of it squared, lay in heaps at the margin of the valley. There were a few crude decaying wooden structures and a larger stone building with a partly collapsed roof at the very end of the road.

"Looks deserted enough," said Floyd. "Let's go."

As Dave walked, his well-worn hiking boots clumping on the hard surface, he looked carefully at the cobblestones that made up the road.

A good deal of hard work went into this road. The stones fit closely together. You couldn't fit a blade of grass between the joints!

Since no one came rushing out at their approach, Floyd gave the "OK" and they split up to search the ruins. Dave went into the dilapidated stone building. Climbing over piles of rubble, he slid his body over broken beams from the collapsed roof, which looked like broken ribs and slowly worked his way to the back corner of the building. He was about to go back when a patch of brown caught his eye. It looked like a piece of fabric. He reached his hand in between two sections of broken slate, but the fabric eluded his grasp. Using one of his crossbow bolts, he was able to snag a corner and pull it out. The cloth was brown vellum, heavily stained and badly weathered. In the dim light he could not make out any writing or figures, but decided to keep it for Floyd to examine. He carefully folded the swatch and put it into his pocket.

Dave heard Floyd calling to him from outside. He worked his way back to the doorway, and found the snow now falling so heavily, visibility was only a few feet. The dark clouds and heavy snowfall made it seem like twilight. He moved toward the sound of Floyd's voice.

"We've seen enough," said Floyd. "Let's go back."

"I found something," said Dave.

"What did you find?" asked Floyd, peering up at the sky with a grimace.

Dave pulled the vellum out of his pocket and thrust it into Floyd's hands. "I found a skin or something. It may be a message or a map."

"I can't make anything out in this light," muttered Floyd, turning the vellum over in his hand. "Did it have anything on it?"

"Not that I could tell," said Dave.

The distant howl of a wolf sounded.

Floyd gave it back. "We've got to go. We'll look at it tonight at camp."

With that, the two headed back to join Al and Stan who waited on the road. Together, they trudged back through the snow. This time they made directly for the others on the ridge since the snow had reduced visibility to such an extent that Floyd said he was no longer worried about being spotted from the road. As they climbed up to the ridge, they heard another wolf howl. By now, snow was collecting in knee-deep drifts.

Floyd steered them east, back down the valley, the way they had come. The party moved in single file, toiling through the deepening white, choosing bare, windblown sections of bedrock as their path whenever possible. Snow continued to fall, and soon a thick blanket covered the entire landscape, masking any terrain markers they might have recognized. Time and again, one of them would stumble into chest-deep snow filled depressions, where he would be forced to remain until the others could pull him out.

Their progress was painfully slow. Dave lost all track of time and wondered how far they had come after so much exertion.

Finally, when Dwight stumbled into a hole and all but disappeared from view, Floyd called out that he'd had enough. Pulling Dwight to safety, the group searched for his crossbow in the dim light, and then huddled by a large juniper—out of the howling wind—to talk.

"We're going to have to stop," said Floyd. "We need to get out of the snow. Let's cut some of these junipers down and build a fire over by that cliff wall." He pointed to a dark shadow to their right.

They struggled to the cliff wall, unloaded their packs, and began to gather branches from junipers and stunted pine trees growing in nearby thickets, while Floyd searched for shelter. The best they could do was a rock shelf about five feet wide and two feet off the ground. An overhanging cliff supporting two pine trees with low hanging branches provided some protection against the wind and the snow.

The needed firewood now gathered, they piled it in a circle about the rock face. The snow was drifting around their small dell and was already waist deep. They were trapped!

But the resinous wood caught easily, and they soon had a blazing fire going to boil some of the potatoes they had gathered the previous day. Remnants of a large grouse, which Dave had felled with a bolt from his crossbow at the campsite two nights before, rounded out the meal.

"Let's have a look at your find," said Floyd after dinner.

"Find?" queried Stan.

"Yeah, Dave found a scrap of vellum. Maybe it has something on it."

Dave pulled it out and looked at the vellum in the firelight. There may have been some faint lines on it at one time, but he could barely make anything out. He passed it around. Stan said he thought it was a useless scrap, while others thought they recognized a map or some characters, but when pressed they could not agree on what they saw.

"You're Rorschaching a bunch of stains," scoffed Stan.

Floyd gave the vellum back to Dave. "Keep it in a safe place. I can't help but feel that this is valuable."

Dave pulled his waterproof money belt out from under his shirt. He took out the picture of his family, his most precious possession. The picture always gave him a pang of homesickness. He carefully folded the vellum, placed it beside the picture in the money belt and then fastened it around his waist. The others settled in for the night. Al took the end of the shelf, leaving a gap for him next to Glenn. Dave squeezed himself between his two friends despite Glenn's grumpy protestations, and soon fell asleep.

Dave woke early the next morning as a drop of water dripped off the cliff, full onto his face. He looked around, memories of the previous night flooding back. A shaft of bright sunlight broke through the snow-clad tree branches of their hollow and played against the cliff wall. He stood up and tried to look out, but the snowdrift surrounding their hollow was too high. Dave shielded his eyes from the bright sunlight and looked up. Blue sky. Then he looked at the rock face, dubiously.

I'm going to have to beat this thing sometime.

Taking a deep breath, he put his foot into a crevice and began to climb away from the snow-enshrouded hollow. The wind had been so violent during the night that the cliff side had been completely scoured of snow.

Move my hand; move my foot. Remember, always three solid holds, and I'll be all right.

He inched his way up. Although he knew this was a technically easy climb, when he reached a ledge about twenty feet up, he was shaking so badly he had to stop.

Sitting with his back to the cliff, his feet pulled up against his chest, Dave looked to the east. The snow was very deep. Only the tops of the taller junipers showed through, like miniature Christmas trees.

The sun was well above the horizon, and the green of the conifer forest far to the east could be seen in the distance. He looked back the way they had come. Motion up the valley, toward the crest of the pass, caught his eye. A tiny dot—black against the white snow—was moving in their direction. Dave watched for some time as it moved, then hesitated, and then moved again, but always in their direction. He periodically lost sight of it as it disappeared behind clumps of juniper. As the thing came closer, rounding a patch of junipers, Dave saw that it was a large, long-legged wolf-like creature, padding along with its head down, as if snuffling for a trail with its long, narrow muzzle.

Dave called down to Floyd. "Floyd, there seems to be a very large wolf of some sort approaching our camp."

Dave's call woke Floyd out of a sound sleep, and it took him a few seconds to realize that Dave's voice was not coming from their camp but from the cliff above him. "Where is it?" asked Floyd.

"It's about 200 yards northwest of us."

As Dave called out, the wolf stopped and looked in his direction. It looked intently at the cliff face for some time. Finally, it spotted Dave up in the rocks. Then the wolf settled on its haunches and let out a series of ear piercing howls. These were soon answered by howls echoing from farther up the valley. In a few minutes, Dave saw a distant group of brown and black dots appear above the crest of the pass and move in their direction.

"I don't like the looks of this, Floyd. That wolf has summoned company. They look like they mean trouble, since they're not backing away."

"All right, Dave. I'll come up and have a look," said Floyd, who at the sound of the howls appeared to be thoroughly awake.

"Bring up a rope and my binoculars, please," said Dave. "I have a bad feeling about this."

In a less than a minute, Floyd had also climbed to Dave's perch. The lone wolf still sat on its haunches, eying them intently.

Much nearer now, the binoculars revealed ten more wolves bounding through the snow.

"Let's get everyone up here until we're sure we know what's going on," said Floyd.

"What are those things?" asked Dave. "They look like wolves but they're much bigger than I would have imagined." He fastened the rope to a rock projection, and the others climbed up onto the ledge, carrying their backpacks. Al had packed up Dave's gear, fastened Dave's pack to the rope, and then followed the pack up the rock face, climbing as nimbly as a mountain goat. By the time everyone was safely on the ledge, the other wolves, yapping, howling, and snarling, had joined the alpha wolf.

After a few minutes, the yapping stopped and the pack began warily to approach the camp in the hollow. The approach of the wolves gave everyone a good chance to examine the beasts at close range.

Floyd exclaimed, "Those monstrosities must weigh at least 200 or 300 pounds. Look at the size of their paws—they're like pillows!"

The creatures were enormous! Some were black and some brown, but all had the long-legged appearance of wolves, with massive, long narrow jaws that looked as if they could easily fasten onto a basketball. Approaching the deserted camp, their red eyes stared hungrily at the explorers perched on the ledge, out of reach.

The beasts broke through the hollow bubble of snow into the camp. While the other wolves snuffled around the site, the pack leader stayed about forty feet away. It circled the camp, glaring continually at the ten travelers, watching their every move. Dave felt a shudder as the obvious malevolence of the creatures washed over him. Dwight raised his crossbow to shoot one of the beasts, but Floyd quietly put his hand on his crossbow and lowered it.

"Let's wait before we start shooting," said Floyd. "We don't yet know what we're dealing with here. The last thing I need is a wounded wolf to worry about."

The wolves, having satisfied themselves with searching the camp, easily jumped out of the hollow, back onto the top of the snow, to rejoin their leader. Yapping and snarling, they milled about. Finally the leader let out a sequence of growls, and the wolves split into two groups. One group headed east along the cliff, while the other headed west. The leader, however, retreated another 100 yards, and then once again sat on its haunches. Floyd handed Dave the binoculars.

"Keep an eye on it! I'm going to climb a little higher to look around."

Dave watched the beast intently with his binoculars. It was licking its paws unconcernedly. However, as Dave continued to watch, it seemed to him that this deliberate grooming by the beast was a sham. He caught a gleam of the beast's eyes every few seconds. It appeared to be checking to be sure they had not moved.

"This isn't good, Floyd. That beast is watching us!"

"I agree with you, Dave; I also don't like the look of this," said Floyd from a ledge another twenty feet up. "Even though the other wolves have gone, I'd rather not chance a visit by that guy by climbing back down to the camp. Besides, with the snow up to our waists, we'd be sitting ducks. Let's work our way along the cliff until we've put a good distance between us and that monstrosity."

"Where have the other wolves gone, I wonder?" muttered Dave. He scanned up and down with the binoculars but couldn't see a trace of them. That was odd, mighty odd! The other men, having begun to climb, were too busy looking for the next handhold to attempt an answer.

Reluctantly, Dave put the binoculars into his pack and looked grimly at the rock face. *How am I ever going to manage this?*

A rope snaked down from above. "You have a heavy pack," called Al. "Tie the rope on and let me give you a hand."

Dave tied the rope on and felt much more confident than he had before. He climbed up to the next ledge, then followed Al and the others.

Trying to traverse the cliff face was difficult, but they were able to climb to a ledge that ran due east across the rock. This ledge climbed slightly, ending abruptly after a few hundred paces. They searched for another ledge and again continued on for a time. Doggedly scrambling forward in this laborious manner, they covered about a mile.

The going had been so slow it was early afternoon when they came upon their first major obstacle. A field of broken rock that had obviously slid off the mountainside sometime in the past blocked their path. They saw no sign of the wolves, or lupi, as Al had named them, so they took a brief rest for lunch.

Lunch over, Floyd roused them to cross the rockslide. Dave felt a growing sense of danger and cautiously unlimbered and armed his crossbow. Picking their way among the rocks, they had progressed about 300 yards—and were just rounding the corner of a house-sized boulder—when the wolf pack struck.

A huge black lupus raced among the smaller boulders, bounded onto a large rock, and leaped onto Floyd, who was in the lead. Floyd just had time to turn his back and duck as he was bowled over by the beast. Dave, who was second in line, reacted quickly, shooting his crossbow bolt into the chest of the wolf at point-blank range. The beast roared and reared up from Floyd's back, pawing the air.

At that same moment, four other creatures raced around the back of the huge boulder and attacked from the rear, leaping onto the backs of the travelers and snapping at their necks. The lead lupus stumbled as a rock shifted under its weight, giving the men just enough time to react before the beasts' weight drove them to the ground.

Al had his sword out in a moment. He rushed at the nearest lupus and thrust the weapon as deep as it would go into the neck of the beast. In doing so, he interrupted its efforts to tear the backpack off its victim, who had wedged himself into a gap between two rocks. The wolf snarled, twisted and tore the sword from Al's grasp. Al tried desperately to free his rifle as the lupus reared back and gathered itself for another spring. The leap never came. The wolf sank to the ground—its carotid artery severed—in a pool of its own blood, which welled in a red torrent around the sword's hilt.

Three of the men, transfixed with terror, were screaming, unable to react. Brandon pulled out his sword and thrust it deep into the neck of a third wolf.

"Use your crossbows!" Dave shouted, and rushed two wolves attacking Kyle Jensen. The nearest wolf released its prey, and gathered itself for a leap at Dave, but lost its footing on the bloodstained rock and fell short. Dave hacked at its forelimb, cutting the tendon. The beast lunged forward, at Dave's arm. A rifle cracked, and the bullet tore a gaping hole in the wolf's chest. Two more shots rang out.

Dave turned, looking for other attackers. Four lupi were down. The fifth was racing away, pursued by crossbow bolts, which scattered harmlessly among the rocks. Floyd fired one last bullet after the fleeing beast, and then stood watching for any further attack.

Adrenaline rush subsiding, the extent of the carnage assailed Dave's senses. Kyle Jensen was dead; a massive bite to his throat had nearly severed his head. The rest were unwounded but shaken. Several of the backpacks were shredded.

"Dave, here, take my rifle and cover that approach around the boulder," said Floyd, woodenly rubbing his aching shoulder, as he indicated the side of the boulder where the lupus had fled. "Al, you take the front approach."

It was late afternoon. The group wrapped Kyle's mangled body in his sleeping bag and first carried, then hoisted it with ropes, to a sloping scree-covered shelf. Digging a shallow grave, they buried him, and then built a cairn of rocks over the site. Al made a small wooden cross, which he stuck into the mound. After washing off the gore and cleaning their weapons in a stream, they were too exhausted to continue, and spent the night huddled on a ledge overlooking the fresh grave.

The noise of dislodged rocks clattering down the mountainside below woke them, but because of the overcast night, they could not see anything in the deep shadows. Sleeping fitfully, they were awakened again later by the noise of snarling and howling.

The next morning, the sun came out and the weather warmed up considerably. The cairn directly below was undisturbed. But much further down the carcasses of the dead lupi that had been at the battle scene were gone. They could see no sign of the other wolves.

Gloom continued to plague the group; they concurred the wilderness had taken on a terrifying aspect, as if a park had turned out to be a coliseum and they were the Christian victims in a spectacle of sacrifice. They agreed no one had slept well, and they ate their food in silence, with none of the cheerful banter that usually characterized their meals. Dave felt as if his world had changed forever. He relived the agonizing moments of combat, and was tormented by the image of the lifeless body of his comrade, soggy with congealing blood.

He was, however, no longer as afraid of climbing as he had been when they first took to the mountainside. The horror of the killing and the repetitive climbing had dulled the fear that had almost paralyzed him at first.

After breakfast, Floyd broke the silence. "If I didn't know better, I'd say those wolves, or lupi, if you will, hit us with a planned, coordinated attack."

"Why do you say 'if I didn't know better'?" said Al. "This is a new world, and we really don't know what to expect. Just because wolves and dogs never showed this kind of intelligence on earth doesn't mean it can't happen here."

"I think we're heading toward the same conclusion, Al. These lupi are intelligent, and we are in as much danger as if we were being hunted by other men."

The travelers digested these comments. The darkness they had experienced with the loss of their comrade took on an added terror as they considered Al's words. "Well, if we were being hunted by humans," said Brendon, "the best thing to do would be to disappear so they couldn't find us."

"How are we going to do that?" asked Dave. "We're on an exposed mountainside with no place to hide, unless we want to 'go to ground' for a long time. There's something else we ought to consider. They may think like humans, but they track scents like wolves. Even if we find cover and reach the trees, and even if they can't see us, they may still follow us faster than we can march."

"Here's what we're going to do," said Floyd. "They can't climb like we can; nor can they use tools. We're going to stay up on the mountainside out of their reach. When we're forced to climb down, we'll look for an open area, since our rifles and crossbows will give us an advantage at a distance. Then we'll hit the woods and head straight back to Botany Bay, disguising our trail as much as possible."

"How are we going to hide our scent?" asked Stan.

"We'll use that creek we saw at the entrance to the valley to cover our tracks," said Floyd.

The sun was warm, and the snow in the valley began to melt. The stone on the mountainside warmed up quickly, helping them a little. Nevertheless, they toiled ten hours along the rock wall, crossing short open spaces only when lookouts were in place to guard against a surprise attack. Throughout this time they never saw the lupi or even heard so much as a wolf howl.

Late that evening, they reached the very promontory that Floyd and Al had used to look toward the great river. Now they looked out over the green lands that ran down to the sea, lost in a haze to the east like a pastel painting in which the distant landscapes are deliberately indistinct. Once again the curious shallow, volcanic cone loomed on the horizon. Across the valley they saw a cascading stream leaping down from a glacier at the summit, while billows of mist rolled eastward in the light wind. This cascade fell into a high glen and then reappeared as the source of the creek they had seen before entering the valley. Unwilling to risk crossing the open meadow to the forest at night, they decided to make camp on the uncomfortable promontory.

Dave woke the next morning with a rock digging into his back. Every limb felt stiff, and he had to stretch to take the kinks out of his strained muscles. The sun was just rising in the east. Out of the corner of his eye he saw movement to his left along the mountain slope, but when he looked more intently, there was nothing to be seen.

Perhaps my overwrought imagination is getting the better of me.

They ate a hurried breakfast and started their descent into the forest. Floyd and Brendon led the way, while Dave and Al, the rear guard, looked over their shoulders. They made their way down the mountainside and then crossed over to the place where they had camped three nights earlier. They heard the snap of a twig behind them but saw nothing. The meadow was now almost free of snow but dotted with many juniper bushes, so there was plenty of cover to hide even a large animal. Ahead of them, the valley ended in a steep slope that descended to the woods below. Dave imagined a wolf leaping out from behind every large juniper bush in their path. They redoubled their pace, urged on by the terror that assailed them.

They reached the lip of the steep incline and made their way down into the valley. Bushes became denser. Reaching the valley floor, Dave looked back up the slope. Silhouetted against the sky was the dark shape of a lupus. Dave plunged into the bushes to escape from predator's sight.

Under their feet, rotten branches snapped as they pushed their way through the undergrowth. Dave's breath was labored; the fear of attack in this closed in space froze his heart. Finally, they came to the creek.

"Let's get across," said Floyd. "Maybe that will throw them off the scent," he added without much conviction. The creek was thirty feet wide, but the margins were only about six inches deep.

For a few hundred feet the nine men walked in the shallows, hoping to disguise their trail. Finding a place where the waters of the creek merged and rushed through a three-foot wide crack in a rock shelf, they crossed, easily leaping the narrow gap, then continued on the north side of the creek. Game trails appeared near the water's edge, and they followed those that shadowed the creek's course. Dave sensed danger was close at hand and felt fear rise with the conviction that they were being followed. Sometimes he thought he heard a branch break or water splash.

The sense of danger became so strong Dave said, "Floyd, I think we're going to be attacked. We have to take cover."

Floyd looked uncertain.

"Floyd, please—"

The other man acquiesced. "All right, let's take a break and set ourselves up in a good defensive position."

They found a place where the creek made a sharp bend north and cut into a steep bluff. Floyd led them across a ford and had them rest at the top of a bluff, facing the creek and giving them a good view north and west. Behind them was a heavy thicket of hawthorns.

Al apparently shared Dave's misgivings; he came and sat by Dave, watching the creek for the approach of the lupi, his rifle cradled in his lap. The others were so relieved by their progress they seemed giddy with excitement.

"Keep an eye out for those wolves! I'm going to have a bite and catch forty winks," laughed Stan derisively. Dave said nothing but scanned the bushes below the bluff and along the creek in an effort to identify the danger that was gnawing at his gut.

Two of the others, still joking at the relief they felt now that they were safe, went down to the creek to refill their canteens. As they were hunched over, four dark shapes, silently and without warning, bounded across the creek and lunged at the two unsuspecting victims.

Dave shouted and fired his crossbow as soon as the wolves broke cover. But his bolt went wide, and the lupi were upon his comrades. With four lupi attacking, the two young men had no chance.

Al's shot was better than Dave's and found its mark in one of the beasts tearing at the body of its victim at the creek. As the other men ran to help Dave and Al, Floyd's shout warned them to watch their backs. Sure enough, two more wolves were creeping through the hawthorn thicket for a sneak attack from the rear. Floyd and two others shot into the thicket, and the wounded lupus bellowed with rage. By now, the three remaining lupi at the creek had left the mangled bodies and were beginning to scramble up the bluff toward the other men. Al fired as rapidly as he could reload, and Dave unleashed two more bolts, which found their marks in the beasts. Tom and Dwight also shot at the creatures. Shoulder to shoulder, they thrust with their swords as the animals exposed their throats and chests, trying to scramble over the steep crest of the bluff. The others joined them now and shot crossbow bolts at the beasts from the side.

Behind them, a particularly massive lupus had wriggled its way through the hawthorn thicket. It had two crossbow bolts buried deep in its chest, yet it still came on. Wild with rage, the huge beast knocked Glenn down. Glenn buried his sword deep in the animal's neck, but the beast managed to snag Glenn's arm in its massive jaw. Al, his rifle magazine empty, rushed up and delivered a blow with his sword to the beast's head, severing its spinal cord.

Finally everything was still. Six wolves lay dead around the men. Floyd, covered with gore from the beasts' wounds, staggered to his feet. To free Glenn's arm from the mouth of the beast, the men had to cut the ligaments in the dead monster's jaw. The creature, already weakened when it had fastened on to Glenn's arm, had not had enough strength to shake him and tear the arm open. Tom began to clean and bandage Glenn's wound.

With Al and Dave to help him, Floyd insisted on going down to the river to look after the others at the bottom of the bluff. Vlad Sowetzky had been killed outright. Brandon Monk had been badly wounded, but Al's shot had prevented the second wolf from finishing him off.

Dave looked up and saw the silhouette of the lupi leader watching them from a rise about 100 yards up the creek. When the leader saw that he had been spotted, he bounded casually into the brush and disappeared from view. Dave's eyes smoldered with anger. "It's time the hunted became the hunter!" he said menacingly.

"I'll go with you," said Al quietly.

Floyd looked as if he was going to object, but changed his mind. "Help us make a safe camp nearby and then you can go, but I want you back by nightfall."

The group bound Brendon's wounds as well as they could. After washing their equipment and tending to their own small wounds, they dug a grave in the soft earth for their dead companion. Then they carried Brendon downstream a few hundred yards and made camp on an island in the middle of the creek. Glenn was able to walk to the campsite with a little assistance.

Within minutes of setting down their packs, Dave and Al were on the trail. Floyd had given Dave his rifle, but held on to Dave's crossbow. The wind was blowing from the west, so they were stalking upwind, which gave them an advantage over the lupi leader. They crept up to the hillock where they had last seen the predator. Reaching it, they peered cautiously over the crest to view the creek bed beyond.

Dave stared for a long time and then boxed Al's arm. In the shadow of some overhanging sumac, they could just make out the dark shadow of the wolf leader. He had apparently taken up an ambush position covering any approach up the creek.

"Now what do we do?" asked Dave. "Can we take a shot?"

"At this range, through brush, I don't think we'd have much chance," said Al. "If we crossed the creek, he would see us…

"I suppose we could just walk into his trap," said Dave, "provoke his attack, and settle him once and for all."

"We can't be assured of provoking an attack," said Al. "It seems to me if I were him, I would only attack if I expected to kill my quarry. If we leave the decision to him, he might accomplish just that or else decide to sneak away to wait for a better chance. No, it's too dangerous. I think we should stay on this side of the creek and creep along out of sight. We can't go too far, but up ahead there's another hillock, and maybe that will bring us close enough to give us a reasonable shot."

Dave assented to Al's plan, and they set out again, heading left, remaining out of sight. When they reached the second hillock, they wormed their way through some scrub pine trees until they saw the creek bed and the other bank almost directly across from them. The wolf leader was still waiting.

"On a silent count of three," whispered Al.

They raised their weapons together, took careful aim, and fired at the same time. There was a blur of motion as the wolf disappeared into the brush on the far side of the creek. Scrambling down and crossing the creek, they cautiously approached the lupus' hiding place. A blood spoor showed that at least one bullet had found its mark. The wolf was not bleeding badly, since the gap between the blood spots was fairly wide, but it made trailing the beast much easier.

The wolf traveled straight back to the high valley, apparently without resting. By about four o'clock in the afternoon, they had covered a great deal of distance, but the blood trail continued to stretch before them.

"Let's turn back," said Al. "The wound must have been minor, since the animal isn't weakening."

"But we have a good trail!" protested Dave. "His wound has to be wearing him out!"

"I know," said Al. "But we promised Floyd we'd be back by nightfall, and we're not going to make it before nightfall now."

Reluctantly Dave agreed to head back. Although they moved as quickly as possible, it was quite dark before they approached the island. They called ahead to alert their comrades of their return.

Floyd came to meet them at the edge of the creek. Stan was waiting with his crossbow.

"Where've you been?" asked Floyd, relieved when he saw they were not hurt.

Al gave a brief account of the hunt.

"So you put a bullet into him. I was worried after I heard the shots and you didn't come back. Just before dark I even sent Stan and Tom after you, but they didn't see any sign of you."

"How's Brendon?" asked Al.

Floyd's face looked troubled in the moonlight. "He doesn't look good to me. We've stopped the bleeding, but he's lost a lot of blood. I was sitting with him when you called."

"May I see him?" asked Al.

"You guys must be starved. Eat the leftovers and then come over and see him."

Dave and Al ate the cold leftovers from supper and then went to see Brendon. In the pale light of the moon Brendon looked paler still. Moaning softly, he asked for water, which Floyd gave to him from a cup at hand. Dave could see that Floyd was exhausted.

"Floyd," said Al, "I'm still keyed up from the hunt. Why don't you sleep now and then relieve me when you wake?"

Floyd protested, but Al insisted. Dave watched Floyd go and decided to stay with Al. Al gripped Brendon's hand and talked to him quietly. His words had a calming effect on Brendon, and his moaning subsided. Dave leaned against a tree and unlimbered his crossbow.

What if that wolf doubles back?

Al and Brendon were in a patch of moonlight. Every few moments, spasms of pain made Brendon tighten his grip on Al's hand. As the time passed, Dave grew so tired that he began to nod off.

He woke in the morning with a start. The sun was already up, and his back hurt where he had slept on a tree root. He saw Floyd leaning over Brendon. Dave got up to stretch his tired muscles. Al, who had fallen asleep, began to wake at all the commotion.

"How is he?" Dave asked about Brendon.

"He's stone cold," said Floyd, his voice breaking with emotion.

"He died during the night," said Al quietly.

"It's my fault—I'm sorry." said Floyd. His face was marked by grief and despair.

"Floyd, you've done all you could," said Al. "Without your leadership, we would never have made it out alive."

Floyd swore under his breath. "I can't believe I let it come to this. Why did I not see the danger until it was too late? Why didn't I believe Dave when he warned me?"

"You did believe Dave, and you picked a defensible position. You're not God, Floyd; you can't see everything. Nor can you go through life without making a few mistakes. I'll say it again: without your leadership we would never have made it out alive."

Floyd sat down heavily beside Brendon's body.

"What kind of a place have we come to, Al? At first, I expected all kinds of problems and trouble, and to my surprise everything seemed to work out better than anyone had any right to expect. We found food. We weren't attacked. There were no killing diseases. It was like living in paradise. Now suddenly we come upon the lupi, which aren't like anything we've seen in our world, and almost a third of my company is dead."

"Floyd, I think there's a lot about this world that we don't know yet" said Al. "Our early success, blessing that it was, made us complacent, and we weren't sufficiently afraid of what came next. Sometimes having a little fear early saves one from experiencing a big fear later on."

They buried Brendon on the island. As Al had done with the others, he fashioned a crude cross and said a few words over the grave.

As for the others, Glenn seemed to be doing quite well; the bleeding in his arm had stopped. With a heavy heart and a deep fear of the future, Dave followed as Floyd led them along the creek, toward the sea. With a start Dave remembered the vellum scrap. Feeling under his clothes for his money belt, he was relieved to realize it was still there.

Chapter 15

New Jerusalem

Although Glenn insisted he was fine and fit to travel, the others fashioned a stretcher for him, from two stout saplings and spare clothes from the packs of the dead. They sorted through the rest of the excess gear, took what they could carry, and buried the rest under a cairn of stones on the island.

When everything was ready, they started out, taking turns carrying Glenn and his pack on the stretcher. The terrain was difficult, and more than once the stretcher-bearers stumbled, almost tossing Glenn onto the ground. After the third stumble Glenn insisted vociferously that it was safer for him to walk. He walked for a short stretch when the terrain allowed but soon tired, so they fell to carrying him again. Their progress was agonizingly slow.

After a week of this, everyone was nearing the limits of their endurance. Their progress slowed further, and they were forced to make camp late in the afternoon when the stretcher-bearers were too tired to continue. Thankfully the weather was warmer again, bringing back a memory of the early fall. Although the trees were bare, in the sheltered glades fall had not yet been completely overwhelmed by winter. They still found plenty of potatoes, and the creek teemed with trout in the deep pools.

The eighth day after the attack, they encountered a barrier. As they climbed a low hill and cleared the trees, they saw a rock wall ahead, about 400 yards high. Although it was made of jumbled rock, it seemed regular and formed the arc of a ring that looked to be several miles in diameter. Directly in front of them was a cleft. At some time in the past, a section of this circular wall had shifted, leaving a narrow channel for the creek to enter.

They debated about the best course of action. The outside edge of this crater was so steep and broken up that it would have to be climbed. Finally Floyd announced they should look for an easy route through the barrier. Failing that, they would walk around it.

They descended from the hill and followed the creek into the barrier wall. On the north side of the creek, a narrow path skirted the edge of the canyon wall. Dave looked up and saw that the walls of the gorge leapt straight up. Already the steep sides cast deep shadows on the creek as it flowed over its stony bed, bubbling and boiling around boulders that had fallen from the heights. The canyon was not straight, but bent to the right. The path seemed too well trodden to be a game trail, so they proceeded with extra caution, Floyd and Al creeping ahead with their rifles. As they rounded a bastion of rock jutting into the creek from the north, the noisy creek became a pool.

They stopped short. Ahead of them a small wooden bridge had been built to cross a gap in the path.

"What do you think?" whispered Floyd.

"It looks like one of ours," said Al, examining the ax cuts on the wood and the wooden spikes holding the timber together.

"They used ironwood for the spikes," continued Al.

"Maybe there's one of our lumber camps ahead," said Dave hopefully, as he crept up from behind to join them.

They proceeded even more cautiously now. When they rounded a bend to the left, they were astonished to see an earth-and-rock dam, about thirty feet high, spanning the narrow gorge and holding back the water to form the long narrow pool they had encountered. They examined the dam wall but could not see where the water left the pool, although the sound of a waterfall could be heard as a muted roar.

Examining the dam in more detail, they saw that it was crowned with a wooden palisade. The path climbed up the north side of the gorge and then crossed a sheer wall of rock into the palisade's rough wooden gate over a drawbridge. The drawbridge was drawn up.

Suddenly, a voice boomed from behind the palisade, "Who are you, and why do you disturb our tranquility?" Stunned, they did not answer immediately, so the voice shouted the question again.

"We are explorers sent out by the colony of Botany Bay. We have been attacked, and several of our members have been killed. We are in need of assistance," shouted Floyd.

There was no response for some time. Finally, a head appeared above the wall of the palisade and said, "Approach the drawbridge so that we can have a look at you. Leave your weapons behind."

Al and Floyd gave their rifles to their companions and then walked up the steep switchback and approached the wall.

"I know you. You're Al Gleeson, aren't you?" said the voice. The face was hooded in shadow. "Gleeson, drop all your weapons and approach the drawbridge. The rest of you stay where you are."

After getting Floyd's agreement, Al gave his pack, sword, and knife belt to him. Then, holding his hands palm outward, he approached the wooden platform opposite the drawbridge. The drawbridge rumbled down, and the gate behind it opened. Al walked in, the gate closed, and the drawbridge was drawn up.

"Now what do we do?" Dave asked Floyd as he rejoined them by the pool, bringing Al's equipment.

"We wait," said Floyd.

"But what if they hold him hostage?" asked Tom.

"We wait!" said Floyd, ending the conversation. As if to emphasize his point, he broke out some food and passed it around to the others.

After about an hour, the drawbridge lowered again, and a young, fine-featured, buckskin-clad man came out. He had a friendly face and was sporting a thin scraggly beard. When he spoke, it was clear that his was the voice they had heard earlier.

"My name is Mark Forsyth," he said, inclining his head courteously. "I've come to bid you welcome as guests. Your companion, Al Gleeson, is known to our bishop. Al has told us of your need and the perils you have encountered, and our bishop has asked me to extend to you the safety of our hearth, even though it's not our custom to provide entry to strangers. Nevertheless, our rules require that you leave your weapons at the door. Will you comply with this request?"

"Strangers?" said Floyd, sounding exasperated. "You know us from Botany Bay. Even though I didn't know your name until today, I recall seeing you in the settlement."

"I also recognize you, of course," said Forsyth. "But we are a religious community that values our privacy, and we fear the interference of Halcyon. You didn't answer my question. Will you relinquish your weapons?"

"Can we speak to Al Gleeson?" asked Floyd.

"If you wish," said Forsyth, seemingly untroubled by the request.

At a signal from Forsyth, Al came down and joined them on the path.

"They want us to give up our weapons," said Floyd.

Al's face was flushed and his eyes were hard, yet his words were calm and controlled. "These people are Dalyites, followers of Dalrymple," said Al. "I believe them to be men of their word, and since they have extended hospitality to us, we need not fear any treachery. However, it's very unusual for them to extend hospitality to strangers. Furthermore, they're afraid of something, so I can't guarantee how easy it will be for us to leave."

"Are you all right? Are you sure?" asked Floyd.

"Yes, I'm sure, Floyd. I'm upset because I met a group I really didn't want to meet—not because our company is in danger."

Floyd put his hand on his chin and looked out over the pond at the palisade. Finally he said, "We'll worry about that later. Glenn needs to rest in a safe place. All this jostling and lugging him about is killing him. Besides, I don't think we could have carried him much farther. Let's do it!"

They crossed the drawbridge and found themselves on a wide wooden platform. In the middle of the platform was a gap where they could see the sluice gate through which the water from the creek poured into the valley beyond. An arch constructed of huge stones formed the end of an underwater drain for the pond.

The sluice had been constructed with great care from cut stone. The stonework was old and well worn by the water plunging through the rock channel and falling another thirty feet to the valley floor. A large wooden tripod made of recently cut wood with pulleys and winches could be used to lower heavy wooden beams into specially made slots in the stone to reduce the flow through the underground channel.

"We have labored day and night to complete this dam and palisade," Forsyth said. "It was a vision of the bishop's. Now we are safe and can live in peace. If we are threatened, we simply shut the sluice gate, raise the level of the water, and the pond will flood all the way to the end of the gorge. The path will become submerged, and access will be very difficult."

"Very well designed," said Floyd, staring at the massive stones that made up the arch of the sluice and formed the slots for the sluice gate. Dave saw that Floyd had a puzzled look on his face. Dave was puzzled too.

There's no way these Dalyites built this! This stonework is too old. They only built the wooden parts. Why are they so afraid? Do they know about the lupi? Is there some other danger we don't know about?

Looking to the east, Dave could see they were in a crater about two miles in diameter. The southern half of the floor of the crater was dotted with small sections of tilled earth in a broad meadow. The northern half of the bowl, in contrast, was covered with trees and dense brush. The creek, which cascaded from the dam to the valley floor, made a broad loop north into the woods and then reappeared, winding through the meadow in broad sweeping curves, until it finally emptied into a lake at the southeastern end of the valley. The gorge was the only break in the circular crater wall. The lake had no apparent outlet.

Forsyth, seeing the direction of Dave's gaze and seemingly reading his thoughts, said, "The creek leaves the crater by an underground channel and emerges on the other side of the crater wall, eventually emptying into Botany Bay."

"Oh, so this is the same creek that empties into our bay!" said Floyd with excitement.

"We're still about three days away, but yes," said Forsyth. "We've searched through your packs and given you what you may keep. Your weapons will be stored here," he said, indicating a small shed, "but now you must come and meet the bishop. He'll welcome you and pronounce his judgment."

That sounds ominous, thought Dave.

Forsyth led them down a switchback path at the back of the dam. The dam had been built atop a natural rockfall, which had partially blocked the creek.

They reached the meadow, crossed a sturdy bridge, and followed a well-traveled road to a tiny village, which was about a mile distant at the edge of the lake. The village consisted of only two buildings, a house-sized church, which the group identified by the large cross, which was attached to the outside, and a second, larger building. This larger building was constructed of cut stone but had a new roof made of turf. One side had a low addition with a separate entrance and a stone well, identifying it as the kitchen.

Approaching the two buildings, they saw that both were festooned with pine, cedar, and holly.

"Didn't you realize today is Christmas Day?" asked Forsyth, noting their curious surprise.

"No!" said Floyd, astounded. "I'm afraid that because of the events of the last few weeks we've lost track of time."

"Your arrival couldn't have come at a more propitious time. We'll be celebrating our Christmas feast today."

They entered the large building adjacent to the church. The main room was square, with a big fireplace on the wall opposite the entrance. A Christmas tree, covered with strips of colored cloth and handmade wooden ornaments, reached nearly to the roof beams in the corner of the common room. An indefinable smell of Christmas in the air reminded Dave of his childhood, bringing with it a longing for family.

The two carrying Glenn's stretcher placed it gently on a bench. Glenn seemed in good spirits and looked eagerly around the room.

Rough wooden furniture surrounded the fireplace. An elderly man with a shock of white hair, his hands behind his back, faced the cheerful fire. When he heard the group enter, he turned to face them, smiled, and approached them with his hands outstretched.

"Welcome to New Jerusalem, and merry Christmas," he said warmly, shaking each hand in turn. Coming at last came to Al, he said, "Welcome home, Albert. Will you give me your hand?"

"I will not!" said Al with anger.

The bishop, with a flush rising on his cheeks, turned back to the others and said in a faltering voice, "As I said, I bid you welcome," then lapsed into an awkward silence.

"New Jerusalem?" asked Dave.

"Pardon me?" said the bishop.

"You called this place New Jerusalem."

"Yes. I know it's a little pretentious," said the bishop, breaking into a smile once more, "but that's what we call our little community." He indicated they were to take seats by the fire, and then gently dismissed Forsyth with, "Thank you, Mark."

"My name is Dalrymple. By the grace of God I am the leader of this community. Before I tell you more about us, as a courtesy to me, your host, I would ask that you indulge me by answering a few questions about yourselves and what brought you here."

Seating himself facing the seven visitors, Dalrymple led the conversation to a discussion of their trip. Glenn obviously felt well enough to join in the conversation. Tactful, skillful, and thorough in his gentle interrogation, Dalrymple asked so many detailed questions it took the better part of an hour to get through them. At that point, two women came in with mashed potatoes and venison for lunch. One of the women left immediately, so they did not catch a glimpse of her face. The second woman served the meal. Though plainly dressed, she was exceedingly beautiful, and the travelers' glances followed her every movement around the room.

Seeing the stretcher lying in the corner, the young woman interrupted the proceedings.

"Who is injured, if I may ask?" she queried.

"Let me introduce Sister Sonja. She is our village physician," said Dalrymple. The men greeted her warmly.

"Glenn Thompson," said Floyd. "He was bitten by a wolf."

"A wolf? I'd better have a look at that right away. He should also have rabies vaccine and a Virostat."

Sister Sonja approached Glenn, examined the crude bandage, and asked, "Can you walk?"

"I can try," said Glenn plaintively.

"Then you'd better follow me."

Glenn staggered as he rose, and Sonja grasped his arm to steady him. He had a pained expression on his face. However, just before he disappeared, he turned back to his companions and beamed from ear to ear. Resuming his look of pain born with fortitude and endurance, he slowly, painfully, limped on Sonja's arm into a side hallway.

"I don't think he's going to be back anytime soon," muttered Floyd, so that only Dave could hear.

After the two had left, Dalrymple returned to his questioning. Finally, when they had described how they had arrived at Dalrymple's valley, Floyd took the initiative.

"We have told you our history since we left Botany Bay more than three months ago," said Floyd. "Mark Forsyth told us that your colony is on Botany Creek and that you're three days from the coast."

"That's correct," said Dalrymple.

"In our turn then," continued Floyd, "we'd like to know what you're doing here, three days from the colony, in this secluded valley."

"That's a fair question," said Dalrymple. "I was—or, I suppose, am—Professor of History at Halcyon. In addition to my academic responsibilities, I'm a person of strong religious convictions, perhaps what you would term a 'fundamentalist,' although I just think of myself as a sincere follower of Christ. I believe our western society—long before the dislocation—was wrong-headed and moving to disaster. I've long wished to set up a small community, sheltered from the headlong rush to social and moral oblivion, but in our twenty-first century that dream seemed impossible to fulfill. My specialty was seventeenth century English history. I wanted to do what the Puritans did in coming to America—to set up a society, under God, free from the decay and manipulation of our modern age. Unfortunately, there really was no 'America' for me, until the dislocation.

"In the first few weeks, I felt I ought to help O'Reilly get Halcyon on its feet, and perhaps I thought I could set up my society within the confines of Halcyon itself. However, as a faculty member I saw Blackmore positioning himself to take over, and God made it clear to me that Blackmore would tolerate people like me on paper, but behind the scenes he'd make every effort to drive us slowly to spiritual extinction. Under him it would become impossible for us to maintain our belief system. His people would slowly grind it out of us. If they didn't succeed with me, then they would certainly educate our faith out of our children.

"As a consequence, as soon as I could, I volunteered for Botany Bay. The people you see here came with me. At first we settled in Botany Bay, but as soon as I saw the Happy Berry users, I knew that big trouble was brewing on the mainland as well. In the Bible, 1 Corinthians, chapter 6, verse 12, the apostle Paul says, *'All things are lawful unto me, but all things are not expedient: all things are lawful for me, but I will not be brought under the power of any.'*" Dalrymple quoted the verse from memory without pausing.

"We are forbidden anything that enslaves. My brothers and my sisters and I take that warning quite literally. We knew it applied to Happy Berries. I knew we had to leave, and so I looked for a way to get us out of town. Happy Berries only grow within a few miles of the coast, so I searched inland to keep my people away from the temptation. At first I volunteered for one of the lumber camps up Botany Creek, but the men of my community and I searched and prayed constantly for a place of seclusion, a *selahammahlekoth*, or 'rock of escape,' if you like, such as the Bible's King David found in the wilderness of Judah.

"I followed Botany Creek, ranging farther and farther with each attempt. Finally, I found it ended at the edge of a steep rock wall in a lake. I was about to turn back when it struck me that there were no streams flowing into this small lake, only Botany Creek flowing out. It was then that I decided to climb the crater wall and saw the valley of New Jerusalem.

"We've been here since the summer, and we've worked day and night to bring our colony into being. Our plan is to maintain our independence, to prevent contamination from the poison that is Halcyon, and especially to keep Halcyon away from our children."

"Where does that leave us?" asked Floyd.

"I knew Albert Gleeson through our meetings at Halcyon." He turned to look at Al. "He's a good and honorable man who speaks the truth, and on that basis I've chosen to trust you. If you come to believe what we believe and seek to escape Halcyon as we do, we'll offer to let you stay as members of our community. On the other hand, if you can't do that, we'll ask of you a solemn oath, that you'll keep our location a secret when you return to Halcyon."

The interview had come to an end. Dalrymple called to a young man walking through the hall; spoke to him quietly, and then addressed his guests.

"We have three double rooms in the bachelor quarters," said Dalrymple. "Mr. Linder, please divide up your companions."

Floyd and Al conferred, and then Floyd divided the six remaining explorers into groups of two, pairing Dave with Al. Preparing to leave, Dave had just moved to pick up their gear when he heard Dalrymple ask to speak to Al. Dave overheard their conversation as he rearranged their gear.

"I'm truly sorry about your brother," said Dalrymple.

"It had been more than a year-and-a-half since Thomas left your group," said Al, anger permeating his voice. "And my parents hadn't heard from him since he disappeared. Do you know why he left you, and left us?"

"No, I can't say that I do," said Dalrymple quietly.

"When we joined the Dalyites, you convinced us to abandon our friends because they were a bad influence. You cut us off from our family for the same reason. After we'd severed all these relationships, he and I did what you said because you were our spiritual leader. But we're not stupid. Even the naïve, like Thomas and I, can eventually see the truth. You were manipulating us. I saw it first. When I left the Dalyites, my relationship to him, the closest friend I had, was also severed. He wouldn't even talk to me. Then when he finally left, he didn't just leave you, but he left his friends, his family, and his faith. And now he's gone because of you and your cursed manipulation."

Dave was so drawn to the conversation that he gave up all pretense of repacking their gear and stared at Dalrymple whose face was a study in profound regret. "I am sorry. Forgive me," Dalrymple implored Al.

Al turned to join Dave and walked away. At the entrance to the hallway, he turned back to Dalrymple, who stood by the fire, a look of pain on his face. Al made as if to speak, but thought better of it, and walked down the hallway, saying, "Come on, Dave."

They found one of the young men, who showed them their quarters at the west end of the building. The mattresses on the stone floor were made of straw. There was no other furniture in the room.

When they had opened up their packs and made themselves at home, Dave said, "Maybe it's none of my business, but I couldn't help overhearing your interchange with Dalrymple back in the hall."

"You're right," said Al. "It isn't any of your business."

"You're right, of course," retorted Dave. "I'm not a Christian, but I thought you folks are supposed to forgive when someone asks you. Am I wrong about that?"

Al turned red but said nothing, continuing to unpack his knapsack. Finally he put the pack aside and turned to face Dave. "No, Dave, you're not wrong. But you do not know what you're asking. My brother—"

"I'm not really asking anything. I just thought that forgiveness was one of the things Christians were supposed to extend to others. Here Dalrymple asks for forgiveness as prettily as one can imagine, and you say no? I guess I don't understand the finer points of Christianity very well."

Al collapsed onto his straw mattress and put his head into his hands.

Dave, worried that he had said too much, went out for a while. He looked at the building. The stonework was old and made of the same stone that formed the walls of the crater, but the wood beams and roof were new. *There's no way they could have built these big structures in the short time they've been here. They must have found the stone shells and finished them off!*

When Dave returned, Al seemed in better spirits and actually thanked him for speaking up. That evening the whole community of thirty people held a Christmas feast. The ten men and twenty women from New Jerusalem, amongst them five married couples, set the feast on long roughhewn tables. For the main course a whole roasted buck was carried in on a spit from the cookhouse. Rough clay pitchers filled with a delicious juice made from wild raspberries graced the table.

Finally, a cake made from acorn flour and honey was served. When everyone had eaten their fill and could eat no more, they sang Christmas carols by heart. Several of the men had guitars, and one played the violin. After caroling the revelers moved tables and chairs aside and exchanged gifts. Somehow, gifts for the travelers appeared amongst those under the tree. Dave received a small leather pouch, cunningly crafted and embroidered. Finally, the evening ended in a square dance, played by the fiddler and called by Dalrymple. Even Glenn took part in the festivities, until he began to boast about his square dancing ability, upon which Sonja sent him to his room. The evening couldn't have been more delightful for the travelers. They had not seen a woman for three months, and dancing with one was sheer delight.

It was very late when the six companions turned in to bed. Al seemed like he needed to talk. "Dave, you were right to admonish me about forgiveness today. I owe you an explanation," said Al. "You see, when I first came to Halcyon, I joined the Dalyites. Dalrymple was an enthusiastic, devoted man, full of religious conviction. He believed in complete and utter separation from the world. By that, he meant from everyone else in the world. Separation was much more important than interaction. I bought into what he said and only made friends with other Dalyites. But as I grew in my own Christian convictions, I realized there was a great deal of social manipulation involved in keeping us in line. We had no freedom. We had no opportunity to decide for ourselves. All questions, even legitimate ones, were taken as a sign of rebellion and apostasy. Finally I left the group, and that estranged my older brother, Thomas."

"I don't get it," said Dave. "If you've seen the light, so to speak, and you've recognized that Christianity is maintained by manipulation and social pressure, why do you still follow it?" Al smiled ruefully. " I suppose at first I did almost abandon everything, or at least I tried to abandon everything. But you know, I knew deep down inside that there was something real there. I couldn't just abandon my beliefs. The author G.K. Chesterton once said that, 'the best case against Christianity is Christians.' I think that's true, but just because someone gets it wrong doesn't mean the whole thing is wrong. One thing I did learn though is that freedom is oh so important. You must let people ask the hard questions about their faith: about pain, about injustice. Let them face up to all of the people who sneer at God; let them face up to their best arguments. Only as you work through that in freedom, can you arrive at a place where faith is genuine."

"Do you think this is going to be a problem for us?" asked Dave. "Will Dalrymple try to keep us here against our wishes so he can control us?"

"No, I do not think so. Dalrymple doesn't lie, and he's not treacherous. He'll keep his word."

"Maybe he's changed," ventured Dave.

"Has he changed?" asked Al. "I think he's doing it again with this colony. That's why he wants to stay away from Halcyon; he wants complete control over these people's lives. In his mind, I think, his control is benevolent, but it's still control."

Dave chose not to respond. He was tired and wanted to sleep. But the sounds of Al's restless tossing and turning told him his friend still had plenty on his mind.

Al tossed and turned, but could not get to sleep. Dave's breathing already had the cadence of a man sinking into deep sleep. Al thoughts kept returning to Dave's rebuke.

I know Dave's right. But what am I to do, Lord?

Reluctantly reaching a decision, Al finally got up and went to the main hall. The fire was still burning merrily. As he approached the blaze, he saw Dalrymple dozing in a chair. Al was about to tiptoe out again when Dalrymple awoke.

"Albert," he said, "I'm afraid I was thinking and fell asleep."

"I came to apologize," said Al. He swallowed hard. "No, that's not quite right. I actually came to ask for forgiveness."

"Forgiveness?"

"Yes," continued Al. "You asked me to forgive you, and I was rude and uncharitable."

"In that case, I forgive you from the bottom of my heart," said Dalrymple.

"And I also forgive you," said Al.

"Well, that's done!" said Dalrymple. "I know you'll be happy here."

"I don't want there to be any misunderstanding," said Al. "I don't think this is the place for me, and I'll need to leave at some point."

Dalrymple's face betrayed his disappointment. "Of course!" he said.

"I'm quite tired," said Al. "I'll think I'll head off to bed." With that he returned to his room and slept soundly.

The days passed swiftly. The people in the valley appeared to have a degree of joy and happiness not encountered in the frenetic culture of Halcyon. Dave and the other explorers raised a new log building next to "city hall," as they called their residence. This new building was to be a library to house the colony's precious books and would eventually become a schoolhouse. The companions helped wherever they could, some cutting lumber in the forest and floating it down the creek to the building site, others raising log cabins for the married couples near their farm plots.

Glenn spent many days in a special room reserved for the sick, adjacent to the unmarried women's quarters. He received no end of good-natured ribbing for this. Sister Sonja watched over him with unceasing care. When he had recovered sufficiently, they could often be seen going for walks together in the meadow or along the shore of the lake.

"What's with Glenn?" asked Dave. "He didn't seem all that sick, yet he's still being looked after."

"Perhaps he's become addicted to the medicine," said Al.

"Perhaps he's finally found a woman that meets his criteria," said Floyd.

"I don't know," said Dave. "Sister Sonja doesn't strike me as a person who meets Glenn's criteria. She has ideas of her own, and she's no slouch. She's much too rigid for him."

"Why do you say that?" asked Al. "Do you really think Glenn knew what he was looking for? I think men rarely speak greater nonsense than when they try to describe the woman they claim is the woman of their dreams!"

"Thus saith the seer who acknowledgeth he knoweth nothing about women!" said Dave solemnly.

Al laughed. "Touché!"

Two weeks later, as they were retrieving lumber that had floated down the creek, the men were told that Dalrymple wanted to see them immediately. They left their work, cleaned up, and hurried over to city hall. Dalrymple was waiting for them. A young man in travel-stained garments was also there, surrounded by many from the village.

"Gentlemen, please sit down," said Dalrymple. "Jared here has just returned from a trading trip to Botany Bay, and he has some disturbing news." Dalrymple also sat down, and gestured to Jared to begin.

"Bishop Dalrymple, brothers, sisters, and guests," began Jared formally with his hands clasped behind his back. "As many of you know, I was sent south with two of our brothers to Botany Bay to trade some of our baskets, weapons, and leather goods for medicine from Halcyon.

"We made the raft trip down the creek without major incident. After we'd finished our trading, we were searching for a buyer of the raft when trouble started."

"What kind of trouble?" interrupted Floyd.

"It became apparent soon after we reached Botany Bay, that there had been a great deal of trouble with Happy Berry users. Some of these people who'd been using the berries for more than six months had begun to change. Many of them had become so unruly that they'd been driven out of town or locked up in one of the log buildings until Governor O'Reilly could get some help from Halcyon. He'd run out of the medicine they use to control the addiction."

"Sedovarin!" said Dave under his breath.

"You said they'd begun to change," said Floyd. "Did you see them?"

Jared shuffled his feet and looked uncomfortable. "I'm ashamed to say it," resumed Jared. "I was curious and wanted to see these fellows I had heard about in the town. I saw them in their makeshift prison. They were terrible to behold. At one moment they growled and spat like cornered animals, yet at another they spoke like men. The whites of their eyes had become yellow-red from the berries, and they seem to have a constant supply of adrenaline-charged strength that's beyond ordinary men. They'd leap up the side of their wooden cage with a strength I wouldn't have thought possible."

"On our final day, a band of these 'renegades,' as the townspeople called them, that had been hiding in the woods and living off the land to the south raided the town for food and broke the other renegades out of prison. It seemed to me that many of the townspeople that had a grudge against O'Reilly also took part in the rioting even though they'd not been using Happy Berries for long. When the violence started, we fled in panic, leaving the area as quickly as possible. We hurried back to warn our brothers and sisters that God's judgment has begun to fall on Halcyon."

"But this is not a judgment of God," said Dave, exasperated. "This is their own stupid fault for not listening to Uncle Charlie, I mean Governor O'Reilly!"

"O'Reilly is your uncle!" blurted Dalrymple.

"What are you going to do?" asked Floyd, turning to Dalrymple.

"Do?" answered Dalrymple. "We'll stay to our purpose. We'll build a refuge here for those who, at God's leading, come here and want to obey His law."

"But what about those people in Botany Bay?" asked Al.

"Albert, you know better that anyone here," said Dalrymple, "that the people of Botany Bay are experiencing natural justice. They've disobeyed the law by using Happy Berries, which led to their enslavement. Now their earlier decisions are coming home to cause them grief and trouble. They have sown, and the crop is coming in. They've made their bed, and now they must sleep in it."

"But where's the grace in this?" asked Al. "Shouldn't we, as God's people, help them even if they've brought this upon themselves? Aren't there innocents among the guilty?"

"That's why I called you here," said Dalrymple, "The time of decision has come. You must now decide to join our family and promise to obey our laws and our leadership, or you must leave, taking an oath never to reveal our location to others. Which will it be?"

Floyd stood up. "I'm going back!" he said. "Who's coming with me?"

He looked around. Al stood up immediately, followed by Dave. Dwight, Stan, and Tom stood up more slowly. Glenn averted his eyes.

"All right!" said Dalrymple, reaching for a Bible. He administered an oath, which was repeated by the six in unison, and then they left to pack up their things.

Dave had to get some answers from Glenn, so he stayed behind.

"Let's go for a walk," Dave said to Glenn.

As they walked Dave asked, "Are you going or staying?"

"I'm staying," said Glenn.

"Are you sure you know what you're doing?" asked Dave. "These people here are not at all like you. Whatever happened to the Glenn philosophy of 'live life to the fullest'? How are you going to do that here?"

Glenn answered slowly, "Dave, I don't rightly know myself. I know that I'm in love with Sonja—"

"So that's it!" exclaimed Dave.

"No, wait a minute," interrupted Glenn in turn. "I know what you think, but it's not like that. I love Sonja, but I'm not at all sure she loves me."

"I care about you, Glenn, and I know how you think, and I just don't want you throwing your life away because you have your hormones up about this woman. Dalrymple isn't going to let you leave if you stay after today. Furthermore, remember the woman of your dreams who was going to satisfy your every whim and desire? Well, Sonja doesn't fit the bill. Sonja has a mind of her own, and her religion is more important to her than you are. You're making a big mistake."

"Dave," said Glenn, "everything I said and believed back then was nonsense. I see that now. You're absolutely right; Sonja loves her God more than she cares about me. Even when she cares for me, she does it out of kindness, since she doesn't need me at all. But she's a woman of character, and she's worth going after. Even if I never win her and I'm left with this ache in my chest, it'll have been worth it. I'm not worthy of her, but I have to try to be worthy of her. I've never been surer of anything in my life. I'm going to try to win her. I already know I'll probably fail. I can't let this go by without at least trying."

What's happened to Glenn? Has he gone mad?

There was nothing more to be said. Dave just shook his head in disbelief.

Chapter 16

Natural Justice

In an hour the explorers were wending their way up the narrow defile out of New Jerusalem. Glenn walked with them, but he'd been pensive during the whole trip from the village, and they all felt the sorrow of the impending separation. When they reached the mouth of the canyon they stopped to say their farewells.

Dave had had a change of heart and wanted to leave his friend on a positive note. "When a woman of quality like Sonja takes an interest in a bonehead like you, I think you have to go for it," said Dave. "I don't know what's gotten into her, and she clearly hasn't heard your bizarre and startling theory on womanhood, but I'd seal her fate before she comes to her senses, if I were you."

With that they thumped Glenn on the back and wished him goodbye.

Leaving the canyon entrance, the six retraced their steps up the creek until they found a ford. After crossing the creek, they began the long journey around the outer rim of the crater.

"There must be another exit from this place," said Dave.

"Why do you say that?" asked Al.

"Remember what Jared said about loading their stuff on a raft and floating it down to Botany Bay? Well, I can't imagine they'd lug all that stuff through here, and then to the outside lake. Anyway, I saw the party arrive, and they came from the east, not through the gorge."

"Really!" said Floyd. "I guess they want to keep the other entrance a secret; otherwise they could have saved us a lot of time and energy by not making us walk around this blooming crater."

They hiked on for another forty-five minutes before coming to the small lake Dalrymple had mentioned. They followed the bank of the meandering creek. Within a few hundred feet, a tributary joined Botany Creek from the south, swelling the creek to the size of a small river in the spring thaw.

All day they journeyed to the coast, following the creek and crossing the occasional tributary. The thought was constantly on Dave's mind that if things had gone badly in Botany Bay, they would arrive too late. It would be a week after the riots had started before they could get back to the mouth of the creek, by his reckoning.

That evening, after it had grown too dark to walk through the bush, they stopped on an island, exhausted. Al roused himself to build a fire and began to warm some of their provisions for supper. When they had eaten and had some Halcyon tea, they felt refreshed.

"I really miss Glenn," said Dave at last. "I feel our family group is breaking up. Why is it that you only really appreciate people when they're absent? I can think now of things I wanted to say to my friend, yet I never said them when we were together."

"Why indeed!" said Al. "Maybe these times of separation are as necessary as the times of togetherness."

"Leave it to Al to always have an answer," said Floyd.

"The ideal woman—" began Tom, imitating Glenn's voice so accurately that everyone broke into laughter. Tom finished the complete Glenn monologue with a little help from the others, and then the group grew silent. For his part, Dave was remembering the time that now seemed so long ago, when there were still ten of them, and the future seemed brighter and more hopeful than it did tonight.

Stan broke the silence. "Dave, you did remember to bring that old stained parchment you found at the quarry, didn't you?"

"You mean the vellum. Of course! Why?"

"I was afraid you might've forgotten it because we left in such a rush. Could I see it?"

Dave felt an odd reluctance to show it to him. Ever since the confrontation between Stan and Al at the Willow Pond, he'd never quite trusted him. Still, he had no reason to refuse.

"Sure." Dave pulled the money belt out from under his shirt, carefully unwrapped the vellum, and handed it over to Stan, who unfolded it and held it up to the fire.

"What do you see?" asked Floyd.

"Nothin'," said Stan, "nothin' at all. Still, I think it's important since it's clear proof that we met the remnants of a primitive civilization of sorts."

When Stan finally handed the scrap back undamaged, Dave inwardly breathed a sigh of relief.

They didn't bother putting up their tents but slept on the ground and resumed their grueling march as soon as it became light enough to walk.

For the next two days, they moved as swiftly as they could. At the end of the second day, the swollen creek foamed through a narrow cut, then, its fury spent, moved tranquilly toward the sea. The weather showed signs of an early spring, and birds could be seen everywhere, gathering grass and twigs for nests.

At last they approached Botany Bay. They crossed to the north side of Botany Creek, and as they came within sight of the town, moved quietly, using what cover they could find to shelter their approach from prying eyes. Finally, they reached a stand of basswood on a low hill, separated from the town by 200 yards of brush and the creek. As they crept to the top and looked toward the buildings, they saw smoke filling the air, but everything was quiet. Dave wanted to go straight in, but Floyd insisted on caution. Looking around for a suitable place to make camp, they suddenly heard cries as the din of battle arose in the town. The noise quickly subsided, and all was quiet again.

They hid their packs in a hawthorn thicket. Al, being the lightest, climbed the largest linden tree in the vicinity to get a better view, and became lost in the highest branches above for some time. When he returned, they all wormed their way into the thicket, to confer unobserved and undisturbed.

"So what's the story?" whispered Floyd.

"The town is on fire. Much of it's already been destroyed. The stockade is well defended but under sporadic attack from the south side. I think I've seen O'Reilly on the stockade walls encouraging the defenders. O'Reilly's made a lot of improvements to the fort's defenses since we left."

"What about the creek?"

"As far as I could tell, the creek side of the fort hasn't yet been attacked. That's not too surprising. With the current high water levels, the wall of the fort is only about ten feet from the water's edge, and any attackers would be easy to kill on that narrow strip of land."

Edward Makalo was bone tired and was pretty sure he was going to die; if not tonight, then tomorrow or the next day. He was on guard duty on top of the Botany Bay stockade waiting for the next attack by the renegades. Everyone else, except Bronson, the other sentry, was trying to get a little bit of rest.

His grandfather, an Igbo fighter from the Nigerian civil war, has been called Atu-egwuonwu before he changed his name to Makalo on emmigrating to the United States. Atu-egwuonwu meant "do not have fear of death" yet Edward was very afraid.

He forced his mind back to his duty and trudged along the north wall of the stockade which was only 10 feet from Botany Creek. The renegades never attacked from this side, but who knew what they would do next?

Movement caught Edward's eye. A large bush, uprooted by the spring flood, slowly drifted down the creek. There was something odd about the bush, but he couldn't put his finger on it in the fog of his tired thought. Still he stopped and watched intently. When the bush reached some reeds next to the stockade, it snagged and stopped. Slowly a dark shape emerged and stealthily approached the stockage wall. Makalo unlimbered his crossbow and was about to shout the alarm when he saw the figure throw a bundle over the wall and re-treat silently back to his hiding place in the bush. Edward swallowed his shout and went to the bundle, adrenaline making him alert for an attack. He carried the bundle to the corner of the stockade where a small lantern was burning. He read a few lines and then rushed down the ladder as fast as he could to pound on O'Reilly's door. He heard commotion inside and O'Reilly appeared at the door rubbing sleep from his eyes.

"Edward, is your watch done already?"

"Bronson is still on guard, but you've got to see this right away." He thrust the paper and the bundle at O'Reilly.

O'Reilly started to read. "Praise the Lord we have a chance."

"Pardon?" said Edward.

"I was just mumbling to myself, Edward. It's from my nephew. He and five others are across the creek and have a plan to get us out of here. Take me upstairs and show me where you found this."

Edward walked briskly across the fort courtyard and led the way up the ladder. From the exact spot where he had picked up the parcel he pointed to the bush snagged in the reeds.

O'Reilly leaned over the wall and called in muted tones, "Dave, Dave is that you?"

After he had thrown his clothing bundle over the wall, Dave returned to his hiding place to wait. He had deliberately made the bundle bulky to that a sentry could not help but stumble over it even in the dark. A long delay at this point could be disastrous.

A sentry approached and picked up the bundle and then moved off. The initial elation at seeing the sentry gave way to concern as the interminable wait began to grate on him.

Something has to happen now. What's taking so long? Maybe Uncle Charlie is already dead.

An ice cold hand gripped his heart at that thought.

Two men approached the edge of the parapet and Uncle Charlie's voice said, "Dave, Dave is that you?"

"Yes, Uncle Charlie," said Dave. "Let me come up and we can talk."

"Give me a minute while I look for a ladder or a rope," said O'Reilly.

"I've got one. I can get up, if you keep your trigger-happy crossbowmen from shooting me."

"Come up and be quick about it before the renegades find out you're here."

Throwing a line up to O'Reilly, Dave disentangled the ladder from the floating island and slowly let it be pulled up the wall of the stockade. Once it was fast, he tested the strength of the rungs and climbed up, pulling the ladder after him.

Dave looked around. The sentry was haggard, weary, desperate, but O'Reilly's eyes glowed at Dave's appearance. "Thank God you're here! It's good to see you, son!" said O'Reilly, clapping him on the back. "I was afraid the renegades had found you. How are the others?"

"They're here; at least, some are here," said Dave. "But what's going on here, Uncle?"

"We're in bad shape—under continual attack. It started about a week ago when a bunch of renegades broke into town and freed some others we'd locked up. We drove them out and had peace for a few days, but three days ago they attacked in force, scattered or killed many, and drove about 200 of us into the stockade. We've been fighting for our lives ever since. We're completely out of ammunition and almost out of arrows."

"What started this?" Dave asked.

"I made an earnest, desperate attempt to contain the spread of the Happy Berry addiction, but it had already become too deeply rooted for me to stop it. At first it was just an addiction, but then the longtime users went berserk; they became violent and out of control and began destroying everything in their path. Now the addiction has affected such a large part of our population, our village has been destroyed. We've no choice but to try to get out of here."

"How many are here?" asked Dave.

"We still have about 200 crammed into this small space."

"Are there any others who are not renegades left on the mainland?"

"There may be," said O'Reilly, "but we have no way of reaching them. We need to get out while we can. Crazy as the renegades are, they've grown to hate us non addicts, and I don't think they'll stop the attacks until they kill us."

"Well, we have a plan, such as it is," said Dave.

"What kind of plan?" asked O'Reilly.

After Dave had explained their idea, O'Reilly said, "It's a long shot and very risky." He paced up and down. Finally he turned and Dave could see O'Reilly had made up his mind. "We've been holding out hoping against hope that Halcyon would send a rescue force after our daily radio reports had gone silent, but no one has come. We're at the end of our rope and we can't hold out much longer. Let's do it."

"Okay," said Dave, "I need five men; all good swimmers and reasonably handy with a sailboat." When these arrived, Dave spoke to them briefly. After checking that the bank of the creek was still clear, the five crept down the ladder and quietly swam across the creek where Al led them into the brush.

Dave stooped as he walked the parapet and peered under cover at the renegades outside the stockade. When he showed too much of himself on one occasion he heard the twang of a bow and the thud of several rocks as they careened off the wall near his head. Dave had seen enough. It was clear the renegades couldn't approach the back of the stockade under cover, and they were not organized enough to occupy the far bank of the creek. Indeed, most were ransacking and pillaging Botany Bay, enjoying all the beer and food they could find. Dave went back to the part of the stockade by the creek.

Time went by slowly as Dave paced back and forth, looking anxiously for any sign of renegades near the creek. *Come on, guys, hurry it up!*

Finally, as he turned toward the bay Dave saw a bright glow. He ran to the wall. In the distance, near Boomerang Island, he could see a fire. This was the signal he'd been waiting for.

Okay, they've torched the bridge! Let's hope it distracts the renegades enough to let us get away.

Dave told O'Reilly they should get ready, then ran back to watch the creek. When Al reappeared on the far bank, Dave climbed down using his ladder. Al threw a rope across the creek. Dave first lashed the rope to the raft, and then leaving some slack, he lashed the end of the rope securely to a tree stump on the bank. Al pulled the rope taut so the raft was pulled into the middle of the stream. Upstream Dave saw the several logs drifting down from the lumber mill up the creek. They snagged on the raft and gradually filled the space across the creek with a little help from Al and Dave. Dave lashed two logs to the stout rope to keep the logs from turning in the water. Al did the same at his end. *So far, so good!*

He gave a wave to the top of the stockade, and as men began to climb down the ladder, O'Reilly handed poles and planks down to Dave. The third one slipped with a crash, and everyone held their breath, but the renegades remained quiet.

Dave crept to the water's edge. He peered up and down the creek. Still no one! He raised the first plank and balanced it on the raft. He added a second. Carrying two more planks, he tested the strength of the bridge and then put down the next two planks. He tried the planks onto the logs with short pieces of rope and tested the crude plank bridge. Satisfied, he crept back to the palisade and waved for the start of the evacuation.

As soon as the first group of men was down, O'Reilly began sending down the women. Dave climbed back up to the parapet, and it was time to empty the stockade. O'Reilly and Dave remained with the last group of men to create the impression that the fort was still heavily defended. However, just as the last of the men climbed over the back wall and were slipping out, the renegades launched another of their periodic attacks, running close to the wall and throwing firebrands, stones, and spears over the wall. The ruse to distract the renegades had failed. The sham defense could not stand up to their determined onslaught, and fires started all over the fort with no one left to put them out.

"We'd better make a run for it!" hissed O'Reilly. "I think our jig is up. If any of these renegades has enough brains to figure out what our lack of defense means, it won't be long until they press the attack to the creek." With that they ducked down and ran along the parapet to the back where a defender was waiting by the ladder.

"Still all clear," the guard said.

"Let's get out of here!" said O'Reilly.

They climbed down the ladder and ran across the pontoon bridge. As Dave held the ladder for O'Reilly, he saw the first renegades reach the top of the front wall. Seeing Dave escaping, they shouted to their companions.

When O'Reilly reached the bank and began to head across the planks, Dave, who was right behind him, grabbed the ladder, yanked it down, and then began running across the pontoon bridge. The first renegade, who was already on top of the wall, jumped down to the bank without hesitating.

Those renegades are fearless!

Dave glanced back just in time to see him land and go over on his ankle.

As the last one to cross the bridge, Dave cut the rope and fit an arrow onto his crossbow while O'Reilly pushed the bridge away from the bank with a pole. With the raft free, the whole mass of planks began to move again, but the first renegade was already charging across the raft, limping as he came. Dave's bolt hit the renegade in the shoulder and knocked him into the water. The logs and raft drifted to the far bank, still tied to the rope.

Al had come back for Dave and O'Reilly.

"This way!" he said and began running away from the creek, along a path through the trees. Within five minutes, the three emerged from the forest onto a narrow spit of rock, where the fugitives were gathered.

Dave ran across the narrow isthmus to the rocky outcropping and climbed on top. The first sailboat with three others in tow had already arrived. Farther off, he could see more sailboats in groups of four, making their way towards them from the far side of Boomerang Island. In the distance, the plank bridge from Boomerang Island to the mainland was ablaze. There were also fires on the island itself, where some of the storage sheds were on fire.

Floyd had twenty refugees forming a line with the women getting first crack at a spot in the sailboats. The rest, armed with crossbows and rifles had taken up defensive positions on the isthmus. "Take it easy," said Floyd. "Dwight make sure that there are no more than 7 in a sailboat. Have the sailboats stand clear as soon as they're loaded to make room for the other boats." As each boat loaded and cast off, Dwight would designate another group to take their place in line ready for embarkation.

It would take thirty-two sailboats to carry everyone away. Only eight men had been sent to ferry the boats over to the isthmus, so it turned out to be an agonizingly slow process. Thankfully the renegades hadn't found them yet. Dave was beginning to hope that they'd either given up, or were in such a drug induced stupor they couldn't make out the direction in which the fugitives had escaped.

This hope proved false. A small band of refugees was still waiting for the last boats when a howl broke out in the woods and an answering howl could be heard from a large band of renegades moving along the shore toward the mouth of Botany Creek.

Can I really bring myself to shoot someone? What if I know them?

Dave had deliberately shot to wound at the creek, but here it would come down to a duel to the death. He looked over at Al beside him and wondered how Al, Christian that he was, would handle the same difficult choice.

All wondering stopped, however, when the renegades broke from the trees and charged the isthmus at full speed, shrieking at the top of their lungs, their red-yellow eyes luminous in the early morning light.

Dave shot bolt after bolt, replacing the arrows as quickly as he could. When his last arrow had been spent, he grasped his staff in his left hand and his sword in his right. Floyd and Al had expended all of their ammunition and thrown their rifles away.

Another band attacked across the narrow rock of the isthmus, now slippery with blood. With a bloodcurdling shriek, a disheveled renegade with torn clothes and wielding a club lunged at Dave. Dave deflected the blow and then in one motion drove the butt end of his staff into the renegade's midsection. The renegade grunted, staggered and stumbled into the roundhouse swing of another renegade's club. The blow dropped Dave's opponent like a stone. Silence. The other renegades were also dead.

Dave looked down at the body at his feet. Blood was oozing from the back of his head. The blank eyes stared up, lifeless, through the matted and tangled hair. It was the contorted face of Darryl Wyndhurst, almost unrecognizable in its ferocity. But there could be no mistake; it was Darryl Wyndhurst.

Dave felt the gorge rising in his throat.

"Are you all right?" asked Al.

"Yeah, I'll be fine," said Dave in a thick voice.

To take his mind off Wyndhurst he looked for the boats. Four more had cast off, but the final two were still far away. Fortunately the attack from the woods had not been coordinated with the attack along the shore, and the former had been repelled before the shore reinforcements had crossed the mouth of Botany Creek.

Just then they heard the cry of additional renegades gathering for another determined assault on the isthmus. "We'll have to swim for it!" O'Reilly shouted, his voice booming above the din. "Leave your weapons and get into the water!" He knocked down the first of three renegades that charged across the isthmus.

One by one the defenders threw down their weapons and dove into the water to swim for the two approaching sailboats. Finally only O'Reilly and Dave were left. Another renegade charged. "Now, you go!" said O'Reilly. Dave felt a pang of regret as he threw his weapons into the sea and dove out as far as he could. When he surfaced, he saw O'Reilly whack a renegade on the head with his club, throw his weapons away, and run for the water. But another renegade charged from the bushes and hurled his spear at O'Reilly. Dave saw his uncle stumble then fall down a step of rock to the shore. Three arrows fired from a nearby boat buried themselves in the chest of the renegade before he could finish O'Reilly off. With a final effort, O'Reilly slid himself head first off the rock into the sea.

Dave swam for his uncle's still body floating in the water. The spear had become dislodged, and in the morning light, dark blood was staining the water. Dave rolled O'Reilly onto his back, hooked his left arm under his uncle's chin, and swam with all his might for the last boat. When the boat was within thirty feet, someone threw him a line and hauled the two men up and onto the boat. Off their bow, Dave could see Floyd's boat, which had come back to cover them, and had saved O'Reilly from the killing blow.

The boats sailed for Halcyon. Dave, sick with dread, made his uncle as comfortable as he could in the bottom of the boat, using a fresh T-shirt to staunch the flow of blood from the wound in his back. Tears rolled down Dave's cheeks as he grasped his uncle's hand tightly.

He couldn't remember when he had last cried. Even the deadly attacks of the lupi hadn't affected him like this.

O'Reilly stirred, opened his eyes, and reached up with his other hand to grasp Dave's left arm. "Dave!" he said hoarsely, his eyes unnaturally bright. "Dave!" he said again, louder this time.

"I'm here, Uncle Charlie."

"Do you have some water?" The request burned Dave like a hot iron.

"I'm sorry, we don't have any." Dave said haltingly. How could he not have water at a time like this!

O'Reilly licked his cracked lips, in endeavoring to speak. "Never mind; listen to what I have to say. I'm going to die." O'Reilly spoke with great difficulty, each raspy word forced from his dry throat.

"Uncle Charlie, you can't die. You're going to be all right."

"Listen to me, Dave. You've got to listen to me!" O'Reilly squeezed his arm firmly.

"I'm listening," said Dave.

"I only have a short time—listen to me," he repeated weakly. "I just have to say … seek after God … the Bible … search for answers to your … big questions."

Bewildered, Dave answered, "Sure I will, Uncle Charlie."

O'Reilly made an effort to speak again, squeezing his eyes shut to still the pain.

"I want to warn you about Blackmore," he rasped.

"What about Blackmore?" asked Dave, more bewildered by the moment.

"Blackmore's a tyrant. He manipulates people … he brainwashes … don't trust him … don't let him get you in his clutches!" O'Reilly tried to say more, but Dave couldn't' make out the words.

O'Reilly's breathing became more labored. He seemed to fall into a light sleep, from which he woke to be reassured that Dave was still there, but he never spoke again. He died before they reached Halcyon.

Why this deathbed monolog? Uncle Charlie was a churchgoer, but he never seemed to take it seriously. Was he afraid to die and wanted to have God as an imaginary friend by his side at the end? That doesn't seem like Uncle Charlie. Was it delirium brought on by oxygen deprivation? Maybe that was it.

———

Blackmore and the Halcyon dignitaries accorded O'Reilly honors in death that they had denied him in life. On a cold, stormy spring day,

Dave stood with a party of senators and friends at the new Halcyon cemetery. He had never felt so miserable and lonely in his life.

Walking back toward his dormitory, he felt a hand on his shoulder. Turning, he was surprised to see Bertrand Hoffstetter. It had been almost a year since Dave had met him at the hospital, but Dave's feelings toward him had not changed. There was definitely something oily and unsavory about the man.

"I'm sorry to hear about your uncle," Hoffstetter said in a perfunctory tone.

"Thank you," said Dave, trying his best to keep his voice civil.

"I know just the thing to keep your mind off this tragedy," continued Hoffstetter.

"You've lost me," said Dave.

"I wanted to thank you for bringing back that vellum. It was of the greatest value."

"It was?" asked Dave. "There was something on it?"

"It's amazing what ultraviolet light will do with faded documents," mused Hoffstetter. "But never mind that now. As I was saying, I know just the thing to help you get over the death of your uncle; it may help you make an important contribution to Halcyon—perhaps the greatest contribution yet. I would like you to lead an expedition to explore the Halcyon River."

I don't believe it. Of all the gall. Hoffstetter has the nerve to talk to me about another trip on a day like this!

"Professor Hoffstetter, my uncle has just passed away! I'm in no mood for exploration right now," said Dave icily.

Hoffstetter frowned. "Of course, of course. I'll write down a number where I can be reached. I've come into some information that promises a great advantage to the hardy explorer and to Halcyon, but I need someone with the courage and the skill to exploit it." He gestured toward Dave. "Perhaps, after this calamity, as you put it so aptly, you may welcome a challenge so suited to your unique—"

"Then why don't you go?" asked Dave, cutting him off. He was very close to losing his temper.

"Ah, of course, I would under other circumstances. But I'm not young, and I'm needed here. They're counting on me to get us home. No, they'd never let me go on the expedition I have in mind. But then again, I may go—later."

"You'll have to excuse me, Professor Hoffstetter. I will consider your offer, and I'll call you if I change my mind," said Dave. His body language spoke "no" much more eloquently than the polite fiction of his answer. He took the piece of paper that Hoffstetter held out to him, turned, and walked away.

Chapter 17

The Inner Circle Decides

Darwin Blackmore was annoyed. Two of his companions from the university senate, Trevor Huxley and Jonathon Hobbs, were in a heated argument over who was to blame for the loss of the Botany Bay colony to the renegades. Always careful about his deportment, Blackmore took a moment to admire the original Cezanne on the oak paneled wall of his study. What had been a loan to Halcyon from the Baltimore Museum of Art had now become part of his private collection, thanks to the dislocation.

"Gentlemen, gentlemen," said Blackmore, "please stop your quarreling for a moment and let us step back from the immediate situation." His commanding voice brought the room to silence. "I do not think we could have anticipated the devastating effect of Happy Berries on the population. How many people did we lose, Jonathan?"

Jonathan Hobbs was a sociologist. Tall and gaunt, his thin fingers were folded in front of him. "We lost about 1,500 people. Most of those who are addicted to Happy Berries are now roaming the mainland in battle frenzy. The rest are missing and presumed dead."

"Are we still able to use the mainland for lumber, Huxley?" Blackmore asked. Huxley was a short, overweight man and an excellent administrator. He had become Blackmore's chief of staff.

"We can, but to do so is very expensive in terms of both men and money," said Huxley.

Lydia Pendergast, an austere looking biologist with short, cropped hair, shifted her position and flashed her eyes at Huxley in anger.

"I mean *people* and money," said Huxley, looking briefly at Pendergast. "We can only risk it with an armed guard; go in and out quickly, and even then, we can expect resistance. Last week we took heavy casualties; the renegades attacked while we were cutting trees close to the mouth of the Halcyon River."

"We have a real opportunity here," said Pendergast, her voice acerbic. "The active compound in Happy Berries makes the renegades very strong. If only we could eliminate the long-term effects that drive people crazy, this compound could be used to control the undesirable elements of our population, and also in the directed evolution of our species."

"I see your point," said Blackmore, annoyed at the digression, "and that needs further investigation. But right now we need to focus on the situation at hand. We could attempt to recapture Botany Bay, or we could attempt to leapfrog the coast and proceed up the Halcyon River as our esteemed colleague Professor Hoffstetter has been urging." Blackmore nodded in Hoffstetter's direction.

Hoffstetter responded with a nod and a wan smile. Blackmore gestured to Hoffstetter to intercede.

"What was the report back from Linder on the exploration?" Hoffstetter asked Hobbs.

"Linder reported that the coastal lands were bounded by swamp to the south and mountains to the east."

"What do you think, Trevor? Can we get through those mountains, even if we take the coast back?" continued Hoffstetter.

"There was one valley that wasn't well explored because of an animal attack that killed three members of the exploration team, but Linder was convinced the road they found would lead us through."

"Well, gentlemen, doesn't it seem to you that even if we expended our forces at great cost to recapture Botany Bay and the coast, we would still have to mount a river expedition to get beyond the mountains? Even if that pass proves able to take us through the mountains, the long trek to the pass through dense terrain and then the danger of the wolves, or lupi as Linder called them, would make that route very long, very slow, and very dangerous at best."

"But what about the distance?" asked Hobbs. "Botany Bay is only six miles away, and *that* presented logistical problems to us. Who knows how far up the river we'd have to go to find the resources we need! If we were to build a colony there, think of the problems involved in supplying such an outpost."

"You've touched on an eminently practical point, Jonathan," responded Hoffstetter, "but I have two other reasons for suggesting the river expedition at this point in time. First of all, even if we recapture Botany Bay, at great cost, the Happy Berries are still there, and in a few months we'll face the same problem with addiction all over again. If we wait, two positive outcomes may be expected. Many of the renegades, mad as they are, will die of exposure or kill each other. Furthermore, as Lydia has pointed out, we'll turn our chemists, biochemists, and pharmacists loose on this new drug, and perhaps in a year's time we'll have a benign derivative that we could hand out to our population without the danger of negative side effects. I'm so convinced this is the right course, I want to be part of the expedition we send out."

Hobbs was not so easily persuaded. "Won't we encounter the same danger of Happy Berries farther up the river?"

"I read Linder's report carefully," said Hoffstetter with an arrogant emphasis on the word *carefully*. "He stated that Happy Berries disappeared a few miles from the coast. It's likely that any colony founded farther upriver will be free of that blight. Finally," said Hoffstetter, "I need not remind you about the contents of the map that Schuster brought back. I won't speak openly of them, since even these walls may have ears, but we should, shall we say, take advantage of that valuable information."

"You're right, Bertrand," said Blackmore, "to not speak of the contents of the map openly. That information must be kept secret. Don't mention it again, even here!"

The conversation rambled on for some time, but in the end, Hoffstetter's arguments proved irrefutable and carried the day. When the inner circle finally left for dinner, there was unanimity their next best move would be to explore the Halcyon River. Preparations would begin as soon as possible so that the expedition could leave that spring.

Chapter 18

The Halcyon River Gambit

It had been almost three weeks since Dave had returned to Halcyon. At Floyd's request he would be joining the Halcyon River expedition the next day. Going over his supplies for the third time, Dave wanted to be sure he had everything he would need. His steel crossbow had been giving him trouble, so he rechecked the mechanism to ensure it worked flawlessly.

He glanced over at Al; since Glenn had remained in New Jerusalem, they had become roommates. Things were working out well between them; they continued to enjoy an easy companionship. The only thing Dave didn't really "get" about his friend was his devotion to the Bible. He read it every day. He was reading it now. Al seemed to sense Dave's gaze on him and looked up. Taking off his glasses, he rubbed the day old stubble on his chin.

"I was thinking of inviting Tom and Dwight over for Bible study and prayer," Al said, "if you don't object."

Why would I object? They're my friends too. Why does this request bother me?

But Dave's response to Al betrayed none of his inner turmoil. "No problem," he said. "I thought you were meeting over at the Student Union building."

"We were," said Al. "In fact, we had a group of about thirty meeting in a booked room at the SUB. But last week a representative from campus patrol stopped by and told us we had to stop meeting there, and we'd no longer be permitted to book a room. Apparently when the Halcyon Society for Freedom and Liberty found out we were holding a Bible study, they complained to the senate that we were using public property for religious purposes. The senate decided that since Halcyon is a secular society and needs to be careful about the separation of Church and state, they had no alternative but to ask us to stop meeting on public property. The patrolman pointed out that if we were allowed to use public property for a Bible study, then students of other religious persuasions would conclude that the government of Halcyon was endorsing our particular religion, and that would make students feel uncomfortable. Since we had no place to meet, we decided as a group to split up into small cell groups and meet in our dorm rooms. So here we are."

"Sounds kind of stupid to me," said Dave. "The Church of Universal Enlightenment holds dances at the SUB all the time. Why aren't they stopped?"

"I tried that argument," said Al. They told me those dances were charitable events for improving morale and therefore exempt. You're right; the rules aren't applied very uniformly."

Dave shrugged his shoulders.

"I should point out," said Al, "that we won't inform the senate we're meeting here, since they may claim that this dorm room is also a public place."

"No problem," said Dave. "Your secret is safe with me! I may head over to the party."

Dave felt guilty. Uncle Charlie's last words still bothered him. He had wanted to do what Uncle Charlie had asked. At first he had tried reading the Bible, but Genesis made no sense to him. He never really decided to give up on his promise; he'd just drifted away. Too much to do—parties, getting caught up on the news, the fun of watching television again after months in the bush—he just stopped trying. And here was Al, reminding him about his broken promise. Guilt and more guilt. He had to get away.

Dave stepped out into the chilly night air. The sound of crickets was broken by the mournful song of the opera bird. The birdsong brought some comfort; it reminded him of some of the good times they'd had on the mainland during their exploration expedition. But inevitably his thoughts turned to the friends he had lost. As he walked past dormitory Schopenhauer, which had recently been converted into a daycare center, he could hear the sounds of infants and toddlers who were having trouble falling asleep. There had been a spate of new births following the dislocation, but hardly any marriages. Since the young mothers were working and going to the classes that had resumed, they had little time to look after their infants, and the senate had needed to make daycare a priority. The students called it "the Stay-care Center" since the children never left, and the mothers could stay with them overnight when they desired to do so. Things had changed a great deal since he had left for Botany Bay and since Blackmore had taken over. All these reforms—was this what O'Reilly had tried to warn him about?

When Dave arrived at the gymnasium, the booze was already flowing. Many of the participants were drunk and behaving wildly. Dave began to regret that he'd come at all. In the first days after he had returned from the mainland, getting together with fellow students at these parties had been about the only thing that had stood between him and despair. But now the parties had lost their luster. Sponsored by the Church of Universal Enlightenment, members expounded that the gatherings were the perfect example of the importance of love, the central virtue of all faiths. Along the far wall, Dave saw a group of young men and women working on their latest assigned project from the mandatory sex education classes, another one of the innovations introduced by Blackmore.

They look remarkably like prostitutes, and that's really not far off the mark. Things have changed quite a lot in the last six months.

After speaking to a couple of friends, Dave left the party and walked to the harbor. It was one of his favorite places, and he unconsciously returned here, as he often had in the past, to a rock on the hillside overlooking the bay. He loved to look at the sea. The sound of the waves lapping against the boats and the call of the gulls diminished his sense of loss and isolation, and the rank despair he'd felt after O'Reilly had died.

The university sailboats were moored in neat groups at the wharf, looking like the fronds of a palm leaf. Far off to the right, he could see the truncated bridge, dimly lit by road lights.

As he sat watching the lighthouse blink far off at the entrance to the bay, Dave thought about the children growing up in the Stay-care Center, and what it would be like to grow up in an orphanage or school. From your earliest days, you'd be associating with kids in cliques and gangs. You'd never have anybody to whom you really belonged and who cared enough about you to scold you or to make you buck up, he thought. *They'll never know what they missed.*

Thinking about his own parents made him gloomy. He rose and walked to the gym. A vigorous workout in the weight room kept him from thinking any more about his lost family, Uncle Charlie, and the life that would never come again.

He realized with a start how much he was looking forward to leaving Halcyon tomorrow. There was something dark and oppressive about the university that he couldn't quite articulate. He felt he was in a dream, in which someone was warning him of danger; and yet he couldn't understand the language and so couldn't heed the warning. He only hoped he would awaken before it was too late.

Chapter 19

The Expedition Sets Out

Early the next morning, the Halcyon River expedition set out from the wharf in West Harbor Bay. Eager to get underway, Dave walked with Al to the harbor before sunrise. He checked that their supplies were properly stowed, and then sat on the wharf waiting for the sun to come up. Al went off in search of Floyd to see if he could be of help.

The day dawned bright and sunny with a few cumulus clouds punctuating the blue canopy and the moon already high in the sky. Dave was in high spirits, breathing in the sea air like a man who had been confined to a dungeon for many years. How he longed to be underway. How he longed to be away from Halcyon!

His eyes strayed to the bay. The water in the bay was calm, but past the lens—the gap between Lighthouse Point and Causeway Point—the wind made the sea choppy. He looked at the boats. This expedition, much smaller than the one that had set out to found Botany Bay, consisted of only five cat-rigged dinghies with three people per dinghy.

Al's hail interrupted Dave's thoughts.

"Dave!"

He wasn't alone. A pretty young woman with auburn hair and fine features walked beside him. Dave thought her army fatigues didn't do justice to her figure. Her beautiful green eyes were particularly striking, but behind them lingered a smoldering anger that discouraged friendly banter. She looked vaguely familiar.

"Dave, let me introduce Pamela Lowental. She'll be sailing with us," said Al.

"How do you do?" said Dave.

"Nice to meet you," said Pam, shaking Dave's hand.

She seems a little nervous. I guess that's understandable.

"May I help you stow your gear?" he asked.

Pam's face brightened and she thanked him, handing over her knapsack and bedroll. Dave carefully stowed her gear in the water-proof compartment in the bow of the dinghy.

By now everyone had arrived, and Floyd, the expedition leader, called them all together for final instructions. "If you look on your map," he said, waving a sheet of paper in the air, "at the area sur-rounding Halcyon, you can see that the Halcyon River is almost com-pletely unexplored. We've explored the southern bank and the river mouth, and a few brave souls have ventured partway up the river, but we know nothing about the terrain once we travel more than a day away from Halcyon.

"Our plan is to head northwest directly to the mouth of the river and then travel up the main channel. We'll fill in our map as we go along. During the trip it's imperative we stay in visual contact. I have an outboard motor and enough fuel for an emergency, but not much more. I can't afford any false alarms. Signal with a flare if you get into trouble. For safety's sake we'll camp on islands, since we don't know how far upriver the renegades have penetrated. If we get separated, stay in the main channel and check islands for our campsite. Any ques-tions?"

There were none. As the dinghy commander, Al had the tiller, and Dave had the mainsail, while Pam, the least experienced sailor, controlled the jib. The wind was blowing gently from the west, and the other boats began to leave the wharf and sail in a northwesterly direction.

Pam was watching the other boats set sail and grew more and more agitated. Suddenly she turned to Al and Dave. "I'm afraid I've never sailed before," she confessed. "I missed the training film, and I'm not sure what I'm supposed to do."

Al looked at Dave, as if to offer him the option to take up the explanation, but Dave motioned with his hands to decline.

"That's okay," said Al. "I'll explain as we go along."

It was their turn to leave the wharf, and Dave raised the mainsail. The dinghy gathered way. "Pam, you're controlling the jib," continued Al. "Right now with the wind coming from the west, the jib is being pressed toward the right, or starboard side of the boat." The breeze was gentle, and they moved at a leisurely pace. "Pam, I'm afraid you're going to have to learn some sailing jargon for us to communicate effectively in the boat. When you're facing toward the bow, I mean the front of the dinghy, the right side of the boat is starboard and the left is port. To leave the bay we ought to sail straight west, but we can't do that since the wind is coming out of the west. So we're sailing as close to westward as we can, roughly west by northwest, and that's called 'sailing on the port tack' since the wind is coming over our port side. In a few minutes we're going to tack, which means we'll turn the bow of the boat through the wind. If we do it right we'll be sailing roughly west by southwest, and we'll sail right out of the bay. One more thing; it's always good to use the ebbing tide to leave the bay. Low tide occurs at about 8:40 this morning, and will help us make the run through the lens. High tide will occur at 14:30 this afternoon, and will actually help us run upriver since the tide will be running against the river current."

Al had been talking while keeping an eye on the other boats. Dave looked up at Pam after examining the mainsail. She was staring into space and had a frozen, disinterested look on her face.

Al's the best friend anyone could hope for, but unless he learns to cut down his explanations, he's never going to find a girlfriend.

They were just passing the shipyards on West Harbor Bay. Several of the new Viking longboats were already afloat, and five more were under construction on the shore. The masts on the floating boats hadn't yet been stepped, but they seemed seaworthy.

When it was time for them to come about, Al warned Dave and Pam, and put the tiller over. The boom swung across. On Al's command Pam put the jib over. The tack was well timed; they managed to clear Lighthouse Point and reach the open water of the channel.

As the day warmed up, the wind shifted so it was gently blowing from the north. The steady breeze down the channel allowed them to sail for the mouth of the Halcyon River without tacking. Within twenty minutes they were in sight of the first channel islands, and fellow students waved from the shoreline gardens that ran down to the water's edge. Since the loss of the mainland, these small islands were all that were left of Halcyon's expansion.

With the help of the tide, progress up the river mouth proceeded rapidly. By late morning, the breeze had slackened and was again coming out of the west. They had left the estuary behind. At this point the river was still two miles wide and the current was relatively weak. There was plenty of room for long tacks, so even this westerly wind proved favorable. This part of the river had been explored, so the expedition did not take time to investigate the numerous islands. At one point, when their dinghy came close to the northern shore, Al pointed out some large alligator-like creatures basking in the sun on the swampy shore. The alligators sent a shiver of dread through Dave. What if these alligators were like the lupi—dangerously intelligent? Looking at them more closely, as they sunned themselves on the muddy bank, he noticed they didn't really exude an overwhelming aura of intelligence. *I guess those carnivores are part of the reason we never spent too much time exploring the swamps to the north of the Halcyon River.* He thrust the thoughts about the alligators and lupi from his mind.

The journey settled down to a predictable routine of tacking back and forth in endless succession as they clawed to windward. For Dave it was becoming boring. Although he and Al had spent months together exploring the mainland, rooming with Al for the past three weeks had afforded him the opportunity of seeing his friend when he was alone and not in a group. There were many personal questions he'd never asked Al. Now was as good a time as any.

"So what made you go into chemistry?" Dave asked.

"I was always interested in science," said Al, "and when I learned the simple rules that explain how atoms combine to form molecules and give rise to the world as we know it, why, it gave me such a profound sense of beauty and order. I had this sense I was looking at God's toolbox. Why do you ask?"

"I guess I thought with your interest in the Bible that you'd go into theology and become a priest or a minister."

Al chuckled. "We all have to take theology," Al said to Dave, "or at least comparative religions, as part of our study here at Halcyon. Having taken those courses, do they make you want to go on in a study of theology?" Al's tone made Dave take his eyes from the boat ahead and look at his friend. Al raised an eyebrow quizzically. He had an uncomfortable way of moving conversations in a direction that Dave didn't want them to go. Sometimes it helped to go on the offensive.

"No. Basically I came away with the feeling that religion—all religion—is a crutch for people who can't face up to the fact of death or the vicissitudes of life. So they make up nice, happy stories to keep themselves from waking up in the middle of the night in a cold sweat. I guess God is an imaginary friend for adults."

He didn't add that he'd been thinking about O'Reilly's last words a great deal. They still seemed so baffling and out of character. Why had he said what he had about God?

"So religion is wishful thinking?" responded Al. "What did they teach you about hell in comparative religion?"

"Hell is a barbaric concept used to scare people into Christianity."

"Well, don't you see the apparent contradiction? If Christianity were an invention motivated by wishful thinking, why would the inventors come up with a concept like hell, which no one in his right mind would wish for?"

Dave was startled by something he saw in the water as he turned back to his duty as lookout.

"Floating tree straight ahead!" he shouted.

"I see it!" said Al.

Checking for the position of the nearest boats, Al called out instructions.

"Smartly now; we're going to tack. Tiller over!"

The dinghy came into the wind, and the boom started to swing across. Dave had the presence of mind to duck just before he could be clobbered by the boom.

"Pam, get the jib over to the other side to help bring us about!" bellowed Al.

Pam, who had been listening instead of keeping watch, was a little slow in reacting. Nonetheless, the bow came round, and they sailed past their nearest neighbor, calling a warning about the floating tree.

Despite the warning, the boat behind them was too busy watching their frantic tack and ran straight into the floating tree. The other boats stayed clear. Floyd, ever watchful, tacked immediately and was able to double back to help the snagged boat.

After they had freed the tangled tackle, Floyd ordered a stop for lunch while he checked the fouled dinghy for damage. He directed everyone to a small island near the southern shore of the river. A single reach on the starboard tack brought them to the north side of the island. The island, which was shaped like a dagger that pointed west, was heavily wooded with large oaks and linden trees. They pulled into a cove at the east end of the island.

After tying the sailboats to one another and fastening the two end boats to stout trees, Floyd gave further instruction. That they were close to the mainland, and within reach of the renegades, was clearly on Floyd's mind.

"Team one, stay with the boats. Teams two, three, and four, set up camp. Gleeson, you take team five and search the island for hazards. Use your whistle if you get into trouble."

"Let's go! Take your weapons," Al said, unlimbering his crossbow and belting on his short sword.

Dave climbed over the next boat to shore and helped Pam and Al as they climbed to the bank. They unlimbered their crossbows.

"All right, Dave, you work your way up the northern shore," said Al.

"Pam, you take the southern shore, and I'll work up the middle of the island. Remember Floyd's instructions: if you get into trouble, use your whistle—but only in an emergency. I don't want the whole world knowing we're here. If you find something interesting, hoot like an owl."

"I don't know, Gleeson; I think making like an opera bird would be more appropriate. We don't even know if this place has owls," said Dave with mock seriousness. "At least, I've never seen an owl."

"All right, Schuster, you go ahead and flaunt your operatic talents and give us a rousing rendition of something from Verde if you see something interesting!"

Dave and Pam had the easier missions of following the shoreline, while Al had to bushwhack through the dense brush in the middle of the island. Hiking along the near shore, Dave knew from personal experience that meeting a gang of renegades or surprising a pack of lupi was the most serious danger, but he didn't relish stumbling into one of the alligators either. Then again, there might be all kinds of dangerous predators in this new world that they didn't even know about. Almost anything could be waiting for him around the next bend.

The first section he searched curved away from the cove to the right. Oak trees came right down to the water's edge. However, the trees were big enough that there was little undergrowth. After crossing the oak grove, he encountered a large rock face that stretched transversely across the island. He walked inland until he came to a large crevice filled with broken boulders. Using his arms to haul himself up when footholds were inaccessible, he made the ascent easily. After reaching the top of the ridge, he doubled back to the island's edge and continued along the shore.

The rest of the island appeared to be quite rocky, with the center higher than the fringes. Nevertheless, the shore was very steep, even sheer in places, but thankfully the rock reduced the undergrowth and he was able to make rapid progress. After another 400 yards, the island ended at a rocky elevation shaped like the forecastle of a ship. Since he'd made such good time, he reached the pinnacle first and was able to see Al struggling up the center spine 100 yards back. There was no sign of Pam, since her shoreline was densely wooded.

Dave pulled out his mirror and was able to get Al's attention with a light flash. He gave Al the thumbs up sign. Al waved back to him, and then changed direction to join Pam.

Dave descended by another route and noticed the entrance to a cave in the rock wall. It was an enlargement of a crack that had not been visible from below or from the first route he had taken up to the rock pinnacle. This chance to explore was too much to pass up. Dave entered the cave and waited while his eyes adjusted to the gloom. He didn't want to corner a cave bear or trap a mountain lion. Surprisingly it was much brighter in the cave than he had expected. There was enough broken rock wedged into the fissure in the roof of the cave that light was able to filter down between the gaps and fill the inside of the cave with twilight rather than the pitch black he had anticipated.

He advanced farther into the cave. The passage took a turn to the right. After the first turn there was a trickle of water into a still pool that almost filled this chamber of the cave. His feet were scrunching on round pebbles that looked vaguely familiar in the dim light. Skirting the pool, Dave entered yet another chamber.

What he saw made him catch his breath. He quietly backed out of the chamber, returned to the cave entrance, and hooted like an owl.

He was beginning to think Al might have returned to camp, when Al and Pam appeared out of the woods below, their crossbows at ready. "You'd better come and see this," Dave said.

He led them to the inner chamber. There on the floor, in a pool of light from a crevice high above, lay a skeleton, partly buried in the marble-shaped pebbles. The skeleton was clearly hominid but didn't look like the human skeletons Dave had seen. The head was too small, and the jaw had features that appeared more apelike than human.

Pam knelt down to examine the remains more closely, but she did not touch or disturb the bones. After a few moments she said, "This is a hominid, but definitely not human. There are bits of cloth about, and I think I see evidence of a crude tool belt. There's something strangely familiar about this skeleton, but I can't put my finger on it."

Dave reached down and picked up a handful of pebbles and showed them to Al. They exchanged glances but said nothing. Dave felt a growing sense of foreboding, and from the agitation in Al's face, Dave knew he was feeling it too.

Chapter 20

The Discovery

The discovery of the remains created quite a stir back at camp. Floyd decided it was of sufficient importance to delay their journey upriver. Fortunately they had a student paleontologist along to take charge of the excavation and recovery of the bones.

Dave and Al guided Sue Burkholder, the paleontologist, and two others back to the cave. After a preliminary investigation, she carefully packed up the skeleton in a blanket. Under her watchful supervision her two companions carried the prize back to camp on the litter they'd assembled from two oars and some rope. Al and Dave followed at a distance.

"What do you think?" Dave asked quietly. "Is this what made the quarry and road we saw up in the pass?"

Al didn't answer right away but thrust his hands into his pockets and frowned. "I suppose it could be. I guess I'd assumed the road builders would look more like us. This thing is much more like an ape."

"Did that floor remind you of anything?" asked Dave.

"What do you mean?" asked Al.

"Did the gravel on the floor remind you of anything?"

"You mean, like the gravel at the mouth of the worm caves?"

"Exactly!"

"But there was no hole, no passage," said Al.

"True, so maybe I'm wrong, but I'm still going to be glad to get off this island," said Dave.

Dave and Al spoke privately about their suspicions to Floyd. He didn't want to worry the others, so the three of them decided to take turns keeping watch.

The following morning all fifteen explorers huddled around the remains. "As far as I can tell," said Sue Burkholder, "this is a complete skeleton of a hominid that looks very much like *Australopithecus afarensis*, or 'Lucy.' This skeleton is a male, and the bones are not mineralized."

"So what does this mean? How did it get here?" asked one of the others.

"I'm not sure what it means," Burkholder said. "In spite of the similarity, I don't see how it could be *Australopithecus afarensis*. This skeleton is not old, since there are still bits of clothing about. We've seen evidence for a similar evolution here. I suppose it's possible this species still exists here. Even if this is the case, I wouldn't think it would pose much of a threat to Halcyon; with a brain of maybe 650 cc, it can't be that intelligent." There were chuckles around the circle.

Floyd interrupted, "Nonetheless, this is an extremely important discovery, and we can't risk losing the bones by taking them upriver. I'm going to call the base on the radio and send you back with the remains. The other four boats will continue upstream." Burkholder nodded.

"What do you need in order to carry the bones back?" Floyd asked.

"The bones look to be in pretty good shape," said Burkholder. "I'll wrap them up in this blanket and get them back to Halcyon as soon as possible. That's the best we can do."

"All right, let's pack up. I'd like to make up the time lost by this delay, so let's be ready to go in twenty minutes."

An hour later they watched the Burkholder sailboat head downstream while those left behind put the final touches on their preparations, and then set out.

Dave was in tearing high spirits. In the first part of the continuing journey, the talk in Dave's boat centered on the discovery of the "Mr. Lucy" skeleton, as Dave had nicknamed it. This alias didn't sit well with Pam, who seemed to know quite a bit about paleontology and viewed Dave's offhanded naming convention as paleontological sacrilege.

"Look, Pam," said Dave, putting on his best professorial air, "isn't it the prerogative of the discoverer to name the skeleton? Well I'm the discoverer of this one, and I want to name it Mr. Lucy!"

"Dave," said Pam, turning around from the bow to throw him a glance that could have soured fresh milk. "You're not really a paleontologist, so you shouldn't be allowed to name the skeleton in the first place. Besides, 'Mr. Lucy' is a stupid name!"

"Stupid name!" mocked Dave in shocked disbelief. "You're talking to the greatest living paleontologist this world has ever seen—"

"What are you talking about?"

"Who else has made a paleontological discovery like this? Come to think of it, nobody, not even Professor MacMillan, has made any paleontological discovery here—so I'm it, the paleontological 'Big Cheese,' so to speak."

A series of expressions flashed across Pam's face. Finally she turned her back to Dave so swiftly her auburn hair whipped around. Dave could see her body language was the only rebuttal he was going to get.

Feeling smug, Dave looked for a way to keep his splendid debating streak going, and to pass the endless, dreary miles that lay ahead. After a couple of minutes of silence, he continued in a more serious tone.

"Hey, Al, when I took comparative religions with Schweitzer, he pointed out that the Christian claim that God is all powerful is a fallacy."

"Where did that come from? What do you mean?"

"Well," continued Dave, *"all powerful* means there is nothing he can't do, right?"

"Yeah—I guess so," said Al, suspicious he was being set up.

"So can God make a rock so heavy he *can't* lift it?"

The boat ahead of them had tacked, and they followed it to keep station. When they had settled on the new tack, Al returned to Dave's question.

"I see what you're saying, Dave. If God makes this hypothetical rock and then can't lift it, he's not all powerful because he can't lift the rock. On the other hand, if he makes this humongous rock but *can* lift it, he's not all powerful because that means he was incapable of making a rock so large that he couldn't lift it. Have I understood the sense of your question?"

Dave nodded, disappointed. The complete surprise he was hoping for had not materialized.

"I've wrestled with this before," continued Al. "The problem with your question is that you're automatically converting an infinite property to a finite one by the way you ask your question." Al was starting to warm to the subject. "Let's assume that God could make a rock of any size. However, to carry out the test 'can I lift it?' he has to make a rock of a particular size, that is to say, a finite size. As soon as he makes a rock, it becomes finite, and now he will be able to lift it."

"I think you're trying to confuse me," said Dave, annoyed.

"Let's go at it another way then," said Al, oblivious to Dave's annoyance. "Human beings do not have many attributes that we could think of as infinite. But one that might do is our ability to think of large numbers. Let me rephrase your question in our context. Can you think of a number so large that you can't add three to it?"

"That doesn't seem quite the same," said Dave.

"Thinking of a large number is equivalent to God making a large rock. There is no limit to the number of zeros you can put after a one, just as there's no limit to the size of rock God could make. But as soon as you pick a number, you will be able to add three to it. Adding three to the number is equivalent to God lifting the rock."

Disappointed, Dave said lamely, "I'll have to think about it."

Everyone fell silent, keeping a sharp eye on the river. For the rest of the day, the journey upstream remained uneventful. Every once in a while, Floyd stopped the convoy to report to base, or to make an addition to his maps after consulting with some of the others. He seemed determined to make up for lost time, however, and even though they encountered several islands with promising campsites, he passed them by. Finally, as the sun was going down, they came to a relatively large, U-shaped island, whose arms faced downstream. Using the deep bay to get the boats out of the current, they approached land, startling a flock of pheasants feeding in a grassy meadow.

This time Floyd sent two boat crews to search the two arms of the island, while the other two crews set up camp. Floyd's crew was assigned to exploration. Dave's crew remained behind on camp duty

After unloading their supplies, the explorers left. Dave and the others searched in the gathering twilight for a sheltered location and firewood. A spot near a rock shelf would offer protection to the fire pit on two sides, and they built a low wall, completing the fire ring. The new matches made at Halcyon worked well, and in a short time fir kindling mixed with dry moss gave them a cheerful blaze that drove away the lengthening shadows. They set up tents and began to make supper. They had an abundance of dried fish and a dried, smoked meat similar to pemmican. Al, Pam, and Dave prepared the best meal they could using their limited provisions.

When the explorers returned without finding anything, everyone settled down to supper. Some made the meal more substantial by eating a portion of their "pemmican" rations along with the soup and biscuits.

Dave ate heartily. Hunger and the exertion of the day made the simple meal much tastier than he had expected. Even the tea was a welcome and fitting end to the meal.

After supper, he refilled his cup and moved off to a rock promontory on the northern arm of the island for some peace and quiet. The night was dark, since the moon wouldn't rise for many hours. The sky tonight was clear and magnificently studded with stars. He heard bullfrogs croaking along the water's edge and the rustle of a small animal in the woods. He thought about the day and his two companions in the boat.

Al was a strange creature; he seemed a mass of contradictions. On the one hand he was exactly the right sort to have along on a trip like this. He was dependable and knowledgeable and could be relied upon in a tight place. On the other hand, he had this irrational religious streak that colored his every thought. In Dave's mind, anyone who took religion seriously was a fundamentalist. Dave had always rationalized the zeal and fervor of fundamentalists by convincing himself they were brainwashed and controlled by their leadership. How else could they believe the crazy things they did? But Al didn't really fit that mold. He seemed intelligent enough. But how could he be so out of step with what everyone else knew to be true? Everyone except Uncle O'Reilly.

His thoughts turned to Pam. She was a good-looking woman. He realized he already liked her and that was why he'd teased her with such relish. But he was smart enough to realize that he probably hadn't done his cause much good this afternoon.

Dave returned to camp, where the three cleaned up the cooking pots, then prepared to turn in. Halcyon under Blackmore had a strict policy of treating men and women exactly the same, so it was an unspoken expectation that as crew, they would sleep in the same tent. Although special considerations of privacy for women (or men) were frowned upon by Halcyon's new policy, Al gave Pam a chance to be in the tent alone before he and Dave joined her. Such became the unspoken pattern of behavior for their team.

The next day the southern mountains marched right to the edge of the river, towering impassable cliffs forming the left bank. The party passed into territory—that to their knowledge—had never been seen by previous explorers from Halcyon.

———————

Although the terrain varied, the next two weeks passed in monotonous repetition: long grueling days of sailing and exploration, followed by evenings passed on a convenient island. After days of fine weather the spring rains came, and everyone sat cold, wet, and miserable in their boats. Even though they had ponchos, it was almost impossible to remain dry.

After five days of rain, cloud, and cold weather, the sun reappeared, and everyone brightened. Even Pam seemed to have grown more cheerful, and Dave saw her smiling from time to time.

The river turned south, and for some time now the mountains had effectively blocked their radio communication to Halcyon. At the end of two weeks, they had traveled about 300 miles upstream.

The monotony of the sailing was coming to an end. As they approached a bend in the river, the lead boat began signaling frantically, indicating they had found something of significance. All the boats immediately altered course to see what was causing the commotion. When Dave's boat approached the others, he saw in the distance along the southern shore a stone jetty. Fastened to the jetty was a sailboat with familiar Halcyon markings. The sailboat was full of water from the recent rain but otherwise was in good condition.

Floyd signaled the boats to gather some 100 yards offshore. They waited to see if anyone appeared or came back to the boat, periodically attempting to hail the shore to bring anyone who might be there, out into the open.

Finally, convinced that no one was going to appear on the jetty, Floyd signaled the gathered boats to draw closer. Glancing frequently back to shore, as if he expected trouble at any moment, Floyd said, "We've been out of touch with Halcyon for almost two weeks, since the mountains blocked our signal. The boat on the jetty definitely looks like one of ours. I don't know how it got here. As far as I know, no one's been sent this far up the river. The boat looks like it's been abandoned for some time, and any survivors may be ill or injured, if they're still around at all. I'm going to go ashore first with Al. The rest of you stay with the boats. Dave, you're in charge while I'm gone. If there's any trouble, don't be a fool and come after us. Get into the open water and reassess the situation. Reporting back is more important than trying to rescue us. We really don't know what's going on here, so we'd better assume the worst. That's an order!"

Dave didn't answer.

Floyd scowled at Dave. "Dave, I need to know that you're going to carry out my order. Are you going to do what I ask and get the team home if we get into trouble?"

Dave looked Floyd square in the face.

"Well?" said Floyd, staring right back.

"I'll do what you ask, Floyd. At the first sign of serious trouble you're on your own and I'll take them back downriver."

Floyd looked relieved and signaled for the two boats to put in at the jetty.

Floyd and Al left their boats at the jetty, ready to cast off at the first sign of trouble. While Floyd and Al's boat stayed moored to the jetty, the other two boats pulled offshore. Experienced now, Pam was well able to handle the jib and the mainsail if necessary. Dave sat in the stern, keeping a sharp eye out for danger.

But he was disappointed. *Why didn't Floyd take me? Doesn't he trust me?*

As soon as the thought formed, he felt ashamed of his jealousy and resolved to do the best he could looking after the expedition. If something happened to Floyd and Al, he was the only other one with much experience in the backwoods of this place, and they'd need him to get out.

But nothing happened to Al and Floyd; they returned after an hour. Floyd signaled the rest of the boats to tie up at the jetty then brought everyone up to date. "Al and I traveled a well made stone road back to some stone buildings in the trees. We found the remains of a camp. The camp hadn't been ransacked, but it appeared to have been deserted several weeks ago. We looked through the things at the camp, but we couldn't find any personal effects to give us a clue about what had happened or who'd made the camp.

"Here comes the kicker. The road doesn't end, but heads towards the mountains that you can see in the distance. We traveled up the road about half a mile to a rise on top of a rocky ridge. From there, we saw a walled city nestled up against the mountains."

There was a collective intake of breath as everyone began thinking about the implications of their findings.

"Is it inhabited?" asked Dave.

"We don't know," said Floyd. "We looked at it through our binoculars. The road leading up to the gate was deserted and there was no one on the walls. The main gate was a rubble heap. It certainly looked deserted, but that doesn't prove anything."

"What do we do now?" one of the others asked.

Floyd glanced toward the mountains then turned and pointed to an island. "Even though things look to be peaceful, I want to err on the side of safety. I suggest we head to that island in mid-channel and hide our boats on the far side. We'll take this abandoned sailboat along, even though that may leave a calling card that we were here. If there are enemies about, I don't want to leave them any obvious means of ambushing us in our sleep. I suppose we could send someone downriver, back to the place where the radio last worked, and hope we can contact Halcyon, but I don't want to take that chance right now. I think we'll do some exploring and then make a decision about reporting back."

Later that night, Floyd pulled Al and Dave aside from the rest of the group. "What do you guys think about all of this?" he whispered.

"Floyd, I don't know what to make of it," Al admitted. "The jetty was built by someone who knows stonework. It looks like the handiwork of the same people who built the quarry road. And remember the stone sluice at New Jerusalem? Maybe these things were all built by the same people. There's a road heading off to who knows where. If there's a civilization about, why has it taken us a year to discover it, or at least make contact with it? What really bothers me though is that campsite. You didn't tell the others, but that campsite didn't look to me to be the work of someone on an ordinary camping trip. From the sheds they'd built, I'd say they planned to stay awhile. I can't help thinking that Halcyon or someone at Halcyon tried to send an expedition up here before and they didn't come back. If this is official, why weren't we told? If it's not official, why would someone go to all that trouble? Then there's that silent city we saw up on the mountainside."

Floyd cursed softly. "Why couldn't they tell us? Why send us out under a pretense?"

"The fact that whoever built the camp has disappeared can't be good," added Dave.

They walked together in silence for a long time. Floyd sighed. "Our suspicion that the higher-ups at Halcyon have been less than candid with us is one of the reasons I'm not rushing to report back.

This is an incredibly important discovery. I should be delighted to have a chance to conduct this kind of an exploration. Nevertheless, I have a very bad feeling about it. I don't like our situation one bit, and I don't like it that we weren't told everything."

Chapter 21

Fort Linderhof

The next morning Floyd scanned the shore from the island, then led the expedition back to the jetty. Instead of landing, however, he rowed his boat along the southern bank, inspecting the shore. Half a mile upstream from the jetty, the river flowed past a mountain spur that had been sheared off by the river's passage. When Floyd saw it, he paused for several minutes as if he were carefully evaluating the rock formation, and then waved for the other boats to approach shore.

He told the others to take a break but to remain vigilant as he and Al set out to scout the formation. Al followed Floyd through the bush, crossbow and rifle at the ready. From experience, he knew to guard on the right and rear while Floyd guarded the front and left. The bush was dense, and tangled vines snagged their weapons.

They found a game trail that led toward the spur. After climbing a short distance, the game trail suddenly descended to a creek, which fell to the river below by a series of cataracts. Floyd and Al took a break and filled their water bottles.

"How are we going to cross this creek?" asked Floyd, taking a long draught of the cool, clear water.

Al looked up and down the creek bed. "I think we could use that fallen tree. It'll be a little challenging to get off the trunk on the far side, but it should be possible."

"How are we going to get back?"

"We can lean a small sapling against the fallen tree in a pinch. The vantage point from the heights will also let us look for an easier route back."

"Okay, let's do it!" said Floyd.

Al slung the crossbow over his shoulder and climbed up onto the large tree trunk. He walked along the trunk without much difficulty until he reached a large vertical branch about two-thirds of the way across. Using his short sword as a machete, he cut some of the smaller branches out of the way and then swung around the larger branch. Not realizing that he'd snagged his crossbow, he was pulled back, tee-tered for a moment, and then lost his balance. He grabbed at the near-est small branch, but it couldn't hold his weight and Al pitched twenty feet into the creek. He bobbed back to the surface sputtering but was quickly swept over a small waterfall into the next pool.

Floyd had been watching intently and reacted as soon as he saw Al's fall. Moving toward the lower pool, he fought his way through the underbrush and so didn't arrive until Al was already pulling himself out on the far side. Still carrying his crossbow and short sword, Al gave a thumbs up and a grin to show Floyd he was unhurt. Floyd re-turned to the fallen tree and crossed to the other side without incident.

"Are you okay?" Floyd asked when he sat down beside Al.

"Yes, I'm fine. The pool I fell into was quite deep, and I didn't hit bottom. The ride over the waterfall was exciting, but the lower pool was also deep. Fortunately, I was able to escape the undertow without too much trouble."

"Okay, Tarzan, let's take a break," suggested Floyd.

"I'm really okay. I had a chance to catch my breath while you were crossing over. Let's keep going. If we sit longer, I'm just going to get cold."

They started to climb again. "Floyd!" said Al.

"Yeah?"

"Let's keep this mishap our little secret," said Al sheepishly.

"Oh, I don't know. I may save this little tidbit for a rainy day! How the great Al Gleeson, 'woodsman extraordinaire,' stumbled over a branch and managed to give himself a dunking!"

Al rolled his eyes at the good-natured teasing.

The climb grew steeper, and rock began to protrude through the earth. Finally the trees thinned, and they found themselves climbing over bare rock, exclaiming at the view. They could see the boats below in the small cove. Farther off, there were the jetty and the ruined buildings.

"Look, there it is!" Al pointed. Floyd looked at the walled city nestled against the steep cliffs of the mountain. This "city" (it still wasn't clear to Al exactly how large it was) was situated on the same mountain spur on which they stood. "Do you think it's inhabited?" asked Al.

"If it is, then why haven't we had company?" responded Floyd. He took his binoculars out of his knapsack and searched the battlements, as if looking for some sign of life, but evidently saw nothing and handed the binoculars to Al.

The strange, alien nature of this new world struck Al with overwhelming power as he looked at the ruined, lifeless city. The place seemed haunted. *How do I really know the rules that govern this place? What if its inhabitants are invisible, or ghosts, or something worse? How could I really know? Is it rational to extrapolate from what I know in my world?*

Al heard the voices of his teachers, friends, and colleagues scoff at his thoughts and urge him to reject these ideas as outlandish and improbable, but Al was a theist, and he fought that rising tide in his mind with everything he could muster. *No I will be free to face the universe as it is. I will not just accept the programming that has been drummed into me my whole life. I believe in a universe governed by natural law, but there is room in my understanding of the real for the supernatural and for phenomena beyond the reach of my five senses.*

A quiet voice, in contrast to the chorus of voices from his upbringing, kept prodding him with "what if?" Eventually he had to concede to himself that invisible beings were a possibility. It frightened him, but he remembered that the God who had made his familiar, home world had also made this one, and that thought helped him to feel at home in this strange place despite the uncertainty.

Floyd and Al drew their eyes away from the eerie mountain city, focusing once again on the task at hand. "I have to believe there's something dangerous about this place," said Floyd. "If we read the signs at the abandoned camp right, we've had three explorers disappear without a trace. I've thought about going directly back to Halcyon, but that would leave a lot of work undone and questions unanswered. I think we should just make camp in a place that's more defensible than in the open, near the jetty. The rock outcropping I saw this morning from the island may do."

The rock Floyd had seen proved to be a mesa, separated from the main spur by a deep chasm. They could hear a creek gurgling at the bottom. "I think this creek joins the one we just crossed near the river," said Floyd. "If this channel is deep enough, then this may be what I've been looking for."

"Okay, I see that," said Al. "We could make a rope bridge to cross the chasm, but what happens if we face trouble? Won't we be cut off? Won't our refuge become a trap? Let's look around first and see what our options are. Maybe there's a way we could be safe on the mainland and still have a backdoor escape route."

They moved along the crevice. After about 300 yards, they came to a small ravine that formed the channel for the creek as it tumbled down the mountain spur and disappeared into the chasm. Beyond the creek, the chasm bent north, and they could see the river. This western section of the crevice was much shallower than the southern leg containing the creek.

"This might work. The mesa is completely surrounded—cliff and river on one side, chasm on the other," mused Al.

"We could climb across here," said Floyd, pointing at the relatively shallow boulder-choked depression on the west end of the mesa.

"I wouldn't want to do it at night, but by daylight it should be easy enough. If an enemy tried to approach the camp by that route, we could stop them if we had warning that they were making the attempt."

"What if they cut down one of the trees?" asked Floyd.

"There are a few that are big enough, but we'd hear them," said Al. "If they made ladders they could get across quickly, but we can't stop everything. We don't have enough people."

"What about an escape route?" asked Floyd.

"Well," responded Al, "we could make a rope ladder and get into the shallow crevice on the west side, then follow the bottom of the crevice down to the shore. Maybe in a pinch we could even jump into the river and swim for the boats. The water at the edge of the cliff's very deep."

"Okay, let's do it!" said Floyd.

A suitable plan now in place, they headed back to the cove to inform the others. After Floyd had explained their plan, six of them returned to the mesa, now dubbed "Fort Linderhof" by the party, while the rest guarded the supplies at the cove.

Meanwhile, Al and Dave hiked up to the second creek and crossed it farther upstream. Then Al began his descent into the west crevice. Dave guided the safety rope as he went down. When Al reached the bottom, he released the safety rope and began the much more perilous ascent on the other side. It took about fifteen minutes, but he accomplished it with little difficulty.

While Al was completing the climb, the others began to assemble a rope bridge. When Al had hiked back along the chasm, Floyd threw him a light line, and Al hauled the rope bridge across. It consisted of a heavy foot rope, two lighter hand lines, and rope cross members tied transversely to all three ropes at intervals of about two feet. When they'd hauled the bridge across, they disentangled the ropes and fastened it to supports. Floyd insisted on testing the makeshift bridge first. He crossed safely in seconds, so the other three followed, one at a time.

The others had already begun exploring Fort Linderhof. The fort was a flat rock mesa about three acres in size with a few sturdy oaks sparsely spaced along the top. A large shallow bowl at the west end of the mesa collected rainwater in a small, deep pond. In contrast to the rest of the mesa, which was mostly bare rock, the pool supported trees and grass, so this sheltered hollow was ideally suited for a campsite.

After they had thoroughly explored the mesa, they headed back to the cove. It was now about noon, and the team at the cove had just begun lunch preparations.

The group spent the afternoon moving supplies up to Fort Linderhof. Initially they lugged them up the newly cut path, but it proved to be much easier to haul supplies directly up from the boats using a pulley salvaged from the abandoned sailboat. They found a small rock shelf, level with the river, on the northern wall of the mesa. This shelf also solved the problem of a backdoor escape route. By dropping a heavy rock as an anchor into the water and fastening the other end of the anchor rope to a tree clinging to the rock face about the shelf, they were able to keep the sailboats accessible without exposing them to attack.

After they secured the boats and constructed a second, much longer, rope ladder for access to this shelf, they set up camp on the mesa and had supper. Later, talk turned to their situation.

"I think we did a good day's work," said Floyd. "We've established a well protected camp here. Tomorrow I'm going to send out two parties to explore the region. I've already talked to their leaders, but I wanted everyone to know. Gleeson, Schuster, and Lowental are going to hike cross-country to that city nestled against the mountain. Jackson, Taylor, and Smith are going to follow the road to see where it leads. My guess is that it will also lead to the walled city. Gleeson, when you get to the fortress, signal by Morse code with your mirror so we know you're safe. Jackson, I don't know if you'll get high enough on the mountain to be able to use your mirror, but we'll keep a lookout for your signal. If you have trouble and it's safe to do so, send up a flare. If you're in real trouble and need to be rescued, send up two flares. While you're gone, the two teams here will take turns making a thorough search of the surrounding area. We'll always leave one team behind on the rock watching for your sign. Any questions? No? OK then, good luck!"

Later that evening Pam found Al sitting on a rock at the edge of the cliff, looking north out over the river.

"Mind if I join you?" she asked.

"No, not at all," said Al, shifting over to make room for her.

"I've been meaning to ask you something," said Pam.

"Sure, go ahead."

"Remember back on our second day, when Dave and I had that argument about 'Mr. Lucy'?"

"How could I forget," chuckled Al.

"Well, remember afterward when Dave leveled his sights on you and asked you that question about God?"

"Oh, you mean the one about 'can God make a rock so large he can't lift it?'"

"Yeah," said Pam. "I was wondering, are you a member of the Church of Universal Enlightenment?"

"No!" said Al vehemently, "I'm a Christian, but I'm most definitely *not* a member of the CUE."

Al paused then went on in a softer tone. "I guess I should explain myself a little bit. I should say that early on, I went to their meetings. Are you a member of the CUE, Pam?"

"No, I'm not really anything. You were going to tell me about the CUE."

"All right," said Al. "When I first came to Halcyon as a new student, I was really lonely. My older brother, Thomas, encouraged me to join a group on campus called the Dalyites. At first it was wonderful. What the group leader, Professor Dalrymple, said made sense, and he had a way of applying the Bible to everyday life. In retrospect I think Dalrymple meant well, but fear drove him to control the group. It was as if he smothered all joy, freedom, and honesty in his headlong rush to impose biblical behavior on everyone in the group for their own good. Every fun activity and every joy at its root was regarded with suspicion and as a temptation. At first, loyalty to my brother and a respect for authority compelled me to go along, but over time the dreary absence of all joy caused me to slowly wilt and die on the inside.

"Finally, it was my own Bible reading that freed me. I was praying alone one day when it struck me that God is, first and foremost, a God of freedom. Hell is a monument to the lengths he's willing to go to let us truly be free and choose for ourselves, even if in choosing we decide we want nothing to do with Him."

Al stopped. "I'm sorry, Pam. Very long answers to short questions is a character flaw of mine. You probably just wanted a 'yes or no' answer."

Pam didn't contradict him but just laughed gently. "Go on, tell me more; I'm interested," she said.

"Well, in the end I dissociated myself from the Dalrymple movement and felt a tremendous sense of relief as I did so. Of course, they warned me of the dire consequences of my apostasy, but I had such a sense of relief and new life that their words did not have much effect on me."

"What did you do then?" asked Pam.

"I left the Dalyites, causing a major rift with Thomas, my brother. I tried going to the Church of Universal Enlightenment. At first it felt like a refuge from the rules and shackles of Dalyism. The CUE talked a great deal about 'love,' but I learned pretty quickly that what was really being preached was unconstrained sex. So it seemed to me then that I had run from the frigid, frostbitten Niflheim of Dalyism to the scalding hell of the Church of Universal Enlightenment! I learned that whether you go where everything is forbidden or where everything is allowed, the destinations are very nearly the same. Both leave you in a drab featureless landscape where everything becomes insipid."

"But you're not like that now. What happened?"

"The Dalyites call themselves Christian, and so do the CUE. Of course the CUE also call themselves enlightened Buddhists, Hindus, Muslims, and atheists at the same time. They feel they can speak for all these groups.

"I knew I was a Christian, but I did not seem to fit in anywhere. For a while I simply hung out by myself. I had a few friends who did not make a big point about calling themselves Christians, but, like me, they had this sense that things were not right, that they did not fit in, and that, frankly, they didn't want to fit in. I kept reading my Bible, and gradually things became clearer, and I began to see the bits in Dalyism and the CUE that were right, and much in both that was wrong!

"So in the end I do not really fit in anywhere. My brother, Thomas, ended up so broken by the Dalyites that he abandoned all of his beliefs and the university as well. For me the process of being cut off from the institution of the Church became complete with the dislocation. There isn't a church or Christian group for me to relate to now. I just have a close family of friends, and we look after each other.

"So how about you, Pam? What's your story?"

Pam fidgeted as if uncertain whether she should share the details, then finally said, "After the dislocation, I was desperately lonely. I'd never had a good relationship with my parents, who saw me as a burden, but I missed my sister terribly. When I first came to Halcyon, I used to call her almost every day. The dislocation changed all that. At first I cried myself to sleep every night, but over time, I settled into a routine of classes, work, and survival, and the ache dulled. I think I completely missed the overthrow of O'Reilly, because I was still terribly despondent then.

"But you know, something curious has happened. This trip has made me feel truly alive. I don't recall feeling like this since I was a small child and the world was full of wonder and discovery. I've begun to realize how drab and insipid life at Halcyon had become! Since we left on this trip and have had to struggle to stay alive, I've felt closer to my comrades than I ever did at Halcyon. I feel as if I'm waking from a drugged sleep. I don't want to go back.

"I said 'insipid' just now, but I think it's more than that," she added. Soon words came out in a jumble as Pam obviously warmed to her subject. "What you said about the Dalyites and the CUE has set me to thinking—I can't get over the contrast. In Halcyon, nothing is forbidden, but everything is manipulated. From what you said, Al, when you were with Dalrymple, at least everything was black and white. His rules were in your face, and you had to either agree to them or rebel. Under Blackmore, all of our rebellion and independence is being slowly but inexorably educated out of us. Our minds are changed for us little by little by a wearing repetition that grinds down our resistance until we mouth the lesson against our will. On this expedition we have orders and rules, and I've never been happier than to obey them, because I know our survival depends on the obedience. I don't dread the danger tomorrow nearly as much as I dread the fog of Halcyon."

They spoke long into the night and Al felt the comfort of friendship and understanding. Much later, he lay awake in his tent. Pam and Dave's gentle, shallow breathing told him they'd fallen asleep. Pam's comments about the oppression at Halcyon made Al think back over his time there, before the dislocation. He remembered one afternoon in Professor Kinnerton's genetics class, just after he'd completed an assignment on the implications arising out of the elucidation of the human genome.

"Mr. Gleeson, stand up, please."

Kinnerton had handed Al his term paper with a large "D" scrawled across the front.

"In future I will ask you to keep your religious drivel out of our genetics class. I have painstakingly pointed out to you how genetics has incontrovertibly demonstrated the very close relationship between *Homo sapiens* and our nearest hominid neighbors. Has the fact that we have about 97 percent of our DNA in common with chimpanzees escaped you? How can you still argue that we are special and have a soul when we are so obviously animals?"

In anger Al had responded, "I accept the 97 percent evidence, even though, of course, I have not been able to verify it."

"That's big of you!"

"With due respect, sir, the 97 percent is precisely the problem. Are chimpanzees 97 percent of the way to splitting the atom? Are they 97 percent of the way to writing their first sonnet?"

Someone had tittered in the back of the room.

"Are bonobos 97 percent of the way to putting the first bonobo on the moon? Is there an orangutan somewhere with a simian Mona Lisa 97 percent finished? Do we see evidence of mercy, justice, or compassion in monkeys? Is there an ape somewhere wondering who made everything and why there are trees, rocks, and songbirds? A writer I like, C. S. Lewis, once said that so much of what we do as people 'gives value *to* survival rather than has value for survival.' Isn't the gap so much wider than the 3 percent disparity in the respective DNA sequences?"

At that point, Kinnerton had stomped out, publicly scorning Al. It still stung.

Pam's perceptive comments on Halcyon really had him thinking. So much of what Pam said was true. Halcyon really was an oppressive place. Somehow, having no rules and true freedom were not really the same thing! The apparent freedom of Halcyon was the freedom of a rat in a maze. Halcyon let people do what they wanted so the powers behind Halcyon could use that data to reprogram their subjects in the direction they wanted. Like all scientists, they needed unbiased data so they could evaluate the current deeply held beliefs and assumptions of their subjects and so know the degree to which their programming had succeeded. A society that allowed freedom of speech and action provided them with precisely that data.

Kinnerton's attack then had just been a part of the manipulation process. The fact that an *ad hominem* attack like that still stung now showed it had in part worked, but he hadn't seen it at the time.

Al's troubled mind gradually relaxed into fitful sleep.

Chapter 22

The City of the Dead

The two teams started off at dawn the following morning. Al, Dave, and Pam headed directly up the spur, crossing patches of bare solid rock pitted by erosion interspersed by tree filled hollows. Late in the morning, after struggling through the uneven topography, they came out of a hollow and saw the city across a shallow valley. It was nestled against a vertical mountain wall that was more than a thousand feet in height. The outer ramparts formed three sides of a rough rectangle. A road, climbing out of a deeper valley to the east, ran along the top of a ledge of rock under the shadow of the wall and entered the fortress city through a broken gate.

Behind the outer wall, farther back in the city, a second wall rose several hundred feet above the rampart, forming a smaller enclosed area, like a citadel. Against the cliff, the top of a high turreted keep made of jet-black stone was just visible.

"That must be the road from the jetty," said Al, pointing to the road disappearing into a valley to their left. "The stonework on the road looks identical to what we saw at the river."

"If that's true, Jackson, Taylor, and Smith ought to have arrived ahead of us," concluded Dave.

They headed for the main gate. This stretch of their journey was more open than any they had yet encountered since they had left Linderhof. Whether it was a consequence of the poor soil or some malevolent influence emanating from the city, no living thing grew in the shallow, elongated valley that fronted the gate, except a thorny, gorse-like bush that clung tenaciously to their clothes whenever they chanced to brush against it. The gorse bushes were so troublesome that they gave up trying to cross the valley directly and instead skirted the edge, joining the road at the point where it began to climb. Thus they traveled half a mile on the road under the shadow of the rampart. The wall was higher than it had looked, and they felt naked and exposed; any defender on the wall could kill them with a well-thrown stone. And so they raced to the front gate in fear.

When they finally reached the gate, Al called a halt and looked into the city. The gate had at one time been a long tunnel about a hundred feet in length. The roof of the tunnel and the adjoining wall had collapsed so that large blocks of stone were scattered about. Dave positioned himself inside the walls on a large flat boulder that gave him a good view of the utterly deserted city streets, while Pam watched outside.

Inside the gate, the street was bordered with row upon row of houses, some with collapsed roofs. Each house shared its sidewalls with its neighbors so that only the street or the occasional narrow walkway made an intermittent gap. The windows had no glass.

The main avenue that came through the gate continued into the heart of the city, becoming increasingly narrow and winding as the houses closed in on it. Just inside the gate, this main road crossed a second road, which appeared to follow the outer rampart all the way around the fortress.

Al said he was reluctant to enter the heart of the city and so turned left and searched buildings across from the outer rampart. With Al out of sight, Dave became aware of the unearthly silence. Even the wind seemed unable to reach into this city.

In five minutes Al returned and motioned Dave to follow him as he walked back out through the broken entrance. When they rejoined Pam, she seemed relieved that they had returned.

"As far as I can see, this city has been deserted for a long time," said Al. "I saw wood that had almost completely decayed, and the dust in the buildings looks undisturbed. This is what I propose: I'm going to scale this wall and try to signal the base with my mirror. Then if I have Linder's go ahead, I believe we should explore the city. We'll be in and out before nightfall and back to the base a few hours after that. Any comments?"

Dave said, "Up until now we've been traveling very slowly because we've been very cautious. Now that we're inside the gates, we don't really have an escape route. I'd prefer to go for speed so that we can get in and out as quickly as possible."

"What do you think, Pam?" asked Al.

"I'm with Dave. This place gives me the creeps; the faster we get in and out, the better."

"All right then, let's do it!"

Pam and Dave resumed their guard positions while Al began climbing the broken wall. After he had been gone for about half an hour, he reappeared.

"Come and join me on the wall," he called.

Pam and Dave hauled all of their supplies to the top of the rock pile. They fastened Al's pack and crossbow to the line so he could haul it up. Pam's equipment went next. Al offered to guide Pam and asked her to fasten the rope to her climbing harness. Dave helped her up onto the first rock ledge. Wearing her climbing harness and listening to Al's instructions about footholds and safe grips, Pam began the ascent.

After a few minutes without mishap, Pam reached the upper edge, and Al hoisted her over the top.

Dave's pack and crossbow came next. But his old fear of climbing returned, and he felt especially self-conscious since Pam had managed very well under Al's direction. Putting on a brave front, Dave tried to climb without the rope Al offered, becoming so afraid at one point, that he wanted to call for a rope, but Pam's concerned face peering down at him convinced him to go on. Relief washed over him as he reached for Al's hand at the top.

"I made contact with the base," said Al. "They told me that they haven't heard from the other party. Maybe I'm wrong about the road after all."

"Maybe they've found something really interesting that diverted them," volunteered Pam.

"Could be," said Al, "but I think we should exercise extra caution. Floyd agrees we should press on. I want to be as careful as possible, but as Dave pointed out, it would be better for us to move quickly, find the Taylor team if they're here, and get out before nightfall. My plan is to walk along the top of the wall all the way to the rock face. There's a tower at the end, and I hope to reach the cobblestone road just before it enters the citadel. That way we can look down on the lower tier of the city from above, without having to move among all those abandoned buildings."

"Isn't this a longer route?" asked Dave.

"Yes, but it has the advantage that if we stay near the outer parapet, the width of the wall will make us invisible from the city's lower tier. We'll still be in full view of the upper wall, but that can't be helped. I think it shouldn't take us more than thirty minutes to get to the far end of the wall if we walk fast, and we can't get lost while we're up here."

They moved quickly along the wall for about 200 yards to the first of the towers. Entering the tower through an arch, they could see a heavy wooden door lying where it had rotted from its iron hinges. Inside the door there was a circular stairway connecting the top of the tower with the street.

"This would have saved us a lot of time!" said Al, gesturing at the stairs.

"Then we wouldn't have had the exhilaration of the climb," said Pam, smiling.

They continued along the parapet and through three more towers until they were facing the mountainside. The wall did not butt directly up against the cliff face, but made a sharp turn to the right, gradually closing the gap to the cliff at an acute angle.

"This is a well-designed fortification," said Al. "If anyone tried to scale the rock face to get up to the wall, they'd be under fire from this section of the wall the whole time. It would be hard to surprise the defenders if they remained vigilant."

"Nevertheless, it looks like someone did break in, judging by the rubble at the front gate," remarked Pam.

They made the final trek to the last tower without incident. Below them they saw the cobblestone road climbing up to the citadel wall and another gate, which seemed undisturbed. As they entered the citadel, they saw that it was quite different from the lower tier. The cobblestone road entered a large square like a parade ground. Against the mountain rock face, at the southern end of the square, there was a huge tower made of black stone. The gate to the tower was open, but the opening, large enough to be a train tunnel, was so dark, it looked like the entrance to a cave.

Dave looked about the square. Around it were the ruins of what once must have been impressive buildings. On some, the large circular columns had collapsed, while others were mostly intact. The dark window and door openings looked like the eye and mouth holes of huge stone skulls.

"Let's explore that black tower," said Al quietly. "It seems to be the most important building. After that it'll be time for us to head home."

They approached the entrance to the tower. It was crowned with a sharply pointed arch, above which a hideous stone beast glared with bared fangs into the square. Entering, they could see they were in a tunnel with smooth walls that ran straight into the mountain.

At that moment a shape separated from the shadows further up the tunnel. The humanoid shape was about five feet tall. Clothed in hides, it had a small head with disproportionately large jaws, but it walked upright and used its apelike hands to wield the crude club it carried. Stopping as it saw them, it tilted its head back, gave an ear-piercing howl and then charged with a lumbering jerky motion. Its face displayed a cold, bloodless snarl but no fear. Al raised his crossbow and began to back out of the tower.

Dave shouted, "There are more behind us in the square!" The shadows of several more apemen darkened the entrance.

"Up the stairs!" yelled Al.

They reached the first landing by the time the apeman, with club raised, had rounded the corner and began lumbering up the stairs. Dave's bolt tore into its body, knocking it down. But the creature's demeanor did not change; it rose and continued the attack. A second bolt knocked it down again, and this time, it lay unmoving.

Still hoping to escape, the trio started back down the stairs when four more apemen entered the base of the tower. Howling, the beasts attempted to climb the stairs, but tripped over the body and fell in a heap.

"Get upstairs quick!" said Al.

Pam led the way while Dave and Al covered their retreat. Racing up the stairs, they emerged at the top of the tower, some 500 feet above the square. Dave and Al prepared to face the apemen lumbering after them.

Pam ran along the parapet toward the mountainside.

"I've found an escape!" she shouted, and stepped onto a narrow rock ledge.

"Let's go!" said Al.

He and Dave fired their crossbows, and then Al raced to join Pam. But Dave hesitated.

I'll never be able to keep up on the ledge; besides, the apemen are too close.

He turned towards the attackers to buy his friends more time. Pulling his sword from its sheath, he swung at the first apeman that approached, making a deep gash across its arm.

———————

Pam carefully moved along the ledge, followed closely by Al. After traveling a dozen feet, Al realized Dave was not with them. He turned around, retraced his steps to the parapet and looked on in horror as one of the apemen struck Dave in the head. When Dave collapsed, the others hoisted his limp body and began carrying it down the stairs.

Al felt an urge to fling himself at the apemen, but that would have meant abandoning Pam. He had no choice but to return to the ledge. With a heavy heart and inwardly raging, he turned back to Pam. When Pam saw him turn, she realized Dave wasn't joining them. A look of fear and horror crossed her face.

"Where's Dave?" she asked.

"They got him. Keep moving!"

Pam froze.

"He's dead. Keep moving!" Al shouted.

Slowly, Pam turned as sobs racked her body. Al gently placed a hand on her shoulder. "Pam, we'll have time for tears later. We need to keep moving. We need to warn the others."

Some apemen had followed them out onto the ledge. But despite their appearance, they did not have the agility of apes. They proceeded along the ledge for a few feet, then first one and then the others fell to the rocks far below, their bodies bouncing off the mountainside, leaving a red stain wherever they hit. After a dozen had fallen, the others clustered at the tower parapet but did not venture onto the ledge.

Pam led the way along the mountain face, her sobbing interspersed with expressions of helpless rage. Traversing the sheer wall demanded they summon their composure and focus on the climb. Only when they finally reached a broader ledge with a cave did they allow themselves to relax their concentration. Pam looked back into the citadel. The apemen were not following, but were carrying the bodies of their fallen comrades back into the tower entrance.

After a few moments rest, the two companions woodenly resumed their climb. The sheer stone wall now bent south to make a deep cleft in the mountainside and they lost sight of the hideous tower. Looking down, they could see the western end of the city, as quiet and deserted as before.

Rounding the corner was difficult; there were few handholds, and they had to carry their equipment. Pam, who was proving to be an excellent climber, unerringly picked the best route over the rock wall. Al recalled the help he'd given her in scaling the outer rampart, a trivial exercise compared to this climb.

She really didn't need my help on the outer wall. She can climb much better than I can! But she took my silly instructions without comment.

High up on the other side of this stone rampart they eventually reached a wide ledge that sloped back into the mountain. The steepness of the slope, and its depth, kept them safely hidden.

Pam had reached the end of her endurance. Falling to her knees, she sank back, wrapping her arms about her knees as great sobs again shook her body. Al put his arm around her shoulder but could not think of anything to say. Tears welled up in his eyes, but they were silent tears. He remembered the attack of the lupi. How many graves had he dug? How many prayers had he said over the mounds?

They sat like this for a while, until Pam's sobbing gradually subsided. She hadn't seen Dave fall under the clubs of the apemen, so Al told her how Dave had obviously made a stand at the tower door, only to be killed by the attackers. Pam wiped her eyes and tried valiantly to suppress her shudders. Eventually, Al took his arm away and began rummaging through his pack for some food. The simple act of taking some food and water gave them both a sense of normalcy and helped restore their emotions.

Chapter 23

Attack

"Should we keep going or head back to the tower and make a run for it?" asked Al, after they had been sitting quietly for a few minutes.

Pam quailed. Al sensed a shiver pass through her.

"Al, I couldn't face those creatures again. They weren't animal—and they weren't human. They seemed so—unnatural. I can't go back—especially not at night."

"Then we should go on?" asked Al. "What if they follow us and come upon us in the dark?"

Even in the waning light, Al could see the color drain from her face. Pam moved to get up, but her legs were obviously too stiff. Al also felt weary—from the tension of their escape and the emotional trauma of Dave's death.

Finally he pulled himself up and helped Pam to her feet. At the back of the ledge was a crevice, a chimney that extended out of sight. It would be a difficult climb, but the lower stages, at least, were manageable. However, even now the shadow was so deep in the cleft that they could not see the handholds.

In the end, they spent the night huddled on the ledge under a shallow overhang that provided them with some protection from the wind. There were no stars, and the night air filled with the oppressive heaviness of an impending thunderstorm. The lightning flashes and loud crashes of thunder were terrifying on the exposed mountainside. In the momentary brilliance of the lightning flashes, they thought they saw apemen creeping toward them in the flickering shadows on the rock face. They waited in fear. The apemen never came.

Al prayed a silent prayer that they would both remain calm. He told Pam every silly joke he could remember. Many of them were old chestnuts, and Pam must have thought him a fool for trying them out on her at a time like this, but the jokes had their desired effect. Pam actually started to giggle softly, and time passed more quickly as they forgot the shadows and the danger. Eventually, through sheer exhaustion, they fell into a restless sleep.

Dawn found them so cramped and cold they could hardly move. Stretching gingerly, the pain at first was excruciating, but soon they were able to have a few mouthfuls of water and a bit of cold breakfast. Both were anxious to leave their precarious perch, so Pam, silently acknowledged as the better climber, led the way up the broken rock face of the chimney.

An hour later they were standing on a broad ledge with the city far below. They had climbed well beyond the western wall of the city and were now searching for a way down. The ledge, like a sword slash in the side of the mountain, ran down at a forty-five degree angle in the direction they wanted to go but carried them around a mountain spur that put them completely out of sight of the city.

The going became easier since the mountainside was not as steep here, but they had to go slowly since the ledge ended in a steep field of boulders and one false step could result in a fall.

By early afternoon they were finally off the mountain, about a mile west of the city. Tired as they were, they made all possible haste back to Fort Linderhof.

At about suppertime, they approached their camp, exhausted. A guard on alert waved and then ran back to the hollow. Soon Floyd and several others came to meet them across the rope bridge.

"Where's Dave?" asked Floyd.

Al hung his head and wiped his eyes. "Dead!" he said wearily.

Floyd was visibly shocked at the news and took a moment to recover his composure. "What happened?" asked Floyd.

"It's a long story, and we'd better get across the bridge," said Al.

A few minutes later, Pam and Al were hungrily helping themselves to the food set before them and drinking Halcyon tea. Almost everyone had gathered around. Floyd even had to chase the lookout back to his post by the rope bridge.

Pam and Al took turns explaining their journey in detail. There was a perceptible intake of breath as Al described Dave's final act of courage, which had obviously allowed his and Pam's escape. He dismissed the return journey with a few words and then fell silent.

Floyd's eyes smoldered.

"The other party encountered the same type of apemen you did," Floyd said. "They were trapped for a while. Fortunately it happened on the open road and they were able to take up a safe position, beat off the apemen, and disengage without taking any casualties. What are they, do you think, these 'apemen'?"

Pam answered. "They seem to have some primitive means of communication, and they coordinate their attacks. I guess they have some intelligence, but they're impervious to pain and they don't really get angry. It's not that they are devoid of emotion; it's as if the emotion they exhibit is a parody or a sham. It's almost as if they were zombies."

"They have another curious behavior," added Al. "They always carry their dead away. After several had fallen off the ledge, we saw others come back to the bottom of the cliff and carry off the bodies."

"Hmm," said Floyd, "do you think they might attack us here?"

"They might," said Al. "They didn't follow us, but we had outclimbed them. We're more exposed here, and it's possible they may make an attempt. This is a defensible position, but if they come in sufficient numbers to surround us, we could be in a desperate situation."

Floyd addressed the group. "We'll double the watch. I want all the sailboats filled with provisions. I want our ropes fastened and ready to go, in case we have to make our escape. I'm going to make up our new watch schedules. Pam, you and Al get some sleep."

Al walked slowly back to their tent. The images of Dave's last stand came back to him and filled him with remorse. It should have been him. He was the leader. He should have stayed back and fought the apemen!

Al took his sleeping bag out of the tent and found a spot under a small pine tree. He used his raincoat to make an improvised lean-to and placed his belongings next to his sleeping bag. As he turned around, Pam was standing by the tent watching him. It looked as if she were going to say something but changed her mind. She lifted the tent flap, turned and wished him a good night, and disappeared into the tent.

———

It was a clear night. Dark shadows shambled over the rocks toward Fort Linderhof. The first shadow reached the rope bridge and began to cross.

A voice called out, "Who goes there?"

In silence the shadow continued to cross the bridge. Floyd's axe flashed in the moonlight, and the main rope parted. The apeman held onto one of the hand ropes. Two more axe strokes and the hand ropes parted, sending the apeman into the depths. A dull thud sounded as his body landed on the rocks far below.

Other apemen approached the chasm carrying long, roughly made ladders. Speeding up as they neared the edge, they lowered the front ends of the ladders to the ground, lofting them vertically with the help of poles and letting them fall across the yawning gorge. Five ladders thudded, bridging the gap, and the apemen began to lumber across. Occasionally, one would overbalance and fall into the depths; others fell as they took hits from crossbow bolts or rifle shots. Still they advanced in silent ferocity. The bullets quickly spent, the few crossbowmen would not be able to hold off the attack for long.

Floyd brought up a crew of six men. Using ropes and pry poles, they knocked one ladder after another to the bottom of the chasm. When the last ladder had fallen, the remaining apemen retreated as silently as they had come. "We're almost out of arrows," said Floyd in a loud voice. "If they launch another attack, we'll be fighting hand-to-hand, and they'll overwhelm us. We must get out of here now."

Having ordered their retreat, he had the group pack up their remaining things and begin the slow process of going down the rope ladder to the boats. Most of the people were already down when the apemen reappeared, supplied with fresh ladders. Again, as before, they propelled the ladders over the chasm and began climbing onto them almost before they hit the ground. Al, Floyd, and three others tried to knock the ladders off, taking aim with their crossbows at any apemen that came across. When the last bolt had been shot and the apemen had crossed at the far end of the mesa, Al and the others raced back across the mesa toward the riverside precipice and jumped into the void.

Al hit the river feet first, his crossbow jarring his shoulder. Time slowed to a crawl as he sank into the water's inky blackness. Seeing the faint shimmer of air bubbles rising, he kicked vigorously to follow them. On the surface, Al saw the ghostly shadow of a boat approaching. Arms dragged him aboard, and then the boat paddled swiftly and silently into the predawn twilight.

Chapter 24

Return to Halcyon

The wearying journey back to Halcyon passed uneventfully. Floyd kept them going with all possible speed, camping on islands they had used before. Finally they saw the mouth of the river and the familiar islands in the channel. Once clear of the mountains, Floyd radioed ahead, so a small welcoming party, including the chancellor and most of the senate, was at the harbor to greet them. The chancellor spoke a few words, and then the newly arrived adventurers were hustled off for a debriefing that took the rest of that day.

Al's session had all the characteristics of an interrogation. He was repeatedly questioned about his trip to the deserted city with a succession of crossexaminers phrasing the same questions using different words, as if they wanted him to recant or catch him in an inconsistency. Toward the end of the day, their questions turned to his religious beliefs and the possible impact these beliefs might have had on the performance of his duty.

It wasn't until later that night, after he had been released, that the fatigue of the journey, with all its rigors, loss, and uncertainty, settled on Al. Not wanting to go back to his empty dorm room alone, he walked by himself for a while. He turned into the library, hoping to find the feeling of familiarity. But the comfortable sense of being at home among the books at first eluded him. Then he reached his old study table and saw his friend Dwight at his usual place.

Seeing Al, Dwight's face lit up. They traded punches.

"Man, am I glad to see you!" said Al.

"Likewise. Your exploits on the river expedition are all over campus. I thought you would have had your fill of adventure after our brush with the lupi. You'll have to tell me about things over a cup of tea."

"I'd love to. Why don't we find Tom and make our reunion complete?" Al suggested.

Dwight's face betrayed a look of concern. "I'm afraid he's not doing very well," he said guardedly.

"What's up?" said Al.

"It's a long story."

"I've got lots of time." They headed for the cafeteria.

"Well," began Dwight, "it all started shortly after you left. Tom started seeing this incredibly beautiful woman named Cynthia, Cynthia Dodson. He told me at first he was very concerned about her spiritual state. You know me, I'm always a bit of a cynic, so I gave him one of my inscrutable stares that says 'yeah, right!' and left it at that. Well a few weeks later, I find out he's spending nights with her.

"Now here's the real kicker. After this development, he began to avoid me. When I finally cornered him, he told me he's having all these intellectual troubles about the reliability of the Bible. He brought up a number of old chestnuts, and we talked about them for a while. I got exasperated, because I knew it was all a smoke screen. I lost my temper and told him his gonads had far more to do with his doubts than his brain did! Needless to say, that didn't go over very well!"

The weight of this blow on top of everything else seemed too much for Al. "How can this be! We're being destroyed little by little. Where's the Lord in all this? Why doesn't he stop it? Why isn't he working? Why isn't he answering!"

Leaving the question unanswered, Dwight continued in a quieter voice. "Anyway," he said, "a week after I told Tom off, Cynthia dumped him for someone else. Tom has a new girlfriend and really wants nothing more to do with me."

Dwight wanted to know about the adventure, so Al filled him in on the details. Later, when he finally returned to his room, although exhausted Al was unable to sleep. He knelt beside his bed and prayed to the God that almost no one seemed to believe in any more.

God, where are you? Why aren't you working? I thought Dave was really coming around to think about you, and you let those apemen kill him. For every step forward, we go two steps back, and you don't seem to care!

The next morning, Al checked the Halcyon work schedule to find Tom's work assignment. He was working on one of the kelp-harvesting trawlers and would return from the kelp fields about two o'clock in the afternoon. Al waited for him at the wharf on the east side of the island.

As Tom came through the gate and saw Al, his face registered surprise.

"How are you, Tom?" said Al.

"I'm fine," said Tom woodenly. "How about you?"

"I just got back from the expedition, and I wanted to see you."

Tom nodded.

"I know you're just off your shift," said Al, "but could we go for tea, or what passes as tea, and talk for a while?"

"I'd like that," said Tom, but his voice and manner contradicted his words.

Tom warmed up as they remembered mutual acquaintances, talked about their adventure with the lupi, and Al recounted details of the most recent river exploration. They had been sitting for some time at the cafeteria, and Tom was already on his third beer when Al ended his tale. "I've heard there have been some changes in your life since I left on the expedition," said Al.

Tom's eyes hardened. "You've been talking to Dwight."

"Yes," said Al.

"Listen, Al," said Tom, with some bitterness, "all my life, I feel like I've lived in a state of puritanical repression. And now I have a gorgeous girlfriend, Lynn Whitford, and I'm having the time of my life. I'd like for us to continue to be friends, but I don't want you telling me what I can and can't do."

"Tom, hear me out. I'm not here to tell you what you can or can't do. You're a grownup and have a God-given right to make your own decisions about things. That doesn't mean we won't disagree or that I don't care. We've been friends for a long time, and I just don't want our friendship destroyed, because of Lynn or anyone else."

Tom's eyes softened. "Al, I've just gotten off my shift and I'm really tired. Maybe I'm overreacting. I've got to get some rest, but I'm glad that you went out of your way to see me. Maybe when I'm less tired we can talk some more?" With that, Tom got up, clapped Al on the back, and left.

Al sat for a few minutes mulling over their conversation.

Why do I do that to people, especially a friend like Tom? Why did he feel criticized just because I asked about Lynn? How do I let him know that although I think he's making a big mistake, I'm still his friend and his decisions aren't going to change that? One step forward, two steps back!

Al finished his tea, rose wearily from his seat at the table, and went back to his room.

Chapter 25

The Inner Circle Meets

Blackmore finished sipping his martini and looked around his oak paneled drawing room. They had an important decision to make, and he half listened to the discussion while he thought about the proposal. Finally he looked at Hoffstetter intently. "So, Bertrand," he said, "you're urging us to launch an immediate expedition to seize the mountain city. What do the rest of you think of that?"

Huxley was ready for the question. "I'm inclined to agree with him. The deserted city is well fortified and may hold knowledge that could be very useful to us. I don't see the apemen as a problem. Sure, they overwhelmed a handful of explorers, but we have a technological advantage over the apemen, and with sufficient numbers we should easily prevail."

Hobbs was agitated by Huxley's response. "But what about the risks?" he asked. "Our supply line to this new city will be very long. We've only now built our first versions of the Viking longboat. What if the apemen defeat our expeditionary force?"

"We need to plan carefully," responded Huxley, "but I think we could be ready in a month. We'll send our twenty-five longboats upriver and establish a base, not on the mainland but on this island they talked about," he said pointing to a newly drawn map on the wall. "The apemen have no watercraft, and our island is unassailable. From there we can fortify Fort Linderhof and make our push to the city when we're strong enough. As far as supplies go, we have enough food here now, and we can set up a ferry service using the longboats so that supplies arrive every week."

Blackmore leaned forward and made a steeple of his fingers. "I think the potential benefits outweigh the risks. There's another reason I think this journey is worth the risk. We're more intelligent than these brutes, but they have language and rudimentary organization. Just think of the resource they could be if we apply ourselves to controlling them or, shall we say, to domesticating them. They could take over many of our menial tasks, and they don't have the intelligence to be a threat to us."

His point had struck home. Everyone was nodding in agreement. "There's another issue we need to think about," he continued. "Albert Gleeson and Pamela Lowental have become celebrities because of their exploits in the city. Is this a problem for us?"

Lydia Pendergast's eyes had hardened at Gleeson's name. "I don't think Lowental is a problem, but Gleeson is another story. He's a schizophrenic, receiving messages from and talking to God. I don't want a person like that gaining influence in Halcyon or participating in another of our expeditions."

"But how can we legitimately deny him a role in this new expedition," said Hobbs, "when he's a hero? He has the allegiance of the expedition members."

"I thought we might discredit Gleeson for abandoning Schuster," said Pendergast, "but the facts weren't on our side. Instead I think we should call Gleeson in for another interview and have Boyd from psychiatry listen to him. Boyd believes religion is a psychosis, and I'm sure he'd feel that he would be doing Gleeson and our society a great service by enrolling Gleeson in a treatment program so as to free him from this mental illness. If Boyd institutionalizes him, then we could, if we were asked, publicly lament the effects of post-traumatic stress syndrome on Gleeson while expressing our hope that Boyd will heal Halcyon's hero."

Blackmore smiled; he'd heard enough. The conversation had come around to the point he'd waited for, so he got up out of his chair. "We've decided then. Bertrand, you'll propose to the senate that we launch this expeditionary force as soon as possible. The rest of us will support your proposal. I don't fully trust Linder, so we'll find a new leader. We'll also work to cure Gleeson from his psychosis to our benefit and the benefit of our fragile society." He said this last phrase with a sly smile.

Blackmore led the way to the dining hall for their meal together. Food always tasted better after a decision had been reached.

Chapter 26

Resolve

The Halcyon University Hospital was a large steel and glass building designed to provide a pleasant, bright, open atmosphere for convalescing patients. As a medical student, Pam knew the building well and did not need to ask directions to the psych ward. Here she met her first surprise. Instead of the open passageway to the psych wing she had expected, she found a receptionist sitting in front of a locked door.

"May I help you?" asked the pretty blonde receptionist.

"Er, yes. I'm here to see Mr. Albert Gleeson."

"And your name is?" asked the receptionist.

"Isn't it visiting hours?" asked Pam sweetly.

"I'm afraid visiting hours no longer—" the receptionist stopped herself. "I'm afraid visiting hours don't apply to the psych ward."

"In that case, my name is Pam Lowental."

"One moment please!"

The receptionist pushed on a button under her desk, unlocking the solid door, and then went into the psych ward. The lock clicked, seconds after the door had swung shut. After a few minutes, the door opened and the receptionist returned with a corpulent man with a full, graying beard.

"Ms. Lowental?" he said, extending his hand with a wan synthetic smile. "You must remember me. I am Jonathan Boyd, professor of psychiatry. I taught you Psych 101."

"Yes, of course, Dr. Boyd," said Pam. Pam had disliked him when he had taught her, and now she found herself disliking him even more.

"Please come to my office," said Boyd. He went through the door ahead of Pam and walked briskly to his office at the end of a side corridor. Opening the door to his office and gesturing to a chair, Boyd walked around his desk, piled high with reports. He didn't sit in his office chair but moved some papers and sat on the side of his desk, folded his arms, and looked at her appraisingly.

Pam began to feel intimidated by the extended silence, but she had been through too much to be frightened into speaking first, and so she met his gaze with pursed lips.

"Ms. Jensen tells me you want to see Albert Gleeson. May I ask why?" said Boyd at last.

"Who's Ms. Jensen?" asked Pam.

"My receptionist, of course," answered Boyd smoothly.

"Why is the psych ward locked up? It never used to—" said Pam in a calm voice.

"We have had to impose, er," interrupted Boyd, "a rather limited security for the safety of our patients. I'm afraid the stress of the dislocation and the recent calamity at Botany Bay has pushed many borderline psychotic people over the edge."

Remembering his unanswered question, Boyd began again. "Why do you want to see Albert Gleeson?"

"Albert Gleeson and I were partners," said Pam, "in the recent river expedition. We had a close call in the city that we found—"

"Of course!" interrupted Boyd again. "Your exploits are being discussed all over Halcyon."

"Naturally, when Albert disappeared about two weeks ago," continued Pam, "I made inquiries through my contacts in the medical school and I learned he was being detained in the psych ward."

"Detained is hardly the word!" laughed Boyd. Turning more serious and leaning over the desk, he continued. "I'm afraid Albert is a deeply troubled young man. He has for some time now been borderline schizophrenic. For example, he believes he talks to God and that God answers him. It's difficult to say when this psychosis will turn violent, but it will inevitably do so, and therefore I've had to confine him for his own protection as well as for the safety of others. These are very difficult cases," said Boyd. "Those without the proper psychiatric training are often fooled, since the schizophrenics truly believe they're hearing the voice of God. It's essential that we intervene before the schizophrenia becomes too deeply ingrained."

Pam was hard-pressed to conceal her surprise. Al was about the sanest individual she'd ever met. She had no doubt whatsoever about his sanity. The more Boyd spoke about Gleeson's psychosis, the more convinced Pam became that it was Halcyon—and the mindset that had produced Halcyon—that was warped and demented.

What if Al's right about God?

That thought came unbidden, and it frightened her. She felt as if she stood in front of a doorway. Her mind and her heart bade her go in to see what she might find, but she was afraid if once she crossed that threshold, she might never go back. Her mind returned to Boyd, who had continued talking.

"...and so I'm afraid I can't let you see him," he concluded.

"There's something else I haven't told you," she interrupted, panic making her play her last card.

"And what would that be?" asked Boyd.

"I'm carrying Al Gleeson's baby," she lied. "I had promised to give him Al's last name, but I need to see Al for myself before I can make that determination. I don't want the child associated with a lunatic."

"Now, now, we don't use that term," reprimanded Boyd. "Hmm, this gives me some hope for Gleeson. I've always felt these psychoses are a byproduct of celibacy, and to hear that Gleeson—well, let me say I have even more reason for hope. Pamela, I'll tell you what I'll do. In view of your situation, and in view of the fact that you're a medical student, I'll make an exception and let you see Mr. Gleeson briefly. But you must promise that this is an exception and that you'll not ask to see him again."

Reluctantly Pam said, "I promise."

She was about to get up when Boyd said, "Does Mr. Gleeson know about your son in the Halcyon Daycare Center?"

Cold dread froze Pam's heart. "No, Albert doesn't know about my son."

"Of course not!" said Boyd. "That's really none of his business. How you exercise your sexual freedom really has nothing to do with him. Nonetheless, some men, especially those with a more puritanical bent, can be unreasonably jealous. I think you've been wise to keep that information from him."

Boyd spoke briefly on the intercom, and an orderly appeared. "Please take Ms. Lowental to Mr. Al Gleeson's room and give her five minutes alone with him."

He's threatening me! He's letting me know that he'll tell Al if I try to see him again.

The orderly led Pam to a door and unlocked it with a key. Holding the door open, he said, "Five minutes! I'll lock the door so that other patients don't wander in."

Al looked pale against the white sheets. He slept while an IV quietly dripped a clear liquid into his arm. Pam pulled a chair next to his bed, took his hand in both of hers, and gently called his name. There was no response. "Al, oh Al, what have they done to you!" she whispered. She put her hand on his forehead and gently stroked his hair. "Al, please wake up! Please wake up!"

Al stirred. She called again. Suddenly Al opened his eyes and tried to lift himself up in bed, but could not. He looked at Pam but did not recognize her. "Somebody loves me, but I can't remember who it is. Somebody loves me, but I can't remember who it is." This last sentence died in a whisper as Al sank back onto his pillow.

Tears welled up in her eyes. "I love you, Al! I love you!" She kissed him gently on the lips and cried quietly as she held his hand, waiting for the orderly to return.

Anger welled up within her. She had to get Al out of here somehow. How could she pull it off? Who would help her? Who could she trust? Where would they go so they would be safe? Otherwise wouldn't she end up drugged, in the room next to him?

She cautiously turned the lever to unlock the door and peered up and down the hallway. Although she heard voices, there was no one to be seen. She quietly closed the door and turned right to explore the hallway.

There must be another way out!

She walked slowly and deliberately and tried to look as if she were lost. At the far end of the hallway there was an exit sign that was no longer lit (bulbs were saved for critical purposes only). She approached a door labeled "Fire Exit." A fire extinguisher and stretcher were attached to the wall next to the door.

"May I help you?" The nametag on the pretty blonde's uniform read Lynn Whitford.

"Help me? Yes, you can. I was visiting a patient and I'm looking for a way out. Could you direct me back to the entrance?" answered Pam politely.

Whitford frowned. A curt "Please follow me!" was all she said.

Pam stepped through the door to the reception area. The receptionist was across the room placing some documents into a filing cabinet and had her back turned to Pam. Pam walked behind the receptionist's chair, glanced at the desk, and then walked back to her chair to pick up her coat. "Thank you!" said Pam sweetly as she folded her coat across her arm and proceeded down the corridor.

The television set in the cafeteria was blaring. "A healthy sex life is a wonderful antidote to stress," said the student talk show hostess. She introduced her panel of Halcyon celebrities. They filled in the time between the canned films that the Halcyon television station broadcast on campus.

Pam approached a table with a single occupant. "Tom Chartrand?" she said.

"Yes," replied Tom.

"My name is Pam Lowental. I've heard that you're a friend of Al Gleeson's, and I need your help."

Chapter 27

Exodus

Dwight Larsen used one of those US quarters—still in circulation on campus—for a pay phone, and punched in the number written on the piece of paper he held. Crackling the paper near the mouthpiece as he spoke, he said, "Fred, this is Dr. Boyd."

"Yes, Dr. Boyd, I can hardly hear you," answered the voice at the other end.

"My line's bad too. I think all these phones are starting to give up the ghost. Listen, Fred, I need you to do something for me. I need to unload some equipment at the loading dock. The med student that's helping me isn't strong enough to get the box off the truck. If I send her up to you, can you come down to help me get this unloaded? There's no one else to ask. I'd be deeply grateful."

"Sure, Dr. Boyd," said Fred hesitantly.

"Thanks, I appreciate it!" Dwight hung up the phone.

Pam, dressed in her medical student uniform, walked down the corridor and approached the desk of the security guard. She held out her hand and smiled. "My name is Pam Lalond. Dr. Boyd sent me to take your place for a few minutes. I'm afraid I wasn't much help to him unloading the truck downstairs."

Fred smiled. "I'm not really supposed to leave my post. I'll tell you what I'll do. Give me your phone number and promise to have a drink with me this week, and you have a deal."

Pam hesitated, and then taking a piece of paper, she wrote down a number, handed the paper to Fred, and smiled at him. "See you in a few minutes," said Fred as he ambled down the corridor.

Pam took his place at the desk. On the right was a half eaten sandwich. Next to it was a well-worn library book. Two figures came down the hallway pushing a large white laundry cart. Pam looked up, relieved as she recognized Tom Chartrand and Dwight Larsen. "He's gone," said Pam, stating the obvious.

"Yes," said Tom. "We saw him heading towards to the main elevator."

"We'd better hurry," said Dwight.

Pam quickly located the electronic lock under the desk and unlocked the psych ward door. Tom held the door open as Dwight maneuvered the awkward cart through the entrance, and then waited for Pam to follow. Pam took the lead, striding confidently down the hallway to an unmarked door. She turned the handle and smiled with relief at Tom as the door opened. Al was still sleeping peacefully. They pushed the laundry cart into the room, and then Pam locked the door from the inside. They had just begun emptying the cart to make room for Al when the sounds of approaching voices made them freeze. Someone stopped outside the door, and the handle wiggled.

"It's locked!" they heard Jonathan Boyd say from the other side of the door. "I'll wait here. Fred, run to the nurse's station and get all of the keys. We're going to check every room, starting with this one."

"What are we going to do?" whispered Pam.

"Quick! Shove that laundry cart against the far wall and then everyone in!" whispered Dwight urgently.

Al was the single occupant in a two-bed room. Each bed had a privacy curtain. They pushed the laundry basket to the far corner of the room, so that it was partly screened by a curtain. Dwight climbed into the laundry basket first. Tom jumped in on top of him, landing heavily on his friend. Dwight let out a muffled groan. "Sorry!" whispered Tom.

By this time Pam had also climbed on top. "Can you guys get a little lower? I'm still sticking out the top, and they'll see me!" Pam hissed. Tom rearranged himself, and Pam hastily pulled a blanket and some towels over her.

It isn't very good, but it will have to do. God, if you're there, we could use your help!

A key sounded in the lock. The door creaked open and heavy footsteps approached Al's bed.

"Hmm, it looks undisturbed. This can't be the reason for the fraud. Fred, you hurry back to the entrance and wait for the campus police. Detain everyone who wants to leave, even if it's the chancellor himself. Marjorie, bring your keys and come with me. We're going to check every room in the psych ward until we get to the bottom of this!" said Boyd.

After the door closed and was locked from the outside, Pam climbed out of the basket. Tom, who had been bent into an uncomfortable conformation, needed a hand to step out of the tight space. "Boy, you're awfully heav—" Tom stopped awkwardly, leaving the sentence unfinished.

Pam felt herself blushing. "Watch it!" she said with mock seriousness. "And help me get Dwight out."

When Dwight emerged, he looked at Tom. "Boy, Tom, you're really going to have to lay off that cafeteria food. Halcyon's struggling to put enough food on the table, but you seem to be getting more than your share."

"All right, all right! What are we going to do about Al? That security guard is watching for our escape," said Tom.

"We go to plan B," said Pam.

"There's a plan B?" asked Dwight.

"Yeah, and there's no time to explain. Help me get Al into the laundry basket," urged Pam. She deftly unhooked the IV line from Al's arm while Dwight and Tom gently lifted him into the laundry basket. Al moaned softly.

Pam unlocked the door and cautiously opened it a crack. She didn't see or hear anyone, so she opened it wider. After peering up and down the corridor, she waved to the others to follow. She strode down the hallway, and Dwight and Tom followed as quietly and rapidly as they could, pushing the laundry cart.

Pam came to a door marked "Fire Exit." She opened a cabinet and took down a stretcher. Dwight and Tom laid Al's body on it. After pushing the laundry cart against the wall, Pam opened the fire exit door and held it for Dwight and Tom as they carried Al into the stairwell. Pam squeezed past them and led the way downstairs. They descended three more floors and finally came to a door marked "Exit to Outside; Alarm Will Sound."

Pam whispered, "When we get outside, find some place to hide Al. I'm going to run to the front and get the car. Keep a lookout for me!"

Pam gave a thumbs up and pushed the door open. There was no alarm to be heard, but she knew that if the system still functioned, they'd be lighting up someone's console somewhere.

Turning left, she raced as fast as she could along the building. When she came to the front entrance, she slowed to a walk as she emerged from the shadows. There were several people either hurrying into the hospital or leaving their shift late, but anyone who caught a glimpse would have seen only a young woman heading home after a long shift at the hospital.

At this time of night the parking lot was mostly deserted. She found her borrowed car in the dark, secluded corner where they had parked it. She climbed in, and giving a quick prayer of thanks for the noiseless electric motor, backed out of her spot, and headed toward the service entrance where Tom and Dwight were supposed to be waiting with the helpless Al. But the back of the hospital was deserted. She saw no trace of Dwight or Tom.

As she circled back for a second look, Tom stepped out of some shrubs and signaled her to drive in among the bushes. In the shadows of the greenery, she saw Dwight crouching beside a body on the ground.

Dwight and Tom lifted Al into the seat beside Pam, folded up the stretcher and put it in the trunk. After they had climbed into the back seats, Pam started off towards the harbor, putting distance between themselves and the hospital just as the fire escape door burst open and beams of light stabbed into the darkness. Again Pam blessed the quiet electric motor of the car.

When Pam reached the harbor, she jumped out and raced to the top of the hill. Expectancy and hope were replaced with despair when she saw the empty pier. They were too late! The invasion force heading for the deserted city had obviously left early, and now there was no escape.

Chapter 28

Rescue

When Dave decided to give his friends time to escape, he knew he didn't have much chance of surviving the apemen's attack. Nevertheless, if the move was going to cost him his life, Dave was determined to sell it dearly. After felling the first apeman, Dave swung his sword at a second, inflicting a long deep gash through its shoulder and into the chest. The blade stuck on the bone, so that Dave had to forcefully wrench his blade free. This delay proved disastrous. The press of bodies was so severe Dave couldn't swing his sword quickly enough to keep the apemen off the landing. A blow from behind staggered him. Dave momentarily lost consciousness.

The next moment a dozen hands grabbed him and hoisted him into the air. Coming out of his mental fog, Dave realized he was being carried down the stairs of the tower. The apemen were talking to each other in slow guttural monotones. They seemed neither infuriated by his resistance nor elated by their success.

At the bottom of the stairs, they proceeded with Dave, feet first, into the long tunnel leading under the mountain. The first section of the tunnel appeared manmade. About thirty feet in diameter and constructed of the same smooth black stone as the tower itself, it led into a wider chamber, lit by a shaft of sunlight coming through a fissure high on the mountainside.

Dave had recovered his senses enough to fear for his life. He tried to struggle but couldn't break the iron grip of the apemen. Craning his neck and looking forward, Dave saw another party carrying a dead apeman about thirty yards ahead. Dave was terribly frightened. The apemen behaved like living machines, grinding out some program without feeling or conscience. He used to make fun of those who prayed in desperate situations, accusing them of wishful thinking, but he succumbed to that temptation now and prayed feverishly for rescue to a God he had never believed existed.

The party of apemen entered another chamber, with an arched doorway at the far end. At that moment something extraordinary happened. An arrow thudded into the chest of the lead apeman. He bellowed and collapsed. This first arrow was followed by a flurry of arrows, which felled the remaining apemen in the party. Miraculously, none of the arrows hit Dave. His carriers stumbled, and Dave tumbled to the ground, instinctively breaking his fall with his arms. He rolled to a sitting position, automatically rubbing his wrists where the iron grip of the apemen had held him as if in steel manacles. Some of the apemen from the party ahead of him dropped their load to the ground, turned around, and lumbered toward him. He was startled by a touch on his arm and a furry face beside him. He jumped away, and the pain of his sudden movement inflamed the wound on the back of his head. He felt a stabbing pain, and his vision blurred. He felt the touch on his arm again. The touch was cool and a thought, not his own, entered his consciousness.

Come follow me. There is great danger here!

Dave's vision cleared.

This thing is trying to speak to me!

He realized it had been this small creature and its companions, roughly half his size, who had fired the arrows that had freed him.

The apemen were now dangerously close. There was no time to lose. He had to take a chance and trust these rescuers.

Dave followed the creature as quickly as he could, hoping it wouldn't ask him to follow through an impossibly small hole. The creatures were mammalian, about three feet tall, and had long prehensile tails with a knob or tuft at the end. Their glistening fur was dark, but they wore clothing, which looked like primitive leather body armor. They carried belts with knives, small bows and quivers of arrows over their backs. For all his fear of his ferocious pursuers, Dave smiled at the appearance of these creatures that had saved him.

His guide led him into a crevice at the side of the chamber. The crevice became a high, narrow passage that climbed steeply. Thirty feet into the passage, Dave was dismayed to see the creature disappear into a very small opening. He looked at the hole dubiously but decided he had to try it, even if he became stuck. Dave squirmed through the opening and down a narrow tunnel, which ended in a gallery of sorts.

As he climbed out and stretched himself to his full height, he saw about twenty of the creatures waiting for him. They all had bows in their hands and knives in their belts but didn't seem to be afraid of him. One of them slowly approached and placed its hand on his arm. Again, he received a communication.

You must come with us! You are not safe here; they will try and get you. Follow us. Do not be afraid, for we are brothers.

What an odd thing to say! How could we be brothers? I'm sure you're much more closely related to a raccoon or a badger than to me.

At that moment some of the lumbering apemen emerged from the tunnel. Dave's furry companions quickly formed ranks and began shooting.

It can't be!

The furry creatures shot rapidly with their arms. The tuft of fur on the end of their prehensile tails was actually a third hand, which they used to pull arrows from their quivers, ready for the next volley. This additional hand was so alien, so unexpected, that it filled him with a kind of revulsion. Several of the apemen fell but were quickly replaced by others.

Finally one of the furry creatures gave a cry of command, and a group of them retreated to a ledge at the far end of the gallery. At a second command, Dave, urged by the rest of the troop, mastered himself and climbed behind the rear guard to an opening at the very back of the gallery. Together, Dave and the troop began another climb up a long side passage. It was not a difficult climb but changed direction several times inside the mountain wall. Dave was completely disoriented by the many turns and side passages. Sometimes he felt a breath of fresh air. Other times, he heard the sound of dripping water. His furry companions ignored the side passages and kept to the main tunnel with single-minded determination.

They emerged onto a large shelf, which overlooked a hidden valley inside the mountain, hundreds of feet below. The mountain, like the throat of an extinct volcano, was nearly vertical, with a circular opening to the sky 2,000 feet above the valley floor. The valley floor, which was about two miles across, was filled with subdued daylight and was covered with mounds. Some of these mounds were gray, while others were a sickly green in the dull light.

Dave could see apemen lumbering back and forth across the valley floor. They were carrying the bodies of their dead into the cavern in the manner of a funeral procession, six pallbearers per body. Stopping beside a green mound, they would deposit the body on the ground. As the bearers retreated, the mound would open up, like a poisonous green rose moving from bud to flower in a matter of seconds. A long green appendage would reach out, grasp the body of the lifeless apeman, and lift it easily into the center of the mound. Unlike a rose, the inside was the same rancid green as the outside. The open plant intensified the pungent, sickly smell of death that filled the cavern. In a few moments the leaves would close on the body and the mound would resume its nearly spherical shape. *Good grief! Is that what they had intended for me?* One of the furry creatures touched Dave's arm, interrupting his thoughts and beckoned him to follow.

The next part of the journey took several hours. The furry companions took out several luminous gourds, which they held high above their heads using the hands at the end of their tails. In the places where the natural greenish glow of the caverns faded, these gourds provided enough light to negotiate the dark passages. There were so many side passages that Dave wouldn't have been able to retrace his steps. At one point they crossed a ledge that skirted the wall of a very large, dark cavern, so large that the gourd lights did not find either the roof or the distant walls.

When they had crossed this treacherous ledge, the party halted and the creatures began speaking to one another in low voices. One of them approached Dave with a luminous gourd, a skin of water, and food that had the consistency of rough cornbread. The creature put the food next to Dave and placed its hand on his arm.

Eat and drink. You will need your strength for the rest of your journey.

After a short break, the party resumed their journey. They entered a long shaft littered with broken rocks and boulders. Every now and then, a deep crevice would open up at their feet, and they would pick their way along the shaft wall to the other side. Their gradual descent took them ever closer to a dull vibration like the roll of continuous thunder, which increased in intensity with every step.

Finally they entered a cavern. A river shot out of an opening high on the cavern wall and plunged like thunder into a wide subterranean lake. A number of the creatures pulled several boats from behind a large rock over golden sand to the lake. After an animated discussion among the little folk, complete with frequent finger pointing in Dave's direction, two of the creatures beckoned him to the largest boat, which another two creatures steadied in the shallow water. They motioned for him to climb in and lie down. He climbed in, but refused the humiliation of lying down. His recalcitrance caused further animated discussion. Finally they seemed to give up, climbed onto the bow and stern of the boat, and began to paddle down the lake. The other boats were swifter and soon passed them.

Rounding the bend, Dave saw a dull patch of daylight in the distance. This patch grew steadily until the boat emerged into the evening gloom. The lake was long and narrow, winding through the long mountain valley like a snake. On the right the mountains rose steeply. Across the lake, on the left, a village of thatched huts was nestled at the base of tree-clad hills. The paddlers made good speed since the gusting wind was behind them.

As they approached the wharf, villagers gathered along the shore. A few feet out, the paddlers stopped, and the villagers welcomed them with joyous song. The weary paddlers answered with a song of their own. The singers had unexpectedly deep voices for creatures of such small stature. The effect, carrying easily over the water, was one of a mass choir jubilant to be reunited after an absence involving risks as real as they were necessary. This experience changed Dave's view of the creatures. Despite their difference in size and looks, they were kindred spirits, because they obviously appreciated beautiful music with a reverence that touched on the core of what made Dave human. Somehow they did not seem as alien as before.

The welcome complete, the boats pulled alongside the wharf, and everyone disembarked. A creature came alongside Dave and placed its hand on his arm, telling him to follow. The creature took him to one of many thatched huts on a promontory in that part of the village closest to the cave entrance. The thatched structure proved to be more of a veranda than a hut. At the back was a low square entrance to a tunnel, which Dave surmised was the creature's living quarters. The family was just sitting down to a meal. They gestured for Dave to join them. There was no table. Everything was spread out on a large blanket, picnic style.

The creatures seemed to have a love of food completely disproportionate to their size. There were vegetables, fish, some kind of fowl, and a large side of something that reminded Dave of ham. The adult creatures ate more than Dave, and even the cubs seemed more than able to hold their own. Just as Dave thought the meal was over, nuts and pastry were brought out and passed around.

After the meal, all of the cubs gathered around an old grizzled creature, who spoke to them at length by the fire pit. While the children were entertained, the adults of the village began construction of a much larger dwelling, which was completely closed in, unlike the open veranda that Dave was enjoying. The rapidity of their movements as they tied poles and sheaves of grass together, and the song that they sang as they worked, made the task go quickly.

The construction complete, the creatures led Dave into his new one room home. After gesturing his thanks, he lay down on the grass mat they had provided for him and was asleep almost before they left. Even a frightful crack of thunder in the mountains did not interrupt his untroubled sleep.

Chapter 29

Higher Education

Dave awoke the next morning to the squeals of animals chasing each other. He looked around at the grass and pole walls, and then at the mat that he had slept on, and the memories of the previous night came flooding back. He had slept soundly and felt thoroughly refreshed, although his head still ached a little.

He opened the door and heard the cubs squealing as they raced around the house in some game of hide-and-seek. Two others were wrestling. They wrestled like two small boys, grabbing at each other's shoulders and trying to throw one another down. But their curious third hands were balled into hairy fists at the end of their tails, and every once in a while a fist would come whipping by like a club and land a solid wallop on the opponent's back.

After Dave had watched for a short time, one of the adult creatures (he could tell she was a female by her attire) working on a garment on the veranda in the next dwelling noticed him, put down her work, and came toward him tentatively. Dave knew she was trying to communicate, and so he let her touch his arm. A message came into his mind: **Come and eat!**

He followed the creature to the veranda, where yesterday's picnic blanket had been replaced by a child's play table, complete with tiny chairs. It was the family table, but it would not answer for him.

The creature did not realize the problem until she saw Dave and the table together. She disappeared into the entrance of their den at the back of the veranda and soon returned with another creature, the two of them dragging a large wooden structure, intricately carved. Dave went over to help and lifted the waist high structure easily, since it was very light. This set off more chatter among the creatures. They returned to the burrow and carried out a small empty armoire, which was approximately the right height for a seat.

Dave sat down at his new table and watched as the creatures brought him breakfast, eggs and delicious mashed potatoes seasoned with a sauce he'd never tasted before. There was honey and milk, but he very much missed his morning cup of tea. He had more than enough food to eat, but no sooner had he finished than the creatures brought the same amount of food again. He waved it away, using pantomime to show that he really couldn't eat any more.

When they were finally convinced, they took away the food and replaced it with a jug of brown liquid. Dave settled back, leaning against the support pole of the veranda. The veranda was on the side of a hill overlooking the lake. A green meadow that formed a broad step in the side of the hill stretched out before him, dotted with yellow buttercups, dandelions, and daffodils. At the foot of the hill, cubs were frolicking at the water's edge, diving into the lake with reckless abandon amid the shrieking of their peers. Off to his right, a dark mountain loomed menacingly. At the base he could just make out the tunnel from yesterday's journey. Off to the left, he could barely make out the other cottages in the village. The village had been planned so that each cottage was hidden among the trees and separated by gardens, providing a good deal of privacy.

When he had finished the brown drink, a creature approached and gingerly touched his arm. **Please come with me.**

He followed the creature up the hill to a large tree, where it climbed a ladder into the tree, beckoning Dave to follow. He gingerly put his foot on the rung, expecting it to collapse under his weight, but it was surprisingly strong and carried him without even noticeably bending. When he reached the top, he came to a large platform that provided a wonderful view of the lake and the village.

The creature sat down on the mat in the center of the platform and beckoned Dave to sit down as well. It handed him a small section of slate and a piece of chalk.

So, my "higher education" begins! It amused him that the pupil towered over the teacher to a ridiculous degree.

The creature pointed to himself and said, "Hanomer."

Dave pointed to himself and said, "Dave."

The creature next pointed to himself and then to various dwellings around the village and said, "Hansa."

———————

Two months had passed since Dave had been rescued by the Hansa. To his way of thinking he had become fluent in their tongue, even though Hanomer informed him he had a long way to go if he were to develop his gifts as a composer and a poet.

Dave was sitting on his veranda drinking his morning siph, the brown drink he had had when he'd first arrived in the village. Siph had become one of his favorites, and he enjoyed some every day. No one would come to visit before he had finished his siph and had had his morning time of tranquility, as they called it. It was customary to allow everyone, even the children, a time of quiet reflection in the morning, and it was considered rude and inappropriate to disturb the morning tranquility unless there was an emergency. Dave listened as the birds sang, and saw the glint of the sun on the lake below him. His heart was filled with a quiet joy he did not really understand. He did not delve into this too deeply, for fear of destroying the magic of the moment by introspection.

He took out his crossbow and short sword. They were the wonder of the village. Even though they were held in great esteem, they had been returned to him as soon as they knew he was a friend. The new bolts he had fabricated while at the village were carefully unwrapped. The crude iron heads looked impotent next to the steel bolts he had brought from Halcyon.

"Hello, friend Dave!" said Hanomer, bowing low. The Hansa normally spoke using audible speech, reserving touch mediated telepathy for times when absolute quiet was demanded.

"Greetings, friend Hanomer," said Dave, rising and returning the bow. "Please come and take a seat."

"Why are you dressed for battle, friend Hanomer?" asked Dave after Hanomer had settled.

"I have come to tell you we cannot meet today for our lesson."

"Where are you going, friend Hanomer?"

"A rokash has been spotted in the next valley," said Hanomer.

"What is a rokash?" asked Dave.

"A rokash is a creature from the elder days. It stands about fifty hands high. It runs and leaps on two powerful legs. It has a large head with powerful jaws and can kill with jaw, claw, or tail," said Hanomer.

"I would like to go along," said Dave, yearning for an adventure after two months of study.

"That would be foolish, friend Dave, since the rokash is exceedingly dangerous, and your skill in the hunt is not yet highly developed."

"Not highly developed!" exclaimed Dave. "Among my people I'm considered a woodsman of the first order." Hanomer did not answer. "Your people have rescued me and shown me hospitality these past two months. The code of honor of my people demands that I contribute in some small way to the defense of the village," continued Dave.

Hanomer was thinking. Dave knew that a call to honor was the strongest argument he could make. Finally Hanomer said, "Honor makes a strong call on any man, and there is justice in your claim. We take some of the older boys along and leave them with guards so they can observe without getting themselves and others into danger. You may stay with them. That should satisfy the claims of honor."

Dave began to protest, but Hanomer raised his little hand. "Stay!" he said. "To ask for more is to endanger the whole company. The rokash will know that you have little woodcraft and will target you first. The hunt is already very dangerous. If you were to hunt the rokash you would not only put yourself but the whole company into even greater danger. Surely the code of honor of your people cannot demand that?"

Sometimes the kindness and generosity of Hanomer made Dave forget that he could be as tough as an old tree root when the situation demanded it. "I accept your offer with thanks, friend Hanomer. When do we leave?"

"Get your weapons, food, and water skin. The others are gathering in the upper town meadow even as we speak," said Hanomer.

While Hanomer proceeded to the gathering, Dave quickly strapped on his sword belt and picked up his crossbow. He hunted and found his heavy boots but could not find his water skin. Endowyn, Hanomer's wife, came with a water skin and a food pack, which Dave gratefully stuffed into his knapsack. He had started to run off when Endowyn called to him and gave him his hat.

"Dave, do not let your impetuosity get the better of you!" she warned, standing with her hands upon her hips, her prehensile tail twitching.

"I'll be good!" he called as he hurried up the path leading to the town meadow. He was the last one to arrive, and everyone had already organized themselves into companies. The most skilled of the Hansa were chosen as the trackers. Theirs was the most dangerous assignment, as they might encounter the rokash on their own without support. Next would come three hunting parties. Since a rokash was too powerful to be killed by one Hansa alone, the nearest hunting party would run to support the scout and try to kill the rokash. Finally, Dave's party was under the control of three older Hansa, veterans who had seen many hunts. They would find a high place with good sightlines and try to follow the progress of the hunt. If they saw the rokash from their perch, they would use a horn to let everyone know. A complicated sequence of horn calls, akin to Morse code, would direct the hunting party to the right place.

The scouts melted noiselessly into the wood. One hunting party started down the main trail leading to the next valley, while the two other hunting parties took up positions to the right and left of the trail. Finally, Dave's party started down the main trail. The trail climbed steadily through a fir wood, weaving around the huge tree trunks, some eight feet in diameter.

After several hours they entered a clearing. Ahead of them loomed a cliff wall rising a thousand feet into the sky, but riven as if by an axe blow. The expedition headed for this narrow defile, which led to the next valley.

When Dave reached the defile, he saw it was about 300 feet wide at the mouth, with walls rising almost vertically for the full 1,000 feet. Strewn with rock fallen from the mountainside, the defile narrowed after a few hundred yards to a mere thirty feet. Beyond this throat, the pass widened and the trail wound its way around larger boulders, which had been loosened by the snows and fallen from the mountainside far above them.

Although it was going to be a hot, sunny day, the steep walls filled the defile with shadow, and the air was cool. When Dave emerged from the pass, a narrow valley clad in fir and pine stretched out before him. The mountain wall on his right proved to be a spur, which gradually diminished in size as it ran north. The wall on his left curved around and ran northwest, forming the far boundary of the valley. Looking down the valley to the northwest, Dave saw in the distance a river dotted with islands, some of them quite large in size.

"What is that river?" asked Dave in Hansean.

"That is Pishon the Great," answered Greeomer, one of the party leaders. "It runs east to the great sea."

Speaking to the party in general, Greeomer said in a much louder voice, "We will stop here and watch while the scouts search the upper end of the valley."

The younger Hansa climbed the cliff on either side of the defile, looking for signs of the rokash, since special honor was attached to the first one to spot it. The three veteran guards took up positions so that they covered all of the approaches to their position with their weapons. Dave watched for a while but soon grew restless for action. He had begun to climb along the base of the western cliff wall when he heard Greeomer calling him.

"Friend Dave, I know you are restless and long to be on the hunt, but you must remain close by. If you wander off, we will have to search for you, and you could endanger everyone here."

Dave did not want to give Hanomer any reason to regret bringing him, so he returned to the entrance of the defile and climbed upon a large rock. He scanned the valley floor and could not see a single Hansa. *That wood is so dense an army could hide down there and no one would ever know it!*

Finally, after about half an hour, a shrill birdcall rang up the valley. The three guards left their position and waved for everyone to join them. Greeomer said, "The scouts have combed the upper end of the valley, and there is no sign of the rokash. It may be that it has already left the valley. Since they are working their way down away from us, we will move to our next observation post." As he said this, he pointed to a grassy hillock that rose out of the valley floor about a mile away.

They began their descent and entered the trees. The floor was choked with fallen trees and dense undergrowth, but the guards deftly followed a game trail running in the general direction of the hillock. Dave was the second last of the party, with only the trailing guard behind him.

They hadn't been on the trail for more than five minutes when Dave heard a whooshing sound followed by a thud behind him. He turned in time to see a large reptilian shape land on the trailing guard, bring the guard to the ground as if he were a twig, and bite him in half with one snap of its jaws.

Time seemed to move in slow motion for Dave. The rokash was about eighteen feet long and had long, powerful hind legs ending in six-inch talons. The head was crocodilian, with red eyes set forward. The front limbs were shorter and clawed. It finished eating the guard with a second bite and then turned its red eyes toward Dave, who was already shouting for help as he unlimbered his crossbow. Out of the corner of his eye he saw Greeomer running toward the rokash.

Greeomer's first arrow flew wide as he shot on the run while racing to place himself between Dave and the monster. The rokash's tail lashed out and sent Greeomer tumbling into the bushes. Dave heard a frantic horn call echoing across the valley from nearby. The rokash turned to look for Greeomer.

Dave felt a tremendous urge to fling down his weapons and run for cover as quickly as he could. The brutal death of his companion was still fresh in his mind, and fear rolled over him. He knew he couldn't aim properly. Yet in the midst of swelling terror, he cried in his heart for help and found there was another quieter voice within him, telling him to stand his ground and fire at the monster, even if it cost him his life. An ember of courage flamed into life.

"If I'm to die, let me die standing my ground defending my friends," he said aloud.

The sound of Dave's voice attracted the rokash's attention, and it transfixed him with its red eyes as it gathered itself for another leap. Dave's inner debate had ended; his growing resolve stilled the trembling in his limbs. His first bolt entered the beast just inside its left forelimb, disappearing, barb, shaft, and feather. Dave ran to put a tree between himself and the rokash just as it leaped fifteen feet into the air. The jump went wide as the monster landed with a bellow of pain. Dave fitted a second bolt onto the string. With the speed of a striking snake the rokash turned and rushed toward him. He fired the second bolt as the monster reached the tree. Drawing his sword and dropping his crossbow, Dave backed into a thicket of trembling aspen, hoping the bulk of the rokash would hinder its approach through the saplings.

Bleeding from wounds in neck and chest, the rokash charged into the aspen thicket with terrifying speed and power, snapping the saplings as it came. Dave saw a third arrow sticking in its back as it stretched itself out to lunge for him with its jaws. With two hands on his sword, Dave swung with all his might at the snout. The blade bit, but hit bone and stopped.

The fetid breath of the monster filled him with nausea as the beast careened forward, then lay still. Dave was thrown backward and pinned underneath a tangle of saplings that had been toppled by the wild, terrifying charge of the carnivore.

The rokash did not move. Dave saw Lanomer, the third guard, approach the carcass and prod it a few times with his knife to convince himself it was dead. He quickly came to Dave and began to free him from the sapling that pinned him to the ground. Another Hansa joined the work, and Dave heard other voices speaking excitedly as they entered the clearing. Finally, Lanomer was able to lift enough of the tree trunk to let Dave wriggle out. Dave stood up, towering over Lanomer, and checked to see if he was hurt. He had a few bruises but was otherwise unharmed.

Then he remembered Greeomer, flung into the bushes by the rokash. Lanomer must have seen it also, since he was already moving in that direction. Dave followed him. They found Greeomer lying in some chokecherry bushes. Lanomer was examining Greeomer's chest. "I think several of his ribs are cracked or broken by the blow from the rokash's tail. We need to fabricate a litter, since I doubt he will be able to walk," said Lanomer.

Hanomer approached. Dave and Lanomer explained what had happened and how the guard had been killed. "Oy!" went up Hanomer's cry. "Our joy at the death of the rokash is mingled with grief at the death of a friend and comrade."

They gathered the weapons and remains of their fallen comrade. Even the ground that had collected his spilled blood was taken up and buried along with the weapons and remains in an open glade. Over the burial spot they built a cairn and transplanted yellow forest flowers to the fresh barrow.

The Hansa would not eat the rokash meat. They took its teeth and talons and wrapped them up carefully. Over the place where the rokash had fallen in the aspen grove, they cut down the remaining saplings and built a large pyre and burned the foul-smelling carcass to ash. The company stood solemnly around the burning, grief displacing the merriment that the Hansa would otherwise have felt at such a time. As the carcass burned to embers, everyone, except those on guard duty, laid down to sleep by the fire.

Dave could not sleep. The moon, just rising in the east, was beginning to cast its light on the great river in the valley below. He thought about the day, about the nearness of death and the courage of his Hansa friends. He realized with a start that he naturally thought of them as human, even though they were not. He no longer saw their furry faces, their tails, or their short stature; they were just friends and family. Where did their good nature and joy come from? They were not especially smart. They knew very little about mathematics beyond arithmetic and little about chemistry beyond herb lore. They would not be highly regarded at Halcyon. When he thought about the experiments that would be conducted on the Hansa at Halcyon if their kind were ever captured, he shuddered. Whatever else happens, he must not deliver his Hansa friends to the experimenters at Halcyon!

In the morning they sang a song of lamentation for their fallen comrade and then broke camp. Hanomer had to hurry back to the village to tell the widow of her husband's death. He asked Dave to go with him while the others carried Greeomer on a litter back to the village.

As Dave and Hanomer were climbing back to the narrow defile that led toward the village, Dave asked, "What were you singing about in the song of lamentation?"

"We were rejoicing that Clanomer had left the shadow lands and returned to his true home. But we were also grieved that we will be parted from our brother for a good while and that his wife, children, and grandchildren will miss him deeply."

"I don't understand what you mean by the shadow lands. This valley receives quite a lot of sun," said Dave.

"You do not understand about the shadow lands because you are a mere shadow yourself, friend Dave," said Hanomer.

"What do you mean by that?" stammered Dave.

"Each partial answer brings a host of new questions. If I am to give a partial answer to each new question, we will never get anywhere. Now that your language education is adequate, perhaps I should teach you some of our history," said Hanomer. "This place isn't real," continued Hanomer, "if you take my meaning. In our poetry we talk about this place as if it's a dream or a picture of the real world, which the Creator has made. The things we like, we like because they remind us dimly of the beauty of the real world."

"I don't mean to be rude, Hanomer, but a lot of the things your people believe about this world are wrong. At Halcyon, we have machines and instruments that have given us much knowledge about the world that is frankly beyond you. We know what stars are. We know about—" He wanted to say atoms and molecules, but there were no words. "We know deep things about matter, what causes disease. We also know how to build weapons beyond your wildest imaginings. Back home we had vehicles that could move like the wind for great distances."

"I know you big people are much cleverer than us Hansa. We are a simple folk. We do not have much interest in building machines and instruments, and even if we did, in these shadow lands, we have been given neither the gift nor the interest to explore the knowledge these may bring. But what we have is a love for poetry and the ability to see into the heart of things and rejoice in them as the work of the Creator.

"On the other hand, your people desire power, knowledge, and control for their own sake. Therefore the shadow lands hold a great danger for you. You can choose to make the shadow lands anything you want them to be. When you choose to stop honoring the Creator, you find yourselves living in a dreadful world in which the Creator has no part. You have a longing that cannot be stilled, but the longing unfulfilled only makes you try to fill it with the paltry things that power can bring."

When they reached the village, Hanomer went straight to Clanomer's house and, bidding Dave to wait, entered the burrow alone.

The sad news spread quickly, and the entire village took up the lament. Dave returned to his cottage to think over all that he had heard.

Chapter 30

The Dream

A week later the sharp pain of Clanomer's passing had been blunted to a dull sorrow. His absence was daily noted by his family, friends, and indeed the whole village. At every turn his absence and the loss to the village was acknowledged. Yet in a curious way, the Hansa knew how to celebrate Clanomer's passing and the village's loss without descending into despondency. Deep down Dave marveled that their inherent joy and optimism was undiminished.

Nothing brought home more clearly to Dave this Hansa ability to sorrow on a bed of joy than the announcement that a celebration would be held in the town meadow to commemorate the death of the rokash. Dave expected a dull evening, more of a wake than a celebration. And indeed, the festivities began slowly and solemnly with food and drink. But soon, to Dave's surprise, the younger Hansa were dancing, slowly and quietly at first, and then with much more vigor, laughter, and exuberance. Everyone remarked how Clanomer's place in the village dance was empty, but the joy and laughter could not be suppressed. After everyone had eaten and drunk their fill, the clan chief, Hanomer, rose to speak to the assembled villagers.

"We are remembering the loss of our friend Clanomer and how he gave his life to save those of his companions."

Hanomer bowed his head, and silence fell on the gathering as everyone shared a moment of remembering. Then Hanomer looked up.

"We are also here to honor the hero who vanquished the rokash. We will make him champion of our village."

Dave was still thinking of Clanomer and reliving those terrifying moments with the rokash when his musings were disturbed by the sound of his name, and he roused himself to see all eyes turned toward him. Hanomer beckoned him to come to the center of the circle by the bonfire. "Here is the hero!" said Hanomer, and there was loud table thumping, clapping, and cheering as Dave came into the light. He was delighted by the unexpected honor.

Three sturdy Hansa came forward. One was carrying a tray while the other two carried a large shrouded object. Hanomer took a necklace of rokash teeth from the tray and gestured to Dave to kneel so that he could hang it around his neck. There was loud cheering as Dave received his trophy. Next the shrouded object was brought to Hanomer and Dave. The shroud was removed, revealing a four-foot wooden carving of a rokash about to spring. Around the base of the carving were the remaining teeth and the talons of the beast.

Then the bard of the village came forward and the crowd quieted down. The bard began singing softly. Dave marveled. Hansean was a language far superior at rendering images, to any human tongue he had heard. The lyrics transported Dave back to the valley, and the images of that day filled his mind like a vivid dream. The bard sang:

From mountains cold
And caverns deep
The rokash came
To kill and eat.

With stealth it crept
Through larch and fir
It leapt and killed
Brave Clanomer.

The rokash turned
And fixed its gaze
On one who faced it
Strong and brave.

The rokash leapt
The arrow sang
With hideous voice
The death roar rang.

Rokomer pinned
By mighty foe
The rokash killed
By his last blow.

Dave was stirred from his reverie. "Who is Rokomer?" he asked.

"That is your new name. It is short for 'rokash slayer,'" said Hanomer.

Dave was stunned, but he had no time to think about what had happened. Many of the younger Hansa came to him, asking him over and over again to tell the story of the rokash. He was a poor storyteller by Hansa standards, but he did his best.

After he had told the tale again and again, Dave headed for bed.

In his dream, Dave was standing in a hospital room at the foot of a bed. He saw himself lying on the bed in front of him—at least, the corpse looked like him. He and the corpse were bathed in a wonderful bright light. The light emanated from a hallway. The hallway was a tunnel, and he walked toward this wonderful light, so much brighter than noon sunlight that it hurt his eyes. Even so, it filled him with expectation and delight. He felt a deep longing to go to the light; he felt as if he were going home.

He left the tunnel and emerged onto a broad heath bathed in even brighter sunlight. He looked down, and his limbs and body were made of glass filled with tendrils of brown smoke, without organs or bones. As he looked across the heath he saw others. Some were a deep gray color; others seemed more transparent than he. All were walking toward the light, which emanated, not from a sun in the sky, but from a mountain range far in the distance.

At first the walk was a delight. He enjoyed the smell of the heather, and his longing for the light added a spring to his step. His sense of going home to the light filled him with longing to reach the mountains. As he walked, the light grew stronger and stronger. Some of the others that had been walking with him stopped, and he walked by without speaking to them. Others, who were already stopped when he approached, turned back and began walking away from the light.

The light grew so intense that it began to burn him. Wherever the brown smoky discoloration in his glass body was strongest, the burning pain was most intense. He still wanted to go home to the light, but he had to be clear as glass to get there, and he was not.

With each step the little smoky discoloration that had not mattered at first mattered more and more as the intensity grew. He began to despair. He had so far to go. He was like a dirty projector bulb. If the smoke in his glass body burned now, what would it be like as he approached the mountains that were his destination and home? He seemed to be two people: one loved the heather and intensely longed for the light and the mountains; the other wanted to escape the terrible burning that the light caused.

He stopped, and a battle raged within him. On the one hand his desire for the light was intense, so that even the thought of stopping the journey was unbearable. On the other hand, the pain of the burning was so great he simply could not go on. What was the use! He had so far to go. Finally, his desire to go home to the mountains was overcome by his desire to escape the unbearable burning.

His ego rose as a third voice in his mind. *I choose to be tough and strong like steel. I do not need to go home to the mountain. I cannot change the light, but I can kill my desire for it!*

It came into his mind that he had grown in power since he had left his old body. In his old life, he could not wipe away feelings and desires; but now things were different. If he chose, he could wipe away the desire for the mountains forever, since that was something inside him. Once erased, like a beautiful story wiped from a blackboard, that desire would be gone forever.

He chose; his loneliness and longing for the mountains were wiped away, never to be remembered. When they vanished, he also lost his enjoyment of the heather, the sunlight, and the smell of spring. The place no longer looked like the path to home, and the very things he had enjoyed now angered and offended him. He turned and began to walk away from the repelling light. A part of him had died, but it was a different death from what he had seen in the hospital room.

The scene in the dream changed; much time had passed. Dave was sitting in a vast circle of beings. He was filled with a monumental boredom. He loathed himself and those around him. He was defined by his loathing. Nothing was left to give him delight. By conscious choice, he had slowly erased everything that had once been wholesome and good, because it caused him pain and reminded him of the mountains and the light, which he loathed above all. Now he was left with a vast hatred for himself, for others, but especially for that Being who had made him.

A sepulchral voice spoke in the gloom. He hated that voice—but then Dave hated everything. "We have destroyed everything else that reminded us of Him. We have nothing left to destroy, but our hate for Him has grown like a towering mountain. Let us punish Him who made us. From the heart of hell we will stab Him who still loves us. We will dig a great pit and fill it with burning pain. We will climb in, to our torment, and it will feed our hate. It will reduce our boredom. Each stab of pain we feel will bring pain to Him who created us, and this is how we will punish Him. His love for us is the only weapon we have to torment Him."

And so the dreadful work began on the lake of fire. Driven by hate, they toiled ceaselessly. Their hate for Him continued to grow.

Dave woke up in a sweat and shuddered as he thought about his terrible dream. He went outside to reassure himself that the world was as he remembered it. The day was overcast and somber, like his mood. A hawk circled in the air currents looking for breakfast. He hadn't prayed since that brief cry for help when the apemen had seized him, but he tried to pray now. He stood with his palms flat against each other, but words wouldn't come to him.

"Begging your pardon, Rokomer, there's trouble in the dead city." He turned to see Hanomer standing beside him.

"What kind of trouble?" asked Dave.

"Come have a quick breakfast," said Hanomer. "Then you ought to come with us and see. I will tell you the scout's report on the way."

Chapter 31

City Point

The waterfront was dimly lit by a row of electric lamps running the length of the wharf. A mist from the cool water made the scene indistinct, as if seen through a camera lens coated with Vaseline. Pam scanned the hazy pool of light around the wharf. The boats were gone. They had left without them! Panic began to rise in her mind.

What do we do now? Where do we go? How can I hide Al on this island?

Just as another wave of despair washed over her, she heard the faint sound of oars in the water. A boat with six oarsmen and a coxswain crept into the pool of light and continued to pull until it bumped into the side of the wharf with a gentle clunk. A man, indistinct in the mist, climbed out and scanned the shore.

"Pam!" the man called quietly.

Floyd!

He began to walk along the wharf and repeated his call with increased urgency.

Pam roused herself, left the shadows, and ran to Floyd, relief pouring over her. "We were so afraid you'd left!" she said.

Pam saw concern on Floyd's face in the dim lamplight. "The expedition left early because of the favorable wind. Obedient to orders, we did leave along with them," he said, smiling mischievously. "However we had trouble with our sail just beyond the point, and the other boats sailed on ahead. I think our equipment trouble would have continued until I found you. I'm sorry I gave you such a scare." Floyd peered into the gloom. "Did you get him?"

"Yes," said Pam.

"Then we'd better get back to the boat," said Floyd, "and get underway as soon as possible. Everyone on board is part of the conspiracy, but no one else in the fleet must know."

Dwight and Tom appeared from the shadows, carrying Al.

"Are we glad to see you!" said Dwight to Floyd as he carried the stretcher along the wharf.

Pam looked into the boat. Five faces were smiling up at her, but she didn't recognize any of them. In the back, one of the oarsmen was hunched over, tying his shoe. Floyd and Pam helped Dwight and Tom hand the stretcher to the oarsmen, who placed it gently down amidships, resting on the rowing benches. Floyd held the gunwale while Tom and Dwight took seats beside the stretcher. Pam climbed to the back of the boat and sat on the last rowing bench so she could steady Al's head. As Floyd began to swing the boat around, the rower beside Pam lifted his head, smiled, put his arm around her waist and gave her a squeeze.

"Hi, honey," he said in a low ominous voice. "It's been too long."

Pam stiffened as she heard the familiar voice. Anger mingled with fear and dread rushed into her mind like water bursting a dam.

"Don't touch me! Don't ever touch me again."

———————

Al awoke in a dark place. He tried to get up, but weakness and nausea made him fall back. Even before he was able to focus, he could tell from the rocking motion and the creaking of the rigging that he was in a boat and the boat was underway. He raised his head and looked about the hold. In the gloom he saw his pack and gear next to him. He managed to open the top of his backpack and find his notebook. Seeing his things made him feel more at home. There wasn't enough light to read.

He was so tired. He let his head fall back on his pillow again. Clasping his journal tightly to his chest, he squeezed his eyes shut and searched for memories. He remembered his interview with Jonathan Boyd. After that there were hazy visions of Pam and Dwight and many other people he didn't recognize. A feeling of loneliness descended on him. He began to talk to God in his mind, telling him how he felt and asking for help, even for those in the other world he'd left behind as a result of the dislocation, and he was comforted.

For Al, God formed a link to his old world. He could pray for his parents and siblings and know something was being done. His fatigue hung over him like a cloud. Presently even the mental strain of praying began to be too much for him. The sedative, which lingered in his body, made him fall asleep again.

When he next awoke, a bright shaft of sunlight from an overhead hatch was lighting up a large coiled cable in front of him.

"You're awake," said a familiar voice. He turned and saw Pam sitting beside him. She looked different somehow. Her hair was tied back in a ponytail, except for a rebellious wisp that fell across her forehead.

It was her smile. She hadn't smiled at all when he first met her. *Her smile lights up even the darkened hold of this ship. She's even more beautiful than I remember.*

But there was something else. A cloud of worry hovered about her that she couldn't completely conceal. He could see it in her eyes and in the tightness around the edge of her mouth when she smiled. If anything, the care—mingled with tenderness—etched on her face made her even more beautiful.

He closed his eyes, and when he reopened them Pam was looking down at his jacket in her lap, smoothing it absent-mindedly. He watched her without saying anything, as if she were a much-loved painting.

"Where am I?" asked Al at last.

Pam looked up, startled, but her smile broadened when she saw he was awake enough to converse.

"You're on the Falcon, a Viking longboat under the command of Floyd Linder."

"I feel so strange," said Al. "I don't even know how I got here. The last thing I remember is an interview with Boyd, the psychiatrist."

"It's no wonder," said Pam. "Boyd kept you under sedation in the psych ward."

"Under sedation!" said Al slowly. He still had trouble forming his words. "How long have I been under?"

"It's been a little more than two weeks. We had a devil of a time finding out where you were and an even harder time getting you out!"

Pam gave him a brief description of their escape. Al nodded, his scattered visions and memories falling into place, as Pam recounted their journey to the wharf and then out to sea.

"Where are we going?" he asked.

"We're part of the invasion force to seize and hold the ruined city that we discovered."

A feeling of dread rushed in upon him. "What? When was this decided?" he asked, half rising from his bed.

"Hush now! I've talked far too much already. If it were anyone but me, your doctor would have told them in no uncertain terms to let you rest. There will be time for long explanations later when you're better rested. Now you need to have something to eat."

Pam helped Al sit up and brought him a meal consisting of seaweed, herring filets, and water. Al insisted on eating on his own, but his hands were still so uncoordinated he spilled as much as he was able to spoon into his mouth.

"My turn!" said Pam. She took the plate away from him and fed him rapidly and efficiently. Al's ravenous hunger made even this simple fare seem tasty.

Pam said nothing while he wolfed down the food. She fed him a second plateful, after which he tried to rise but couldn't. He felt as weak as a child and couldn't push himself off the bed.

"Pam, help me get up. I can't stand lying here any longer."

"Al, you're crazy! The sedative is still in your system," Pam protested.

But Al was so insistent she relented.

"All right, I'll help you walk a little. You'd probably get up and try to walk anyway as soon as I was out of sight."

Al smiled. "Hmm, you know me too well!"

Pam helped him up, warning him to keep his head down. He stretched out his hand to shield his head from the deck beams. At 5' 8" Pam could just stand up straight on the lower deck, but Al, was 5' 11', and so had to duck to avoid every deck beam. He could barely walk, and Pam had to support him as he shuffled his way back and forth, tracing a six-foot circular path in the bowels of the boat. Nevertheless, the exercise seemed to do him some good, and he grew steadier as he continued walking back and forth. Finally, he decided to try to go up on deck. After struggling up the ladder, he came out of the hold into brilliant sunshine.

They were on the Halcyon River. With a string of other vessels ahead, theirs seemed to be the last boat. Familiar faces from their previous voyage welcomed Al with warm handshakes and claps on the back. He was surprised to see Dwight and Tom among the crew. He hadn't realized that they had come too. Others were new; he nodded to them, and they returned in kind. He tired quickly but took the time to say "Thank you!" to Floyd, Tom, and Dwight.

The boat was much bigger than Al had realized from his constrained perspective in the aft hold, and he soon determined that a much larger hold in the bow housed the crew when they were not on watch.

The next morning, as Al was back in the aft hold, sitting in a patch of sunlight reading his journal, he heard steps on the ladder. Hoping it was Pam, Al looked up and saw a crewman, descending with his back to Al. The large man seemed familiar. When he turned, Al recognized him. It was Stan Bigelow.

"Hey, how are you, Al?" said Stan, offering his hand.

Al was pleased and shook it warmly. He and Stan had had their differences, and Al was glad to be able to make peace.

"I'm on the mend. I did not know you were part of this, Stan. Thanks for helping me out!"

"No problem, Al. Pam means a lot to me, and so I wanted to help. Besides, I couldn't let an opportunity to be of service pass me by. After all, that's what comrades are for, right?"

Al smiled at him and searched his face.

Is he mocking me?

"Well, I'd better get back to the rowers' bench. I just wanted to say hello, since I'd heard you were up."

With that he patted Al on the shoulder and climbed back up on deck.

Five minutes later, Al was trying to write in his journal, but his thoughts kept returning to Stan. *What did Stan mean by "Pam means a lot to me"?*

He heard someone else climb down the ladder. This time, it was Pam. He smiled.

Pam looked at him critically, hands on hips, and then sat on a box in a beam of light.

"I see you've been up and about," she said. "I hope you're not overdoing it." "Yes, I feel much stronger today," said Al. "Honestly, I've been behaving myself!"

"Yeah, sure." Pam looked at the open journal he was holding. "Whatcha working on?"

"I had some time to amuse myself, since I am not up to rowing yet, so I thought I'd doodle."

"May I see it?" asked Pam. Al reddened but handed the notebook over without comment. He'd been working on a poem. Pam started to read it out loud.

The Day the World Changed

"Halcyon proudly strode ahead
The future sure in glory bright
Fearing neither God nor man
Forbidden knowledge—keen delight.

"Without remorse they toiled and dug
We can—we will! Their keening cry
No bound or limit stayed their quest
Until the blinding change of sky.

"And now despair has gripped my soul
All friends and soul mates stripped away
I'm chained to foes who warp my mind
Who chafe and grind till spirit fray.

"I cried to Him from deep despair
For solace to my wounded soul
The silent torment grew and grew
No whisper came to make me whole.

"A tiny light I saw afar
Beauty past the ken of men
The light cast shadows in my gloom
I'd learned to love and dream again!

"She filled me with such sharp delight
Her laugh, her smile, that wisp of hair
She knew not how much joy she brought
She lifted me from deep despair.

"You may forever stay afar
Yet love and beauty mingled sing
Your song that wakened up my soul
And taught me new to love my King.

"A day of warmth was my request
He answered with a blessed spring
I prayed and sought a crust of bread
He raised me up and made me king."

Pam's voice faltered, and Al saw her turn crimson in the sunlight. She swallowed hard and answered in a quiet, low voice. "I'm sorry, Albert. I shouldn't have barged in and so cavalierly read your journal. This poem - it's beautiful, but very personal." With that she thrust the notebook back at Al and rushed up the ladder.

Al tried to speak, but no words came. For once he didn't know what to say.

I've really done it now! I've scared her away. Whatever possessed me to imagine that she could ever love a clumsy oaf like me!

The next few days followed a familiar routine. Al spent the day walking and exercising on deck and gradually regaining his strength. Determined not to frighten Pam again, he was careful not to appear too eager to enter into conversation with her. Pam still brought him his meals below decks, but she said nothing more. Their times were awkward and filled with uncomfortable silences. Every time she came, Al wanted to take away the wall that had grown between them, but he didn't know what to say.

The boat made rapid progress. Unlike the previous voyage, they did not camp during the journey upriver but kept moving at the best possible speed. When the wind was favorable, the crew was able to relax, but when it was not, the crewmen took turns rowing. After three days, Al took his turn at the rower's bench, joining the crew in the forward berth when his watch was up. Now there was even less of a chance of talking to Pam privately.

It was a bright sunny day when they arrived at the stone pier and the road to the dead city. However, instead of moving to Fort Linderhof, the expedition stopped at the large island previously used as their campsite.

The island was shaped like a linden leaf with the stem and a large piece ripped out the bottom end. Twenty-five longboats were crowded into this eastern bay, hull to hull. Planks were placed from boat to boat, and the crews began unloading their supplies. Each boat's company was assigned a separate campsite on the island. The center of the island had a rocky plateau that provided an excellent view of the jetty and Fort Linderhof. This plateau became the command center and home of the First Platoon. Floyd located the Twenty-fifth, his own platoon, on the west tip of the island, well removed from the others.

Al had kept his scraggly beard from the hospital and wore a toque as he helped unload the longboat in the hope that he wouldn't be recognized. No one seemed to take any notice of him, and he made four uneventful trips from the boat to the campsite and then helped set up the tents. Al, Dwight, and Tom would occupy a tent set apart from the rest in a small glade. Floyd obviously didn't want to draw attention to the fact that his platoon had twenty-nine members rather than the twenty-five had by all the others.

When the tents were set up, Al decided he had to talk to Pam alone, even if he risked frightening her off for good. He'd had no chance of doing so on board the ship because of the crowded conditions, but he felt so agitated by the change in their relationship that he wanted to do or say something to at least try to return to their former friendship.

Pam's tent was in the main glade, and Al went back there now. After the arduous unloading, everyone was lounging around, waiting for the inevitable orders for their next move. Al spotted Pam sitting with five other girls, chatting and laughing, at one end of the glade. He winced inwardly, but setting his jaw and putting his hands in his pocket, he sauntered over, trying his best to give the impression of nonchalance.

He failed. The conversation stopped as he approached, and six faces turned towards him. Pam's face had the hint of a smile, but the other five had broad knowing smirks; they knew what he was about. He felt the color rise in his face.

"Pam, could I speak to you for a few minutes?" His voice quavered as he spoke.

She rose immediately, "Of course!" She walked directly to him, and Al saw the smiles around the circle broaden even further.

They said nothing for a while until they reached the western shore of the island and walked along a stretch of sandy beach.

"Pam," said Al, "I wanted to thank you again for rescuing me from Boyd's captivity."

She turned to look him full in the face, a hint of disappointment or even sadness about her eyes and mouth. "I'm your friend, Al. Of course I'd try to rescue you," she said softly and reproachfully.

Another silence. "Is that what you wanted to tell me?" asked Pam.

"That's part of it," said Al. "But there's something else. I'm sorry I embarrassed you with that poem—"

"I wasn't embarrassed!" said Pam. "After I read it, I knew I'd had no business taking it and reading it without permission. It was an intrusion, and I'm sorry."

"But why has such a wall gone up between us? Things aren't the same."

Pam put her hand on his arm. "Al, you're in great danger here, and seeing me is only making your danger greater. We need to stay apart." She looked up past his shoulder and her eyes widened.

"What do you mean?" asked Al.

"I've got to go!" She started to run away. She turned suddenly. "I'm sorry!" She turned and ran back to camp.

Al turned around to see what had startled Pam. In the distance he saw Stan with a scowl on his face.

Why didn't she want Stan to see us?

He remembered Stan's statement in the ship, and the realization struck like a blow.

What a fool I've been! How could I be so blind? So that's what Stan meant by "Pam means a lot to me." Am I so weak in her eyes that she has to protect me from Stan's wrath?

Al didn't go back to camp but morosely sat on a log by the shore and looked west, watching the sun make its way toward the western horizon. He thought about Pam, about how much he cared for her, and the unexpected turn of events. He half expected Stan to come over and tell him to "stay away from my girlfriend." He was angry enough that he wished Stan would come over. But Stan did not.

———

Events began to move even more quickly than Al had anticipated. That evening, the expedition commander called a meeting of the platoon commanders at the headquarters. When Floyd returned, he called everyone together around the campfire.

"I have some news. Seven ships are heading back to Halcyon with skeleton crews of six to become our supply line. In about two weeks, a ship ought to be arriving every two days. Three platoons will be sent to retake and hold Fort Linderhof. We'll join that group, since we discovered the place. Our plan is to move to the deserted city in

force and hold it. I don't know why the 'higher-ups' think this place is so important, but we're going to try very hard to control it."

"Who's in charge of the expedition?" asked one of the newcomers.

"Glenn MacDonald. You may remember he's second in command of the naval base on Halcyon Island. He's brought a crew from the installation. They make up the first four crack platoons. The First, Second, and Third platoons will be joining us at Fort Linderhof with Duncan McTavish, MacDonald's lieutenant, leading us to Linderhof. Any other questions?"

There were no further questions. "Okay, then, get some sleep now. We move at 0600 sharp," he said. The group dispersed.

When the three friends were lying in their bedrolls, Tom said, "This place still has bad memories for you, doesn't it, Al?"

"Am I that easy to read?"

Tom just chuckled in response.

"Yes, you're right, Tom," continued Al. "I can still see Dave being overwhelmed by the apemen. It was horrible. Now we're going back there, and I'm afraid. The fear of that place is beginning to gnaw at my gut. I don't really think these cowboys from the naval station know what they're getting into."

The next morning was overcast, promising rain. Four of the longboats were made ready as the four platoons gathered on the island shore. Duncan McTavish, the commander of this small expedition to Fort Linderhof, looked on in silence while Glenn MacDonald, the expedition commander, addressed the four platoons.

"We've been observing the shore," he said, "and we've seen no sign of life. Don't use your rifles unless you absolutely must, since our ammunition is limited. If you do fire off a shot, make sure you pick up your expended shell casings. We can recharge them. If the shore is clear, move up to Fort Linderhof and secure it. Set up the winch and the rope ladder so we can resupply you or even evacuate you using the river in case of trouble. It's important you make Linderhof as secure as possible so we can make our move toward the city."

The quiet optimism of MacDonald and McTavish filled Al with dread, but he said nothing, remaining quietly in the background with the rest of the Twenty-fifth Platoon.

Their landing was not opposed; they didn't see a single apeman. Even at Fort Linderhof, there wasn't a single corpse to be found from the many killed during the previous assault. When Al peered into the chasm, he saw no evidence of any bodies. To a keen observer, only broken weapons, black with dried blood, and empty shell casings indicated that a battle had recently taken place there.

The crew put the winch and rope ladder in place, and hauled supplies up from the boats to the Fort Linderhof mesa. The slow process of preparing the fort for an assault on the city began to take shape. Floyd's platoon worked on fortifying the mesa while scouting parties led by the First, Second, and Third platoons ranged to within sight of the city. There was no sign of any apemen or any other opposition. Even animal life seemed absent from the rocky spur that stretched from the deserted city to Fort Linderhof.

One particularly curious development for Al was the appearance of Bertrand Hoffstetter at Fort Linderhof. Al hadn't been aware that the physicist and senator had been part of the expedition, but seeing Hoffstetter Al assumed his cover would be blown and he'd have to report to McTavish to explain his presence on the mission. Fortunately, the summons never came.

Although people displayed deference to Hoffstetter because of his status as a senator, his shipmates disliked him for his arrogance and air of superiority. Nevertheless, he seemed unaffected by the muted hostility and set up a tent by himself on the west side of the plateau. Hoffstetter passed close by Al on several occasions but appeared to take no notice of him, or perhaps he deliberately chose to not recognize him. Al wondered if he'd worried unnecessarily.

Chapter 32

Return to the City
of the Dead

The initial scouting having shown no sign of opposition, McTavish proceeded, with all haste, to move his four platoons to take control of the dead city. Four new platoons were to take their place at Fort Linderhof and cover their retreat in case of attack while the advance party moved on the deserted city. Four small scouting parties from the First Platoon set out very early in the morning.

This expedition had fuel cells to power short-range radios. By 8:00 a.m., Fort Linderhof received a communication from City Point, the name given to the island base that they were to proceed. The three remaining platoons, heavily laden with supplies, hurried down the path to the road. Marching quickly, they waved to the scouts who'd taken up observation positions along the way.

At about 10:00 a.m., they reached the broken main gate of the city. Several soldiers from the first platoon ascended to the top of the first tower and set up a winch. They hauled supplies up onto the outer wall, and made their base camp on top of the wall near the main gate.

Floyd's platoon set up camp, while the other three platoons hurried off along the wall, retracing the route Dave, Pam, and Al had taken to the citadel. With a radio link established, Floyd was to report every hour to the main headquarters at City Point.

Nothing happened for about forty-five minutes. Suddenly a tremendous explosion shattered the silence of the city. A cloud of dust rose from the mountainside. Floyd rushed to the radio and called headquarters. He returned, relief on his face.

"They were sent to blow up the tower and block the cave entrance," he said. "That was the explosion we heard. Those cowboys could have told us what they were up to rather than scaring the living crap out of us!" he exclaimed.

Everyone went back to the task of setting up camp and barricading the top of the wall against attack. An hour later, the three platoons returned. Obviously weary, dusty, and stressed, the terrifying strain of the dead city showed on their faces.

Once camp was established, Floyd's platoon left the city to collect firewood. Lugging wood made for hard work and a long day. Al was getting hungry; he could smell the fires burning on top of the wall and the meals being prepared by the other platoons. The sun had begun to poke through the overcast sky, but now more clouds began to move in from the west, and soon the whole sky was overcast again.

Late in the afternoon, a shout came from the wall that supper was ready. Al and Pam had not exchanged more than a couple of words all day. Al found her presence increasingly awkward, for although he wanted to speak to her, he dreaded another rebuff. Stan's constant menacing presence only made things worse.

They ate by platoons. Floyd's platoon ate in silence. Al's dread of this place had grown throughout the day. He thought, at first, that it was due to the memory of his last trip, but he also saw dread in the drawn and fearful faces of his companions. A nameless fear gnawed at the whole company. The only exception seemed to be Hoffstetter, who had come with the First Platoon. His face was enlivened by eagerness and impatience rather than fear.

Finally, after supper, in the early evening, McTavish called the four platoons together and stood on the outer parapet facing them.

"We're going to spend the night here," he said. "Tomorrow, if all is well, another four platoons will join us, and we'll move to the citadel. I think we successfully blocked the tunnel, so we should be safe from attack from that quarter. Once we're in the citadel, we'll rig an escape route along the mountain wall in case we have any serious trouble. In any case, we ought to be able to barricade the inner gate and man that wall with our people. Any questions?"

Al could feel the fear in the company. He wanted to pack up his gear—no, hang it all, leave his gear—and rush back to Fort Linderhof.

Floyd was the only one with the courage to ask questions. "Why are we here? What are we looking for?"

"I haven't been told," said McTavish. "I only know that I'm to secure the citadel and make it a base of operations. I'm a soldier, and I'm going to obey those orders without question."

"Maybe the senator," said Floyd, gesturing at Hoffstetter, "could tell us why the senate is so interested in this city?"

McTavish scowled and opened his mouth, but Hoffstetter waved him to silence.

"Surely you can see," said Hoffstetter, "how extraordinary a find this city represents to our community of Halcyon! A wholly alien city on our planet! This changes everything. The people of Halcyon, isolated and vulnerable as we are, must know without delay if this city or its potential inhabitants represent a danger to our small community. Then perhaps, with this early knowledge, we can take steps to build a defense. On the positive side, what if there are archeological and technological advances to be discovered here? We could learn much that could help us adapt to this world."

Beet red with rage, McTavish could contain himself no longer. "We're here to obey the senate, not question them. Let's have no more questions!

"The Second Platoon will take the first watch, followed by the Third. The Twenty-fifth takes the morning watch. Dismissed! Linder, could I see you for a minute, please?"

Al returned with the rest of his platoon to their camp on the wall nearest the main gate. As the dusk deepened, the company's feelings of fear and despair increased palpably, and there was none of the cheerful banter that normally accompanied their time together.

Fifteen minutes later Floyd returned, his expression livid. He sat beside Al. "McTavish reamed me out for challenging his authority with my impertinent question. He thinks we made up the story about the apemen." He took off his hat and slapped it across his knee. "Since we have no military training, he figures we were so scared by this city we made up the story to save face."

"That's ridiculous!" said Al.

"I know, I know, but as McTavish pointed out, there are no bodies, no bones, or even skeletons. There were none in the upper city either!"

"But they carried them off! We saw that in the citadel," interrupted Al. "How does he explain the weapons?"

"He doesn't. His explanation doesn't really hold together, but it means he doesn't really trust our platoon. We will continue to get these 'support assignments' to keep us out of the way, and because McTavish doesn't take our situation as seriously as he should, we're all in more danger than before."

"And everything we say," ventured Al, "will be taken as further evidence of our undisciplined paranoia and so will be disregarded?"

"That's right," said Floyd.

Al tried to get some sleep. However, the feeling of dread was so real that he couldn't close his eyes. He left the tent. The darkness was so complete he couldn't see either the inner or outer parapet of the wall. He made his way by feel to the outer wall and looked into the inky blackness toward Fort Linderhof. The dull glow of a distant fire at the fort was some comfort. The time passed slowly.

He heard Tom whispering, "Are you out here, Al?"

"I'm over here," Al said softly. He felt an outstretched hand touch him as a shape loomed beside him.

"I couldn't sleep either," said Tom. "Where did Dave get killed?"

"Over by that tower that McTavish blew up. I do not want to talk about that now. Let's wait until morning."

They sat in silence for a minute.

"Tom?"

"Yeah?"

"Thanks for coming to get me."

"I'm your friend," said Tom. "Of course I was going to come and get you. Anyway, it was Pam. She was the one who found out where you were, recruited us, and organized our little conspiracy. That's one determined woman when she makes up her mind."

"No kidding. Anyway, I wanted to say thanks."

"You're right about one thing though," said Tom slowly and deliberately.

"What's that?"

"My relationship with you and Dwight has changed. I've thought about it quite a bit since our last conversation."

"So why has our friendship changed?" asked Al.

"I guess from where I sit, I thought you were taking liberties with our friendship to put an oar in where it wasn't wanted. I don't mean to be rude, but both you and Dwight are legalistic and don't approve of my relationship with Lynn. I figured that was my business and none of yours, and I wanted to spare us all the embarrassment of tiptoeing around this disagreement."

"You're right, of course, about our disagreement, but why does that make us legalistic?"

There was a pause in the conversation. The utter darkness made this conversation almost like talking on the telephone. One had to glean all information about the other person's reactions from their voice alone.

"If Lynn and I love each other," said Tom haltingly, "and we want to sleep together, what's wrong with that? We just want to have a good time. Prove to me that it's wrong. Making up arbitrary rules to say it's wrong is legalistic."

Al's feet scraped on the rock as he sat on a step. "Is anything wrong with anything?" he said.

"What?" said Tom.

"I'm trying to answer your question. Is there anything, anything at all, that is wrong?"

"Of course there is!"

"Like what?" said Al.

"Well," said Tom, "like murder, rape, stealing, genocide. What's your point?" Tom's voice had grown louder.

"Well, let's take murder," said Al softly, as if he were discussing the weather, "what's really wrong with murder? Prove to me that murder is wrong without being legalistic."

"For one thing, you're hurting someone. Lynn and I aren't hurting anyone."

"Aren't you? But let's leave you and Lynn for the moment. Getting back to murder, I concede of course that someone gets hurt when you murder them, but so what? What's wrong with hurting people?" This conversation was taking the edge off Al's fear of the place.

"You're kidding me, right?" said Tom. "Everyone knows that murder is wrong. How would you like it if someone murdered you or your friends? How can you question if it's wrong?"

"You know that both you and I think murder is a terrible thing, but I want to understand how one can reasonably get there without being, as you put it, legalistic," said Al. "Maybe your revulsion and my revulsion to murder are just a feeling or an emotion on our part. It might simply be my biochemistry that makes the cessation of life unpleasant. However, we began this conversation with the statement you made asking me to prove to you that sleeping with Lynn is wrong. I simply wanted an example, the simplest possible example, that there can be one thing that can be proven wrong without resorting to rules. Show me how you prove that anything is wrong. Even horrendous deeds like murder, rape, or genocide. Saying 'everyone agrees that it's wrong' doesn't prove it to be wrong. At the risk of preaching, things can really only be wrong if there is some kind of moral or ethical law outside ourselves, akin to the physical laws, which we offend by breaking that law. If morality is real, you and I have to discover it, not invent it. If morality and virtue are relative and made up arbitrarily, there is not a single act that can be demonstrated to be wrong by trying to answer the question 'what's wrong with this or that act or behavior?'"

Silence. Finally, not wishing to leave it there, Al began again. "Tom, I'm sorry I went on so long. I'd be lying if I said that I didn't believe what you and Lynn are doing is wrong, but I sincerely believe it's equally wrong for me to use our friendship to punish you for your actions. If my assessment is wrong, you and Lynn will be fine. If my assessment is right, then wrong actions will bring bad consequences, and in that case, as your friend, I would want to be there to help in any way I can. Can't we agree to disagree about your relationship with Lynn and maintain our friendship?"

"Al, when you disapprove of my relationship with Lynn, you're disapproving of and rejecting me. How can we go on from there?"

"Tom, if we don't go on from there, won't we just be two solitudes, unable to discuss or share? We can't have friendship without honesty. We have to work through this. As far as I'm concerned, I've put my oar in, spoken my mind, and done my duty by you as your friend. Now let's move on. My silence doesn't mean I've changed my mind—only that I want to move on."

By unspoken agreement they decided to talk about something else. Al and Tom were still talking when Lyle McGrath, the leader of the Third Platoon, came to hand over responsibilities for the next watch to them.

Floyd's platoon took over the watch along the wall. There was not a star to be seen, and the early morning was even darker than before. Al and Tom were given the east end of the encampment, just past one of the watchtowers, where a crude wall of broken stone and branches had been erected to hinder a potential attack by enemies creeping along the top of the wall.

Floyd came to show Al and Tom their guard position. They walked past the tents of the First Platoon. By the light of a lantern inside a tent, they could see Hoffstetter's corpulent silhouette against the fabric. He was holding an oblong object about the length of his forearm the way a mother would hold a baby. They heard soft songs in a language they did not understand. Al looked at Floyd questioningly, and Floyd shrugged his shoulders.

Leaving this solitary light, they made their way by feel to their guard position, staying close to the outer parapet. They had to pass through the darker gloom of one of the towers, and Al felt the hackles rise on the back of his neck as the draft coming up the tower stairs from the dead city below blew against his face.

"This is it," said Floyd. "Your job is to make sure nothing creeps along the wall or climbs up the stairs in the tower. Good luck!" They heard him pick his way back toward the light, seeing the silhouette of his frame against the dull light from Hoffstetter's tent.

Al wanted to talk about what they had seen in Hoffstetter's tent, but he was afraid to speak for fear of alerting an approaching enemy. They stood at their post, seeing nothing, but straining their ears for any sound. There were noises, some from outside the city wall. A stone rattled below inside the dead city and echoed hollowly among the stone buildings. But silence followed. This sequence of noise, followed by fear, followed by silence was wearing on their nerves.

At last the east lightened, and Al could see his hands and the end of his crossbow. As the light grew, he looked back along the wall to the camp and saw Hoffstetter making his way slowly toward them.

"He's up early," said Tom, gesturing with his crossbow toward the ambling figure.

"Perhaps he didn't sleep at all," said Al. "I wonder what he wants. He hasn't given our platoon the time of day until now. He spends almost all of his time with McTavish and his subordinate—what's his name?"

"His name is Jim Wilson," said Tom.

By this time Hoffstetter had reached Tom and Al. He looked directly at Al, smiled, and held out his hand.

"Al Gleeson, if I'm not mistaken," said Hoffstetter.

Al reluctantly took his hand and felt himself blushing.

"Senator Hoffstetter!" said Al.

"So I get to speak again to the famous Al Gleeson," said Hoffstetter, "the hero of the first expedition to this place. I never forget a face."

Al shifted position uncomfortably, dreading the next question about his presence here. It never came.

"I'm very interested in the apemen," continued Hoffstetter. "Would you tell me about them?"

"There's not much to tell," said Al. "Since we haven't seen any, I think McTavish has begun to wonder if they exist at all."

Hoffstetter laughed easily. The laugh, in Al's mind contrived and intended to simulate friendship, increased Al's distrust of the man. Hoffstetter kept looking at Al, expecting more, so Al felt compelled to go on.

"There's not much to tell," repeated Al. "They're shorter than we are and look something like the pictures we see of hominid reconstructions. We shot several as they attacked. They kept coming until they had been so damaged that they couldn't continue. The curious thing is they weren't like animals. Animals show emotion and run to protect themselves. These seemed more like machines."

"Where'd they come from?"

"I'm not really sure. If I had to guess, I'd guess they came out of the tunnel that McTavish blew up yesterday. We were trapped in a tower when they arrived, so we didn't really see where they came from."

"Hmmm," said Hoffstetter, "although I'm a physicist, I'm very interested in human evolution. I used all my pull as a senator to be allowed to look at these pre-humans first hand. I'd been hoping we'd see some by now."

Al extended his hand to Hoffstetter.

"Well, Professor Hoffstetter, we're likely to see the apemen soon enough, although I'm pretty sure we'll wish we hadn't seen them. Thank you for stopping by to say hello. I think McTavish would want us to keep attentive, so we should get back to our sentry duty."

Hoffstetter's eyes hardened, but he took Al's hand and then also shook Tom's.

Then he smiled. "Of course, duty calls. If anything further comes to mind, please come and see me." With that he strode back to camp.

"Why is he here anyway? Shouldn't he be trying to get us home?" said Tom.

"There's more to this than he's telling us. I wish I knew what it was." And Al turned to scan the wall once again.

Chapter 33

The Citadel

Just as the light grew stronger, a drizzle began. They hastily built a campfire in the tower, and everyone took turns warming up their breakfast. After breakfast, they broke camp as quickly as they could and began the trek along the wall. Apparently, when McTavish had contacted headquarters at City Point, the decision had been made to move as quickly as possible to the citadel and not wait for the reinforcements. The drizzle probably had something to do with this change of plans.

The Twenty-fifth Platoon was in the rear and had been given the task of carrying as much firewood as they could manage. When they reached the last tower by the mountainside, the First Platoon scouted the citadel while the Second guarded the road from the last tower to the citadel gates. Within ten minutes McTavish reappeared and waved them all in.

When they had gathered just inside the citadel gates, McTavish began issuing orders. He had to shout to be heard over the steady rain. The First and Second platoons were to make a thorough search of every building. The Third Platoon was divided in half. One half was ordered to guard the rubble heap blocking the tunnel, and the other half was asked to guard the citadel gate and see if they could close it and fortify it. Finally, Floyd's platoon was told to find a way to rig climbing ropes up the mountain face to provide a backdoor escape route out of the citadel in case they were trapped.

As the group dispersed, Floyd asked Al and Pam to oversee the escape construction. Doing so would be awkward; they had been avoiding each other since their walk at City Point. Al tried to appear nonchalant, as if nothing were wrong.

"What do you think, Pam?" he asked.

Pam put her hands on her hips and thought for a moment.

"We know where the ledge is, but we're not sure where we'll be trapped. Why not set up two escape routes, one from the citadel wall and one from the rubble heap?"

"That's good!" said Al. "We should also find a position that we could man to cover our retreat, since we have more than 100 people to get up the mountainside."

They placed pitons and ropes from the top of the rubble heap to the ledge they had used during their previous escape. They also placed ropes and pitons from the top of the citadel wall up the mountainside as a second access point for an escape. They then climbed to a higher ledge, which backed into a shallow cave. At the back of this cave there was a small, deep pool. Although no visible spring flowed into the pool, a small stream flowed out and ran out of the cave, cascading down rock fissures, alternately appearing and disappearing from view until it bubbled into a small pool on the west side of the citadel square.

This ledge was ideal as a lookout post. One could survey the whole citadel and even see the main gate. Roughhewn seats in the stone indicated that this had been used for such a purpose at a previous time.

Working together did much to relieve the tension between them. Both Pam and Al were so engrossed in their work they forgot the recent past for a time, and talked eagerly about the next phase of the project.

By late afternoon the rain had stopped and the ropes for the escape route were in place.

The First and Second platoons chose to occupy two buildings on the plaza near the main citadel gate. McTavish decided he would use a building at the southwest side of the plaza as his headquarters and assigned the building next to his to Floyd's Twenty-fifth Platoon. There was a tower back of Floyd's building and a stair to the west citadel wall. McTavish asked each platoon to organize their own sentry schedule. Floyd was given responsibility for the lookout ledge and the west portion of the wall.

As evening came, the clouds had cleared and the moon was already high over Halcyon. The next day would see another four platoons enter the city.

Early in the morning, during the third watch, Al was on the lookout ledge while Tom and Dwight were patrolling the west wall. In the pale, pre-dawn light, Al saw two dark figures cross the plaza toward the tower rubble. One of them looked to be Hoffstetter, by his ponderous size and curious shuffling gait. He couldn't be sure of the other. They began climbing the rubble as if looking for something.

This seems very odd. Should I raise the alarm? For what? Maybe McTavish sent them to look for something? At four in the morning? McTavish already thinks I'm a civilian who bolts at every shadow. Do I really want to add to that?

Eventually Al lost sight of them in the shadows of the rubble. He did not see them reappear.

Soon the sun was up, and a short time later, there was a flurry of activity as the camp started to rouse.

Floyd came up to the lookout and said, "We can't find Jim Wilson."

"Is Hoffstetter still here?" asked Al.

"Why? Do you know something?"

"During my watch I thought I saw Hoffstetter and another guy search for something at the tower rubble heap. I lost them in the shadows and didn't see where they went. Maybe the second person was Wilson?"

"You'd better go and report it to McTavish," said Floyd. "I'll relieve you and watch for you here at the lookout post."

Al climbed down and went looking for McTavish. At first the adjutant informed Al the platoon commander was busy. But Al insisted, so the assistant relented and let him in.

McTavish looked up from a crude map of the city he was studying and said rather brusquely, "What can I do for you?"

"Linder sent me down," said Al. "I've been up at the lookout, and I have some information that might be useful."

"Go on."

"It was early in the morning, before first light. I saw two people crossing the square to the rubble heap. They climbed about the heap as if searching for something, and then I lost them in the shadows. Although I kept watching, I never did see them go back the way they came."

"Did you recognize either of them?" asked McTavish.

"One of them looked like Hoffstetter, but I wasn't sure about the other one. Hoffstetter wouldn't also be missing, would he?"

"You know about Wilson, do you?"

"Yes, Linder told me."

McTavish then called an aide and asked for a thorough search for Hoffstetter.

"If it's all right with you," said Al, "I'd like to return to my post, since Linder is standing in for me."

"Yes, of course," said McTavish. "Thank you," he added perfunctorily, without gratitude.

As McTavish turned his eyes back to the map, Al made his way out of the building, across the square, and back up to the lookout. He told Floyd of his conversation with McTavish and then resumed his sentry duties. When the bell sounded that his watch was over, he returned to his room and met Floyd just coming to see him. They sat down on a stone bench in the corner.

"As you might have guessed," said Floyd, "Hoffstetter is also missing."

"What does this all mean?" asked Al. "Where could they have gone?"

The two said nothing for a few moments.

"I think I would have seen them if they'd left the rubble heap. Could they have become trapped in the rubble?"

"Maybe they found a way into the tunnel," said Floyd. "Why don't we look where you think you saw them?"

They crossed the square and made their way toward the rubble heap. At Al's direction they began at the bottom and searched. The broken stone was treacherous, and some pieces shifted when they put their weight on them. Finally, near the top they found a large section of the tower that had collapsed. By worming their way through a window, they found an open space in the rubble. They squeezed through gaps between large blocks of stone for about thirty feet until they came upon a larger pocket, which was lit by a greenish glow. The glow came from an opening that looked into a long tunnel.

"So this is where they went," said Floyd. "Why would they come here?"

"And why would Wilson go with Hoffstetter?" asked Al. "I can see Hoffstetter being a little cracked, but why Wilson?"

Floyd grimaced. "I don't know. I really don't know," he said. "Now what do we do?"

"Right now everything is conjecture," said Al. "We really aren't sure that Wilson and Hoffstetter went inside. I've already gone to McTavish once. If we go again we'll reinforce his conviction that we're not good enough to be part of a military operation."

"I guess you're right," said Floyd. "If he really takes your story seriously, he'll send some one here to investigate, and then he'll know as much as we know now. Let's wait and see what McTavish does. Eventually we'll have to tell him. Should we block up this hole?"

"I'd like to!" said Al. "But if we do, how will Wilson and Hoffstetter get back if they find their way back to the tunnel? I think the best we can do is wait for McTavish to act on what I told him, and keep an eye on the rubble hole from the lookout."

McTavish ordered Floyd's platoon to stand guard over the citadel while the other three platoons searched the lower city, house to house. Late in the afternoon, four more platoons arrived from City Point and were given another large building to use as their barracks.

Since Al had the second dogwatch from 16:00 to 18:00 for the coming evening and had agreed to take the midnight to 04:00 watch for Stan, he slept until early in the afternoon, had a bite to eat, and then caught up on the latest news. There was still no sign of Wilson or Hoffstetter. Much of the lower city remained to be searched, but there was no trace of recent human activity anywhere.

Al climbed back up to the perch a little before his watch was due to start, to relieve Pam, who had the watch before him. She seemed quite on edge. They talked for a few minutes. She'd not seen or heard anything, but she'd had the uncomfortable feeling that she was being watched.

She said good night and made her way back down. Al watched her longingly until she was out of sight. He knew better than to dwell on her and forced himself to deliberately look around the citadel. He also had the uncomfortable feeling that he was being watched.

The moon was just setting. Al could see the dark figures of the sentries on the citadel wall below him. Occasionally the moonlight glinted from a crossbow or a drawn blade.

"Al!" a voice whispered from behind him.

Al froze. A chill crept along his spine.

"Al, it's me, Dave."

Almost against his will, Al forced himself to turn around. The cave behind him was pitch black. A large figure loomed. Al stifled a cry. He tried to speak, but his voice quavered.

"Is that really you, Dave? It can't be! You're alive?"

"Yes, I'm alive," Dave said quietly as he walked out and sat down beside Al. Al saw a large figure towering above him in the starlight. Steeling himself he grabbed his arm and felt buckskin. They clapped each other on the back, and Al felt the air squeezed from his lungs as he was crushed in a bear hug. It was Dave. If anything, he seemed quieter and stronger than before, and there was an aura of confidence about him that was communicated by his bearing. He was stern and dignified, like an ancient king coming to a parley, yet at the same time young and full of health.

Al was filled with sudden joy and grabbed his arm again. "I thought you were dead!"

"I know," said Dave. "After the apemen got me, I thought I was dead too."

"Why all the secrecy?" said Al. "Why didn't you rejoin us as soon as we came?"

"I met some friends. Listen, Al, you're in great danger—"

"I know, the apemen," said Al.

"No!" said Dave. "A much bigger danger even than the apemen. Hoffstetter has betrayed you."

"What are you talking about?" asked Al.

Dave took a deep breath. "Let me tell you my whole story. Let me tell it to you from the beginning and then you'll understand. Then we've got to decide what to do about it."

Chapter 34

Taking Possession

So Dave recounted his story from the time of his capture to the present. After telling of his rescue by the apemen, his education by the Hansa, and his adventure with the rokash, he told Al about the most recent part of his story. He remembered clearly how Hanomer had told him that the expedition had arrived on the great river and how he and Hanomer had set out to investigate.

Dave and Hanomer paddled up the lake to the tunnel leading into the mountain, and landed on the beach by the subterranean waterfall. On the way, Hanomer told Dave what had happened.

"One of our scouts was on the great river yesterday, and he saw many large boats. They landed at the quay opposite the dead city and began to set up camp. I fear they are up to some mischief."

"Hanomer," said Dave, "you've been reluctant to talk about the dead city and the apemen. Is there anything you want to tell me?"

Hanomer was silent and became introspective, as the Hansa often did, as if listening to a voice Dave couldn't hear. Finally, he said, "I will tell you, but the whole tale is far too long for this journey. I will tell you some, if you promise not to ply me with questions while I'm telling you the story. You are hasty, Dave, and often destroy a good tale with too many questions."

"All right," said Dave, hopeful that he might get some of his questions answered.

"Many long years ago there was a city of men here—men very much like you," he said.

"You mean, there are others like me here—"

"You promised not to interrupt with questions!" said Hanomer.

"Okay, okay!" said Dave, completely bewildered by this new revelation.

"They worshipped the Creator and took delight in growing things. Although they made some things out of metal, their real skill and creativity was directed toward bending plants and animals to their will. They were koibanthu, or 'life changers' in your tongue. They could not make anything wholly new, but they could mold and change plants and animals to their own purpose. While their purpose remained pure and they served the Creator, their plant and animal creations were good. In those days there was friendship between our people and theirs.

"Eventually, though, other men came from across the sea and taught them many new skills, and some of them grew proud of their power over living things so that they began to produce plants and animals for their own selfish purposes. They began to care more for power than beauty, and they grew more and more bent and twisted in their ways. Their creations began to follow their hearts, and some of their creations were evil, designed only to kill and destroy, like the rokash you killed.

"Gradually darkness descended upon the men of the city, and a great sorcerer arose whose skill with plants and animals exceeded that of all that had preceded him there. He made alliance with the men of the pit, that is to say the men from across the sea. His name was Meglir. He became king of the city and drove out those who opposed him. The Hansa gave refuge to the fugitives. Meglir developed the korpa, or 'death plant' as we call it. It is the great plant that grows in the dark that you have seen in the cavern. It can take the fresh corpse of a man and reanimate him into an apeman. Apemen have no spirit within them. They feel no pain, have no will, and no ability to distinguish good from evil. They are commanded by Meglir and his lieutenants.

"Over time, Meglir killed all of his enemies and transformed them into apemen. However, bands of men that had been driven from the dead city gathered around it and attacked the roving bands of apemen. They built a great fortress, Torburg, and for many years fought the long fight. Gradually the strength of the resistance grew and raids gave way to a siege of the city. Men came from other cities to join our men and the Hansa for a great battle at the gates of the dead city. While the men battered the main gate with a great catapult, the Hansa led a host of men through the mountains and into the citadel. Finally we drove Meglir deep into the cave, but we could not destroy the cave. The more we fought inside the cave, the more corpses Meglir had to make into apemen. In the end, the alliance of men and Hansa gave up the attack and set a guard over the cave. We watched and utterly destroyed any apemen that wandered out.

"As the years went by, the numbers of men dwindled and the remainder grew weary of the vigil. At one point Meglir unleashed a great plague that killed almost all of the men, but left the apemen unharmed. As the plague ravaged, a few far from the city packed up their families and left. They went up the river, and we do not know where they have gone."

"So why do you keep watching?" asked Dave.

Hanomer looked genuinely perplexed. "I do not understand why you even need to ask that question. The real puzzle to me and my kin is why the men left. They had a duty to perform and ought to have stayed at their post! If they had all died from the plague, then they would have died doing their duty. What greater privilege is there for man or Hansa?"

"But if it's hopeless, doesn't one need to give up at some point, since to continue would be foolhardy?" asked Dave.

Hanomer paused and thought. "I guess we are different from men," said Hanomer at last. "We do not forget, and we are loyal. We promised to defend against this evil, and we will do so. Men are much cleverer and more gifted than we are. In some of the men the blood of the Old Ones ran true, and they had great power to heal disease and to reshape plants and animals into new creations. Men and Hansa were much stronger together than the Hansa are alone, but we have taken an oath to fight this evil, and we continue to do so even though the men have broken faith. Neither the passing of generations nor the futility of our fight in any way diminishes our obligation to do our duty. For many long years and generations of Hansa we have fought the long fight."

Hanomer told Dave more of the history of the elder days. Time passed quickly. They did not follow the old route to the long dead throat of the huge volcano but took a side passage, which rapidly began to climb. Here the passage was lit by the same green light that Dave had noted earlier.

"Is this luminous green plant on the walls of these caverns the product of the arts of these 'life changers'?" asked Dave.

"Yes," said Hanomer, "as are the light gourds we carry. We are now in part of the vast underground greenhouses that the men used at the time of their ascendancy before the dark years came."

"Did they cut these passages then?"

"In a manner of speaking, yes," said Hanomer. "They bred rock borers, huge worms that gnawed many of these passages through the living stone. I am told that feral rock borers can still be found in the deep places of this mountain, endlessly cutting channels and passageways. Let us hope we do not meet one."

Hanomer told Dave many more things of their history as they made their way through the mountain. The passage ended in a long stairway cut into the wall of an irregular chimney. Hanomer ran up the stairs. The stairs were three feet wide and irregular in height. As Dave looked down, he saw that they had come in at one of many side passage entrances and that the stairs descended beyond the entry point so that the bottom was beyond his sight.

Hanomer continued to climb, and Dave had to quicken his pace to keep from being left behind. Periodically they passed openings leading to other side passages. Finally he caught up to Hanomer as he waited by a passageway. Hanomer signaled Dave to follow as he entered the passage.

After several hundred yards, they came out on a wide ledge. Far below them spread the citadel and the dead city. They were almost directly above the tower that led to the tunnel and cavern of the apemen. Several hundred yards below, they could see a group of men kneeling with crossbows and rifles pointed at the tower. Others were moving in and around it with some purpose in mind.

Dave could see from their livery that these people were from Halcyon. Looking into the distance, he observed another large group of figures moving on the outer wall of the dead city near the gate. There were about twenty people directly below, others among the citadel buildings, and still more on the outer wall.

As if reading Dave's thoughts, Hanomer said, "There are more of your people on the outer wall. They have also established a camp on a rock fortress by the river."

"Your eyesight is much better than mine, friend Hanomer. I think that rock outcrop you refer to is what we called 'Fort Linderhof' in honor of our expedition leader."

The activity below continued for some time. Finally, there was a shout of "Fire in the hole!" and all the men ran across the square to take cover in the buildings.

"I think we'd better move back!" said Dave.

Hanomer followed his direction without objection. Within seconds there was an explosion that shook the mountainside, sending dust and rocks past the ledge of their perch. After the dust had settled, Dave and Hanomer cautiously approached the edge of the ledge. The tower leading to the tunnel had been completely demolished. Several members of the party inspected the ruins of the tower, and apparently satisfied, hurried out the gate of the citadel.

"Look how they hurry," said Hanomer. "They feel the oppressive evil resident in this place."

"I wonder what they're planning to do?" said Dave. "Why would they come back here?"

"This place is full of danger," said Hanomer. "If they think to contain the apemen by sealing the tunnel, they're miscalculating; there are many passages out of the inner cavern. There is some mischief being planned here. I think, friend Dave, we need to watch. Maybe we will be called upon to help!"

Dave and Hanomer made camp on the ledge, just inside the passage opening. They ate some smoked fish and several of the small travel loaves that were a Hansa specialty. They placed their light gourds in the sunshine and watered them so they would be replenished for the night.

As darkness fell, Dave felt the oppressive brooding of the dead city. Hanomer told him more of Hansa customs and celebrations to keep Dave's mind from being overwhelmed by the evil spirit of the city. The night was exceedingly dark. Dave saw a single fire on the outer wall and a distant glow at Fort Linderhof, but nothing else. Finally Dave fell asleep, and Hanomer watched. Early in the morning, before first light, Hanomer woke Dave to watch and took his own turn to sleep.

Sitting alone in the dark, Dave felt anew the evil and oppression of the city. The silence was broken only by the gentle trickle of the stream that issued from another cave below him and fell to the citadel courtyard. His memories turned to that dreadful episode with the apemen. His limbs ached anew at the memory of their iron strength as they had carried him to the death plants.

The first glimmer of light in the east was so welcome that he was almost glad to be here. A steady rain began, and he could see that the party on the wall had begun to move. They retraced the path that he had followed to the citadel. When they finally arrived, Dave and Hanomer were careful to stay hidden as activity below increased. Finally a party approached the pile of rubble from the tower. Two members of the party were deep in conversation, and Dave felt a thrill of joy when he recognized the familiar faces of Al and Pam. He wanted to cry out, but prudence cautioned him to wait.

The party climbed the rubble heap, and began to hammer pitons and fix ropes onto the rock. Then they anchored safety ropes that stretched west beyond the citadel wall, up the mountainside.

"They must be planning an escape route," said Hanomer. "And that must mean they are planning to stay. But why?"

"That's my friend, Al Gleeson," said Dave. "In fact, several in that party hanging the ropes are from my expedition. I wonder if we should let them know we're here?"

"What do you think they would do if they found out about me and my people?" asked Hanomer.

Dave frowned and shifted his position uncomfortably.

"Al would welcome you as a brother," said Dave, "but the others—the others would capture you and carry you back as a prize for study. They have no sense of soul. They see us all as animals. Since you are not human, your freedom would be sacrificed to their pursuit of knowledge. I'm not even sure you would be safe if you were human."

"Then should we not remain hidden, until the need of the hour calls us to act?" said Hanomer.

They continued to watch as the observation post below them was manned and the gate to the citadel was fortified.

―――――――――

Dave was awakened from a sound sleep by Hanomer's persistent tug. *Something strange is going on, Dave. There are two men searching the rubble heap.*

Dave approached the edge on his stomach and peered into the gloom. Dave's friend, on watch in the cave below, had also noticed the two and had stretched himself out on the rock as he watched the two shapes approach the rubble heap. The two figures climbed over the rubble as they looked for something. When they finally neared the top of the heap, they disappeared into the ruined tower.

"Dave!" Hanomer said quietly. "They're looking for a passage into the mountain. I don't like the direction this is taking."

"What's going on? What does all this mean?" whispered Dave.

"There is no time to explain," said Hanomer. "We must get moving to get a view of the main tunnel leading to the underground cavern."

Hanomer rose, entered the tunnel, and then uncovered his light gourd so they could see. Hanomer raced along the passage and down the circular stair. He waited at another horizontal passage while Dave caught up to him. He seemed more anxious than Dave had ever seen him before.

"We must hurry!" Hanomer called over his shoulder as he raced down this side passage. They made excellent time along the tunnel's slight downward incline. Despite Hanomer's small stature he could move with surprising speed. Dave was hard-pressed to keep up.

After about ten minutes Hanomer entered a crack leading off to the right. Dave could barely squeeze through the narrow entrance of this side passage. Fortunately the passage opened out, and after about 100 feet, Dave found himself about 200 yards above the cavern floor. The floor was dotted with sickly gray green mounds—death plants. About 300 yards to his right he could see the inside mouth of the tunnel. In the greenish light he could see two figures. Dave couldn't hear any words, but he could see wild gesticulations. Hoffstetter was waving an object with one hand. From his gestures, it seemed he wanted to take the most direct route across the cavern, through the large mounds of death plants. The more athletic figure seemed to object and preferred to take the longer route along the cavern wall. Finally Hoffstetter spread his hands in resignation and followed his companion, who was creeping along the cave wall. Hoffstetter walked unconcernedly beside his skulking companion. They passed directly below Hanomer and Dave along the cavern wall.

"I had hoped they would turn back, but they are determined to go on!" said Hanomer.

"Shouldn't we call to warn them?" asked Dave.

"We'll alert the apemen to their presence—but yes, call them while they still have a chance to escape."

Dave roared at the top of his lungs, "Get out of the cavern. This is very dangerous. It will cost you your life!"

Hoffstetter's companion stopped as if about to bolt back to the tunnel. However, at this hesitation, Hoffstetter seemed to grow in size and become so menacing in his demeanor that the other was visibly cowed. Hoffstetter pointed straight across the cavern to a large opening in the cavern wall, and the other man crouched and scurried like a beaten cur. He moved ahead of Hoffstetter between the mounds of death plants in the direction Hoffstetter had pointed.

Hanomer shook Dave's arm and retraced his steps to the corridor. He began to run again, and Dave noticed that the corridor was no longer straight but curved to the right slightly. After ten minutes, Hanomer again took a side passage. There was no real opening to the cavern, but there was a crack that was large enough to serve as a window. Dave peered out with Hanomer. The two figures were still moving at a brisk walk between the mounds, heading for the far wall. Hoffstetter's companion was stumbling, while Hoffstetter had him by the collar and hastened him along. From this vantage point Hanomer followed their progress.

"I must see where they are going!" he said, more to himself than to Dave.

Finally Hoffstetter and his companion reached a large vertical shadow on the far wall, plunged into the shadow and disappeared.

Hanomer now became more agitated than Dave had ever seen him before. "Why are they going into the heart of the darkness? What are they up to?

"What's going on?" asked Dave.

"All of the evil and fear of this place emanates from the end of that tunnel they just entered," said Hanomer. "None of the Hansa have ever gone there in living memory, because it is too dangerous. Normally there are many apemen guarding the approach. Now there are none. I need to take a great risk and go there now to see what they are going to do! If I do not come back, you must make your way back to the village—or at least to your people—to tell them what you have seen."

"I want to come along," insisted Dave.

Hanomer did not answer but led the way back toward the main passage they had been using. Partway back Hanomer climbed through a fissure that led into a small chimney. The chimney was narrow, and Dave was able to use the walls to hold himself steady as he descended from foothold to foothold. After about thirty feet, the chimney began to widen. When Dave reached the bend, he saw that the descent was much less steep. His progress was more rapid now, and he was able to reach the cavern floor, where Hanomer waited. He touched Dave's arm.

"Rokomer, I don't know this part of the cavern at all. I have never gone through this tunnel, since it has always been heavily guarded by apemen. Long ago Hansa tried to climb into this tunnel, but none ever returned. Our elders have forbidden the Hansa to try this route again, yet I feel strongly that I must know what your countrymen are doing in there. The cavern is empty of apemen today, and I have never seen it empty in many years of watching the entrance. Still, we must be careful, since we can easily be cut off. I think it best if I go alone the rest of the way into that tunnel."

"No!" whispered Dave. "I want to come along."

Hanomer did not press his objection but shook his head in dismay and lapsed into whispered speech. "Just follow my lead then," he said.

Before proceeding further, Hanomer studied the tunnel carefully. Finally he signaled and descended to the cavern floor. He crossed and then began to climb the cavern wall again. Dave followed him.

After about thirty feet, Dave saw where Hanomer was going. The tunnel was a long, vertical crack stretching 300 feet up the wall and descending through the floor. Some time in the ancient past an earth tremor must have dislodged a large section of the fissure wall. The huge wedge-shaped fragment had slid into the narrowing crack of the fissure, forming the rough floor of the tunnel. The fallen section had left behind a long shelf, or notch, in the wall of the tunnel, some twenty feet above the tunnel floor.

Hanomer climbed up to the shelf and waved for Dave to follow. When Dave reached this shelf, he was able to look down and see the path wind between large boulders of broken rock on the tunnel floor. With Hanomer leading, they crept along the shelf, hugging the wall to remain out of sight.

After about 500 yards, a wall loomed ahead, signifying the end of the notch. They both crept to the edge of the shelf. The path wound among the fallen rocks twenty feet below. At various places along the path, one could see the green sheen of light through great yawning gaps from the deep chasm beneath the wedged fragment of rock that formed the floor of the tunnel. At the end of the tunnel, the rock plug ended prematurely, leaving a wide chasm. Here the path crossed an iron bridge into a smaller cavern. They could not see much of this smaller cavern.

They advanced to the end of the shelf. Although the crack in the ceiling here was much lower than in the entrance, the roof still towered above them by 100 feet. Hanomer climbed across the sheer rock face that confronted them and disappeared around the corner to the left as he reached the inside of the small cavern. Not willing to be left behind, Dave attempted the dangerous traverse, going hand over hand with no footholds. As he rounded the corner, he saw Hanomer crouching on a narrow shelf.

With hands bleeding and cramped from exhaustion, Dave covered the final few feet, then slumped beside Hanomer and tried to get his bearings. This cavern, although not as large as the throat of the volcano, was long and narrow. It contained a lake and a large flat island arranged so that the island appeared to be surrounded by a 100-foot moat. A rock lip or ridge prevented the lake from emptying into the chasm. The first iron bridge ended on the top of this ridge. The path wound down to the lake's edge and then crossed to this island by a second iron bridge.

The island was made of rock and was slightly convex. Five statues, arranged in a pentagon and facing outward, towered some twenty feet in height above the rock surface. The statues had heads like vultures and reptilian bodies. At the apex of the island, stood a black obelisk about a hundred feet high on a base about ten feet square.

The two men were crossing the second bridge. The taller of the two wanted to go back, but at each attempt to leave, he seemed to be dragged forward, against his will. Having crossed the bridge, both figures made their way between the two stone statues nearest it. Finally the tall man stopped before the obelisk and stared at it.

Hoffstetter came up behind him. Dave saw him raise the black object he had been carrying high above his head and strike the tall man a mighty blow on the back of his head so that he fell forward. Hoffstetter then knelt down before the huge obelisk with his head bowed and his arms held aloft. Holding the bloody black thing, he shouted some words that Dave did not recognize.

The large obelisk seemed to pulsate with energy, and the cavern filled with its green cadaverous light. Apemen appeared from the shadows and picked up the body of the slain man. Dave could see that the force of the blow had crushed his skull. Furthermore, he could now see clearly enough to make out the shape of the murder weapon. It was a smaller replica of the huge stone before which the awful act had taken place.

Hoffstetter seemed oblivious to the apemen. He continued chanting and bowing, holding his bloodstained weapon in front of him with both hands as if offering it to the obelisk. The apemen carried the body to a large black spherical object beside the base of the obelisk and set it down. The object was so black that Dave had taken it for a shadow. But the black object began to open, and with large black leaves spreading out like a rosebud opening, a massive black arm reached out from its centre and lifted the body inside as if it were lifting a toy doll. Hoffstetter, rose from the ground and walked over to the plant. Stepping onto the open leaf he walked in, following the arm to the center of the plant. The leaves closed, and both were lost from view.

Hundreds of apemen began to lumber out of the shadows, and some began crossing from the island to the ridge. When Hanomer saw them, he tugged on Dave's arm beckoning him to follow, and began to climb back over the rock face to the ledge with terrible urgency. Dave followed him. It was easier the second time, since the handholds were familiar. They moved quickly along the ledge. When they reached the cavern wall, apemen were approaching their position from several directions.

"While the guardians and the evil one were bending all their will to control their victim, they were blind. Now that the deed is done, the guardians have detected our presence," said Hanomer.

"Who are the guardians?" asked Dave.

Hanomer didn't answer but descended rapidly to the cavern floor. Dave followed, apemen close behind. Hanomer had already crossed the floor and reached the ledge, unlimbering his bow. Dave dealt a blow to the nearest apeman and raced to join Hanomer. Hanomer felled a second with an arrow from the ledge and then kept the apemen off Dave while he climbed. When Dave reached the ledge, they made their way back up the chimney in silence.

Reaching the passage safely, they caught their breath, drank a little water, and had a bite to eat.

"What was that all about?" asked Dave.

"Meglir sought long ago to extend his life as he saw death approaching. The black obelisk is his attempt to preserve life. He has been trapped inside. It is the living death of the undying. His five lieutenants are also trapped in the five statues that surround the obelisk and serve him in their malice. By bringing a victim and committing unspeakable treachery, that fat human has opened himself up to Meglir. Once he leaves the death plant, he will be possessed by Meglir.

"Now I also understand why the cavern was so empty of ape-men," Hanomer went on. "We only made it as far as we did since all the power of Meglir and the guardians was directed at bringing the fat one and the victim to them. The apemen were immobile and hidden away so as not to terrify the victim. We will not get in there so easily again!"

"What does all this mean?" asked Dave.

"Until now, Meglir's power and that of his lieutenants was range limited. The apemen could travel only a short distance from the center of power before Meglir and the lieutenants could no longer control them. Now Meglir, in the fat man's body, will be on the move and can take the apemen anywhere. My village is in danger. Your people are in danger. We must hurry. I need to think what must be done."

Chapter 35

Another Kind of Evil

"And that," said Dave, "brings me up to the present. Hanomer and I decided that we had to warn you what happened."

"What was Hoffstetter thinking, going into that place?" said Al, more to himself than to Dave.

"I don't know. It's clear that the other fellow—what was his name?"

"Jim Wilson"

"It's clear that Jim Wilson," continued Dave, "went along willingly for a while and then couldn't turn back. Hoffstetter, on the other hand, seemed to go willingly the whole time."

"May I meet Hanomer?" asked Al.

"Of course!" said Dave.

He gave a low whistle, and a small furry figure climbed out of the shadows and extended his hand to Al as he approached.

"My name is Hanomer, son of Hallomer. Albert, son of Gleeson, blessings on you and your kin."

Although Al had mentally prepared himself for the surprise of meeting a being of another species, still he was shocked. Hanomer looked to his eyes like a beast. After a moment of awkward silence, Al recovered himself enough to speak.

"Your English is excellent," said Al.

Hanomer bowed.

"The Hansa have a remarkable gift for song, poetry, and languages. This gift carries over to picking up our language. If we speak in English, Hanomer will understand," said Dave. His face became grave and his tone changed. "You're in great danger here. If the ape-men attack, you'll be surrounded and cut off from the Halcyon River."

"Linder tried to dissuade McTavish, our expedition leader, from coming here," said Al, "but McTavish ignored him. I'm afraid we do not have much credibility with McTavish."

"I think I should go and try to persuade him," said Dave.

"That might work," said Al. "Are you going to bring Hanomer?"

Dave considered Al's question. "No," he said slowly. "I think there's a good chance McTavish may lock him up, because Hanomer will be assumed to be an enemy. And we may need Hanomer to rescue us if my advice isn't heeded and the apemen attack."

In the end they agreed that once the platoons were up and about, Dave would come into camp and Al would take him to see McTavish. Dave and Hanomer climbed away from the lookout ledge, and Al was soon relieved by the next sentry.

Shortly after sunrise, Al waited near the stone pool at the foot of the cliff. Dave climbed down and moved silently, taking up his position beside his friend before Al even knew he was coming. The sentries had also not seen Dave arrive, and so they raised no alarm.

Dave still wore some of his Halcyon clothes, but he also wore a buckskin shirt and leather boots tied at the knees. A murmur went up among all who saw him, and they stared at him as Al led his friend across to McTavish's quarters. McTavish's orderly raised an eyebrow when he saw Dave, but he simply told them to take a seat.

After fifteen minutes, another messenger entered breathlessly and whispered into the orderly's ear. The orderly immediately left the waiting area. He returned in a minute with McTavish, who nodded at Al without speaking and gave Dave a long look as he followed the orderly out to the square. Al and Dave looked at each other and then followed McTavish and the others out. Al was filled with a sense of foreboding.

In the center of the square, a crowd had gathered. The crowd parted as McTavish approached. In the center of the crowd stood Hoffstetter!

Fear and revulsion descended on Al.

McTavish went straight to Hoffstetter. "Bertrand, you're back! Where have you been? What happened?"

Hoffstetter turned slowly and fixed his eyes on McTavish. He attempted to smile but it was more of a sneer than a smile. When he spoke it was a thin, hollow voice, devoid of warmth and life.

"I have discovered the secret of the city!" he said. "It's wonderful! We have come to the dawning of a new glorious age, beyond our imagination."

"Where's Wilson?" said McTavish in a quavering voice.

Hoffstetter is getting to him too.

Hoffstetter turned and pointed a fat finger at Dave.

"He killed him!"

Dave went white and took a step back, but all eyes turned towards him and a murmur went up around him.

"Grab him!" a voice shouted, and several from Wilson's platoon lowered their weapons against Dave.

"Wait!" said Al.

McTavish waved Al to silence, then turned towards Dave and demanded, "Who are you?"

"I'm Dave Schuster from the first expedition. I didn't kill Wilson; he did!" Dave could only nod at Hoffstetter since his arms were pinned. His counteraccusation so close on the heels of Hoffstetter's remarks robbed Dave of all credibility.

"You both agree that Wilson is dead," said McTavish coldly. "The fact that you make the claim of murder places you at the scene of the crime. Lock him up," said McTavish, indicating Dave. "Senator Hoffstetter, may I see you in my quarters, please!"

Dave was led to a trap door at the back of McTavish's building and instructed to climb down a rope ladder into a cellar beneath the floor. Guards pulled up the ladder, threw him some heather for a bed and a blanket, and then closed the trap door. He could hear their footsteps retreat.

I guess there's no need to guard me!

Exploring his surroundings, Dave observed the cell had a stone floor, stone walls, and a stone ceiling. There were only two breaks in the stone—the hole in the ceiling that was blocked by the trap door, and a small window in the outer wall. The mountainside was only thirty feet away, and a window had been cut into this wall. Dave saw it would allow easy aim at any besiegers who might try to gain the citadel by scaling the mountainside. He craned forward as far as he could. The citadel wall was high and stood on a tongue of rock. The city was far below.

Much too far to think of escape in that direction.

Nevertheless, the mortar was soft and crumbled as he scratched it with his fingernail.

Dave sat in the corner and thought long and hard about his predicament and about Hoffstetter. He had seen Hoffstetter walk into the plant.

What happened to him? What's his game? I can't sit here like this! I need to find something to do.

The guards had not searched Dave carefully when they had put him in the cellar. He pulled out a small metal blade, a little longer than a nail file, from a tiny sheath on the inside of his leather boot. Loosening the mortar would help pass the time.

Al was bewildered. He had anticipated that McTavish might disbelieve Dave and do nothing, or that he might believe Dave and take action to protect them all, but neither had happened. Hoffstetter's accusation was completely unexpected. Who was he to believe? Since he had become a Christian, Al had tried to speak the truth in every circumstance, even if it seemed counterproductive or painful. One of the consequences of this personal determination had been the sharpening of his ability to detect truthfulness in others. His heart told him now that Dave and Hanomer were telling the truth and that Hoffstetter was lying.

Then there was the raw fear and terror he'd felt in Hoffstetter's presence. He admitted to himself that he had never liked the man, but none of that could explain the terror and revulsion he felt whenever he was near him.

Al returned to his room to think. Sometime later, Floyd came to him, looking upset.

"You'll never believe what happened!" said Floyd.

"What's happened now?" asked Al.

"McTavish just called the platoon commanders into his office. He told them that since Wilson had in all probability been killed, he needed to appoint a successor. So he appointed Hoffstetter second in command!"

Floyd paused to let his words sink in. Al looked grave but did not answer.

Floyd continued. "Can you believe it! McTavish, who only ever trusted his own military people, appointing Hoffstetter as second in command! Even if Hoffstetter is a senator, it goes against everything we know about McTavish."

"Floyd, none of this is natural or makes sense. Hoffstetter gives me the creeps. How did McTavish look when he talked to you?" asked Al.

"Eh?" said Floyd. "What did you say?"

"How did McTavish look? Was he himself? Was he elated?"

"No," said Floyd. "He looked wrung out and even sickly. Not at all the McTavish I remember. I thought it was the news of Wilson's death."

Hoffstetter wasted no time setting up his headquarters just outside McTavish's residence and office. He used his influence and previous connections to surround himself with a dozen allies—from the three platoons who took up residence near Hoffstetter's quarters—as his personal bodyguards. He selected no one from Floyd's platoon.

By the next morning the picture had changed completely. During the night hundreds of apemen had taken up positions outside the citadel walls. When Floyd's sentries spotted these creatures, he asked Al to accompany him to McTavish's office, hoping McTavish would ask Al to report on his conversation with Dave. When they reached McTavish's building they asked the orderly if they could speak to McTavish. But instead of McTavish, Hoffstetter appeared. Al felt the same chill he'd felt the day before.

"You're looking for McTavish" said Hoffstetter's sepulchral voice. "He's feeling poorly—stress from poor Wilson's death. He's unavailable, but you may speak to me."

My report is of the greatest urgency," said Floyd icily. "I must see McTavish!"

"Must?" said Hoffstetter tersely. "I think not. Commander McTavish cannot be disturbed. He's given me strict orders to that effect, and I will carry them out."

Hoffstetter looked at his bodyguards, who rose from their places in the waiting room and closed in around Floyd and Al.

Hoffstetter called his orderly.

"Please tell everyone to assemble on the parade ground," he said.

To Floyd and Al he said, "Come with me!"

Hoffstetter marched directly to the crumbled tower and climbed partway up so all could see him.

His voice boomed out. "Commander McTavish has asked me to address a few words to you on his behalf. We are reaching the dawn of a new, glorious age," he said. "Do not fear the servants that have gathered outside the walls. I have discovered the secret of this city. They will not harm us. They will protect us and serve us."

A murmur ran through the crowd.

"To show you that you have nothing to fear," said Hoffstetter, "I will go out to them and show you that they will obey my commands. I will have them bring us wood and food from the forest. I will have them bring stone and timber to strengthen the citadel gate."

With that Hoffstetter walked to the makeshift citadel gate, had it opened, and walked down the road to where a large group of apemen were standing. He gave orders, and the apemen lumbered off to obey his commands.

Chapter 36

A Conspiracy Unmasked

The Twenty-fifth Platoon gathered for their evening meal, posting two platoon members as lookouts in the hall just outside their quarters. If anyone came, they would greet the visitors loudly, warning the conspirators within.

"We have to get out of here!" said Al.

"Are things really that bad?" asked Stan. "Anyway, where would we escape to? Could we go back to the island or back to Halcyon?"

"The answer to both questions is 'I do not know.' I haven't thought that far ahead. This place is now inundated with apemen. This can't be good."

"Maybe Hoffstetter can control them like he says. Maybe they'll become our 'hewers of wood and drawers of water,'" said Stan.

Al hadn't expected this much opposition. It underlined, once again, that in some minds he was not a full-fledged, trusted member of the platoon, despite his previous experience with the apemen.

"For my part, I think we've got to get out of here," said Floyd. "Stanford, you weren't there when these apemen attacked. I don't want to go through that again. I don't trust Hoffstetter. What has he done with McTavish? I say, let's pull out and get to the island and warn them."

"What about Schuster?" asked Al. "What did they do with him?"

"I heard they took him back to Fort Linderhof," said Stan.

"Linderhof!" said Floyd. "Why didn't we know about that? Why didn't we see them leave?"

Stan shrugged his shoulders. "I guess they took him out by night through the town. They control the main citadel gate, and we weren't watching closely from the wall."

There was stunned silence at the thought of Dave's disappearance.

"I'm all for getting out," said Pam at last, "the sooner the better. You know Hoffstetter has set the apemen to reopen the tunnel. Think about it; McTavish goes to all the trouble to blow up the tower and block the tunnel, and then Hoffstetter, supposedly under McTavish's orders, reopens it. I think McTavish has been taken out."

They discussed Pam's suspicion. As their murmuring died down, Al looked around the group, many were nodding their assent to Floyd.

"Yeah, let's go!" said a voice summarizing the general assent. With that settled, Floyd took a deep breath and began to plan their escape.

The next night Al was again up at the lookout, while the Twenty-fifth manned the wall nearest the mountain. All day, apemen had been working incessantly to remove rubble from the tunnel. They were as tireless in their dedication to this menial task as they had been unrelenting in battle. Floyd, afraid that somehow their escape plans would become known, had only confided in Al and Pam with respect to the exact moment of their escape. Everyone was to be ready to go at a moment's notice. Tonight was the night, and Floyd was now going around personally giving word to the whole platoon to depart.

Al kept watch as the members of the Twenty-fifth began their escape using the route mapped out with ropes across the mountainside. As leader, Floyd had volunteered to go first. Pam went with him, since only she and Al had ever crossed the mountain face before. Now they were doing it by night. Al's task was to stay prominently at his post and then join them as soon as the last team member was on his way.

Al guessed more than half of the group had begun the treacherous climb, and every few minutes one or two more joined them on the rock face. Seeing a figure climbing toward him, a chill went up his spine. Relief replaced fear when he realized the climber was Stan.

"What are you doing here, Stan?" asked Al.

"Linder told me to stay with you so you don't have to manage the climb by yourself," said Stan.

"Well, that's thoughtful of Linder. Might I suggest that you back farther into the cave and stay out of sight, since I'm supposed to be here alone? We don't want to arouse suspicion, do we?"

"That's a good idea!" said Stan.

Al took up his sentry position and watched as more shadows crept up the wall. Suddenly he felt a rope snap around his neck. Jerking back violently, his left hand involuntarily grabbed for the rope—but it was too tight. He could feel himself starting to black out. In desperation he reached for his ankle, pulled out his boot knife and jabbed at the body behind him. There was a yelp of pain, and the rope around his neck loosened. Tearing off the noose, Al whipped around to see Stan on one knee, clutching his leg. Three apemen, dripping wet, came out of the shadows of the cave and closed their iron grip around Al's arms. The strength of the apemen was horrible. Two of them lifted Al off his feet and carried him, marching methodically into the pool at the back of the cave. He struggled violently and kicked one of them solidly in the back of the leg, causing the apeman to stumble. But the third apeman grabbed Al's legs, and the three continued their march into the pool.

Al felt the cold water close over his head as the apemen marched relentlessly forward, never relaxing their grip. With their iron shod boots and iron clubs, the apemen were so heavy they immediately sank to the bottom of the pool and had to keep Al from floating to the surface. The water was pitch black. Al began to pray, preparing himself for death as the searing pain of anoxia wracked his frame. Just as his body was about to force his mouth open in a desperate attempt to gulp for air, his head broke water. Al gasped, gulping air into his lungs. Breathing hard as they emerged from the icy water, Al could see by the faint green phosphorescence of the walls that they were in a large tunnel. The apemen walked down the tunnel without a word. After fifteen minutes of passages and stairs, they emerged into the dark square of the citadel. Crossing the square, they entered McTavish's building, and then shambled to the back of the building in the dark.

Al was completely disoriented. They came to an opening even darker than the darkness of the building. Al was hurled down, falling heavily and awkwardly on a soft pile of heather. He groaned from the pain of the fall and the exhaustion of his struggle against the apemen as he heard the sound of the trap door closing.

"Who's there?" said a familiar voice tinged with fear.

"Dave! It's me—Al!"

In the dim light from a nearby window slit, Al could see the dark figure of his friend gingerly approach the pile of heather that had broken his fall.

"Are you all right?" asked Dave. "Can you move your arms and legs?"

"I think I'm all right," said Al. "So this is where they put you!"

"Yeah," said Dave, a hint of resignation in his voice. "It's a little late for visiting hours. What are you doing, dropping in like this?"

"Dave, I'm in pain, and your stupid, inappropriate jokes are adding to it. Now stow it and help me try to stand up!"

"Wow, Al gets mad!" Dave said, then added contritely, "I was so glad to hear your voice, the comments just kind of oozed out of me."

With Dave's help, Al staggered to the wall with the outside window. Dave had bundled more heather into a crude bench, and the fragrance of the heather filled the night air. Settling against the wall, they heard footsteps and then the trap door creaked open, a light shining through its opening. It grew brighter, and a head, shrouded in shadows, poked through the opening in the ceiling. The torch beam played along the wall until it caught them in the light.

"Enjoying your new accommodations?" Stan laughed derisively.

"Why did you do it?" asked Al. "Why did you betray us?"

"Payback stinks, doesn't it? You thought you could push me around and get away with it because you had Big Dave to back you up. Now look at you. I don't forget. I just wait my time, and then I strike.

"By the way, there's another thing you ought to know. Pam's mine. You made a big mistake when you went after her. Did she tell you that we had a son together? He's back in Halcyon?" Stan laughed again. "I thought not! You should see your face now, you big stupid fool. She was just playing you, knowing full well that she was coming back to me. You're such a sucker!"

"Shut up, Stan, if you know what's good for you!" said Dave ominously.

"Gee, Big Dave, exactly what do you have in mind?"

Quick as a snake Dave's arm coiled back, and he snapped his wrist. Something hit Stan in the face. Stan dropped his flashlight with a howl.

"You'll pay for this!" Stan growled.

"Better write it down," said Dave. "As soon as I get a chance I plan on adding to the total. Waste of a good mostly rotten apple."

The trap door slammed with a loud thud. Dave crawled over, grabbed the flashlight, turned it off, and put it between them in the heather.

Chapter 37

The Prison Pit

Stan's footsteps echoed on the stone floor as he retreated through the dark corridor above them. Dave looked at Al. In the faint light coming through the window slit he could see Al's head was bowed. A faint groan escaped from his lips.

"Al, are you okay?" asked Dave.

There was a long pause. Dave wanted to speak again, thought better of it, and bit back his desire to fill the empty silence with words—any words.

"Dave," said Al at last, "I can't talk right now. I just need time, time—"

Dave slammed his fist into the palm of his left hand, and the snap of the impact sounded loud in the darkness.

I wish I had Stan here right now. What a rokash he is! He needs someone to rearrange his face.

His lapse into Hansa lingo surprised him. To take his mind off Stan, Dave looked into the blackness across the room and then periodically looked back at Al. He was still huddled with his head in his hands, but he made no sound. It seemed to Dave that he could see his friend's despair from the inside. He felt a depth of camaraderie and compassion towards Al that surprised him.

Dave tried praying to the great darkness that Someone, Anyone—assuming there was Someone out there—would reach down and comfort Al, since he didn't know what to say.

———

"Dave, are you awake?"

"Yeah, Al, I'm awake. Are you all right?"

"As right as I can be. By the way, thanks for understanding and giving me a chance to pull myself together. I guess I needed to process what I had just heard."

"I'm glad I did right," said Dave. "I don't really know how to help in circumstances like this."

"Keeping quiet was just what I needed."

"Do you think what Stan said was true?" asked Dave.

"I don't know. I just don't know. Stan's a liar—a very good liar. Any good liar knows that mixing in a little bit of truth makes the lie stronger. I just don't know which parts are true and which parts he made up to drive the knife in. Still, Pam has been acting strangely enough ever since we started this trip upriver that I have to admit something's going on."

"What are you going to do, Al?"

"Do? I'm pretty sure I know what I should do, but I do not know if I can bring myself to do it. When Stan talked, it was as if a black hole was opening up at my feet and I fell in. Right now blackness is all around me, and I do not care about what I should do. I do not care about anything except the blackness."

Dave was quiet for a while. He tried to think.

"Sounds to me like you love her," said Dave at last.

"How can I love her? We hardly know each other. Our relationship consists of a trip in a sailboat and a few minutes of talking while I was half out of my mind with sedatives. Besides, when I tried in my bumbling way to let her know I cared about her, she rebuffed me."

"Al, none of that matters. The time doesn't matter; the activities don't matter. It's clear to me that you're in love with her and that's the 'black hole.' Now admit it and try to climb out of it. We have to get out of here, and we need our focus and determination to try to do something to that end."

"What do you have in mind?" asked Al heavily.

"Look, I know the Hansa. They'll try to do something. We need to count on them and do what we can."

"How could they possibly help?" said Al. "We're in the middle of a small army of armed men, and now apemen are also patrolling the square."

"I don't know," said Dave. "I only know they're going to try something and we need to be ready. The hole in the ceiling is about twelve feet up. I could never reach it myself, but with two of us maybe we could get up there. Stan closed the trap door in a hurry. Maybe he didn't lock it."

"So what do I need to do?" asked Al wearily.

"I'm too heavy for you," said Dave, "but maybe you could stand on my shoulders?"

Al took off his boots, and Dave made a stirrup with his hands. By main strength Dave lifted Al up until he reached the ceiling.

"Okay, Dave, I've reached the ceiling, and I can steady myself against the opening. I'm going to try to stand on your shoulders. Steady my ankles."

Dave crouched, and Al placed first one foot and then the other on Dave's shoulders. Dave looked up and saw him pressing against the trap door. He tried to lift it. It moved slightly but didn't open.

"Brace yourself," said Al, "I'm going to push against the door with all my might."

Al pushed hard, and Dave straightened up, pushing with his powerful legs.

"Stop!" shouted Al. "It's no good!"

They regrouped and tried again and again, but the trap door wouldn't budge.

"When Stan left," said Al, "the trap door must have fallen and locked on its own. I can't budge it."

"Okay," said Dave, "we move to plan B."

"There's a plan B?"

"I was working on plan B before you came. I had no chance to get out the trap door, but I noticed that the mortar around the window slit is soft and friable. I already have two blocks loose." Al followed Dave to the window, and Dave pulled out two stone blocks and placed them on the floor. Dave pulled a small, thin blade out of his boot and got back to work. They took turns, and the work progressed rapidly.

After they had switched places a couple of times, Dave asked, "Aren't you supposed to try to convert me or something, Al?"

"What do you mean?"

"You're a Christian; you know what I mean. Ask me to pray a prayer 'asking Jesus into my heart' to keep me from going to hell."

Al started to laugh, gently at first and then louder.

"What's so funny?" asked Dave.

"God sure has a sense of humor," said Al. "You want to talk about a subject that I'd rather talk about than anything else, and here I am moping in my black hole. It's as if God is saying to me, 'Al, it's not all about you. You have things to do, and here you are feeling sorry for yourself.'"

Al stood up, leaned against the wall and watched Dave scrape at the mortar. "I'm sorry. I didn't mean to laugh. Do you know what it means to be a Christian?"

"I suppose it means being a do-gooder and joining a church—right?"

"I won't say no," said Al, "since those things are certainly part of it. But as far as I can tell, they're not the central things."

"So what is the heart of the matter?" asked Dave.

"It's my best understanding that a Christian is a Christ follower. In other words, when I became a Christian, I decided to live the way he wants me to live."

"So how does that work? Does He send instructions?"

"In a way, I suppose. I get a lot just reading about Christ's life in the Bible and then figuring out how it would apply today."

"Well, if God created the world and has all that power, why is everything so indirect and so mysterious? Why doesn't he paint his instructions in bright glowing letters on that stone wall over there? It should be easy for him. If he's really there, why not make his presence unmistakable?"

"Good question, Dave. As I see it, there are two ways for God to make us into robots. The obvious way would be for him to control our every thought and action to such a degree that we thought we were making all our own decisions, but there he would be, the invisible hand in the background, pulling all of our strings."

"Okay, I can see that," said Dave. "What's the second way?"

"Well, the second way would be to make his presence and will so compelling that although I *could* make my own decisions, he would be so overwhelming I couldn't get away from him. If he did what you said and confronted you with glowing letters on our cell wall, how could you ever choose to disbelieve in him? He wouldn't leave you that option. He has to leave things so there's a reasonable amount of evidence, but the evidence isn't compelling. That way as you come to him hoping it's true, and it becomes more compelling, you can choose to follow him completely, or you can choose to turn your back on him and come up with another explanation that leaves him out but also holds together well enough to be believable. This way you have to choose, because for whatever reason, he considers the freewill relationship to be of paramount importance."

"So what happens if I turn my back?" Dave was almost afraid to ask this questions since the memory of his dream gripped him so strongly he almost thought he was back in it.

"In a letter that Paul, an early Christian, wrote to other Christians in Rome, he talked about people who knew God as creator but didn't honor him as such. When they chose to disbelieve, it seems as if even the evidence they'd seen before became hard to see. When they closed the shutters, the whole room became dark, and they grew more comfortable in their darkness."

Now Dave was really frightened. One way or another he was going to shut down this conversation. "It sounds like a lot of rationalization to me. I think I need to think about it. Can you scrape for a while? I need to take a nap."

Well before sunrise, when the cell was still quite dark and they both rested, exhausted, against the outer wall, they felt evil come before it arrived. It was as if darkness itself approached, preceded by fear so strong it was like the odor accompanying a decaying corpse. The fear washed over Dave and caused his limbs to tremble. Luckily Al had replaced the loose stones before he had also decided to catch up on some sleep.

They heard the trap latch click and then open up. The flickering light from a torch shone through the opening. Hoffstetter appeared at the hole in the ceiling, kneeling and looking down at them.

"Where are the others?" hissed Hoffstetter.

His voice had changed. He no longer sounded like the Hoffstetter Dave knew. When he fixed his eyes, red from the torchlight, on Dave, waves of fear and doubt assailed him anew, and it took Dave's whole will to stop his knees from shaking. His lips were dry. He clenched his teeth with all his might to keep the answer from being torn out of him.

"They're gone," said Al haltingly.

"That I already know," said Hoffstetter menacingly. "Where are those vermin, the Hansa? I want their village—tell me!"

An all-consuming dread tortured Dave's mind; he wanted to cry out and raised his arm as if to ward off a blow. Al put his hand on Dave's arm, and the wave of terror diminished.

"Who are you?" asked Al, turning back to Hoffstetter.

"I am beyond you, little man!" Hoffstetter sneered arrogantly. "I am the power under the mountain."

"Where's Hoffstetter?" asked Al.

"Oh, he's still here. I honor him by using his body. I leave a little place for his little mind. I have been planning this for a long time. Did you really think that your coming to our world was Hoffstetter's accident? I called him. He came because he wants to serve me, as he should. If you choose to serve me, you can have things you never dreamed of, but you must help me find the Hansa and show me how to conquer your island."

Dave didn't have the energy to respond; Al also remained silent.

"I will give you time to think about it," said Hoffstetter's mouth. Without another word, Hoffstetter's body rose and closed the trap door. They could hear his boots receding on the stones above.

"Whew!" said Al. "We've got to get out of here! Do you really think the Hansa will come?"

"They'll come—I'd stake my life on it."

"I think," said Al soberly, "those are precisely the stakes that we are placing on this bet."

They went back to the window and worked furiously to loosen more stones around the narrow opening.

They worked steadily on the mortar for several hours. With the trap door closed they knew they would have some warning if one of the guards were to check up on them.

"Dave, you seem different," Al said at last as he worked a stone loose.

Dave paused for a second and then resumed scraping mortar. He felt the same fear rise up in him again that he felt at their last conversation. Yet deep inside, he knew he had to talk about this, and Al was a fellow he could trust.

"I believe I am different," he said at last. "It's hard for me to describe. It's as if I've come to question everything I believed about our world, the people in it, and even who I am."

"What caused the change?" asked Al.

"I'm not really sure. I think it was partly just getting away from Halcyon. Halcyon is like an educational narcotic. I've come to realize that I lived in a controlled environment where the teachers, administrators, and important people spoke constantly about freedom, about how wonderful we are, and how we should pursue our own whims and desires. And yet the whole system, the whole culture, was designed to be inimical to freedom and independent thought. Only certain approved thoughts were considered courageous, expansive, or innovative. Many of the ideas that really mattered—such as 'Who am I? 'Why am I here?' 'Is there really a mind behind the universe?' and 'What does it mean to be good, and why should I really bother trying to be good?'—those questions, although not directly suppressed through edicts, were ground out of me. I was told they're stupid questions asked by stupid people and they lead to inhumanity, that they're arrogant, intolerant questions. But no one ever asked, 'What are the possible answers?' and 'Are any of these answers true?'"

"I know what you mean," said Al. "I've felt the same, nameless oppression while in Halcyon. But what changed your mind about these things?"

Dave smiled ruefully. "Then there was this dream I had…"

"What dream?" asked Al, his voice betraying his interest.

"I dreamt that I was standing by a hospital bed and my dead body was lying in the bed."

When Dave finished the whole story about the dream, Al shook his head. "That's amazing, Dave. I remember when I was in first year I had a friend who was an atheist but who was quite knowledgeable about the Bible. When he learned that I was a Christian, he showed me the passage in the biblical book called Revelation about the lake of fire. He asked, 'How could you worship a God who would send me to place like that just because I don't believe in Him?' His comment has always bothered me. Maybe there's a side to this I've never considered before. From the perspective of your dream, you were the one who dug the pit, because of your overwhelming hatred towards God."

Dave had the sinking feeling that he, Al, and Al's atheist friend were the ogres who made hell possible. Who knew what Dave Schuster would be like after a thousand, maybe ten thousand, years of moral decay and degeneration?

"You know," said Dave, "you really scared me earlier when you talked about the gift we've been given to control our own reality. That's what I did in my dream. In my dream, I could choose to kill a part of myself. When I walked away from the mountain and the light, I closed a portal that let me connect to God. When all those were gone, and only hate and self-loathing were left, I was the one who created the lake of fire. Can we really be like that?"

Al worked another stone loose. Then he stopped and said, "You know, Dave, there is great evil in this world. Some we do to each other, but much we do to ourselves. When we torment ourselves or give ourselves up to addiction, who will rescue us then? Don't we have many instances where we act against our own best interests? I guess people think of sin as breaking a series of rules, but I think sin also has many of the attributes of a disease of the soul. When sin takes hold, it slowly takes over our lives, and we do horrible things to ourselves. I do not know if my theology is right on this point, but perhaps, given our self-annihilating condition and our extreme hatred of God, we may eventually even go so far as to dig the lake of fire. Who knows? I'm personally convinced that the Bible is truer than I can imagine, but I'm also convinced that I'm wrong about a lot of things that I think the Bible says. I'm sure I harbor a thousand heresies. May God forgive me!"

Dave had worried his thoughts about the dream might be right. He had hoped that Al would talk him out of them. Now what would he do? "So what's the answer?" asked Dave.

"You gave me the answer from your dream," said Al. "We have to be clear as glass to approach the light, and we cannot do that on our own. Someone has to help us."

———

They were finally been able to remove enough stones to enlarge the opening such that even Dave with his broad shoulders could get through. Now what came next? The outside wall was sheer, and the drop to the city below was several hundred feet at this point. The top of the wall was at least fifty feet up. On the other hand, the mountainside was tantalizingly close. Here the wall of the citadel bent back and converged on the mountainside at a shallow angle.

Al and Dave struggled to stack the loose stones back in place so that if a guard looked through the trap door he wouldn't find anything amiss. Dave took off his jacket and hung it out the window as an afterthought. They had just sat down again, leaning against the wall, when they heard a whoosh and a snap as an arrow shattered on the stone wall across the room and fell to the floor. Dave jumped up and grabbed a thin rope that had been attached to the arrow as the weight of the rope began to draw the arrow across the floor toward the window.

"It's Hanomer!" whispered Dave excitedly. "I knew he wouldn't leave us."

He and Al immediately began pulling the stones away. Following the rope in the deepening darkness, they could just see Hanomer below them on the mountainside. He was signaling to them.

"What does he want?" asked Al.

"I think he wants us to make the rope fast and slide down it."

"That rope can't be thicker than a pencil. It will never hold us!" protested Al.

"I think it will," said Dave. "Hanomer wouldn't make a mistake like that. Making ropes is one of their great arts. I'll trust it. If I make it across, so should you."

Dave stretched the rope across the room and wound it three times around an unbroken stone pillar that held up the roof of the room. He made the rope fast with a bowline hitch. Giving it a solid pull to test the hitch, he went back to the window to wave at Hanomer. The rope was pulled and stretched out until it was taut as a bowstring.

Dave took his leather jacket, doubled it up, and placed it under the rope where it rubbed across the window ledge. Next, he took off his belt, doubled it over, and tentatively hung on the rope in the room. It held his weight. He noticed the rope had been greased with tallow.

Hanomer thought of everything!

Dave climbed out onto the window ledge and sat down. He swung the belt around the rope and then wound several times around each wrist. Dave felt his old fear returning as he looked down to the lower city far below. He took a deep breath.

If there's anyone out there, I could sure use some help!

"Here goes!" he said.

He leaned forward onto the rope and used his foot to push himself off the ledge. The rope gave a jerk when it took his full weight, and he shot down the line rapidly. He could hear the hum as the belt slid over the taut cord.

If there's a rock wall at the end of this, I'm dead!

He came rocketing close to the mountain face and entered the shadow. At breakneck speed he splashed into a pool. The impact knocked the wind out of him, and he swallowed water. He felt many hands grab at him and pull him out. As he came up dripping wet, the first face he saw was Hanomer's. They both laughed out loud with relief. Around them were a dozen Hansa.

Dripping wet, Dave climbed to the small ledge, where he could see Al's anxious face. He waved for Al to come on, afraid to shout for fear of alerting the guards. Al slowly positioned himself on the ledge, took a deep breath, and launched himself into the void. The rope hummed at he raced down the line, and Dave got back just in time to pull Al out of the pool, sputtering. They both laughed and clapped each other on the back. It was good to be alive!

Chapter 38

From the Frying Pan into the Fire

Leading the escape from the citadel, Pam and Floyd crawled along the cliff face. Even though it was quite dark, Floyd was amazed at the quiet confidence Pam showed as she picked her way from handhold to handhold. Assembling at the jump-off point, the platoon members were roped together by pairs. Pam and Floyd, roped to each other, were to lead the other teams to a wide ledge where they could rendezvous. Pam led off. After crossing a difficult rock face that carried them around a rock wall and out of sight of the citadel, she finished the last climb that brought her and Floyd to the ledge, and they waited for the others. It was only when the last group arrived that they realized two were missing.

"Where's Al?" Pam asked.

No one knew.

"Stan's also missing."

"I'm going back!" said Pam.

"No way!" said Floyd. "We need you to guide us out. Maybe Al couldn't leave right away. He can get out by himself, since he knows the way. He may have had a good reason for staying."

Floyd could tell Pam didn't believe him. He wondered if he believed it himself, since Stan had always filled him with a sense of unease and foreboding. *No time for that now.*

Pam led the group to the back of the broad ledge and began ascending the chimney that began as a crack at the back. After about an hour, they reached another ledge that angled down into the valley.

"You'll be okay now," said Pam. "This ledge will take you more or less down into the valley if you follow it."

"And just where do you think you're going?" asked Floyd.

"I'm going back for Al."

"You don't have a chance!" said Floyd.

"I can take care of myself," said Pam.

Without another word she disappeared down the chimney into the shadows. Floyd tried to follow her progress visually but could not. He looked into the darkness for a time, undecided about what to do. Finally he turned to the expectant and increasingly anxious group.

"Follow me!"

He walked through the group, which was still peering after Pam, and began to lead them down the sloping ledge to the valley floor. Quickly the few stragglers who were still trying to follow Pam's progress reluctantly followed Floyd.

The trip down the mountainside was slow, but they proceeded as Pam had indicated. The journey across the broken terrain separating the city from Fort Linderhof was also difficult. It was late afternoon when they reached the rock outcropping across from the fort and saw the sentry hail them. Floyd led the way as they hurried to Fort Linderhof.

"Who's in charge?" asked Floyd breathlessly.

"I am!"

It was Huffstetter. They were already too late; Floyd saw that the apemen were all over Fort Linderhof. Floyd and the Twenty-fifth Platoon were taken prisoners before they could even draw a weapon.

Chapter 39

The Council of Granomer

The Hansa moved swiftly through the mountain. A scout returned from one of the side passages and spoke to Hanomer in whispers. Hanomer in turn approached Dave and Al.

"That scout," Hanomer said, "says that one of your females is high up on a ledge above the citadel, watching the city. He did not approach her for fear of frightening her."

"I wonder who that could be?" said Dave.

"I don't need three guesses!" said Al with a laugh. "How many 'females' do we know that would pull a crazy stunt like this?"

"Pam!"

"I'd bet a month's pay on it!" said Al. "We had better go out on the ledge alone and tell her about the Hansa. Hanomer, could you take us there?"

"The scout and I will go with you," said Hanomer.

The scout led them to a vertical fissure and began climbing up the cleft. Handholds and footholds had been cut into the rock at intervals, to aid the ascent. After climbing about 200 feet, the scout entered a horizontal shaft. When Dave reached the opening he saw in the pale light a narrow passage that descended gradually. As he followed the scout he heard the gurgling of water and soon saw a stream bubbling out of the rock. The stream was little more than a rivulet, but the passage was increasing in height so that it was large enough for even Al and Dave to walk upright. The water was cold and clear, and they frequently had to skirt pools whose depths were beyond the reach of their gourd lights. The underground brook disappeared into a fissure, and the passage began to climb gently.

Finally they saw light ahead. Hanomer and the scout stopped, and the scout waved Al and Dave forward. They crept out of the opening to the edge of the ledge and peered over. They seemed to be directly over the tower rubble but much higher up than the sentry ledge and even higher than the ledge that Dave had used with Hanomer. In the middle of the open plaza below, a great crowd of apemen were pulling on ropes. Despite their prodigious strength, whatever they were pulling moved very slowly. Finally a very large wagon came into view, dragged by six rhinoceros-like creatures assisted by the apemen. On the wagon lay a huge statue. The statue had the face of a vulture, staring up into the sky, with clawed and taloned feet.

As Dave saw the horrible statue, he remembered from the nightmare in the cavern and held his breath. He could see the threefold symmetry of the statue, with the other two heads resting on the wagon. *What are they doing with that thing? Are they bringing out all five of the guardians?*

Dave felt Al's hand on his shoulder, and when he turned he saw Al pointing straight down. Thirty feet directly below them, Dave saw a prone figure lying on a ledge. Even from the back he could tell it was Pam.

The scout who had quietly joined them touched Dave's arm and pointed to an easy route down. It was well chosen, since it was off to one side and kept them out of sight until they reached the lower ledge. Al and Dave made the descent as quietly as they could, hoping the gentle breeze would mask the sound of their boots. When they reached the lower ledge, Al put his finger to his lips and crept up behind Pam's prone form. He lunged forward and, quick as a striking snake, clamped his hand over her mouth.

Despite Al's advantage of surprise, Pam whipped around with the speed of a cat and hit him on the side of the head with her elbow. The unexpected blow knocked Al over to his side. Free from his grip over her mouth, Pam pulled a knife out of her boot and sprang to her feet ready to strike. A look of relief, joy and then concern replaced determined ferocity as she dropped her knife with a clatter and rushed over to Al, cradling his bruised head in her arms.

"Al, what have I done?" she whispered.

Dave, arms crossed, leaned against the cliff wall and broke into a grin.

When Pam saw Dave, she gently helped Al lean back against the cliff wall, then sprang to give Dave a hug.

"Dave! I was so glad when I heard that you were alive! Help me with Al and then tell me what's going on," said Pam.

"Don't worry about Al, Pam," said Dave. "It was all his fault. He made the unpardonable mistake of assuming you were a woman."

Pam bristled until she saw the twinkle in Dave's eye, and then softened.

"If I'm not a woman, what am I?" she asked sweetly, fluttering her eyelashes.

"You're somewhere between an Amazon and a tigress. Anyway, I'm sure Al is playing up the injury in order to get you to do the 'cradling his head' thing again. Hadn't you better humor him and get started so that we can get out of here?"

"If you insist," she said. She turned to go back, changed her mind, came back, and gave Dave a kiss on his cheek. "I'm glad you're still the same pesky Dave. I actually missed your needling."

Dave felt himself reddening. Pam smiled in triumph.

She went back to Al while Dave crept back to the ledge and followed the progress below. The stone figure on the wagon had been pulled almost to the citadel gate. Other wagons followed, filled with metal implements that gleamed in the sun and clinked as the procession rolled along. After these came two more heavy wagons in tandem, together they carried a long, worm-like creature, about eight feet in diameter and about fifty feet long.

An earth borer! I wonder what Hoffstetter plans on doing with that? Whatever it means, Hoffstetter's plans were laid long ago. There's no way Hoffstetter—or whoever controls him—put all of this together in the last few days.

Dave had had enough. He crept back from the edge and saw Hanomer waving to them from above. Pam and Al were talking quietly. Dave came over to them, knelt down and spoke softly.

"I think we need to go," said Dave.

"Go where?" asked Pam.

"To the Hansa," said Dave.

"Who are the Hansa?"

"Pam, you're going to be surprised at this," said Al. "Dave has met some creatures, some friendly creatures, that have helped him and may help get us out of here."

A look of fear crossed her face. "What kind of creatures?"

"They're nothing like the apemen. They're waiting for us up there on the rock face," said Dave, pointing. "They won't hurt you. They're smaller than we are and look more like badgers than people—I mean men—but they're trustworthy and won't hurt us."

And so they began to climb, with Dave leading. Al followed, and Pam came up last. When Pam caught her first sight of Hanomer, she was visibly startled. Hanomer approached her slowly and bowed. The gesture was so unmistakably "people" that Pam relaxed and smiled down at the furry creature.

They had little time for introductions or explanations. They rejoined the party and then moved swiftly through the mountain and reached the village by the lake before nightfall. Clouds were moving in from the west, and the sun set in red splendor.

———

The next morning Dave woke to the sound of a light drizzle on the reeds of the roof. He looked over and saw that Al was still snoring softly, and so he crept out onto the veranda. A mist hung over the lake, and the meadow glistened with raindrops. Higher up the mountainside, the rain had turned to snow, and all the trees were clad in a new coat of white.

It felt good to be home. He went to pour himself some siph. Looking out over the lake, he felt his soul drenched with the tranquility of that place that had given him such joy.

Al came out of the hut, yawning and stretching his arms. "What's that you're drinking?" he asked.

"It's a drink the Hansa make called siph. On days like today I like it warmed up. Here, I'll get you some." Dave went over to the fire pit and poured from a clay pot sitting in the embers.

"Hmm, this is good!" said Al, after taking a small sip of the steaming liquid.

Settling back, Al said, "Dave I need to talk to someone."

Dave looked around mischievously. "I guess I'm the only one around, so I'm going to have to do."

"I didn't mean it that way," said Al. "I usually work things out myself, but I need to get your impartial advice."

"Sure," said Dave. "I have to give out my advice freely, since I've never found anyone who wanted to pay me for it."

Al grimaced. "It's about Pam."

"So what about Pam?"

"Remember what Stan said to me? He said he and Pam have a son back in Halcyon."

"Yeah, I remember. I also remember he'd come specifically to stick the knife in after he shafted you."

"I know that was Stan's intent, but still I think I need to leave her alone and bow out of the relationship."

"Hmm. How do you feel about the child?"

"Well, it was quite a shock!"

"I can believe it."

"I'm not very good at explaining this," said Al. "Give me a moment to think."

"I guess I don't really understand. To me it's pretty clear that you two are in love. Whatever happened in the past, she's high quality, so why not go for it? Is it the thought of Stan's child?"

"Sure, the baby bothers me a lot. It bothers me even more that I had to hear about it from Stan. But you know, the baby—I guess I should say "child"—can't help who his father is. No, that's not really what bothers me. How do I tell Pam how I feel?"

Al heard a noise in the brush behind the hut. He looked around but saw nothing. He paused for a moment as he shifted his position. He chose his words carefully. "Should I even be telling her that I love her? Am I not just thinking about myself? Do I have the right?"

"I don't get it," said Dave. "Why wouldn't you have the right to tell her you love her?"

"Well, as I see it," said Al, "in the earliest part of the Old Testament, no distinction was made between sleeping together and being married, since the two happened together. So it seems to me in the biblical sense Pam and Stan are married, and I should respect that."

"I don't know what to say. Your point never occurred to me before," said Dave. "Why are you even talking about the biblical concept of marriage when Stan doesn't even give a fig about the Bible? It seems to me if you follow your thinking to its logical conclusion, you're going to leave Pam stuck with that stinker Stan, and the child without a father. If you don't care enough for her to accept the responsibility of someone else's child, then you should tell her now, break it off, and spare her further heartache. If you love her like you say, then you should talk to her and at least tell her how you feel and let her make the decision. After all, what she does or doesn't do with Stan is her decision, isn't it?"

At that moment Hanomer appeared on the path.

"Come and join us, friend Hanomer," Dave called out. "Have you had breakfast?

"Yes," said Hanomer, "but come to think of it, I could use another bite to eat."

Soon they were all eating and talking.

When Hanomer had finished his second breakfast, he pushed back from the table and waited patiently, as if he had something he wanted to say. Dave stopped talking and looked at Hanomer.

"Friend Hanomer," said Dave, "I can tell this is more than a casual visit. You have something on your mind."

"Friend Dave," Hanomer began, "I cannot stop thinking about the terrible deed we saw under the mountain. I think the power under the mountain has broken out of the wall we had set around it. My heart troubles me, and I fear that perhaps even our village may eventually be in danger."

"Was it not in danger before?" asked Al.

"There was always some danger," said Hanomer. "Before this, the main danger was the apemen, as you call them. They only traveled a certain distance from the cavern, and this village is beyond their range. Now that Meglir has occupied a new host, I don't think anyone is safe anymore. Furthermore, it is probable some men from your company have gone over to him."

"Are you sure men have gone over to Hoffstetter, to the power under the mountain?" asked Dave.

"While we were looking for you, we watched the citadel carefully. Some men were armed; others were enslaved and shackled. It all happened without a fight. We think that about half of the men have gone over to the man you call Hoffstetter. He will lead them to commit greater and greater crimes on the others in your company, by small degrees, so his hold over the traitors will become more and more secure as their evil deeds increase. It is ever so with evil; men can be beguiled into choosing evil deeds for a seemingly good end, only to find that their hearts have changed so that even the good purpose is lost as time goes by."

Hanomer put down his siph, stood, and looked at the tunnel at the end of the lake. "I do not think Meglir knows where we are, and he will have to search long to find us. Still, I will strengthen the lookouts so that we will not be surprised if Meglir's next stroke falls here.

"As for me, my duty is clear: I must take you to the lore masters. They may know what all this means and give council to both you and me."

"Who are the lore masters?" asked Al.

"We do not write many things down," said Hanomer, "but we have a guild of people who remember for us many things that have happened in the past. They recite the songs of old and remember the years of sorrow as well as the years of joy. If there is any knowledge among my people about what happened in the cavern, the lore masters will know."

***

Pam woke from a sound sleep. She heard the quiet chirping of a robin in an apple tree behind Hanomer's house, and remembered where she was. She felt more cheerful than she had at any time since they'd started on their voyage up the river. With a light heart, she went to look for Al. She was walking down the path to Dave's house when she overheard Dave and Al speaking quietly. She stopped.

Should I intrude?

Then she heard Al's voice clearly.

"Sure, the baby bothers me a lot. It bothers me even more that I had to hear about it from Stan. But you know, the baby—I guess I should say "child"—can't help who his father is. No, that's not really what bothers me. How do I tell Pam how I feel?"

Pam choked back a cry as tears welled into her eyes. The moment she had been dreading had come, and Stan had lied to her again and gotten to Al first.

Stumbling back blindly, her thoughts raced through her mind.

He knows about little Thomas! Stan has talked to him and poisoned the well. Now he's trying to figure out how to tell me he's really not interested in raising someone else's child—especially Stan's after all he's done.

She ran back to Hanomer's house just as Hanomer emerged. She did not even greet him as she stifled her sobs, ran to her room and flung herself on the heather mattress. Only then did she give way to her tears, and sobs racked her body.

After a time, she sat up and wiped away her tears. Her disappointment and sense of loss was slowly being replaced by hot anger. *I may have been a fool to fall for Stan, but it's not Thomas' fault. If Al can't bring himself to care for Thomas, then I want no part of him. My son doesn't deserve that!*

Similar thoughts flooded through her. She grew angrier with Al and determined that he would not be given the chance to have pity on her. She would put an end to the relationship herself. She would not let Al humiliate her or her son though his condescending kindness.

I don't know what got into me. How could I put Thomas into the Staycare Center? He should have stayed with me. If he had been with me, I wouldn't be hurt like this. Al would have stayed away without breaking my heart.

Al and Dave were sitting on Dave's veranda ready for their journey. They didn't have much to take along, but what they had was bundled ready to go.

Hanomer and Pam came around the hut. Pam had her few things in a bundle under her arm. Hanomer greeted them, but Pam said nothing. Her face was drawn, and she had streaks down her cheeks.

"Good morning, Pam," said Al after the silence became awkward.

"Good morning," said Pam icily.

I wonder what's eating her?

There wasn't much more time for conversation as Hanomer led them to the village meadow, where the elders were assembled along with a small company of warriors. Within a few minutes the company began their journey to the lore masters. The drizzle had stopped, but all the leaves were wet, so soon they were all drenched. Their path took them up to the mountains along the route Dave had followed for the rokash hunt. But soon they climbed to a ridge and headed southeast. At this point they were above the tree line, and the rocks were covered in a blanket of snow. They crossed a high boulder-strewn pass and continued along a ridge bordered by snow-clad pines, until late in the afternoon.

All this time Al made few attempts at conversation, and Pam maintained a stony silence. Dave met with better success, and soon Dave and Pam were speaking with laughter and enthusiasm. Al thought the laughter on Pam's part was forced, but by now he felt so low that he blamed himself. When they finally called a halt for lunch, Pam went off by herself and sat a stone's throw from the company on a rock outcropping that gave a sweeping view of the trail they had covered.

Seeing Pam alone, Al determined to talk to her. When he approached, he saw Pam's face grow graver.

"May I sit down?" asked Al.

"Sure," said Pam without enthusiasm.

Al unwrapped his lunch, offered her some, and then ate in silence for a few moments.

"Pam," he said at last, "I need to talk. About us."

"About us?" said Pam. "Actually, Al, I've been meaning to talk to you myself."

"You have?"

"Listen, Al, I don't want you to get the wrong idea about my coming back to rescue you."

"Wrong idea?"

"Yeah, the wrong idea. You don't owe me anything. You're a friend, and I wanted to help. But there's something else."

"Something else?"

"I think I've misled you, and I'm sorry."

"Misled me?"

"Yes, you know, given you the impression that there could be something between us, when there can't."

"There can't?"

"No, there can't. We're very different people and have very little in common. You don't value the things that are important to me. Friends value the same things, don't they?"

"I hadn't thought about that—"

"Let me finish," said Pam. "I think it best if we stayed friends but leave it at that. Do you understand?"

"I guess so," said Al, his head spinning at this turn of events. He felt as if his whole world had caved in.

How could I be so stupid? I thought she cared for me! I guess I just do not know how to read women.

Al's thoughts were interrupted when Hanomer called for the company to resume their journey.

———

Dave could tell that something was wrong. Al and Pam avoided one another as they continued on their way. Dave tried to talk to

Al, but there was little opportunity. Besides, Al was clearly not in the mood to talk.

After entering another shallow valley, they came upon a narrow defile that passed between two high bluffs. The cloud cover was so low fog dogged their steps. The walls of the narrow passage—only a few feet apart—climbed on either side until they were lost in the fog. They descended following a well-worn path that picked its way around fallen boulders. When they finally emerged from the fog, Dave saw a broad valley with a long lake that wound between the mountain peaks for as far as his eye could see. He heard a sound—like the continuous roll of thunder—from a waterfall that plunged into the lake from an unseen river in the mountain.

Hanomer pointed to a cluster of green projections rising from the water. Dave looked with astonishment on a grove of trees growing directly out of the lake.

The party descended the slope rapidly by well-used paths, and soon they were standing in a clearing that bordered the edge of the lake. Evidently they had been expected, since boats for their transport out to the village had already landed, and the tree Hansa sang a song of greeting to their visitors. The Hansa from Hanomer's village sang a song in reply.

Having finished the formalities of the introduction, the first group entered the boat. Dave, Pam, and Al were honored by being asked to join the first group to cross the lake. The distance to the trees was about 300 yards. As Dave was paddled across, he observed his surroundings. A strong wind was beginning to disperse the clouds high up on the mountainside. About two miles away, the lake ended in a sheer mountain wall that rose a thousand feet to a high mountain valley nestled between even higher peaks above. A river thundered from glaciers that capped the tops of these towering mountains. In that fall, much of the water was blown into a mist that shrouded the end of the lake. Ahead, the trees that rose out of the bottom of the lake looked like a giant sequoia forest that had been flooded. Such a comparison, however, did not do justice to these trees, since they were much larger than the sequoias he had heard about. The trunks at the level of the water were at least 100 feet in diameter and were spaced several hundred feet apart. As Dave approached, he realized that there was more than one kind of tree here. There was a deciduous tree with smooth bark like a beech. Then there was a conifer like a large Douglas fir with rough bark. When branches of these trees met above the water, they joined and fused as if to help one another stand, rather than fight one another for sunlight. Dave was surprised to see that this joining of branches even occurred with trees of different species. Thus, at the lower levels at least, there was a network of branches that stretched over the whole tree island.

The boats moved silently among the tree trunks that rose to the canopy above them like huge towers. After paddling for a short time under the trees, the boats moored at a large floating raft that was fastened to several of the lower branches. From the floating raft a spiral staircase made of rope and wood ascended high into the treetops. Just as Dave was steeling himself to make the long climb, one of the tree Hansa beckoned him to a large basket. He, Pam, and Al climbed into the basket, and the Hansa began opening water valves on some large gourd-like containers that surrounded the basket. As the basket lightened, it strained against the anchoring ropes. Once the tree Hansa was satisfied that enough water had been released, he closed the gourd valves and unshipped the line. The basket began a smooth ascent.

Al wondered if the cable would hold: what if the tree Hansa had not reckoned with the weight of the big people? But his fears proved groundless and they noiselessly rose until they were opposite a very large platform made from five joined branches of the huge trees. On one side there was a low dais. They were asked by the Hansa to take a seat close to this raised platform.

Dave and Al lingered behind at the water elevator to see how this worked. Dave asked a question in Hansean of one of the tree Hansa, and the fellow, Kellomer, showed him a vine-like tube from one of the trees. After listening to Kellomer's explanation, Dave explained to Al that this was a water vine that collected water from the mist high up on the trees. The Hansa used it to refill the water elevator to take it back down. Dave couldn't ask any more questions, since Hanomer came back to get them and insisted that Dave and Al assume their places before the elders came, in order to avoid a breach of etiquette.

––––––––––

There must have been several water elevators operating, since others from their party began to arrive within a short time. The large clearing began to fill up with Hansa. Some of the Hansa Dave recognized as friends from his village, while others were from the tree village. Finally a very old Hansa appeared, helped by four younger Hansa. They were all clad in golden green robes draped over their diminutive forms, like togas. This elder Hansa was older than any that Dave had seen in his own village.

Hanomer whispered into Dave's ear that this was Granomer, the chief loremaster of the Hansa. It was his responsibility to train his pupils to remember and recite their history.

One of the pupils opened the assembly, and the Hansa stood and sang a song praising the Creator. Finally, the pupil introduced Dave and asked him to recount his adventures from the beginning. Hanomer had already told Dave that Hansa loved a long story and that he should tell everything in great detail. In Hansean, Dave began with a brief description of his own world and the dislocation. He told them in simple language of their technology: of lights and nuclear power and even the weapons they had to kill at a distance. He was surprised that the Hansa did not receive his words with incredulity and skepticism, as would have been the case had a Hansa had told a similar story back on Earth. Hanomer sat with Al and Pam, translating when he could.

The sun had set when Dave finally completed his tale. A time for questions followed. Dave was amazed at the Hansa memory, since his listeners remembered the long presentation in the minutest detail.

Then Hanomer was asked to stand up and give his story. He spoke in Hansean, and it was Dave's turn to translate for Al and Pam.

"Honored assembly, guests, and esteemed lore masters," Hanomer began. At this point he bowed to Granomer, who nodded in return. "It has long been our task to watch the dark place and hunt the apeman. Alas, on my watch we were not as vigilant as we should have been and did not see these men camp upon the outer wall. So it happened that they came to the cave entrance and were attacked by the apeman, and Dave, my friend who has earned the name Rokomer, was captured and destined to go to the death plants.

"Rokomer has already made known to you his friendship to our people, his growth and education in our ways. Still I would say Rokomer and those of his people are like the men we knew before: although these men have great gifts of thought, knowledge, and physical strength, they are also weak and bent. From what Rokomer has said, many, perhaps most, of his people do not honor the Creator, and are in opposition not only to him but also to all that is good in creation.

"Still we have known that we have been sent to befriend men and help them as they struggle against Meglir and the dark powers he commands, and so we were glad that men have returned to the struggle after all this time. However the evil of these men has grown, even beyond our lore. One of them has given himself up as host, thus releasing Meglir the Evil One."

A murmur ran through the crowd.

"The man Rokomer," continued Hanomer, "has already told you about our following the bent one into the bowels of the cavern. What he did not tell you was the remarkable fact that the deep cave was more unguarded than we had ever seen before. All the apemen had drawn back. I risked going where we had never gone before—indeed, where we are forbidden to go by our council's decree." Once again, the crowd murmured.

"The bent one, this Hoffstetter, walked in unimpeded and uninhibited with his victim. So did we. I must say that I did not know what was about to happen, or else I would have tried to save this Wilson while he was still in the main cavern. Hoffstetter took this Wilson past the five guardians to the pillar itself and bowed down and killed him—"

Hanomer's voice trailed off until it became inaudible. His sense of failure, horror, and sadness was palpable, and his fellow Hansa cast down their eyes. Some made quiet murmurs of lamentation.

Dave interrupted the silence and asked in Hansean, "But what actually happened there?"

Granomer, whose head was bowed in sadness, roused himself from his deep thoughts and looked at Dave.

"Young one, the pillar preserved the spirit." He hesitated as though he thought better of it, then shook his head and continued. "No, it is important for you to understand this, so I had better begin at an earlier point that is known to us, but not to you who are recent strangers.

"Many years ago, in a previous age, there were men here, men who looked like you and may indeed be your kindred. They settled in this valley and founded the city that you know, and they had come to honor the Creator. They grew in numbers, and the Hansa were their friends and allies. Their knowledge grew far beyond ours, but not their wisdom. Your people—" here Granomer turned to Dave and nodded to him, "your people, from what you have told me, have grown in their knowledge of dead things: of metals, machines, and stones. These men took a different path. They could make very simple machines and devices but did not go far in this knowledge and could not rival you.

But they learned instead to control and shape living things. These very trees that form our home are products of their wisdom.

"Then a new group of rulers arose who did not seek to honor the Creator. They began to shape animals and plants that were not as wonderful as before. They shaped and molded great worms that could bore through the living rock and so extended the city underground. They grew more bent and began to shape creatures with tooth, claw, and ravenous hunger for sport and amusement. A great battle arose, and the last good king, Aldemir, defeated the Bent-Ones and forbade the making of evil creatures by the life changers. During his reign the city again earned its old name of Tau-en-Nar, the City of Light, when light gourds graced the walls and the streets, and each citizen sought to help his neighbor.

"Our histories tell us Aldemir was merciful and did not kill his enemies but banished them from Tau-en-Nar. Rumors came back to the city that many of the most wicked had gone to a far-off continent, the Black Land, where they were able to mold animals of great size and ferocity. Some bent ones even took on animal form by mixing animal and men by their gifts, which they had bent to do evil. These creatures are hideous in form, but are rational like men.

"After Aldemir, his son, Meglir, took the throne. It was rumored that Aldemir had died under unusual circumstances, but no inquiry was ever made. Meglir reopened communication with the Black Land and drove the people to greater evil than ever before. Those who opposed Meglir rebelled, and we aided the rebels. Meglir the king developed the death plants, which grow only in the darkness of the cavern. When he captured his enemies, if he could not turn them to evil, he would take them to the plants, which would banish their spirits but keep the bodies alive as living machines to do his bidding.

"Meglir had five lieutenants that returned to him from the Black Land, the guardians, who drove his enemies like chaff before him. The guardians had taken the shape of animals, very much like the rokash, with tooth, talon, and claw, and they drove all before them in battle. Meglir also commanded the great wolves, and these too were strong. And so, those who opposed him were defeated and scattered. We were also scattered, since we opposed his evil.

"The rebels that were not killed or captured stayed for a while in hiding and aided us. However, over time they grew weary and went far away to safety to begin life again. But we Hansa stayed true to our calling and opposed him wherever we could. These were to us the darkest years, since we had not the strength or intelligence of men. Still, we did our duty. We hid in the woods and used woodcraft to evade capture. We were not able to defeat him, and we were hunted mercilessly, but the death plants could not take us, as we were not men; nor could he corrupt us, so he just killed us.

"When Meglir had defeated all his enemies, he set his mind to new arts. We learned from slaves we had freed that he sought to achieve immortality by molding a living organism that would keep his body, old and wizened beyond recovery, alive enough that his spirit would remain. He and his five lieutenants entered the loathsome living sepulchers that you saw in the inner cavern and continued to exist in this living death. Meglir continued to rule. He would select a human host who would willingly accept him, and he would possess him. Thus he ruled for hundreds of years. The city was no longer the City of Light but Tar-en-Gorg, the City of Death. But Meglir was increasingly dissatisfied with the hosts that he had available. The mistreatment made many of the hosts defective. Instead of lasting hundreds of years, their lifespan dwindled.

"It was at this time that the People of Light returned from the west. They had grown again to a great host and laid siege to the city, destroying the gate. Then Meglir overreached himself in his pride and fear. Fearing defeat, he worked to warp and distend an organism, thinking to destroy his enemies. He laid his plans too well. Instead of killing only the People of Light, the new organism killed the whole population of men, and now Tar-en-Gorg was truly a dead city. A small remnant fled the disease, and we do not know what happened to them. Meglir barely made it back to his pillar before his host died from the disease. But now Meglir was trapped in his pillar with no hosts to use. Only the apemen remained. We thought our chance had come to end Meglir's dominion forever. Although we tried, we were never able to penetrate the inner cavern to attempt the destruction of the pillar or the guardians. But we did destroy the occasional apeman and kept Meglir in check. Now, for the first time in many long years, he has a new host, and he has many living men to prey upon."

"What's he saying?" asked Al.

Dave, who had stopped translating, gulped and began to translate the remainder of Granomer's history to Pam and Al. His friends sat in stunned silence when he finished.

Then Dave noticed that an animated conversation between Granomer and several of the Hansa was going on, and he realized he had missed the context.

"Then we are in great danger!" said one.

"Yes," said Granomer.

"Then we must fly!" said another.

"The danger is great, but we must not take thought only for ourselves but also for these many men from another world, who I think will bear the brunt of Meglir's lust for power and control."

"What should we do then?" asked a third.

Granomer folded his hands under his chin and closed his eyes. The others respectfully held their peace.

"I think we are safe here for the time being. If Meglir comes over the ridge, he must fight his way through the narrow valley of entrance. Even if he wins that, he must either carry boats or build them to assault our city. If we remain vigilant, we should have warning of his approach. Hanomer, on the other hand, your village is at great risk. We are not strong enough to attack now, but we need to build a refuge, a safe place for these men and a safe place for your people."

Dave stood up and approached the group surrounding Granomer. "Hear me, O Granomer and my Hansa friends," said Dave. "It is clear to me that one of my people has caused great evil. We are a bent race and always tend toward evil. I do not approach to make excuses for our evil, for there are none to justify so great a wrong. No, I approach respectfully, O Granomer, with information that may save your honorable people and mine, though we do not deserve it. I know where Meglir's hammer stroke will fall."

"Where will Meglir strike?" asked Granomer.

"He will strike our home, the island we call Halcyon," said Dave.

"How do you know?" asked Hanomer.

"Remember," said Dave, "that Hoffstetter, or more precisely Meglir, came to us and told us he had called Hoffstetter to this place. The dislocation was not an accident as we thought. If Meglir has moved to bring Halcyon to this world, then surely he has a use for Halcyon, and so it seems reasonable to me that Meglir will move against it."

"What will Halcyon give him?" asked Granomer.

"It struck me when you were speaking," said Dave, "how differently the men developed on Earth—the place we come from—from the way they developed here. We have many weapons made from powders, metal, and wood. The men here have control of living things like nothing I had ever seen before. If Meglir conquers Halcyon, he will have both. He will be a much deadlier foe than he is even now."

A murmur of fear ran through the listeners.

"What did you say?" asked Pam.

Before Dave could answer Pam, Granomer spoke again.

"There is wisdom in what you say, Rokomer, son of Halcyon. It is plain to me now that Meglir will move against Halcyon. Will they be able to resist him if they are warned?"

Dave translated the conversation for Al and Pam, then turned to face Granomer.

"I have spoken to my friends," said Dave, "and we agree that Halcyon will not defend well against Meglir. It is a sad fact but true that the leaders and influencers of Halcyon believe only in power that they can touch, feel, or measure with their mechanical instruments. The power that Meglir wields would be beyond their ken and seem mere folly or superstition to the wise in Halcyon. If we tried to warn them, they would not believe us. They might even imprison us as dangerous people who are sick in the head, who are causing others to despair and panic. They would be wholly blind to the danger that Meglir brings."

Granomer and the other Hansa were deeply troubled by these remarks.

"Yet Halcyon is an island, and Meglir has no boats," said Granomer. "He cannot go there easily, since the apemen are unskilled in such things."

"You are right, O Granomer, that the apemen will not build him boats, but boats are at hand! He will attack my people on the river. If Meglir gets those boats, he will reach Halcyon."

"Do you have kin and friends who would escape Halcyon if they could?" said Granomer.

"Yes," said Dave.

"Then," said Granomer, "our duty is clear. First, we must help those already enslaved to Meglir to escape, and second, we must warn those who are guarding the boats of Meglir's intention.

"First, let us find a place for you and for Hanomer's villagers. Perhaps we can again renew our alliance with men and gather strength to oppose Meglir. Bring the maps!"

In a few moments, a troop of Hansa carried a huge rolled carpet into the room. As they unrolled it, an enormous map was revealed, stunning in its Hansa artistry. In agreement with Hansa custom, they took their boots off and walked across the map to look at it. They found Hanomer's village and also their current location.

"Would you want to move your village to our lake?" asked Granomer.

"Since Halcyon and Meglir count on the River Pishon to access our country and Halcyon," said Hanomer, "I believe we need a strong place that will let us patrol the river."

Hanomer traced a path of twenty miles along the lake on which Granomer's village was located. At the far end was a waterfall that fell to a second lower lake, which emptied into the Halcyon River through a tributary. In the middle of this second lake was a large rocky island that looked like a boot, with flat shallow lands pointing north to the outlet of the lake and a high table top, the last outthrust of the mountains at the south end of the island.

"I think we should go back to the fastness of Torburg," said Hanomer. "Then we can support you if needed, and you can escape to us if you are overrun. We can also watch the river."

"You know well that we have left that isle uninhabited because of the evil men did to your forefathers," said Granomer.

"Perhaps it is time for men and Hansa to redeem that isle by filling that place of bones with new life. Must the enemy be allowed to forever besmirch a place because of evil deeds? It is strong and was destroyed from within by treachery, not from without by attack with weapons."

Granomer's eyes bored into Hanomer.

Finally he said, "Go and do what seems right to you. We are in need of a strong place right now. Torburg was ever strong. May it be so again! I would not leave the slaves of Meglir without help or let Meglir attack the island. Send your people to Lake Tor and let them wait for you there. We must make some attempt to thwart the plans of Meglir. We will meet again tomorrow to discuss what can be done."

Chapter 40

The Storming of Linderhof

The next morning it was decided that Hanomer should return to his village and lead his people to Torburg. It was almost noon when Granomer accompanied the four companions across the lake to bid them farewell. They had reached the shore of the lake and just started on the trail when a band of Hansa came down the path from the pass, leading a stumbling, exhausted, and bedraggled Hansa warrior.

When Hanomer saw him, he rushed to him. "Danomer, what happened?"

Danomer, gulping great volumes of air, was doubled over with his hands on his hips, his tail swishing back and forth over his head in agitation. He struggled to get his words out. "They have attacked!" he croaked.

"Who has attacked?" asked Hanomer, fear edging his voice.

"Meglir has attacked," said Danomer. "He came early in the morning."

Hanomer led the warrior to a rock and made him sit down. Dave gave Danomer a drink from his water skin.

"Now, from the beginning," said Hanomer.

"It was very early in the morning when apemen were spotted creeping down the mountainside. They did not use the tunnel, since they did not have boats, but crawled out from among the rocks like the maggots they are.

"As you told me, Hanomer, I had someone keep watch, so we saw them coming. There were too many for us to fight, so I woke the village and we began our escape. We would have been able to get clean away if it were not for them!" Here he nodded in the direction of Pam, Al, and Dave.

"What happened?" asked Hanomer.

"A small band of men also came with the apemen, and they had thunder sticks that could kill us at a distance. They moved to cut us off from the forest. They killed many of our people as we ran."

Hanomer stood up and paced up and down, his tail twitching, his prehensile hand opening and closing like a fist. He came back and sat down abruptly. "What happened next?"

"We lost about twenty of our people, killed by the thunder sticks. When we reached the woods, we turned to fight. They will not pursue us so rashly now I think."

"What happened next?" asked Dave, forgetting his place.

"Friend Rokomer, I raced ahead to ask for help. The warriors are fighting a rearguard action, but Meglir will not give up. He continues to pursue us."

"Are you sure Meglir is with them?" asked Granomer.

"Yes, O Sage," said Danomer, rising to bow. "I have seen Hoff-stetter's body with my own eyes, and he drives the apemen forward and fills the men with fear as they harry our rear guard."

Granomer turned to one of the younger Hansa. "Call the battle chiefs. We must hold the pass to our valley at all costs." He turned to Hanomer. "Meglir is here. Now is your chance. You must warn the people of his impending attack on the island and have them warn your home city of Halcyon. I will counsel the battle chiefs to send you with guides through the Dimroth pass to the west, and you must warn the men on the island of danger. Perhaps in his hatred for us, Meglir has made a mistake in forsaking the island to attack us."

Dave wasn't convinced Meglir would make that mistake.

"But my people need me," said Hanomer.

"Your people will be safe once we get them through the pass. Danomer can then take them up the lake and down the long stairs to Lake Tor and Torburg. If you reach Rokomer's friends and kin at the island, you can protect them from the counterstroke and warn the people from Halcyon about the danger that they face in Meglir, or Hoffstetter, as they know him."

In the end, it was the battle chiefs who finally convinced Hanomer. And so with a guide and a band of warriors, they set out along the lake for the high Dimroth pass.

Dave, Pam, and twenty of Hanomer's fighters were lying on a hillock some 200 yards west of Fort Linderhof. They had been keeping watch since the previous night. In the daylight, Dave could see that the fort had changed considerably. A stout wooden timber bridge had been constructed across the chasm, and a plank road had been built from the main road. A steady stream of apemen had been carrying sand and gravel out of Fort Linderhof to improve the road. Although Pam and Dave did not understand the origin of the gravel, their alarm grew, for they knew Hoffstetter was preparing some move against City Point, and the sand was somehow bound up with Hoffstetter's scheming.

Upon arriving the previous night, Al had paddled a hastily constructed raft across the river to the island of City Point in order to warn the people there of the impending attack. There had been no sign from Al since he had landed on the island; nor had there been any evidence that the islanders had heeded his warning.

Late in the afternoon, the work on the plank road was finished and the procession of apemen carrying baskets and sacks of gravel out of Fort Linderhof stopped. As the second night approached, an atmosphere of dread and doom filled the hearts of the watchers.

Pam crawled up beside Dave with a worried look on her face.

"No word from Al, I take it?"

"No. I've been on the point watching City Point with my binoculars, and I haven't seen anything. Something should have been happening by now."

Dave felt in his heart that something had gone wrong, but he could see that Pam was already desperately worried about Al, and he didn't want to add to it.

"I guess all we can do right now is pray."

Pam stared at him as if she hadn't heard correctly.

"I guess you're right, Dave; we can always do that. I'd better go back and keep watching. And by the way—thanks!"

Now what could possibly have made me say that? Well, at any rate, I guess it's what Al would have said, and it encouraged her.

He watched Pam slowly make her way back out to the lookout point.

Well after midnight, while Dave was still on watch, he heard the tramp of many feet approaching the fort. The night was dark, and no fires were lit at Linderhof, so he could not see what was happening. Hearing feet on the wooden bridge, he made up his mind to wake Hanomer.

"They are preparing to attack!" he said to Hanomer, shaking him awake.

"How do you know?"

"They've brought many troops. It can only mean one thing."

"How can they attack, friend Rokomer? They have no boats."

Hanomer has a point. Why would Meglir bring so many troops up if he didn't mean to attack? It is either guile or attack. Many troops argue for attack.

They were still debating what to do next when suddenly, they heard the sounds of shouts and clashing steel from the island of City Point. Fires on the island flared up, and Hanomer's keen eyes made out the lumbering figures of apemen grappling with the men from Halcyon on the island.

Without further discussion, Dave began picking his way down in the dark, from the treed hillock to the bare rock beneath. When he reached the rock, he heard a sound behind him and saw that Pam was running at full speed to follow him.

"What are you going to do?" asked Pam.

"I don't know; I'm winging it!" said Dave.

Looking back, he saw the shadows of Hanomer and the Hansa also following, but they made no sound. Dave crept as quietly as he could toward the deep cleft separating Fort Linderhof from the mountain spur. He came to the noisy creek that formed the western protection of Linderhof and began to look for a place to cross.

Dave felt a hand on his arm.

Follow me!

Dave followed Hanomer upstream a short distance, where they crossed, leaping from one large rock to the next. On the other side Hanomer cautiously led them along a shallow ravine, which brought them to within thirty feet of the new wooden bridge and the new plank road.

The east had lightened perceptibly, and Dave could see the dark motionless form of an apeman sentry at the other side of the bridge.

He saw no other signs of life. When they were all together, the Hansa archers shot their arrows at the apeman and brought him down. Dave ran towards the sturdy bridge and crossed at a run, heedless of the noise of his feet on the planks.

The plateau that was Fort Linderhof was deserted, but it was much changed. In the central shallow bowl that used to be their camp, the pond had disappeared. A crude, wooden scaffolding and a winch spanned the slippery bed of the old pond. A wooden ramp descended ahead of him, and Dave could just make out the deep cleft under the winch ramp with the help of the flickering torchlight emanating from the cleft.

He hesitated only a moment to get his bearings in the early light and then ran down the ramp, stopping at the top of an irregular shaft.

A sinkhole! What happened to the water?

Crude irregular steps had been cut into the rock and descended into the depths below. Several apemen lumbered toward him, laboriously climbing up the steps. Dave charged, pulling his sword from his sheath. He swung the blade furiously; the bodies of the apemen were pitched off the steps to the depths below.

Hanomer's voice behind him was filled with wonder. "Since the rokash, you have grown much as a warrior! Even this descent down these steps would have filled the old Rokomer with fear."

Breathing hard, Dave stared in blank amazement. Hanomer was right. His fear of heights had much diminished, and he was quite a different fellow than he had been.

"We must destroy the bodies of the apemen," said Hanomer, "so they are not carried back to the death plants."

"We'll do it later. We don't have time right now. We have to hurry!" said Dave. He turned and continued racing down the stairs.

Reaching the bottom, Dave saw that the shaft ended in a small natural cavern. Ahead of him was another deep shaft, about ten feet in diameter. Light gourds cast their dull yellow light about him. A few flickering torches added their smoky orange light to the yellow light of the gourds.

Like the racing tide overtaking the unwary on the seashore, fear and revulsion suddenly washed over him. He raised his sword hand as if to ward off a blow and turned to his right. Through an opening from a second, larger, cavern, he saw the grotesque vulture-faced figure of a guardian. Dave felt nausea and despair add to the fear that already held him in its grip. He knew it was the guardian. Steeling his mind, he forced his legs to obey and tried to approach the statue, but was opposed by a will so strong it made him reel back. He staggered backwards and would have fallen had he not been steadied by Hanomer's hand. Turning away from the guardian, he saw Pam on the ground, cowering and holding up her hand as if warding off a blow. The panic in his mind grew like a great vast cloud of despair. He wanted to flee. The part of his mind that was still clear knew he was overreacting, but he could not calm himself. It took all of his willpower to keep from bolting back up the stone steps to the open air.

As Dave sank further into despair and terror, he collapsed to his knees, shaking uncontrollably. Out of the corner of his eye he saw the Hansa gather together. Soon, he heard the soft notes of their singing. Dave recognized from the words that it was a song of victory and triumph, praising the power of the Creator. As the notes rose in that smoke filled place, a glimmer of light came into Dave's gloom, and his destruction did not seem as certain as before. As the song proceeded, his felt his courage returning, and the dark despair fall away from his soul. Then, as if a bar of steel had been cut, the oppression of fear vanished. Dave put his hand to his brow like a sleeper wakening from a terrifying dream. He staggered to his feet.

"Can we...can we destroy it?" asked Dave, gesturing to the guardian.

"I know not," said Hanomer. "We have never been this close to a guardian before."

Dave forced himself to walk into the adjacent cavern. He looked up at the grotesque statue towering above him. This cavern was bathed in the same, dim green lichen light he had encountered in the death plant cavern. The guardian was about twenty feet high. It was made of a black material Dave did not recognize. He slowly walked past it, turning to keep an eye on the statue. When he finally turned around to look where he was going, he stopped short in horror. In an open space behind the guardian, in a shallow pit, bodies were strewn about. He heard Pam gasp beside him.

No, it can't be. They can't have killed them all.

One of the bodies stirred and looked up. It was Floyd Linder. Floyd began to wake the others. By this time Hanomer and some of the other Hansa had approached. All of the people in the pit were awake now. Dave could see they were chained together by leg irons.

Hanomer called for tools, and he and the other Hansa lowered themselves into the eight-foot-deep pit and with chisel and hammer made short work of the soft metal chains that bound the prisoners.

As they were considering how to free the Halyconites from the pit, a high-pitched, long, drawn-out wail pierced the air.

The guardian!

The sound grew so loud, so intense Dave covered his ears. But the blood-curdling noise stopped as abruptly as it had started. No one moved. Then, in the distance they heard a new sound; a loud scraping, as if a heavy stone were being dragged over rock.

Pam ran back to the stairs in the first cavern and peered into the shaft descending into the depths. "That awful noise is coming from the shaft," she called. "It sounds like some big machine coming up, but I can't make it out."

Dave left the Hansa to their work of freeing the captives, and raced past the guardian to the shaft where Pam was kneeling. The rumbling, clattering noise continued to come from far below. Finally, they saw the source of the noise. A hideous shape slowly came into view. Worm-like, with a tentacled mouth large enough to swallow a pickup truck, its scales and armor clattered on the rock as it expanded its body to work its way up the shaft to the cavern. Crude wooden ladders had been fastened to the sides of the shaft. These broke like matchsticks as the creature made its way up the shaft. Dave recognized the creature; it was the same one he had seen on the wagons.

"The rock borer!" said Hanomer, who had just joined them. "The guardian has called it."

"Can we kill it?" asked Dave.

"It's very heavily armored. I don't think so," said Hanomer.

The rock borer moved toward them at the rate of a slow walk.

"We could try burning it," said Hanomer.

"No good!" said Dave. "A big fire would plug up the passage. I think this tunnel was used to attack City Point. We need to get down this shaft to get across to the island. But you've given me an idea!"

Just then a Hansa warrior approached. "Friend Hanomer," he said, "we have seen a line of torches leaving the city. They are marching down the road. Meglir is returning!"

"Whatever we do, we must act quickly," said Hanomer. "If the advance scouts from Meglir's army trap us here, we'll all be lost."

Looking at the newly freed captives and gesturing at part of the group, he said, "Half of you, upstairs! Tear down the scaffolding and the crane and throw them down the stairs. The rest of you pile the wood around the feet of the statue."

Fifteen people raced upstairs. Within a minute someone yelled, "Look out below!"

Pieces of scaffolding came crashing down the shaft, landing on the floor of the cavern and splintering as they landed. Meanwhile Hanomer's archers were shooting arrows at the rock borer, but with little effect. Dave and the remainder of the captives began piling the wood scaffolding around the feet of the guardian. One of the Hansa started a fire at the corner of some brush, which someone had thrown down. The smoke from the brush drifted toward the fissures in the ceiling of the cavern, and the flames billowed upward and licking at the beams of the broken scaffolding. More and more wood was thrown around the feet of the hideous statue. As the flames engulfed the stone figure and licked around the vulture head, the hideous statue looked the part of a demon from hell. Suddenly in Dave's mind he heard a scream, more of anger and hate than of terror.

Dave ran to the shaft and looked down at the rock borer. The forward motion of the rock borer had stopped; the creature was making itself longer and thinner so that it slid to the bottom of the shaft. Its tentacles withdrew, and it reversed direction, moving away, retreating around a bend in the shaft.

"Come on!" shouted Dave to the others. He took one of the cables from the pulley system, made it fast, and threw it down the shaft, then raced down the shaft ladders at breakneck speed. Pam was right behind him, with the Hansa bringing up the rear. Reaching the end of the ladders, Dave swung onto the cable and lowered himself hand over hand to the bottom.

"The rock borer has become afraid," said Hanomer. "I don't know how long we have until its hunger for flesh will drive it to pursue us."

"Then we'd better get moving!" said Dave.

Using what remained of the ladders and ropes, Dave and the others made their way to the bottom of the vertical shaft. The shaft made a right-angled turn, then disappeared into pitch blackness. Hanomer appeared, leading the way with a light gourd. The shaft ran straight as an arrow toward the island. The rock borer was nowhere to be seen. It wouldn't do to stumble into it. Afraid of being surprised, Dave proceeded at a slow walk. Within twenty paces he came to a side tunnel, where he saw the stubby tail of the rock borer retreating. It was cutting a new shaft.

Satisfied that the way was clear, Dave took Hanomer's light gourd and raced down the long level passage, leaving Hanomer behind. Soon the passage began to ascend. Up ahead Dave saw the faint light of early sunrise. He burst out of the face of a low cliff that faced north. There were no enemies about, but it was prudent to be careful.

Hanomer emerged from the tunnel. "Hanomer, can your scouts reconnoiter without being seen in this light?" whispered Dave.

Hanomer crept up onto the low hill and looked at the topography. When he came back, he said, "It can be done safely. There is enough cover that they will not be seen."

"Could you send out your scouts then and tell me the situation on the island?" asked Dave.

Since Dave had spoken in Hansean, the Hansa following Hanomer immediately understood and complied, without waiting for Hanomer to respond. By now all the freed captives had arrived. They were armed with clubs and other such weapons as they could find. Some had crude swords taken from the dead apemen, but most had clubs made from the broken scaffolding. When they were all assembled, Dave climbed to the top of the cliff, stretched out on his belly, and looked about the island.

There were fires and bodies everywhere. There were hundreds of apemen, but many were standing still, while others were wandering aimlessly. Looking to the south, Dave could see that the remaining free Halcyonites were still on top of the low hillock that had served as a headquarters. They were being assailed by the turncoats from the citadel who had gone over to Hoffstetter. The free Halcyonites were hard pressed, since they were throwing rocks and sticks while Meglir's men were still firing arrows. There was no gunfire.

Seeing one of the Halcyonites fall with an arrow in his side, Dave didn't wait for Hanomer but ran straight at the turn-coats. Pam and the others followed. Dave ran silently but swiftly and came upon a group of Meglir's men shooting at the Halcyonites from the cover of a grove of trees. Dave was almost on top of them when one of them saw him and, with a cry, turned to shoot. Dave felled him with one blow.

By now Dave's companions were among them, and the turncoats dropped their weapons and ran south toward the river. Dave pursued them to the water's edge but couldn't bring himself to cut any more down now that they were defenseless. Reaching the shore, the turn coats didn't hesitate, but jumped in and began to swim back toward Fort Linderhof.

Dave and his companions ran back toward the hillock where the battle continued. He saw that Hanomer had already arrived, and his accurate arrows were keeping the remaining turncoats pinned down. Dave was just regrouping his company for another charge when the remaining turncoats also broke cover and ran for the river. They passed right past Hanomer's position, but he had too much compassion on the fleeing traitors to shoot them in the back. In they end they too escaped into the river.

Now that the heat of battle was over, Dave felt very tired. Still, he knew reinforcements would be coming, and if they gained the tunnel they could easily overwhelm his meager forces.

"Hanomer, if those reinforcements reach the tunnel, we'll have a tough fight on our hands. If they break out of the tunnel, we'll be lost."

"Dave, scouts have just reported back that the many apemen are leaderless and wandering aimlessly about the island. If Meglir is with the relieving force or if the guardian recovers control, the apemen will attack. We should destroy them now!"

"All right. Set six of your best archers to guard the tunnel entrance. Have the rest hunt down, and destroy the apemen before they become a threat."

"What are you going to do, Dave?"

"I'm going to try to get the holdouts on the hill to stop fighting so they can help us deal with Meglir. I think they still have explosives, the materials they used to destroy the tower in the citadel, and we may be able to seal the tunnel."

Hanomer ran off, shouting orders for the Hansa to cover the tunnel, and to begin the hunt for the apemen.

Dave shouted to the Halcyonites barricaded on top of the hill.

"This is Dave Schuster. I'm on your side. I am not your enemy. All of the traitors have fled to the river. More are coming to attack. I need your help to stop them."

A voice he didn't recognize answered back. "If what you say is true, come up here to talk, but you must come unarmed."

Dave began to unbuckle his sword belt. "Don't go up there, Dave," said Pam, clutching his arm. "You don't know if you can trust them. We don't even know what they've done to Al."

"I know, Pam, but I don't have any choice. I've got to convince them to plug that tunnel, or we'll all be dead."

He started to walk up the hill, his hands raised above his head. Pam started to follow him.

"No, Pam, not both of us. I think you need to look for Al. He's got to be here somewhere. I'm sure they wouldn't have harmed him, even if they didn't believe his story."

Pam hesitated. He could see she was wavering. There were tears in her eyes. Finally, she turned and ran to look for Al.

Dave resumed his walk up the slope, raising his hands in the air. There were bodies of apemen and some Halcyonites scattered on the grass. At the top, a crude barricade had been constructed, and the ugly barrel of a gun was pointed at his chest. As he came close, two men rushed out, dragged Dave behind the barricade, and threw him on the ground. Dave did not resist while they tied his hands behind his back and hobbled his feet.

"All right, Schuster, tell your furry buddies to keep their distance or you're dead."

"You've got to listen to me; you're in danger!"

Someone kneeled on his neck and the voice said, "You tell your buddies to keep their distance, or so help me, I'm gonna kill yah."

Just then a shout rang out. "It's me, MacDonald. Don't shoot. I'm unarmed, and I'm coming up."

In a few seconds Dave heard the sound of someone climbing over the barricade.

"Commander, am I glad to see you!" said a relieved voice.

"Let Schuster go," said MacDonald. "It's all right. He's a friend, and he's rescued us."

"But Commander!"

"That's an order, Norgaard."

Dave felt his hands released. He was lifted to his feet.

Norgaard offered his hand. "No hard feelings, man. I thought you'd gone over to the enemy."

"Yeah, I see your point. ... Al!"

Al had just climbed over the barricade. Dave stepped over to him, and they clasped arms. "Man, are you a sight for sore eyes! I was afraid you'd bought the farm when you went on that hair-brained excursion to the island."

"I knew you'd come!" said Al.

"I was going to leave you for your foolhardy decision to come alone, but Pam would have none of it!" Dave said, smiling broadly.

"It's my fault," said MacDonald. "I didn't believe him. This attack would have succeeded if you hadn't come."

"Listen, Glenn," said Dave, "I mean, Commander MacDonald. We're not out of the woods yet."

"What do you mean?"

"When we attacked there was another force moving down the road from the Dead City. If they get into the tunnel and break out, we'll be finished. We just don't have enough to hold them off."

"I don't know the tactical situation. What do you suggest, Dave?"

"Give me a second," said Dave. He walked to the barricade and called for Hanomer.

His friend came up the hill quickly. The soldiers couldn't help staring at the furry creature. Dave went to him and knelt down, held the Hansa's shoulders, and asked, "What's the tactical situation on the ground?"

In English Hanomer replied, "I have set a guard at the tunnel entrance. We must hold off the apemen and turncoats as long as we can, and then try to make our escape."

"No, wait a minute," said Dave.

He turned to MacDonald. "Commander, do you have a demolition team?"

"Yes; why? Of course! You want to blow the tunnel. Can you buy us the time?"

"Get the demolition team moving as fast as you can. We'll take up positions in the tunnel."

Dave raced down the hill and picked up his crossbow and sword. As Dave and Hanomer were organizing their forces by the tunnel entrance, the Hansa scouts returned and reported that all the apemen on the island were leaderless and could easily be destroyed. A large number of survivors from the island had also been located in a compound nearby. They had been destined for Hoffstetter's chain gangs.

Chapter 41

A New Beginning

Dave, Hanomer, and Al held council with the Hansa at the tunnel entrance. When their old friends from the platoon saw them, they came over to join them. Gradually others joined as well. A murmur of surprise rose from those who had never before seen the Hansa.

"We have to get off this island," Dave said to those assembled.

"Why?" asked Daniel Johnson, the platoon commander in charge of Fort Linderhof. "We've won, haven't we?"

"We haven't won," said Dave. "We only have a reprieve. The apemen have stopped fighting only because we destroyed the guardian. When Meglir, that is to say Hoffstetter, arrives from the Dead City, he will regain control over the apemen, and the battle will resume."

At that moment a scout emerged from the tunnel. "Meglir is approaching down the road with many apemen and a contingent of his men!" announced the scout in Hansean.

"We need to do two things," said Dave, "first, destroy any of the wandering apemen, and second, block up the tunnel. Commander MacDonald is organizing the demolition expedition. Who's coming with me to hold off the apemen and the traitors while the explosives are set?"

"I'm coming!" said Johnson, his eyes smoldering.

Hanomer sent half his men to destroy the wandering apemen before Meglir could regain control of them, and then followed Al down into the tunnel.

"Wait!" said Johnson. "We didn't bring any solar packs and flash-lights."

"No need," said Dave. "You'll see."

Dave led the way. He and the Hansa pulled out their light gourds. The tunnel sloped rapidly downward, and they could see perhaps fifty feet ahead in the light cast by the gourds. They met with no opposition. Finally, they came to the side tunnel to which the rock borer had fled when the guardian's hold had been broken.

"Why did the rock borer flee, Hanomer?" whispered Dave. "When we encountered them before, they attacked us."

"Let us pray he does not do so again, since we cannot easily defeat it. I think, friend Dave, the rock borer was in the power of the guardian, and when the guardian's will was broken with the song and the fire, fear and pain drove the rock borer into hiding. It will remember its hunger soon."

Hanomer turned toward the far entrance. "Meglir has come."

Just then the first of the demolition team arrived and packed plastic explosives into a crack in the wall.

"Here they come," said Dave as the first apemen began lumbering up the passage. Dave and the Hansa began to shoot their arrows, and every arrow found its mark. Still the apemen kept coming.

"Back away," said Dave. He was down to his last six arrows. If they had to fight with their swords, he was going to lose a lot of his people in these close quarters. Just then he heard the scraping, grinding sound of the rock borer moving up the side passage. The giant form of the borer came around the passage, crushing the apemen in its path. Its tentacles pulled their bodies into its maw one by one, then extended towards Dave as it filled the whole of the tunnel.

Dave sent the others back and retreated just ahead of the giant monster. There was nothing he could do to stop it.

The passage was beginning to slope upwards when Dave felt Al's hand on his arm. "Fire in the hole!" shouted Al.

Dave and Al sprinted up the passage as fast as they could. As they cleared the entrance, MacDonald waved to them from behind a rock pile. They dove for cover. MacDonald nodded to a soldier, who threw a switch.

The ground rocked. Dust and debris blew out of the tunnel entrance. Climbing out from their hiding place, they saw that the end of the tunnel had completely caved in.

"We did it, sir!" said a breathless soldier. "The tunnel must have collapsed. We saw evidence for the explosion in the river."

"Thank God!" said MacDonald. He and Dave hurried back to Headquarters Hill. MacDonald used his binoculars to follow the activity at Fort Linderhof for a while. Satisfied at last, MacDonald smiled.

The river was brown with silt from the explosion. Debris from the collapsed tunnel slowly floated by on the gentle current.

Al was tired. Very tired. But he had to find Pam. He asked Hanomer if he had seen her. Hanomer said she had gone to the east end of the island hunting for apemen.

Al moved east quickly. If there were still apemen about, Meglir's proximity would mean that they would attack. When he reached the woods at the eastern end of the island he was relieved to see Pam walking back with a number of Hansa. Al stopped, not knowing what to do.

When Pam saw him, she ran up and threw her arms around him. "Oh, Al, I'm so glad you're safe."

Al felt himself turning crimson and only held her gently. She fell away and looked at him. "What's the matter, Al?"

"Listen, Pam, I know I've been too forward lately, and I guess I've taken things for granted."

"I don't understand," said Pam.

"I think I'm saying things badly," said Al.

"No kidding," said Pam. "You're not making any sense at all. What are you trying to say, Al?" She kept her arms around his neck.

"Pam, I want to help you get your little boy back."

"Why would you help me do that? He's not your son."

"You do want him out of the Staycare Center in Halcyon, don't you?"

"Desparately!"

"Well, I want him out too, only we can't get him right now. Things are too dangerous. We need to wait until things calm down and I need to plan." Al looked at Pam. She had a look of complete incredulity.

"You won't owe me anything," he added, "if that's what you're worried about. There are no—"

Pam stopped him with a kiss. Al was bewildered. She stepped back, looked at his face, and burst out laughing. "You don't have a clue, do you, Al?"

"Probably not."

"You really don't know anything about women."

"No, Pam, I really do not know much about women."

"Never mind, my dear, clueless, Al. Despite the fact you know less than nothing about women, I love you, and I'll take my time educating you. Now let's go back and find the others."

I may not know much about women, but I seem to be doing all right.

Yes, quite all right.

MacDonald planned to leave for Halcyon first thing in the morning. Still, they would pass an uneasy night. In case of an amphibious attack, he had posted lookouts all along the southern shore and kept a continuous watch on the far bank from Headquarters Hill.

Floyd's platoon did not have any assigned duties, so they met to discuss their next steps.

"What are we going to do?" asked Floyd. "Al, you're certainly a wanted man back at Halcyon, and many of us may be as well. Do we really want to chance going back there?"

One of the others, Hugh Matthews, spoke up. "Maybe we don't have to go back to Halcyon. My cousin is a Dalyite, and he says they have a stronghold called New Jerusalem on the mainland. I don't know where it is exactly, but I know it's somewhere on Botany Creek. If we find it, I'm sure they'd take us in."

The friends from the first expedition looked at each other, as tempting memories of that place filled their minds.

"I'm not going back either to Halcyon or to New Jerusalem," Dave said quietly. "I'm going to stay with my Hansa friends."

"How are you going to get back to them?" asked Floyd.

"We have to drop Hanomer and his company off anyway. When you drop them off upriver from Fort Linderhof, on your way back to Halcyon, I'll go with them, and I'm sure we won't have any trouble making our way back to the tributary into Lake Tor."

"What about the rest of you?" asked Matthews.

"What about the renegades? Won't we run into them, trying to get to this New Jerusalem place?" asked one of the others.

"We'd have to watch our step, but from what my cousin, Jared, has told me, New Jerusalem has many natural defenses and should be able to hold out against the renegades, even if they find it," answered Matthews hopefully.

"What are you going to do, Al?" asked Floyd.

Al looked at Pam for agreement, and then they stood up. "At first we thought we'd go back to Halcyon, but after looking at it from all angles, we decided we couldn't go back openly. For now we'll be going with Dave to join the Hansa at Torburg."

"But you were a Dalyite once, Al," pleaded Matthews. "You know the areas around Botany Bay. We need you to lead us to New Jerusalem. Why won't you help us?"

Al sighed and then said, "Hugh, I'll do all I can to help you get to New Jerusalem. I can draw you a map that will get you to the headwaters of Botany Creek, but don't ask me to go either to Halcyon or to New Jerusalem.

"I have a dream; I want to live in a place that allows me to worship and honor God without having roadblocks thrown in my way at every step, and where the whole political and educational system is designed to grind my beliefs out of me."

"That's true of Halcyon, but not of New Jerusalem," said Matthews. "They would encourage you to worship God."

"That may be true," said Al, "but what about my friends Dave and Floyd? They don't worship or believe in God. I want to live in a place of complete freedom. Good, honest people ought to belong and be accepted, even if they don't believe. Could they do that in New Jerusalem, where there is so much fear of becoming another Halcyon that honest dissension is taken as rebellion?"

Matthews gave up. "Is anyone coming with me to New Jerusalem?" Six hands went up.

In the end some forty-five souls asked to go with Dave to Torburg, but Tom and Dwight were not among them. Dave spoke to Hanomer, and Hanomer, to Dave's surprise, welcomed the Halcyonites.

"We have always been stronger," said Hanomer, "when our peoples have fought together against the enemy. Let us do so again."

Dave saw Al get up and walk over to Tom.

"You're going back?" asked Al, disappointment coloring his question.

"Yes," said Tom. "Someone who has seen Hoffstetter firsthand needs to warn Halcyon, and we have some unfinished business there. If you ever do come back to Halcyon secretly, maybe you'll need friends on the inside." They shook hands.

"You've been a good friend, Tom," said Al.

Just then Glenn MacDonald walked up to Al and offered his hand. "I did you a great injustice, Al, by locking you up when you came to warn me. I'm sorry!"

Al smiled and shook his hand. "I'm glad that we survived the storm," said Al. "I know you were under tremendous pressure after McTavish and Wilson disappeared."

"I'm not going to make the same mistake twice," said MacDonald. "We're leaving this island and heading back to Halcyon. I have an inkling that not all of you are coming back with us. There are about forty-five of you, and we can't easily manage all the longboats anyway with the few people we have left. Why don't you take three longboats on your journey? Return them to Halcyon when, or if, you ever come back. I'm sure the fees will be reasonable." MacDonald smiled and offered Al his hand again in farewell.

"They're not going to like it!" said Al, shaking MacDonald's hand vigorously.

"There are a lot of things about this unmitigated disaster that they're not going to like back in Halcyon, but I think, in the final analysis, Hoffstetter's treachery will outweigh them all. Anyway, I'm irreplaceable!" With that MacDonald and those going to New Jerusalem headed for the longboats.

An intense period of work ensued. A giant funeral pyre was constructed at the entrance to the underground tunnel. All the bodies, both human and apeman, were burned.

But an atmosphere of dread—that somehow Hoffstetter would cook up some new surprise—hung over all who remained. They worked tirelessly to load the boats and get ready to cast off as soon as possible.

MacDonald sent a group to gather all the surplus supplies, and to divide them equally among the longboats. He generously gave an extra load—intended for the City Point colony—to the new exiles.

Late in the afternoon, everything was set for their departure. Floyd, Al, and Dave had drawn Matthews a map to the headwaters of Botany Creek and warned him about the lupi. Matthews had gained two dozen followers who also wanted to make the attempt. Al and Floyd didn't tell Matthews all they knew about the site of New Jerusalem, since they had promised to keep it secret, but it was clear that through his cousin Jared, Matthews understood enough about the location to find the entrance to the valley on his own.

Dave, Floyd, and Al joined MacDonald on Headquarters Hill. He was looking intently toward Fort Linderhof. "They have that place crowded with apemen. I'm sure they're planning something. No way are we going to spend another night here. We're heading out right now, and I urge you guys to do the same," said MacDonald.

"No need to tell us twice. We just came up to say goodbye before we shove off." After shaking hands all around, the two groups parted ways, wishing each other Godspeed.

The most difficult parting for Dave was saying goodbye to Tom Chartrand and Dwight Larson, who both remained firm in their decision to return to Halcyon. They knew there was a possibility they could be linked to Al's escape, but they were willing to take that chance.

The wind was out of the west as the boats set out. MacDonald's boats rapidly moved downstream and disappeared. The three longboats moving upstream made slow progress. Nevertheless they worked vigorously to get as far away from Fort Linderhof as possible. The Hansa were not much use in rowing, since they were too small, but they were dispersed among the three boats to make sure they would all find their way to Torburg, even if they were separated during the night.

The moon was newly risen and was just beginning to wane. Traveling near the left bank, bright moonlight showed the trees on the shore clearly. After a time they came to a widening of the river dotted with many small islands. Dave remembered this geography from Granomer's map and with the help of the Hansa, easily located the tributary they were seeking, even though it was hidden by an island and heavily wooded promontories.

They were well above Fort Linderhof, but the crew continued to row all night. Sometime before dawn they found themselves in a long lake. They anchored and slept in the boat until the sun rose, and then proceeded up the lake, which Hanomer identified as Lake Tor. Within an hour, Dave, who was in the lead longboat, saw a large island in the distance. The island was shaped like a boot with the toe pointing toward him. At the far end of the island, the top of the boot rose 2,000 feet above the water and ended in a flat snow-covered mesa. A creek cascaded down from the heights into the middle of the island, where the laces of the boot would have been, and emptied into Lake Tor.

So this is Torburg. I wonder why the Hansa have such bad memories of this place?

He did not have much time to wonder. Hanomer pointed to a location on the eastern shore of the lake, where Hansa from his village were camped. Dave's longboat landed on a sandy beach beside the Hansa camp. As Dave climbed out of the boat, Hanomer's wife came through the crowd and ran to meet her husband. Dave also greeted her, kneeling to clasp arms in the Hansa fashion.

Hanomer turned to Dave. "Friend Rokomer, I would like to move my people to the safety of the island as soon as possible. Since Meglir is on the move, he could surprise us here."

"Of course," said Dave. "We have three longboats, and we could move your whole village quickly."

After Hanomer told the Hansa they were going to the island, there were signs of fear but no complaints. They spent the rest of that day transporting the Hansa and their supplies to the island.

Chapter 42

Another Dream

Dave found himself in his recurring nightmare. He was standing in a hospital room at the foot of a bed. On the bed in front of him he saw his own corpse, the lifeless eyes open and fixed on the ceiling. He and the corpse were bathed in a wonderful bright light. He knew this was all a sham. He knew how it would end. Still he walked down the hallway toward the light. Even as it filled him with expectation and delight as it had so many times before, his anger grew at the sham—the raised expectations of the delight of the mountains and his inability to get there. He cried out in anger and shook his fist in the air.

"I'm not going to even try for the mountain anymore. I'm not going to play your game anymore!" he shouted into the tunnel.

Who am I shouting at? I don't even believe in God.

"If you're there, can't you make this dream end differently? Answer me!"

There was no answer. The silence was absolute. All he saw was the light.

Just as I thought.

He left the tunnel and emerged onto a broad heath bathed in even brighter sunlight. He looked down, and his limbs and body were made of glass, filled not with organs or bones, but with tendrils of brown smoke. As he looked across the heath, he saw others. Some were a deep gray color; others seemed more transparent than he. All were walking toward the light, which emanated, not from a sun in the sky, but from a mountain range far in the distance.

At first he was going to join the others, just to experience the early delight of the journey, even though he knew how it would end. But no, he had no chance. It was no use. Why play along with the sham? He started to look around.

Off to his right there was a wooded glen he had never seen before, since he had always directly climbed up onto the broad moor in his eagerness to head for the light. Out of desperation to make the dream end differently, Dave headed for the glen. He walked down a gentle slope through tall beeches, his favorite trees. He heard the sound of water gurgling merrily ahead of him. He came upon a glade, and in the midst of the glade he saw a pool in a round stone basin. At the opposite end of the stone basin was the statue of a lion, its head lifted in agony. In its upraised stone paw was an enormous thorn, and from the wounded paw sprang the spring that fed the pool. The liquid flowing into the pool was the color of Burgundy wine.

The head of the stone lion turned toward him, and the stone lips moved.

"What do you want, my son?" said the lion in a deep, sonorous voice.

"I want to get to the mountains," said Dave, with a note of despair.

"But you cannot," said the lion.

"Why can't I?" asked Dave.

"Absolute Goodness is perilous and deadly. You cannot approach as you are, for the fire of the Goodness would destroy you."

"Then what am I to do?

"Drink of the wine."

Dave knelt down and drank the wine. He had enjoyed some wonderful wines before, but this surpassed them all. He looked at his body, and the stain of the wine had infused him, and now his dull brown was red.

Oh no! This has made things worse!

"You must bathe in the pool," said the stone lion.

Dave wavered.

Oh, what does it matter anyway? Sooner or later I turn back and go to dig the pit.

He stepped over the rim, expecting to touch the bottom of the basin, but there was no bottom. He tried to grab the lip, but he had already overbalanced and plunged in, his hands slipping off the edge. He sank for several feet, then kicked his legs and broke the surface. He found some steps he had not seen before and climbed out. After he stepped out he looked at his body. He held up his hand. It shone with a light that made sunlight seem dull. His whole body shone. He turned to thank the lion, but only a stone statue stood before him.

He left the glade, climbed out of the glen and went to the heather. His body gave off so much light that the heather seemed to exist in twilight. Every once in a while he saw ghostlike figures. Approaching them, they fled in terror and agony at the light coming from his body.

He saw the mountains, and the delight of the mountains filled him with expectation. He walked to the mountains. He was going home.

Chapter 43

Eleytheria

The next weeks were spent organizing the homesteads. Hanomer's village would be located on the low rising hills flanking the high mesa of Torburg, since this terrain was much like the hills of the village they had left. The Halcyonites settled on the flat land near the water's edge. Here there was ample room for fields and gardens. Dave, Al, and Pam worked with some of the Hansa to construct cottages and verandas on the hillside, while other Hansa dug into the earth and rock to make their underground rooms.

Floyd set the Halcyonites to work right away, planting their gardens with the few seeds they had brought from Halcyon and others that the Hansa had given them. So urgent was Floyd's desire to get their first crop in that they lived in tents until they could construct log cabins beside their garden plots.

Dave, Al, and Pam decided to build their small one-room cottages at the base of the foothills on a wide stone terrace where the stream cascaded out of the foothills. In this space between the two villages, they could overlook the fields of the Halcyonites, but were only a few minutes walk from their Hansa friends. They shared a common cooking fire at the edge of a stone ledge that gave them a view of Lake Tor.

On one clear summer's evening, when the garden plots were in and the cottages of the Hansa were complete, the island's new inhabitants decided to have a feast. The Hansa had caught a very large fish, which was roasting over a fire pit in a glen formed by the rushing creek in the midst of the Hansa village. The whole island was invited, and everyone sat together late into the evening, laughing, telling stories, and singing. Although the outcasts from Halcyon knew few Hansa words, several of the Hansa were well enough versed in English to carry on conversations with them.

After everyone had eaten their fill, they all sat around the fire, some quietly conversing, others already dozing.

"What should we call this place?" Floyd asked.

Everyone looked at Al. "Why look at me?"

"The Hansa have their sages," said Dave. "We have to have a sage as well, and you're it."

"I see. I'm no Granomer, but I suppose I should give it a shot. Give me a moment."

They all waited impatiently for Al to speak.

"I think we should call this place Eleytheria, which is derived from the Greek for 'freedom.' That's what this place means to us all."

There was a murmur of agreement.

"We need to have some kind of a leader," said Floyd.

"You've been our leader until now. Why don't you do it?" asked Dave.

"I have a gift for exploration," said Floyd, "but I'm no good as a diplomat or as an administrator. How about Al?"

"We need someone who can represent both the Hansa and those of us from Halcyon," Al said. "I think Dave would be the best man for the job."

Eventually, both the human and Hansa populations of the island of Eleytheria agreed. In democratic elections, they chose Dave as the first mayor of their new community, and designated Al and Hanomer as deputy mayors.

Mayor Schuster and Deputy Mayor Gleeson were relaxing at the mayoralty mansion, a much larger three-roomed Hansa cottage built on the stone terrace overlooking the lower village. It had been symbolic of their newfound freedom that one of Dave's first acts as mayor had been to marry Pam and Al.

"We've come a long way, haven't we, Al?"

"Yes," said Al. "I wouldn't have believed it, but the Hansa are so industrious! Everyone has a cottage or a log cabin, and we even have the first crops from our garden plots. At first I was apprehensive that I would see Meglir's army appearing on the shores of the lake, but since that hasn't happened, I can hope that either he doesn't know where we are, or we are too insignificant for him to care."

Dave gulped down some more siph, a regular gift from Hanomer, then stretched himself out even more comfortably on his homemade deck chair.

"Still," said Dave as he looked up at the high mesa of Torburg, "I won't really feel safe until we reopen the fortress and supply it, so that we could sustain a long siege."

"When are you going to do that?"

"I don't know. Hanomer seems afraid of the place, and until now he's refused to attempt it. I've let it go because we've had so much to do. I should talk to him again."

Dave stared up the mountain slope as if hoping to unearth its secrets.

"Well, Meglir is a worry," said Al. "Still, I feel happier and more content than I can remember feeling since the dislocation."

"You and Pam seem very happy. When I first met her, I remember, she had this touch of sadness."

"Do you remember," said Al, "she started to change soon after we were on the river? I suppose being married is part of it, but somehow I think being away from Halcyon is an even bigger part of it."

"Why is that, Al?" asked Dave. "What was so wrong about Halcyon?"

Al sipped thoughtfully on his tea. "Pam and I were talking about it only this morning. Although we felt the oppression of the place while we were there, we couldn't put it into words until we got away from there and tasted freedom. You really don't know how oppressive that place is until you escape it." Al ran his hand through his hair and leaned forward.

"Halcyon has two major problems. First of all, Hoffstetter and his cronies believed that religion in general, or fundamentalism in particular, was the enemy and was responsible for tyranny and intolerance. By focusing on destroying their enemy, in their arrogance they were blind to their own ruthlessness. As soon as you believe anything to be true, you automatically must believe that contradictory views are false. Tyranny does not originate in a strong conviction of the truth but in an unwillingness to allow others the freedom to disagree.

"It begins with benign condescension. You've heard it expressed over a beer at the Student Union Building: 'Those poor religious fundamentalists! If they only had our intellectual power and education, they'd throw off the shackles of their charlatan leaders and see the world as we see it!' Next, one becomes convinced he must intervene in other people's beliefs and lives for their own safety. 'I must protect those who cannot protect themselves,' such as children from their parents. By that point, one is already well on the road to tyranny."

"But aren't you saying that objective truth is the enemy?" asked Dave. "And doesn't that lead to an even worse position, where everything becomes subjective?"

"Not at all! That is not where I am heading," said Al. "I'm a Christian, and so I very much believe that some things are absolutely true and other things are absolutely false. I also believe that acting on that truth is incredibly important, and not acting on it is dangerous. I admit that might tempt me to take things into my own hands and impose my views on others."

"So what keeps you from doing that?"

"Well, if I truly believe God allows men free will and the right to make their own decisions for good or for ill, then I won't trample on that right to decide, no matter how high the stakes are. I know a lot of religious people disagree, believing that people need to be rescued whether they want to be or not. I just think that's wrong and leads to dishonesty.

"It also leads to Halcyon's second problem. As a theist, I can have a compelling conviction and still believe that others must be allowed the full, unfettered freedom to make up their own minds. Why? Because I believe they have an intrinsic value and so they have a right to choose for good or for ill.

"Materialists, in contrast, believe that human beings are no more than a collection of complex chemical reactions. If materialists believe in some kind of autonomy or intrinsic value, they obtained it somewhere else. It doesn't come from within their philosophy—it can't. They are the ones who tend toward tyranny, because they have no rational basis for allowing people complete freedom. Eventually some altruistic impulse that they experience will trump all other virtues, and they will manipulate others to that end, thinking they are doing good.

"Dave, you're our mayor now," Al went on. "I hope you'll make Eleytheria a place of true freedom, where we're allowed to express our beliefs publicly as well as privately, but where we maintain the deepest respect for those with whom we disagree. A place where we resist using any manipulation to make others believe as we do. Let's hold our convictions firmly. Let's talk about them openly. But in the end, let's allow everyone to choose according to what his conscience dictates. Let's show compassion and caring, regardless of what others believe."

"I'll say 'amen' to that!" said Dave.

They saluted their mugs in agreement.

And as the moon slowly edged above the horizon, the two friends lapsed into a comfortable silence, safe and content in their freedom.

The End

Glossary

Abaddon (A-bah-don): A continent to the east of Halcyon, which consists of a continent-wide crater surrounded by a ring of tall mountains. The bottom of the crater is about 16 kilometers below sea level. The high air pressure at this depth and the warm temperatures sustain many large and unusual life forms, which cannot survive at one atmosphere of pressure. This is the home continent of the Bent-Ones.

Ancients: A race of beings that inhabit the continent of Feiramar. These people were separated by the Great Plague unleashed by Meglir. The *Gurundar* (the contaminated ones) live east of the Lake Tolbar and are not permitted to cross over to the western shores. West of the Lake Tolbar live the *Naromundar* (the pure ones). The two sundered peoples only meet on the Callabar Islands in the middle of the Lake Tolbar. After one of these infrequent meetings the *Narmundarians* who met the *Gurundarians* must stay in quarantine on the islands for 3 months before they can return home.

Bent-Ones: Bent-Ones come from the continent of Abaddon off the east coast of Feiramar. The Bent-Ones only come infrequently to Feiramar. They are ancients who have given themselves over to evil. They bend and shape living things through their arts in support of evil.

Feiramar (FAIR-a-mar): The name of the continent that contains the Hansa and the Ancients. The island of Halcyon is off the east coast of this continent.

Granomer (GRAN-oh-mur): Chief Loremaster of the Hansa. Loremasters store up knowledge for the Hansa since they keep few written records.

Halcyon (hell-SIGH-un): An elite island university off the coast of North Carolina. A misguided physics experiment transported the university to a parallel world.

Hansa (HAN-suh): Hansa are furry bipeds that have a prehensile tail that ends in a hand. Although not overly intelligent, they are given to music and poetry and have a highly developed sense of honor, justice, and are self-sacrificing in their service to others. There are left-handed and right-handed Hansa depending on the handedness of their prehensile tail.

Hanomer (HAN-oh-mur): Is a Hansa chief and friend of Dave Schuster.

Kilk: The Hansa name for apemen.

Korpa (CORE-pah): The Hansa name for the death plants. Death plants are very large cabbage-shaped plants that Meglir developed to transform men into apemen. These plants are destroyed by sunlight and exist in the cavern behind the city of the dead.

Meglir (MEG-leer): Meglir, a great king of the ancients grew corrupt and became a tyrant re-opening ties with the Bent-Ones who live on another continent called Abaddon.

Pishon (PEESH-hawn): The Hansa name for the Halcyon River.

Rokash (ROW-cash): A large bipedal reptilian carnivore about 10 feet tall.

Rokomer (ROW-coe-mur): Dave Schuster's Hansa name bestowed on him after he killed the Rokash.

Siph (SIFF): A golden colored drink made by the Hansa that can be drunk cold or hot.

Tar-en-Nar (TAR-en-nahr): City of Light. The ancient name for the dead city before Meglir corrupted it.

Tar-en-Gorg: (TAR-en-ghorg): City of Death. The name for the Meglir's city once the great plague was unleashed killing most men east of Lake Tolbar. Meglir and his lieutenants ruled through the apemen.

About the Author

The Halcyon Dislocation is Peter Kazmaier's first novel. In writing this work he pursued a life-long dream of writing fast-paced novels that explore the intersection between adventure, science, faith and philosophy.

   J. R. R. Tolkien's *Lord of the Rings* , C. S. Lewis' *The Chronicles of the Narnia* , Stephen R. Lawhead's trilogy, *Song of Albion* and Robert Jordan's *Wheel of Time*™ are among his best-loved books. He also enjoys science fiction classics such as Robert Heinlein's *Tunnel in the Sky*.

   Dr. Kazmaier has spent most of his scientific career as a research scientist in industry. He has been an Adjunct Professor of Chemistry at Queen's University since 1999. He has published more than sixty scientific articles in refereed journals and was awarded the Arthur K. Doolittle award for Best Paper by the American Chemical Society in 1993. Cited as the inventor or co-inventor on more than 150 patents, his strong background in science enables him to bring authentic scientific insight to *The Halcyon Dislocation*.

   Dr. Kazmaier joined the "American Chemical Society" in 1976, the "Chemical Institute of Canada" in 1980, and 'The Word Guild" in 2004.

He married Kathryn in 1976. Together, they make their home in Mississauga near Toronto. They enjoy spending time at their cottage near Seeley's Bay, Ontario on the Rideau Canal.